W9-CQR-708

The
Chalchiuhite Dragon

The
Chalchiuhite Dragon
A Tale of Toltec Times

KENNETH MORRIS

TOR
fantasy

A TOM DOHERTY ASSOCIATES BOOK
NEW YORK

THE CHALCHIUHITE DRAGON

Copyright © 1992 by Theosophical University Press. Afterword and Glossary © 1992 by Douglas A. Anderson. All rights reserved, including the right to reproduce this book, or portions thereof, in any form.

This book was printed on acid-free paper.

A Tor Book
Published by Tom Doherty Associates, Inc.
175 Fifth Avenue
New York, N.Y. 10010

TOR® is a registered trademark of Tom Doherty Associates, Inc.

Library of Congress Cataloging-in-Publication Data

Morris, Kenneth, 1879–1937.
        The Chalchiuhite dragon / Kenneth Morris.
                    p.   cm.
            ISBN 0-312-85264-9
            I. Title.
        PR6025.O7527C54   1992
        813'.54—dc20   91-33406
                                                                                      CIP

First Edition: March 1992

Printed in the United States of America

0 9 8 7 6 5 4 3 2 1

Contents

Preface

On Christmas afternoon in 1925, the one in this world to whom I owed the most asked me to write on a pre-Columbian subject, and when, after some three months of thought and research, I submitted to her the idea of a book on Quetzalcoatl, Katherine Tingley approved. Then Bancroft became my study; a poor authority perhaps, but historicity was not the chief aim. Bancroft disentangled, or thought he had disentangled, from the masses of legend the story of a Great King; this author tried to disentangle from Bancroft the story of a Great Teacher.

The result of Bancroft's labor is as follows: Ceacatl Quetzalcoatl was the son of the Toltec Topiltzin (Divine Emperor, or Pope-Emperor), Nonohualcatl Totepeuh Camaxtli and Chimalman, queen of Huitznahuac (which means the South), whom, at the head of her army of unclad and barbarous Amazons, Nonohualcatl defeated and conquered.

When Ceacatl was nine years old, his father was assassinated by three nobles: Cuilton, Zolton and Apanecatl. King Huemac of Tollan, Nonohualcatl's brother, besieged and captured these three in their lake fortress, and Ceacatl inflicted, or witnessed, their cruel punishment. He was brought up by the Princess Civacoatzin, an elder sister of his father, who seems to have been revered in after ages as the Possessor of a Wisdom.

Grown up, Ceacatl became king of Tollan, and soon after, the Toltec Topiltzin. Then he put down the custom of war, preaching to his people from a mountain top through a "loudspeaker" that caused his voice to be heard over many hundreds of miles and ordaining peace, a life of love, the doctrine we know.

However, Prince Huemac, probably Ceacatl's cousin, was ambitious; his ambitions were fanned by the priesthood of Teotihuacan, the old established church, now San Juan Teotihuacan, seat of the head of the Catholic hierarchy; or it was until the days of Don Plutarco Elias Calles and his successors. For they too have found themselves opposed by the priesthood of Teotihuacan. Huemac raised an army and marched against Tollan; now, would the Prince of Peace belie his teachings? Quetzalcoatl—that was Emperor Ceacatl's God-name, the name of the god he incarnated—would *not* belie his teachings; truth meant more to him than empire, and he "fled" (if you like the word) to Cholula, halfway eastward to Vera Cruz and the Gulf.

The Cholultecs welcomed him as their king, and there, it would appear, his activities as Teacher were intensified during the following nine years. Then Huemac, having consolidated his empire at Tollan—Tula, now; not far northwest of Mexico City—marched against Cholula; and Ceacatl, leaving the city in charge of four of his disciples, "fled" once more.

Whither? Some say to the Serpent's Hole in Goazacoalco. H. P. Blavatsky mentions this place; one gathers from her reference that it was the headquarters of the American branch of the Great White Lodge. Some, on the other hand, say that Ceacatl took ship and crossed the sea, and here it is interesting to note that in Mayapan in Yucatan, there appears a king counterpart to him, with the same character and teachings, by the name of Gucumatz, which name is being interpreted from Maya to Nahua as Quetzalcoatl; and the meaning of both is Plumed Dragon or Serpent.

Quetzalcoatl was the great and consistent pacifist of history. Ah, but you say, he failed; he was driven out, as pacifists always will be. But did he fail? We read that Huemac, swelled now with his easy victories, went conquering far and wide; that the Anahuacs, having tasted the peace of Quetzalcoatl, grew mighty tired of it; that Huemac, somewhere far in the north, was assassinated by his officers; and that the whole empire passed into the power and rule of the four disciples whom Quetzalcoatl had left in charge at Cholula.

That was the plot of the book that was intended at first, but I found the preliminaries too interesting—the matter of Quetzalcoatl's parentage and birth, the Serpent's Hole, Huitznahuac—and it became apparent that the life of Quetzalcoatl must be left for another book. It was enough for this one if I brought him to birth, rearranging things and resifting the legends, endeavoring to see through the crude stories—which the Spaniards, after all, gathered only from the bloodthirsty Aztecs—to the spiritual and the beautiful which might be historically possible, too. For the Aztecs knew well that the Toltecs were far more cultured and gentle than themselves. I would go at least halfway to the stake for it that my city, Huitznahuacan, existed; I know my way through all of its streets and gardens. . . .

When did these things happen? Some think they knew that it was in the eleventh or the sixth century of Christianity, but the truth is that we don't know. Quetzalcoatl was born in a year Ce Acatl; he always is born in a year Ce Acatl. Cortés arrived in Mexico in a year Ce Acatl, which fact helped to paralyze Montezuma's will. Ce Acatl—Reed One—was the fourteenth year in any year-bundle of fifty-two years. It will be noted that the book never says that that particular Ce Acatl was the year of the birth of another of Quetzalcoatl's order, Lao-tse of China, in 604 B.C. but here I am confessing that that is this author's belief. Toltecs were to Aztecs much as Greeks are to ourselves: Quetzalcoatl was the Pythagoras of the Toltecs, and I would let him live in Pythagoras's time, had I my way. A plague upon this foreshortening of history!

The days of a theosophical propagandist, at least in Wales, are not conducive to continuous literary effort, and the novel on the life of the Mexican Prince of Peace is unlikely to be written by this pen.

BOOK I

Peace

1

In the Beginning

It was the Eve of Teotleco, holiest of festivals, the last day in the year House 12 in the holiest year-bundle in history. In a couple of hours the sun would set and the new year, Rabbit 13, begin, let but which pass and we would be in Reed 1, Ce Acatl, the holiest year.

They were sitting at supper in the veranda-like open-room of Shaltemoc's house in Huitznahuacan, with an outlook onto the gardens and neighboring houses below. The sun shone in through the frame of flowering vines that made several panels of the view, for the house faced to the west, as did the main part of the town. The room was well decorated with flowers and greenery from the forest, and the folk who sat supping, each seated on a cushion on the floor at a hassock that served as table, wore an air of holiday and holy day not to be mistaken.

There was something about this sprightliness and genial atmosphere that aroused Pelashil's curiosity. She sensed great things afoot and was watchful for explanations. Not, however, from anyone but Nopaltzin, who interested her hugely. From her place opposite his, she made great love to him in the cooing, eye-illumined manner natural to her three years and undeveloped respect for convention. He was the one, she decided, who both could and ought to make things clear for her; and he should do it.

So the moment that supper was over, she picked up her seat

cushion, waddled across with it in her arms and sat down at his side, letting it be known that she was in need of something—at once, and from him. This was the first time she had seen him, because he had gone away just before she was born and had returned only that very afternoon.

Ketlasho, who was Pelashil's mother and Nopal's sister, knew with clear intuition what the something was that Pelashil needed; in fact, she had known it long before Pelashil spoke. Religion meant much to Ketlasho, and this was religion's holiest season. Nopal, her wonderful brother, could tell the story appropriate to it as none else could. Certainly he was not a priest, she would admit, but then . . . look! He would never marry and have children of his own, would he? As good as a priest, one might say . . .

She wanted the story told because Ilanquey was now seven, of an age to offer flowers that evening at the shrines of Tezcatlipocâ. Therefore the girl ought not only to know the story, but to have it in mind as she made her offering. As for the other two, it could only do them good; and it might be years before Nopal was with them for Teotleco again. She hoped that Pelashil would be good during the telling, and she had some confidence that five-year-old Iztaman, the boy, would be. She and Shaltemoc, her husband, had known the story, of course, ever since their education began, but she hoped they could still thrill to it, especially with Nopal as the teller.

She was at pains herself to make a proper introduction for the tale in her careful, domestic-pious way. They knew, she said, that next month was called Teotleco, the "Arrival of the Gods," and that this was the night when the gods would arrive. That was why they would all go up, when the sun was setting, to the Top of the Town, where Ilanquey would give her flowers to the Soul of the World. Someday Iztaman would give flowers, and Pelashil too, so they all must listen carefully to the wonderful story Nopaltzin was going to tell them. It was the Soul of the World, our Lord Tezcatlipocâ, who would be the first of the gods to arrive.

". . . and you will give your flowers, Ilanquey, dear, to show how glad you are of his coming. Whenever you see flowers, remember that He is the beauty in them, and when you hear music, remember that He is the delightfulness in what you hear. Now Nopaltzin is going to tell you why our Lord will come to Huitznahuacan tonight."

So Nopal began by telling them what it was like before the Rising of the First Sun, reciting the poem as it was written in one of the pictograph books of the priests.

"The Sun," it says, "sat drowsily on the low horizon, nodding, dreaming and nodding, unaware of what he could do, peering out now and again over the world, muttering to himself helplessly. There were neither gods nor men on the mountains, no voices in the valleys. In the blue, unvarying twilight, great white blossoms shone and died unseen.

"Then Citlalicway Teteoinan, the Mighty Mother, hurled down Tecpatl, the Flint-stone, who struck the earth in rocky districts and skipped and slid from boulder to outcropping and from outcropping to boulder. Wherever he struck, there fire was born, until four score-score flames had been kindled and there had leaped up four score-score young, indomitable gods, dancing flamelike on the mountains, singing the Mother's praise. They leaped into being, fire-clad, rainbow-colored, beautiful; they moved like flames along the ridges of the mountains, gliding and dancing. All the time, they were chanting their joy.

"They saw the stars, their brothers, in infinity and regarded them with delight and love. They had their homes in the hollows of the hills; their speech was song; their thought was music; the substance of their being was essential fire. All things seemed to them praiseworthy and excellent. The lily that bloomed was their beloved companion; the snow-white blossoms in the twilight adorned their peace. And thus it was with them through an age, and an age, and the age of ages.

"Then a thought came flying out of the vast and whispered from mind to mind of them, until they hung their beautiful heads and pondered, forgetting to dance from ridge to ridge, forgetting to sing.

"Citlalicway Teteoinan regarded them. 'Children, children, why do you ponder?'

" 'There is no noonday, such as we desire,' said they. 'There is neither morning nor eve. We marvel that our Lord-brother, the

Sun, arises not. Why does he sit there brooding and slothful, peering out distrustfully now and again over the delicate world?'

"The Sun heard and made answer to them: 'There are no men; ye have no men to be your Others. Wherefore should I rise when there are no men?'

"They looked at each other, nodding their astonishment and apprehension. 'That is true,' said they. 'He would rise if there were men.' For seven cycles of time they pondered, and the lily bloomed and they beheld her not; and the snow-white blossoms in the twilight went unsung. 'How shall we make men?' they asked. 'In what manner are men created?'

"Then was wisdom revealed to our Lord Quetzalcoatl. 'Out of fire from heaven and bones from hell they are made,' said he.

"Then was wisdom revealed to our Lord Tezcatlipocâ. 'Our blood is the fire; it is fire from heaven. The blood of the gods is the fire from heaven,' said the Soul of the World.

"None desired to contradict him; all were convinced that it was the truth he told."

Here Nopal paused. So far, he had been quoting directly from the *Book of the Green-Shining Planisphere*. The next incident he abridged. It tells of the raid the gods made on the realms of Mictlantecuhtli, king of Hell, and of how they stole from him the bones of humanities long forgone in ancient universes forgotten. These bones they moistened or kindled with their fire-blood and made thereof a new race of men. Nopal then went on from the book.

"So they made themselves men, their Others. For every Divine, a human being. But the Sun did not rise.

" 'Why do you not rise, O Sun?' said they. 'There might be noon, heaven knows; there might be morning and evening in their beauty. Here are men, our Others, who would worship you. Adorable would be the moment of your rising. Consider that!'

" 'No, no,' said the Sun. 'You know not all things, you gods. Sad will be the moment of my rising; lamentation will be heard in it.'

" 'Dear help you better!' said they. 'Wherefore should it be sad and filled with lamentation? Glad it will be, we should think.'

" 'Sad, sad,' said he. 'Sad and not glad. For when I rise, you will die.'

"They looked at each other doubtfully. 'Die—what is that?' said they. 'There is something in this that is not clear to us.'

" 'Rising, I shall destroy you,' said the Sun.

" 'Alas!' said they. 'You are our enemy! We sought to befriend you; we created you worshipers; we desired your companionship and love. Hateful to us is this grim hostility!' A shadow of deep thoughtfulness had come on them; they had never been thus solemn before. It is not to be said that they were free from grief.

" 'Where I am, you cannot be,' said the Sun. 'This is the truth that I tell you: Compelled I shall be to make war on you, to be terrific, to exterminate you one by one. The men, your Others, will not avail you. The world I shine on, you may not abide in.'

"Then they spoke quietly, answering him. 'It will be better to delay!' said they. 'It will be much better to take counsel over this. Proclaim you not your war upon us, we beseech you! Rise not now, until we have considered!'

" 'You, the gods, invoked my rising, and surely rise I must.' The Sun leaped up from the horizon, armed with his bow and his shining shafts. 'I proclaim my war against you!' said he.

"Then laughed our Lord, the Plumed Dragon; he laughed out loud, making mock of the Sun. 'There is that which is more ancient and abiding than thou art. Against thy war I proclaim my peace!'

" 'Blessed art thou, Lord Quetzalcoatl!' " said the Sun, but none heard him at that time.

Nopal explained, *"Therefore art thou he who preserves the universe in stability, O Plumed Dragon, O Quetzalcoatl Beautiful, O Shining Peace in the Hearts of the Stars!"*

"But the Sun leaped up and came on armed and terrifically singing. Golden was his armor; golden was his person, from the nails of his little fingers to the ends of his hair. He was terrifying, wrathful-compassionate, filling the worlds with a rumor of death. He was gigantic, golden, filling the sky. Amazed were the gods, not desirable their situation. They hated the thought of Mictlantecuhtli's kingdom; they had little understanding, at that time, of death.

"Then laughed our Lord Tezcatlipocâ; the Soul of the World laughed out loud, making mock of fate. 'We are the gods; we are the Radiant. Even if he slay us, it will be glorious to go against him, for behold how beautiful he is, how nobly he advances! As for the kingdom of Mictlantecuhtli—are we not the Immortals, the Sons of the Flame?'

" 'Blessed art thou, Lord Tezcatlipocâ!' said the Sun, but none heard him say it, to be encouraged.

"But what the Soul of the World said made the gods warlike and of great cheer. They saw Tezcatlipocâ go forward and were proud. Singing, they followed the Beautiful Youth where he advanced, a running, leaping, lovely flame, against the Sun . . . and the Sun then slew them one by one, so that the flames vanished here to be kindled elsewhere; they waned into the daylight and were hidden in the beauty of the day, until only our Lord Quetzalcoatl was left.

" 'Why fightest thou not, Lord Plumed Dragon? Why fightest thou not, thou Upholder of the Worlds? Behold thy companions, how brave and beautiful they were, how nobly they died! Emulate them, lest evil be spoken of thee!'

" 'Will evil be spoken indeed?' said our Lord.

" 'Fight, that thou mayest be at peace where they are, and lest I slay thee unresisted and thou comest by shame!'

" 'Shall I come by shame in your deed to heaven?'

" 'Lest the sorrows of man become thy sorrows and thou hast no peace because of them throughout the age of ages!'

"Flaming, miraculous, filling the universe, shooting his beams through the kingdoms of the stars, our Lord the Sun came against our Savior. 'Fight,' said he, 'Lord Plumed Dragon!'

"Without defense stood Quetzalcoatl; without defense and without fear. 'Slay thou him whom slay thou canst!' said he. 'Against thy war I proclaim my peace; slay thou me if mine is the weaker!'

"Then the Sun dropped bow and quiver, and his shafts fell down through space like tears. 'Alas, thou art stronger than I am!' said he. 'For all I loved thee, thou hast defeated me!'

"The Sun wept. 'Ye none of ye knew!' said he. 'I slew them because I loved them, to save them from the griefs of the world

I must shine on; and they hated to be slain, and loved me little. And now thyself hast pronounced thy doom wherefrom I sought to save thee. Where the gods dwell, thou canst not abide; thou shalt be born among men forever in thy cycle; age by age thou shalt oppose men as thou hast me. Against their war thou shalt proclaim thy peace, until thou hast overcome them, O Quetzalcoatl!'

" 'Brother, Lord Brother, I have gained what I desired,' said our Lord. 'I shall conquer mankind at last, even as I have conquered thee.'

"But the Sun sighed in his sorrow, foreseeing grief for the one he loved. 'Brother, Lord Brother, I know not,' said he. 'Men will be more stupid than I am; they will not be so easy to conquer.'

"So our Lord was not slain by the Sun, nor sent into the Hidden with the other gods; but age by age he is born here among men."

That being the end of the first part of the Teotleco story, Nopal paused, but also because he could see that demure Ilanquey was brimming over with a question. As for the other two, Iztaman sat wide-eyed and round-mouthed, while Pelashil, sweet soul, was fast asleep.

"Will he be born next year?" asked Ilanquey.

Her elders saw where her thought had traveled. All the world knew that when Quetzalcoatl incarnates, he is born always in a year Ce Acatl, Reed One, the fourteenth of every year-bundle, and Reed One follows Rabbit 13, naturally.

"Who can tell, dear?" Nopal answered. "He comes when the world needs him, we may be sure. Perhaps it needs him now. But listen to the story of the First Teotleco."

Pelashil awoke, commanded him to proceed, and went to sleep again promptly. Nopal proceeded.

"So now the Sun rose, and there were morning and noon and evening, sunlight and starlight; but they brought no happiness into the world. For men went mourning for their Lost Others; they knew nothing of the war of the gods against the Sun. They wandered the earth disconsolate, seeking the Bright Ones they could not find; and they hated the sunlight that hid from them that which they adored. There was no music among the mountains; the speech of the gods was silenced; men did not know how to imitate the speech of their Lost Others. They listened to the wind in the forests; they listened on the seashore and where waters fell; and sometimes they thought they heard, for a moment, an echo or a dying refrain, but it was hard to tell.

"Now at the end of an age of seeking, the servant of Tezcatlipocâ came to the margin of the sea. The Sun shone far and low in the west beyond the heaving greenness of the waters; the winter clouds hung mournfully roseate and purple; in white and ghostly ranks the waves rode moaning in; the cold spray blew shoreward. There was no hope or pleasure in the world, thought the servant of Tezcatlipocâ. He had come to the rim of the world and found no sign of his Other, and there was no farther to go. The gods, whose presence had made the world delightful, were lost.

"So he paced the wet beach, weeping. With bent head, he paced the sand, the wetly shining, sparsely shell-strewn sand— the wave-lined, weed-rimmed sand, where the cold waves came moaning in, frantic along the sand. The Sun flashed green on the sea rim and was gone from heaven. The waves roared in their grand lamentation along the sand . . . and what was this ghost of fluting that stole through the crash of the waves? What was this specter of light that gleamed and flickered along the sand?

"He stood still and gazed. As if it were a glow on evening waters, lo, there the Beauty at the heart of beauty!—the eyes wherein beauty shines, and enchantment; the cloak of celestial hummingbirds' feathers; the youth that seemed to be eternal; the grace beyond computation by men. As if it were a picture reflected from infinite worlds afar, there stood the semblance of the Soul of the World.

" 'Why do you mourn, my servant, my Other? What causes you to wander, mourning and searching?'

" 'Lacking you, our gods, our Others, we mourn and wander, searching for beauty through the grief-encumbered world.'

" 'If ye spoke not with man-speech but with god-speech as we speak, ye would not wander, ye would not mourn.'

" 'Barren our lips; harsh-sounding the world. How should we achieve it, to speak like the gods?'

"The Master of Beauty spoke and said: 'In the House of the Sun is a thing called Music; had ye that, it would teach ye. Flute and serpent, drum and kettledrum; there they are, unused and useless. Obtain you them and you shall not mourn.'

"The radiance died away. There was only the night-brink over the world. The servant of our Lord was in doubt. The completeness that had seemed to be was incomplete again. He bowed his head and wept; his vision had been of unrealities. Without satisfaction, he was turning away.

"Then out of the edge of the ninth wave's foam a voice spoke to him: 'Come you now upon a voyage with me!' said the Turtle of the Western Billow.

"As well go as not go; there was no satisfaction or complacency in the world. So westward they journeyed, he standing on that sea-lord's carapace. 'Sing, servant of our Lord!' said the Turtle. 'Sing now pleasantly, and it will be better! Speak you in the god-speech, I implore you. Desolate and perilous is this traveling where there is no sweet song.'

" 'Gladly would I sing, but my lips are barren. Song is the speech of the gods, our Others; it is not like our speech. It rises and falls and dances through the universe, and dies away beyond the brink of things. It soars and swoons and trills and ripples and warbles, as keen with delight as the winter stars and as deep and solemn as starless midnight. It is like the wind that rides over the tossing forest when the trees bow down and strain and moan; it is like the mountain runlet among the rushes and pebbles. It is like night seas that thunder on the cliffs, or blue-bright seas of noonday that lisp and whisper and forget.'

"And even as he spoke, he rejoiced and marveled, for although the words had their passage between his own tongue and his teeth, the sound of them in his ears was like the god-speech.

" 'Pleasant is journeying where there is song,' said the Turtle.

"Rank on rank the waves fled by and nodded greeting as they passed. Friendly was the night sky, friendly the sea. *The Soul of the World is at hand,* they thought, and troubled themselves to be courteous. The servant of our Lord mourned no longer; he held converse with his Lord Other. He told out his heart to the Soul of the World, and when he spoke, his speech was the god-speech. So they traveled a long age.

" 'Up through the black-blue depths of the sea, I behold a rosy ray shining,' said he.

" 'Do you behold it already?' asked the Turtle. 'Without doubt, it will be from the eye of Cipactli, the great sea-creature of the Wave beneath the Sun. I may not come into his kingdom.'

"So there they waited. Up came Cipactli through the smothering foam: Cipactli, that vehement ancient, homely of beard and visage; Cipactli of the energies not to be tamed.

" 'I heard singing,' said grand Cipactli. 'I heard glorious sound. Evil on my beard if I heard not the god-speech, and the conversation itself of the Soul of the World.'

" 'It is the Lord Servant of Tezcatlipocâ,' said the Turtle, bowing profoundly. 'Of your courtesy, Lord Cipactli, bear you him whither you know, and he will sing to you on the journey, causing you delight. Yea, delight profound and limitless.' Then he said, 'Servant of our Lord, go you with the venerable Cipactli. Mount you upon this sovereign sea-beast and depart!'

"Cipactli bellowed and wallowed in his glee. 'Come,' said he with lofty courtesy. 'O Singer of God, I know what you seek, even though yourself may know not. Leave therefore this princely turtle and condescend to travel further with me.'

"So he mounted upon Cipactli, and they went forward. And now the rosy eye-beam shone down through the curious gardens of the sea-gods and now up into the dark caverns of the stars; and the sea fled away behind them, and the stars fled eastward overhead, so swift was Cipactli, so vigorous that ancient one, despite the innumerable ages of his life. And ever the voyager desired to praise Tezcatlipocâ, and as he praised, the god-speech resounded over the sea.

"Cipactli, snorting, lunged and glided forward, rejoicing in his profound and antique heart. The waves that wander over the solitary sea and heave themselves gigantically starward bowed, as it were, their heads in assent and reverence, beholding that which the Other of our Lord beheld not and the passage of the All-Beautiful between the stars and the waters.

"They came at last to the source of the Wave beneath the Sun.

'Woe is me!' sighed grand Cipactli. 'I have forgotten whither thou wouldst go.'

" 'To the House of the Sun,' said the servant of Tezcatlipocâ, aware now of what the gods desired of him.

" 'Dear, indeed,' sighed magnanimous Cipactli, 'I cannot go there. I cannot take you!' Tears fell from the eyes of him, salting the saltiness of the sea. 'This it is to be old and feeble,' said he. 'If I were as I once was, a flip of my fluke and thou wert there! But now thou must trust to thy singing.'

So the Other of our Lord sang, and Cipactli searched the deep with his eye-beam and rosily illuminated the enormous foundations of the sea, but there was no help there that he could discover. Then he turned his eye-beam into the dark planisphere and kindled up the vastness beyond the stars . . . and a light shone there like a diadem of stars. And a light shone there like the young moon. And a light shone there, nearing, nearing, like the beaming Sun when he sinks into the sea.

" 'Oh, I saw the eye-ray,' said the Dragon of the Planisphere. 'I heard the singing,' said the Master of the Azure Void. 'What goes forward with you now, Lord Cipactli of the Deep?'

" 'Swimmer of the Empyrean,' said tremendous Cipactli, 'lo, here is the servant of the Soul of the World. He who desireth to journey to the House of the Sun.'

" 'For the sake of his song and of our ancient friendship, he shall journey there,' said the Dragon. 'Mount you upon me, Lord Servant of the Beautiful Youth! Forsake my kinsman, the austere Cipactli, and be enthroned between the azure and the emerald of my wings!'

"The servant of Tezcatlipocâ bade farewell to renowned Cipactli and journeyed with the Dragon toward the House of the Sun, and as he journeyed, he sang. The Sun heard and looked forth and beheld, wing-glinting through the far-off blueness, the Dragon of the Planisphere approaching, and between the azure and the emerald of its pinions, one whom he could not fully recognize. 'For Tezcatlipocâ, I slew,' said he. He watched, pondering deeply. 'I foresee danger in the approach of this singer.'

" 'What are we to do?' asked the officers of his household. 'Command you us, and you know that we shall obey.'

" 'It is rather what ye shall not do,' said the Sun. 'Ye shall not exchange words with yonder singer. For all the delightfulness of his singing, let it be with ye as if ye were aware of nothing.'

" 'Our Lord desires little of us,' said they. 'In our deed to our Lord the Sun, it is little he desires of his proud servants!'

"The servant of Tezcatlipocâ raised a shout as he came to the gates of the Sun. 'I searched the world for my Lost Other; I saw a star shine upon the margin of the sea.'

"They went upon their offices proudly; they remembered that they were the ones whom the Sun trusted, and had never trusted in vain; it was not likely that they would fail him now. But ah, the marvel of the singing against which they must shut hearts and ears!

"He raised his shout a second time: 'Riding the turtle, I traversed the waves.'

"They went about their duties determinedly; they would not fail their Lord. The Beautiful Youth who was singing would not long remain there tormenting them.

"A third time he shouted: 'Cipactli magnanimously carried me. We traversed together the infinite sea.'

"They hung their heads and faltered. How could they pretend they heard nothing when everywhere the ether was alive with song?

" 'Riding the Dragon of Heaven I came!' he cried.

"The grief streamed from the eyes of them. 'Wonderful,' they said, 'is this loveliest of singing, and yet more wonderful is the singer!' For they could not but look forth and behold the Dragon and the one who rode between the beauty of his wings. 'Lo,' they said, 'the eyes wherein shines all enchantment; the cloak of celestial hummingbirds' feathers; the youth of him that would seem to be deathless; the grace beyond computation of ours!' So they spoke, describing the one they saw.

"They said, 'My heart will burst unless I listen to this.' And they said, 'Unless he receives what he desires, a wind, verily, from Mictlan will blow the stars into the sea!'

" 'What is it you desire, O Beautiful Singer? What quest do you follow, Lord Soul of the World?'

" 'Lord Soul of the World' they called him; they spoke but as they saw. He was the Servant of Tezcatlipocâ; they saw him the Soul of the World.

" 'I desire the music that is in the House of the Sun: the drum, the flute, the serpent, and the kettledrum.'

" 'Ah, how heaven would mourn unless you received them! How the Sun would feel injured if you went empty-handed away! What disasters would follow if we impiously stood in the way of your quest!'

"So now is the drum delivered to him, and the serpent of gold, and the flute, and the kettledrum. If he should play now, would not the stars follow him? Would not the Sun bow down in love? He has the flute at his lips; his fingers are on the stops of it; he blows into the delicate flute; he knoweth the science of it that he never learned. What went in breath comes forth music; what was air now is magic; what was nothing now is God. Never would he mourn for his Other again, because with him now is what joins the seen and the invisible, what creates the god-world in the man-world, what breaks down the barriers between this and that.

"He came among men and brought with him the music, and in the music, Tezcatlipocâ. On the Night of Teotleco he came, and in the morning the world was full of the Others again.'

"There," said Nopal. "That is the story. That is why this month is called "The Arrival of the Gods," and why Ilanquey will give her flowers this evening at the shrines of Tezcatlipocâ, and why Queen Shuquentzin will take the new robe to the temple, for tonight in every year there is a new coming of our Lost Others into the world."

The silence that followed awoke Pelashil, who chirruped drowsily to him to go on and then fell asleep again. Ilanquey's mind was aglow; this was "religion," which all grown-up people—and therefore also Ilanquey—were bound to enjoy. Iztaman's mind was peopled with mysterious creatures, sovereigns of dim kingdoms in the sea—whatever "the sea" might mean.

A strain of personal feeling mingled with Ketlasho's religious exaltation. Which of the priests could chant the great story like that? All Huitznahuac should have listened. Shaltemoc no doubt would have said so too, had it been suggested to him, for he was

a great admirer of Nopal. But, meanwhile, there was a matter
that called for correction. She broke the silence with: "Not
Queen Shuquentzin. She is dead these two years. And Ashokentzin is dead."
A glance and a monosyllable from Nopal demanded information. He had been in the city hardly an hour before he began the
telling of the story, and he had heard no Huitznahuatec news for
three years.
"There is no king," Shaltemoc vouchsafed. "The Princess Chimalmatzin is queen these four months. She will make her invocation this evening."
A shadow of perturbation flitted across Nopal's eyes, and a
train of thought of this kind flickered through his brain. At least
it had been some comfort to him in these last three years to tell
himself, "Still we have that grand Ashokentzin!" Chimalman—
he did not think he had ever seen her. She had been a child at
Blue-wind when he started for the north and would be Ashokentzin's great-granddaughter. Where then were Ashokentzin's three
surviving sons—if indeed they still survived: Acatonal, Acamapichtli, and Amaqui? Great men, all three of them . . .
He checked that mood with a timely reminder: Huitznahuacan
was much too far away for even the Toltec Topiltzin's armies to
reach. What difference who was on the throne?
That wise little woman, Ilanquey, whether or not feeling that
he needed a rebuke, spoke sententiously: "In Huitznahuac, we
love our queen."
"Yes?" said Nopal.
Placid, silence-loving Shaltemoc blew from his pipe a ring of
yetl smoke meditatively. "It is true," he said, and after a pause,
"You will see."

2
The Eve of Teotleco

Huitznahuacan, capital of Queen Chimalman's kingdom of Huitznahuac, climbed the lower western slopes of Mishcoatepetl—Cloud-Serpent Mountain—from the valley floor to about two-score man-heights up. The Townmouth, by which it was entered, was not more than a dozen leaps from the river and the bridge, and was the one place in the valley from which one could see the town, because Mishcoatepetl thrust out encircling arms westward that hugged Huitznahuacan to itself. The Townmouth was in the gap between these two hills, wide enough to contain the posthouse and the road, and no more.

Thence, for about five-score long strides, what was called the Street ascended gently as far as the koo of Teteoinan by the market steps on the right and there forked and began to climb in earnest. The northern branch was called the Street of the Tzinitzcan; the southern, the Street of the Quechol. Each wound about and turned and twisted pleasantly and was cobbled and steppered unevenly all the way up with quaint, unexpected landings here and there and little flights of steps, up or down, leading into the big dwelling-dotted garden between the two streets. Huitznahuacan consisted of three such gardens, plus the marketplace and the Top of the Town. There were no lateral streets, but only paths through these gardens.

In a niche on one of the landings on either street stood the stone figure of a bird: a tzinitzcan here, with arched neck, and beak combing its splendid plumage; a quechol there, most royal of its tribe, with proud feathers fluffed out; and from these, the streets had their names. The birds had been there time out of mind, and none knew who had carved them; they appealed to the popular imagination and were held to be symbolic of the city. Huitznahuac was as proud of them as of the streets they adorned or as of Huitznahuacan itself—the only city in the world as far as Huitznahuac knew. It was Ulupi's sacred capital. Whereof the very heart and glory was the Top of the Town, into which either street debouched. This was an open space, well-leveled and kept weedless; twice as long from north to south as the other way; and large enough, probably, to hold the whole population of the kingdom. It was bounded eastward by the House of the Kings on its terrace; on the north, by the koo of Tezcatlipocâ, crowned with his little square temple; on the opposite or southern side, by the koo of Quetzalcoatl, round-templed (these two being the largest and most important koos in the town); and on the west, by a large stage, or platform, forty strides or more deep and about two thirds of a man-height above the level of the arena, which was, in fact, the roof of the Calmecac, or college, where the Huitznahuatec boys were educated. The building itself extended from street to street, having its front in the garden below.

This Top of the Town was the sacred center in which, at least once in each of the eighteen twenty-day "months" into which the year was divided, Huitznahuacan celebrated some deity's festival. The koos and the terrace were of the same height and sloped back at the same angle; each had its wide stairway up the middle, on which the graver part of the audience at such festivals found sitting room, while the younger and more active squatted on the stepless slopes. Palace and temples were one-storied, equal in height, facaded with quaint, much-carved pillars, and silver-washed, as were all of the buildings in the country, with a preparation of gypsum kept polished till they shone. From mid-arena one saw all three, backed by forest-covered mountainside: the two spurs of Mishcoatepetl behind the temples, and Mish-coatepetl himself, forest on forest, crag above precipice, rising steeply skyward behind the House of the Kings.

Toward the Top of the Town all Huitznahuacan was making its way an hour or so later that evening. Shaltemoc's house was in the northern of the three gardens, so they went up by the Street of the Tzinitzcan, and slowly because of the children. Everyone who overtook them had warm greetings for Nopal after his three-year absence, but it was to be noticed that none asked where he had been. He had Pelashil on his shoulder, and in his mind a less comfortable burden: the remains of the apprehension that Shaltemoc's news had aroused. It was entirely absurd, and he resented its insistence; but nevertheless, it kept him aloof. The air was full of the smell of the Huitznahuatec mountains, and his ears savored the dignity of Huitznahuatec speech. Every sight and sound kept singing *home!* to him, and yet—

"Wherever you have been all this time, you will have seen no street like this," Ketlasho broke in reproachfully on his musings.

To that, at any rate, he could smile acquiescence. There were no Streets of the Tzinitzcan in the great cities of the north. Here, in places, as many as eight men could walk abreast, and he had seen armies thunder through the streets of Culhuacan in the north, two-score shouting warriors shoulder to shoulder in line . . .

As they came by the end of the Calmecac, Amaquitzin, the Quetzalcoatl-priest, emerged from that building and hailed him. He was King Ashokentzin's second surviving son and the new queen's great-uncle. He had been Nopal's Quetzalcoatl-teacher at the college, of which he and his elder brother, Acatonal, had been joint heads for decades. A hale old man, clear-cut and serene, widely loved and revered, he was reputed to have a laugh that could be heard from the Middle Market to the Queen's Garden.

Being also bound for the Top of the Town, he walked along with Nopal, telling him about the changes of the last three years, and chiefly about the new queen, of whom he evidently thought very highly. He urged Nopal to make himself known to her without delay, saying that she had heard of him and was interested and that he was the only one of her subjects she did not know. By the time they came to the foot of the palace steps, he had half made an appointment with Nopal to meet him after the evening's events that he might take him up to the House of the Kings and introduce him. But he knew better than to make things too definite, and Nopal, whom he had given little chance to say he would not come, for some reason hoped they would miss one another. He did not want to think about the girl-queen just yet. So Amaquitzin left him, and much as he loved his old teacher, Nopal was not sorry.

His desire was to realize Huitznahuacan, not to be talking or listening much. How near and beautiful, here, was the God-world that had been so far away from him in the north! Palace and temples glowed, warmly reflecting the now-kindling west, where, beyond the Calmecac roof that hid away the town and middle distance, the sun rested on a world-rim of burning, roan-purple mountains, with holy Teotepetl like a white feather in the midst; and overhead were skies, as deep and tender, thought he, as only the Huitznahuatec skies know how to be. And then, in the business of the evening—the giving of offerings at the shrines—how near and beautiful was the God-world!

At every crossroad in the country there was what was called a God-seat, put there for the benefit of deities wandering unseen and that men might have before their eyes reminders of the Invisible Divine. In the arena were four of these, and as always at Teotleco, the Calmecac youths had made green arbors, or shrines, of them, in which the offerings were to be laid. Starting at the southwestern corner, the crowd went around in silence, each person leaving a sprig or a blossom at each shrine.

For Ketlasho, it was a pleasing, important duty to induct her elder daughter into this sacramental custom. Hand in hand, they did their devotions at the shrines. Pelashil, still riding on Nopal's shoulder and though quite lacking in reverence, was resolute against being left out. If she might not yet make an offering, at least (she held) she might speak her friendly mind out loud to the Soul of the World.

When all was finished, the crowd climbed the slopes and disposed itself to watch the play, of which the subject was always the story that Nopal had told the children; but a new thing was made of it annually, and surprises were to be looked for and enjoyed. It began; and the players, as usual, took for granted their audience's imagination. Whatever god was slain by the Sun went through the ritual of dying, then walked across to the palace stairway, where a place had been kept for him, to wait until he should be needed again. It was all more dance than drama, with comic interludes of Cipactli. But though they thus eschewed vulgar realism, it did not fail to suggest to Nopal discomforting thoughts and pictures.

The rest knew nothing about war. He did. Violent or unnatural death of any sort was unknown in Huitznahuac. What would happen to these youths now so gaily playing at being killed if war came their way in earnest? If it should occur to, and be possible for, the tremendous Toltec Topiltzin to come south with his hosts—and with the Otomi priesthood in his train—for example?

Thank the gods, they were too far away to need fear it! The tremendous Toltec Topiltzin would almost certainly die without ever having heard of Huitznahuac—if one had but the common sense to hold that fact in mind, excluding suggestions the play was never meant to give. Come now, attend to Cipactli!

But Cipactli failed to hold him tonight. For talking about the Otomi priesthood—what vastly different things the word *priest* meant, here and in the north!

In Nopal's college days, Amaquitzin had been concerned to teach his pupils how to live: moment by moment masters of their thoughts and feelings, and quite free, because not self-hampered, in action. And then there had been their Tezcatlipocâ-teacher, that greatest of poets, Acatonatzin, whose work had been to awaken in them the Tezcatlipocâ-knowledge, or wisdom, or vision; there was no other way to define that grand and living learning. You learned it through poetry, through music, through silence; from stars, from flowers, from mountains; from the hidden god in yourself and the manifest divineness of the universe. And having learned it, you became a member of the brotherhood of natural things. How to live, and how and what to know: Education meant learning just those two things, and what else could it mean? Those were and must always be the two sides of it: interdependent and mutually complementary, the one not to be attained without the other. You could not live Quetzalcoatl-wise without the Tezcatlipocâ-vision; you could not attain that vision unless you lived the Quetzalcoatl-life. What else that was true could be said about education?

Very little, you would think. Oh, but that was not by any means the way it was in the Anahuacs!

There, as far as he had been able to learn—and Cohuanacotzin had told him much—there was practically no Quetzalcoatl-teaching, only mere rules of conduct, taught out of books and such, categories of "Thou-shalt-nots," nothing real. And for the Tezcatlipocâ-wisdom, they taught a lot of what they called "sciences," which he made out to mean facts about this, that and other subjects—the gods knew what! Or, more probably, the gods knew nothing about it, being above such substitutes for knowledge.

And the gods themselves, at least in Teotihuacan, where one heard most about them, seemed to be things to be feared and worshiped extravagantly, who derived a depraved satisfaction from the self-abasement of men, from hearing human beings call themselves miserable sinners and the like! There appeared to be no time in that mad rush of a northern world to let the Plumed Dragon have his perfect will of men's lives.

Thus Nopal brooded, glad to reassure himself of this better state of things called Huitznahuac. In the north, it had been difficult to believe in Huitznahuac: One had been tempted to think, "I must have imagined that." But here it was, the mountain land where one thinks so little about sins and so much about innate divinity, and kinship with the stars and the mountains. "We are your brothers, O Plumed Dragon! O Soul of the World! O Lords of the Mountains!" said the hymn.

Yes; it was those here who were rich and favored, not the Toltecs, despite the vastness of their myriad cities and the stringent circumstance of their religion. When should one find among them the Soul of the World thus friendly brooding and glowing over the peace of a mountain evening, or to be felt, as now, in the grave happiness of a crowd? From their coming into the arena here, these people had been a part of the holy quiet of the nightfall; they did not affront the divine vastness above and around, as would any concourse in the north. And there were no traces of vice or disease, no signs of wrecked life, among them, such as one so often saw in the Anahuacs; only noble physiques, beauty of form and feature, grave dignity. In the north they *dressed* better, he supposed. One must concede them that, with their rich cottons and plumes for our homely nequen. Yes, but even then . . . was there a mashtli, tilmatli, or gown on man or woman here that had not been made and painted for this occasion as a work of religion? Had not the womenfolk watched the universe for hints of the designs they had used, believing that images from the God-world might be revealed to them through natural things? Did they not hold their art sacred, and was not the result beautiful? And was not beauty the only real riches?

Pelashil, waking from a long nap, cooed and gurgled in his ear. The play was over, and the people were moving down into the arena. Nopal went with the rest, and then his instinct to be alone made him forget that more was to follow. He started homeward and was halfway to the top of the Street of the Tzinitzcan before his brother-in-law overtook him. Just then, too, the place became alive with the grumble and chatter of drums, with which the players had been supplied from below.

Nopal turned and looked up whither Shaltemoc was pointing. There he saw a little group at the head of the palace stairway. "The God's robe," said Shaltemoc, and Nopal understood. Chimalmatzin would take up into the temple the robe she had made for the statue of the Beautiful Youth.

The rest of the family joined them at a dozen strides or so from the koo of Tezcatlipocâ, directly before the stairway to the temple. From that point Nopal watched the procession come down from the palace, headed by the three Royal Uncles, the late king's sons. Sculptural grand faces, he thought, that owed nothing to their trappings: Amaqui's, all serene and kindly wisdom; Acatonal's, keen spiritual insight; Acamapichtli's, command and strength of will. At least they would dominate the girl-queen. She might wear the royal headdress, but it was Acamapitzin who would be king.

The procession came down into the arena, and the crowd opened a lane for it to pass. But it was some distance in front of Nopal, so that even if he had not been preoccupied, he would not have seen much of the queen. What those better-placed saw was a girl of about twenty, her nequen cloaks and gown white all over; copious black hair loose on her shoulders in the style proper to maidenhood; above it, the royal headdress of gold-plated leather shaped like the head of a fish, with the lower jaw broken back and hanging behind. Inches shorter than the princes she followed, she yet looked tall; and her face, beautiful by any standard, showed high potentialities of courage and tenderness. There was something in it of her great-grandfather, Ashokentzin, something also of spiritual kinship to her great-uncles: a suggestion that, latent in her and yet to be discovered, rested a will like Acamapichtli's, a serenity like Amaqui's, a lofty perspicacity like Acatonal's.

The crowd was silent as she passed, but thrilled to her nonetheless, so that she felt as she went a constant increase of that inner wealth she hoped she was bringing to the temple. Its outer symbol was the robe she had made for the statue of Tezcatlipocâ, according to the yearly custom of the queens, her ancestors since the days of Ulupi herself. Four women followed her, carrying it. At the top of the koo, she took it from them and, entering the temple alone, invested the statue with it.

There none ever came but the Tezcatlipocâ-priests and, on these occasions, the queens. She felt the breathless, sweet holiness of the place; it winged the invocation she repeated mentally.

"So be thou clad, but more nobly, in our thoughts and deeds; so make we thy robe, the Visible Universe, Divine!"

She remained there while one might have counted a couple of score-score, directing her thought to the Eternal. On the wall above the statue there hung a flute and a bow, brought to Huitznahuac by her ancestor, Huanhua, who, before ever he came to Queen Ulupi from beyond the western sea, had been, in some far land, a prince, and the servant of Tezcatlipocâ. Huanhua was the same who brought the music from the House of the Sun, but, as most held, in a later life. The flute was that of his Lord Other; the bow was his own, and the world he came from had been famous for it. It was a bow that had never missed its mark, men said. So might she not miss hers, while it was the Soul of the World she aimed at!

Then she went out, and standing before the altar in front of the temple, facing the people below, recited the *Invocation to be Used by One Succeeding to Sovereignty,* from the Ritual. Ashokentzin's reign had been a long one, and only the very old had heard it before; and the voice in which she uttered it was so clear-toned and thrilling that the effect was as if a kind of triumphal magic had been used. The very air seemed vibrant with divinity.

Nopal's eyes were on her as she stood unstirring and gazing into the infinite after the tones of the invocation had died away. Suddenly he caught his breath, for he knew what it was that made her face shine with ecstasy.

Out of the night above there breathed an unearthly, a spiritual, music—flute music, remote, and of stellar quality—that she must have heard before he did, and that blew by and was gone. Perhaps it had not outlasted a dozen heartbeats, or half a dozen, or even a single one, and yet it had revealed eternity, as if he had looked through some infinitesimal fissure in the continuity of time into infinite worlds of wonder. It was gone, and he remembered nothing of the . . . *omnivision* he had possessed while it lasted, except that it *had* been omnivision and that the girl standing up there before the altar had possessed it too, and in fuller measure than he. But Ketlasho, as it chanced, looked down from Chimalman's face to Nopal's while it lasted and tried to draw her husband's attention to the marvel that she saw on both.

The lane through the crowd had formed itself before Nopal was in the world again. He had heard the fluting of Tezcatlipocâ, and the queen had heard it. There could be no Toltec or other troubles in this reign . . . for what could it have been but the same fluting that Ulupi heard at the Teotleco of her accession, to augur the coming of great Huanhua and the serene ages of Huitznahuatec history that followed?

He was called back to his surroundings by a sudden wriggle of excitement on the part of his small, comfortable burden—for he was still carrying Pelashil, who could not let her queen pass without making some manifestation of loyalty. The wriggle came near her undoing, and would have been but for Chimalman.

Small arms were thrown out vigorously; a dusky little plump hand reached and stroked the royal cheek; a crow and a gurgle proclaimed adoration; and the queen caught up the child before she could fall, caught her up with the tenderness and compassion her God-mood had evoked in her; and it was a moment before she realized that this was no miracle, but Shaltemotzin and Ketlashotzin's daughter, whom she must give back to her father now, and she held her out, smiling, as she supposed to Shaltemotzin, from whose shoulder the child had jumped or tumbled. It was not Shaltemotzin, though, but a complete stranger, whose smiling eyes she caught for a moment before going on . . . as this ceremonial occasion demanded she should.

Only . . . she had caught this stranger's eyes, and they had been, she thought, different from any other eyes in the world. And then . . . there were no strangers. How could there be? The idea of a sovereign having subjects she did not know!

For the time being, she had forgotten that there was one such—just one. She might have reasoned from Ketlashotzin's daughter to Ketlashotzin's brother, and no doubt she would presently; but the night and her mood were superrational.

3
The Arrival of the Gods

On the night of the Arrival of the Gods, every priest in Huitz-nahuac watched in his deity's temple for the Divine Event. Thus the Royal Uncle Acatonatzin, being Tezcatlipocâ-priest, watched from the koo of the Soul of the World.

He sat in the doorway of the temple, sinking his thought deeper and deeper into the luminous silence behind the mind and exploring that inwardness for signs of the Beneficent Approach. He knew how to prepare himself for the Teotleco: stilling the mind and leaving it forgotten, while the consciousness ascended ever, gazing into bright infinity for the gathering there and the deepening of a star.

Near the Peak of his Being, an impulse came to him, or he heard a command issued, to "Look down . . ."

And he saw the world of men outstretched below: Huitznahua-can, Huitznahuac, the mountains and forests beyond, an infinity of peopled territories far and near, and all of them glowing with light. Though "the world" to him, as to all of his countrymen, had always meant Huitznahuac and nothing more, this vastness of it, with realization of what the vastness meant, caused him no surprise. "Lands beyond lands beyond lands," he thought—or heard said—"and in all of them happiness and exalted peace. It is humanity after the Rising of the Fifth Sun."

Then, around the limits of his vision, shadows darkened and came encroaching inward until only the small space that was

Huitznahuac was left glowing. "The shadows are ignorance, false religions, passions, and ambitions," said the voice. The picture was terrifying. Dim forms like demons rioted in the dark; he saw men slaughtering men. But even as the shadow converged on it, the light that was Huitznahuac intensified, glowed deep and valiantly against the grim invasion, flashed forth to repel it, and then at last suddenly flared up and broke, shot out rays far into the darkness, and died. But the rays, mingling with the substance of night, maintained themselves in the midst of it, ate into its being and produced light there, so that the darkness went thinning away.

"Time decays in its cycle," said the voice. "The Fifth Sun is not exempt from the fate of its predecessors, but a Star—even Quetzalcoatl, the Morning Star—shall arise from Huitznahuac."

And then the light came upon him: the illumination that was the Teotleco, or the Arrival of his God. . . .

Facing Acatonatzin, with the arena between them, sat his brother, Amaqui, in the doorway of the Temple of the Plumed Dragon. He too rose into the golden silence beyond thought and was at one with the peace wherewith his deity had conquered the Sun in the beginning, and would conquer man before the end.

In that intense, teeming vacuity, life began to quicken, or a star to glow, or motion to uplift itself and thrill outward . . . till, as it were, a Winged Serpent occupied infinity and descended into conditioned existence and the realms of time . . . into Huitznahuac . . . into the flesh.

"Prepare, prepare!" sang the spaces thronged with their hierarchies. "Next year shall be the Ce Acatl!" And Amaquitzin staggered to his feet and fell unconscious, overwhelmed with the glory of the Arrival of his God.

There was but one man whom the Huitznahuatecs considered as holy as, or even holier than, Amaqui: Ameyal, the Tlaloc-priest, the oldest man in all that long-lived nation.

He had begun his career, in days none but he remembered, as Priest of the Plumed Dragon, and Quetzalcoatl-priest he might have remained to that day but that he had insisted, when Amaqui was old enough to take it, on giving up that office to him. The king's son, he thought, rather than the king's cousin, should be the legate of the Lord of Peace. The result was that he raised the priesthood of Tlaloc, not a very high dignity before, to equality with those of Quetzalcoatl and Tezcatlipocâ, and both Amaqui and Acatonal revered him as their teacher and consulted him often on the deeper aspects of their wisdoms. It was said of him that at least a year-sheaf ago, he had forgotten his own existence, that he was like a mountain with its peak above the clouds, and carried his head in skies of timeless universality.

From the doorway of the Temple of Tlaloc, where he sat that night, nothing material was to be seen but a corner of the southern end of the Calmecac roof and the Temple of Tezcatlipocâ beyond; and the moon that drew toward the west made a ghostly glow on those two silvery-polished fragments of architecture. Ameyal was aware of them at first; they helped him into loftier regions, their intrusion on it stressing the vast superhumanness of night.

The stars came up from behind Mishcoatepetl. Above the glimmer of the temple, constellation by constellation, they came; and although they were without him, yet also they were within him. Watching them, enlightenment came.

"Aye," said he. "I must do that tomorrow, that the Great Thing the world is waiting for may come to pass."

4

The Chalchiuhite Dragon

On Teotleco night, the priests remained in the temples only until their gods arrived; then they retired to their homes. Iyaca, the Tlaloc-priest's disciple, missing his master in the morning, went up to the temple in search of him. Finding him asleep in the doorway, he withdrew discreetly to lie in wait.

Waking, Ameyal was in deep humiliation. Fourscore and seven years a priest, and never until now— What priest in all history, until now, had let age and physicality master him on the wonder-night? There had been no Teotleco for him: His god had come and found him sleeping. He remembered taking his seat in the doorway and watching the stars come up from behind the mountain, and nothing more.

But to give way to remorse would be to prevent the grace of one's Divine Other from shining through into the world, and he forbade himself that mood quickly. And there was something— some tremendous duty—that he must do.

Watchful Iyaca had him home and persuaded into breakfasting within a few minutes of his waking, treating him the while with a new profundity of reverence and affection. Iyaca, like the rest of Huitznahuacan, was due to make holiday in the country that day. He was loath to go, but Ameyal, when they had breakfasted, dismissed him in a manner that there was no withstanding. The Tlaloc-priest, though ten years frailer in look than yesterday, and with shame still besieging, but not admitted into, his heart, seemed also of loftier holiness; an impersonal grandeur had descended on him. So Iyaca left him to the gods.

Alone, Ameyal set out at once to do what he had to do. It had not occurred to him to think what it was or where he was to do it. But, without hesitation, he crossed the ravine by the bridge at the bottom of his garden and went up by an easy path through the forest to a place called the Raingods' Glade, which he might visit when he would. Thence he took what was called the Votaries' Path down into the Queen's Garden, with no thought that it was to the Queen's Garden he was going, but with the knowledge that it was there that his tremendous duty was to be done.

The garden lay between the House of the Kings and the rise of the mountain and consisted of two or three acres of land, very unevenly surfaced and sloping down from northeast to southwest. Huitznahuatec monarchs had worked and dreamed and delighted in it since the beginning. From the highest part a stream flowed down in chains of ponds, narrow and deep, with cascades and intervals of rapids between, so arranged that the whole surface was almost as much water as land. There were no wide spaces of either, but the brook divided and intertwisted mazily among rocks golden or copper-green with saxifrage; paths wound between and across deep pools not much wider than themselves. There was a bewilderment of singing or whispering waters; here and there nestled a pond a little wider, with perhaps a statue of recumbent Tlaloc beside it; everywhere were rock plants, water plants, blossoms, rushes, reeds. Right in the midst was a more solid piece of land, sheltered from the north by a high rock ablaze with ruby or purple-chaliced creepers; and here, against the rock, was a low stone seat with raised jaguar heads carved at the ends, and squat, distorted jaguar legs for support.

To this place Ameyal picked his way and sat down—still unaware of where he was, but well aware that here his Mayavel would come to him. Quetzalcoatl would send her; she would come with Quetzalcoatl's symbol of symbols in her hand, and thereby he would know her when she arrived, and the purpose of the ages would be accomplished.

The Mayavel was one of the four Votaresses of Tlaloc, who,

with a fifth, a youth, would climb Mishcoatepetl on behalf of all
Huitznahuac at Tepeilhuitl, the Feast of the Mountains, in the
month of the same name that followed this month of Teotleco;
it was the festival and holy season of the Tlalocs. Four of the
votaries were chosen, according to a rule only the Tlaloc-priest
knew, from the elder students of the Girls' College, and the youth
from the Calmecac; and they should have been chosen, and
under preparation, months since.

But Ameyal, in a silver peace, knew that he was where gods
and men, sun and mountains, depended on him to be. The morning sunlight and silence, the solitude and the shadows of the
forest, the fish flocks—blue, vermilion-speckled silver, ruby-red
and gold-green—that poised themselves or flickered through the
dark water at his feet . . . all of these things were his companions
and part of himself. They shared with him the knowledge that
that was on the brink of happening for which ages had been
waiting, for which he himself had been waiting through the long
years of his life. All the future depended on his being where he
was, to find his Rabbit 13 Mayavel . . . that our Lord might
conquer mankind at last, as of old he had conquered the Sun.

Meanwhile, Chimalman was at her housework. The queen of
Huitznahuac was sweeping her palace. This being the day when
everyone went out into the country, she had packed off her
servants, old Ocotosh and his wife, Eeweesho, to their son's farm
east of the mountain; they had started in a litter soon after dawn,
having in turn sent home the couple of maids whose labors
Eeweesho directed. The Royal Uncles were away touring the
districts. Chimalman herself had been going to Blue-wind, but
after last night, she had decided not to go. She wanted to be alone
with the newly arrived gods.

Eeweesho had laid injunctions on her to do no housecleaning
on Teotleco Day. Everything necessary had been done yesterday,
and would be done again tomorrow. Queens did housework,
true; from Ulupi downward, all of them had been used to sweeping their floors, but Eeweesho had an idea that this queen was
intended otherwise, and had come rather to be worshiped than
to work. Eeweesho and Ocotosh had served her father at Blue-
wind long before she was born. But if one is to be with the gods,

one must work; or, at least, that is the easier way. So Chimalman swept the palace floors.

The last room she came to was the one she lived in except during the rains and the cold weather; it was at the end of the south wing, and on three sides wall-less, pillared, and with balustrades between, except where the steps led down into the garden. (The palace, we should note, was shaped like three sides of a square, the two wings stretching back toward the garden and the mountain, with a terrace between.)

As Chimalman worked here, and when she had nearly finished her work, the clink or dap of some hard thing falling on the floor behind her caught her ear. Turning, she saw lying there the noblest carved chalchiuhite in the world: a little dragon, the symbol of Quetzalcoatl, not much bigger than her thumb. "Now where could that have come from?" she thought, picking it up. The touch of it thrilled her strangely; she had seen chalchiuhites as large or larger, but none so liquidly and glowingly green. It could have fallen from nowhere but the ceiling, or that tlapalizqui bush in the big pot. It seemed to flash in the sunlight, to throb with life in her hand.

Then she saw the Tlaloc-priest out in the garden and thought for a moment that he must have thrown it to her for playful reasons of his own; but she realized that, in any case, he was too far off. But she would question his wisdom about it, for surely it was a treasure of the gods and no ordinary gem. Out she went by the doorless doorway and down the steps into the garden, calling "Ameyatzin!"

But it was an Ameyatzin quite new to her—one, apparently, who did not recognize her. "Child," he said, "have you brought the jewel?"

Awed by his voice and manner, she held it out to him with no more words than "Your Godhead knows. It fell while I was sweeping the sunroom."

He looked at it and bowed, but he did not take it. "Yes," he said, "my god has chosen you. The Plumed Dragon verily has chosen you, that the rays of it may shine into your heart. You are to be the Mayavel of this year's Feast of the Mountains."

Now the fact was that each year since her coming to the

capital, if Chimalman had not envied the Tepeilhuitl votaresses, she had certainly thought them the most fortunate of women. The mountain was, after all, her closest friend, since no human being can be in adorableness quite what a mountain is, though he may be equal in constancy and faith. Blue-wind Mountain, Cloud-Serpent Mountain—their spirit was the same. The gods, in all their ultimate dearness, had always been accessible to her in her childhood on the one, and she had always known that they would be so on the other. But none might ascend most holy Mishcoatepetl except those yearly votaries at the Feast of the Mountains, one of whom she had thought she might never be, because of the way they were chosen. She had not been educated at the Girls' College; her father had taught her at home, which was the custom for the heir to the throne. But now, by the favor of this inspired Ameyatzin, she would go to her great lover, Mishcoatepetl . . . .

"My gratitude is to those who have chosen me," she said. "You will teach me the hymns, Ameyatzin?"

But a change was working in him; he made no answer, but seemed bewildered, and after a while, "My work is finished," he said. "I must go."

He rose to his feet with difficulty, no longer the sublimity he had been, but an old man, dazed and tremulous. She would have taken him into the palace and tended him there, but that he so clearly wished to be at home. So, very slowly, she led him down by the Street of the Quechol and up through the marketplace to his house behind the koo of Tlaloc. There she laid him on his bed, covered him and coaxed him to sleep, then prepared a meal against his waking of what she found in Iyaca's larder.

Later, while they were dining, she discovered that Ameyal knew nothing of what had happened in the garden. This became clear when she asked him to teach her the hymns . . . "since I am to be the Mayavel." He was obviously surprised, but exceedingly happy over it.

"Will you indeed?" said he. "Ah, Tlaloc will be pleased — Tlaloc will be pleased!" Later he brought out the pictoscripts and taught her the Mayavel hymns, and thus they were engaged until Iyaca returned. It was dusk when she left the old priest.

In the Lower Market, she remembered the chalchiuhite dragon, about which she had not thought to question him. She felt for it in her pocket, but it was not there; nor could she find it in the garden when she searched there the next morning. But that night she dreamed that it fell into her heart and shone there until the distant heavens were illumined, and she heard the stars praise it, singing, "Hail, Quetzalcoatl! Hail, Star of the Morning and the Eve!"

5

Eagle Mountain

No, Nopal could not spend Teotleco at Huitznahuacan; and Ketlasho, although disappointed, knew better than to press him. She had rather stressed the information—this was on their return from the Top of the Town—that, all being well, Shollo and Maxio and the children would be in town for Tepeilhuitl, and hadn't Nopal better stay with them until then? He might come in for Tepeilhuitl, he answered, but he must go now. At dawn tomorrow morning.

So Ketlasho, for all her disappointment, let the matter drop. He was Nopal, and you had to be careful not to set up your will against—you did not know what. One of the first lessons she had been taught was to accept the unexplained, especially where Nopal was concerned.

So now she packed a day's rations in his deerskin traveling sack: tamales she could vouch for, and three cherimoyas of the most luscious. And she even refrained from asking what had happened when the queen had made her invocation and the strange light had shone on her face and on his. She had told Shaltemoc about it on their way home. "It was Chimalmatzin who might have been his sister, and both of them gods," she had said. "You never saw such a likeness."

By sunrise on Teotleco morning, Nopal had left the town, crossed the bridge, and was settling down to the steady dog-trot, four miles or more an hour, proper to a day's journey, and also

into a happiness he had not known since he started for the north.
True, he was going to Rainflower Manor, as he had told Ketlasho and Shaltemoc; and Rainflower Manor was his birthplace
and still, nominally, his home. But that was not the prospect that
swelled his heart. He loved Rainflower, but there were two places
among these mountains that he loved still more, and he was
bound for both of them now. Tonight he would be with Quauhtli
at Eagle Hermitage; tomorrow, with Huehuetzin, the Master in
the Serpent's Hole.

And then, perhaps, he would learn why Huehuetzin, having
sent him on that unprecedented journey to the Anahuacs, had
bidden him to so time his return as to be in Huitznahuacan last
night, witness of its wonder. Had Huehuetzin foreknown the
accession of Chimalmatzin at this time, and that the omen of
bright omens would be vouchsafed her, and that Nopal would
hear it too? Probably he had, for the Master was intimate with
the inwardness of things and shared their knowledge with the
rivers and the stars.

How wonderful he had made life for Nopal; how he had
illuminated the years! Twenty-six or seven years it would have
been; it was hard to tell which now. But it must have been in
Reed 12 or Flint 13 of last year-sheaf, when Nopal was three or
four, that his father first took him up Teotepetl, the Mountain
that was God. The day was unforgettable, in whatever year it had
fallen, and Nopal began recalling it to mind as he ran: a good
mental discipline when one was going to the Master.

His father had carried him up through the forest and left him
under the big mahogany tree in the glade, with the command not
to stir whatever happened. And then first the monkeys had come,
and he had had hard work not to be terrified; but, just in time,
the Voice in the Silence had ordered them away. He heard it; and
the monkeys obeyed it; but he was still sure that it had made no
sound. And then the peccaries; and they heard it too, and as he
distinctly remembered, they laughed and came and made friends
with him. And the deer; and the tapir that sniffed at him with
wiggling snout; and lastly, at nightfall, the jaguar. Well he re-
called how its desolating hunting squall had changed into a
cough and a whimper, and then into ecstatic purring, as the

Voice in the Silence became a living man, whose hand had taken his. . . .

Thereafter Nopal had never feared anything, nor lost the sense that came to him on that day of having Unseen Protection always, and the Heart of the Invisible for his companion; for the hand that took his hand, and the voice that said, "Come, Nopalton!" had been the Master's.

He wondered how long he had stayed in the Serpent's Hole that time, both Quauhtli and he waiting on the Master daily and receiving from him endless benediction. Through the months of Quecholli and Panquetzaliztli, he suspected. It was the first of many visits. His absences from home were always arranged by his father and never referred to at Rainflower. At the end of that first visit, Ashopatzin had fetched him from beneath the mahogany tree; and he, eager to tell his news, had begun, "Tatzin . . ." But Tatzin's finger had gone to his lips, and a smile had come to his face that somehow made Nopal understand that he must never speak about his adventures on Teotepetl. And he never had.

Thus when, years later, he had been sent to the Calmecac at Huitznahuacan, and the first boy he met there was Quauhtli, neither had shown by so much as a sign that he had known the other elsewhere; and in all the years since, they had never spoken of the Serpent's Hole except at the Serpent's Hole itself or at Eagle Hermitage.

Thus Nopal mused, running southward and at midday eating his lunch as he ran, until he had left the Road behind him—and the cultivated fields and gardens, and Queen Chimalman's kingdom—and come far into the uninhabited regions beyond. The Heart of Things took hold upon him, as it always did when he approached the Master. An electric joy was growing in the air. He crossed the Quinames' Bridge, where the northern ends of Quiname and Eagle Mountains converge, and took the road that ascends along the eastern flank of Quauhtepetl, Eagle Mountain.

A bridge and a road in these wilds? Yes, built in ancient ages, the Master had told them, by the Quinames, those proud and sorcerous giants who had flourished and fallen with the Fourth Sun. Both now seemed works of nature only, for the mountain and forest gods had so disguised them: the bridge covered deep with soil and jungle, but with the torrent roaring beneath; the road a great scar of bare rock on the mountainside. None ever used it but the Master and his two disciples; the Master very rarely, for these parts were unknown to the Huitznahuatecs, and the nearest forest savages dwelt many months southward.

It was all lit with wonder, and a sense of its holiness grew on Nopal as he went. Over the dark valley floor of treetops below on his left, the sudden flash of a macaw's flaunting scarlets, blues and yellows thrilled him strangely, as if it had been a flaming of inspiration from the God-world.

Near sunset he came to the highest point on the road, just before it swept around onto the southern slope of the mountain. There, climbing a rock by the roadside on his right and pushing aside the fern and undergrowth, he came soon into a great glade edged with precipices on the far side and with a pile of rocks called the Quinames' Altar in the midst, beneath which pile, in a kind of cavern it roofed over, he found fire-sticks, tinder and a torch, and had a light before darkness fell. But he would have needed the light even in broadest daylight, for his way now lay underground by a passage from the end of the cavern and through a maze of what might have been ancient mine-workings, which, since Quiname times, no one had been there to mine. Then he passed up through a long tunnel, stairwayed all its length, and so out into Eagle Hermitage. This was a shallow canyon, rich with the night breath of flowers and vocal with running waters. Turning to his right, he came soon to the head of it, and to the cave; and in the mouth of the cave, there was Quauhtli, expecting him.

Quauhtli of the wonderful physique, the tallest and strongest of the Huitznahuatecs; he whose parentage was unknown and uninquired into; he who had been with the Master since his memory began. And who was now, Nopal soon saw, a nobler and grander Quauhtli than ever he had seen him, so that to come into his presence was almost like coming into the presence of the Master.

Before the fire at the end of the cave they supped, saying very little, for the habit of being silent together was an old one with them. But that impression of Quauhtli's new greatness grew on Nopal, until at last, when the meal was over and the bowls washed and put away, he sought an explanation.

"What is it that has happened?" he asked.

Quauhtli looked across at him, a marvelous light in his eyes; but he answered only, "He said it was you who were first to tell me about the north."

So Nopal leaned forward, chin in palm, and gazed into the fire, collecting and sorting his memories, and presently he began to speak.

6
Nopal in the North

"Having passed through the Canyon at the End of Things," Nopal began, "I was three months on the road, running my best through the forest. It was as the Master said it would be: The people of the lands I went through fed me daily, and I might lie down by night anywhere on the road without fear.

"Then I came into rich, cultivated regions and passed cities every day, and later, every few miles. They were all vastly larger than Huitznahuacan, but not so pleasant to the heart. The people I came among at last were those Toltecs of whom the Saltmen tell their tales. The tales are true, but not true enough. The Chiapanecs never told us more than half."

"The tales about their wars could not have been true," Quauhtli objected.

"They were true," said Nopal. "It is what all those peoples do. They destroy each other's cities and kill each other's men. It is an amazing country. But you shall hear.

"You know, the Master told me which cities I was to visit. They were to be the three most important in the Anahuacs, which is what the northern world is called. The first was to be the capital of their power, he said; the second, the capital of their religion; the third, the capital of their culture. I found that there were three such cities and that their names were Culhuacan, Teotihuacan, and Tollan. Here is a thing that surprised me: the number of languages in the world. Not a word you knew would you hear in the forest, where, I was told, the tribes, or some of them, speak the Quiname language—*the Quiname!"*

"They may be the descendants of those ancient giants," said Quauhtli.

"They are wild men now, with no rag of clothes on them, and their hair matted and unclean. They eat human flesh when they can get it, I was told; but they put food out on the roadside for travelers."

"Still, it may be that they are Quinames," said Quauhtli. The Master taught me the Quiname language at one time, saying that I should need to know it someday. To him, all things were known, I think." His face was covered with his hands while he spoke.

"They are," Nopal agreed. "However, it is our Nahua you will hear again if you go far enough, for the Toltecs speak it. Not as we do; one must speak slowly to be understood by them at first; but after a time, one comes to speak it as they do. I could already talk with them fairly well when I reached Culhuacan, the capital of their power, and found work in the clothmakers' district. In all of their cities, each trade has a district of its own, very few of which are not much larger than Huitznahuacan.

"They make their cloth of a stuff called cotton, which is finer than nequen. Four days in the week I served the cottonmakers in their factories; on the fifth, I would give out their goods in the marketplace in exchange for bags of cocoa beans or quills of gold dust. The guild I worked for gave me such bags or quills for my work, and with these I could, as they say, *buy* what I needed beyond the food they supplied. You know what I was to do for the Master?"

"To wear a badge in your cap?"

"Yes, this one," said Nopal, handing him a chalchiuhite shaped like the one Chimalman found in her sunroom, but smaller.

Quauhtli examined it. "It is not *the* Chalchiuhite Dragon," he said, "because that is said to be as big as a woman's thumb, and to glow and flash."

"What is *the* Chalchiuhite Dragon?"

"He told me a story about it once, I think before you came. It was a gift from the Sun to Quetzalcoatl, when the Sun foretold his fate. Or it may have been that Quetzalcoatl gave it to the Sun; I forget. Anyway, the Sun would throw it down into the world whenever our Lord was about to incarnate among men; and the woman who was to be his mother was to find it, and this would be a sign that our Lord was coming. No doubt the tale has some spiritual meaning. I remember the Master said that it was a living thing, though a green jewel; and that it would be of the size of a woman's thumb."

"But still," Nopal said, "this one might have some connection with . . . the same idea. There may be something— but you shall hear when I come to it.

"Many people in the marketplace used to look curiously at the dragon on my cap, and some seemed on the point of speaking. But none actually did ask the questions I was to expect. I was to stay there for a year, you know. When sixteen months of it had passed, the king of Culhuacan returned from a war he had been waging somewhere. Nonohualcatl Totepeuh Camaxtli is his name, the 'Camaxtli' being the name of their God of War. Besides being king of that city, he is the head of all the Toltec race—his title is Toltec Topiltzin—and all the other kings are his subordinates. I must tell you something about him, because in some ways he is typical of his race. You could not find so puzzling a character here.

"In the first place, it is he, most of all, who is concerned with warmaking. It is his favorite occupation; he goes to it every year, and is famed and praised as a great conqueror. Such a one, I thought at first, must be a tzitzimitl in human guise; but later I saw that to judge these people, you must make yourself in thought one of them, feeling and believing as they do. Things we shudder at are part of their lives and rouse no disgust in them; and yet none of them seemed to me other than human, and most of them I liked. One would not like a human tzitzimitl, but I certainly liked the Toltec Topiltzin.

"On his return to Culhuacan, everyone went out into the streets to welcome him, I with the rest. He came throned in a litter carried on the shoulders of his guards: a huge man—not even you are huger—noble of bearing, magnificent in his plumes and jewelry.

"I found out later that when at Culhuacan, he had the habit of wandering the city by night, meanly dressed, to see for himself how his people live. Right at the end of my stay there, while he was doing this one evening, three men attacked him, and I was able to prevent their killing him. Oh, yes—people do get killed like that in the streets of those cities! I did not know who he was at the time, but the next day he sent for me, and that was how I came to meet the Princess Civacoatzin, his sister. He was . . . well . . . making a great deal of what I had done when she came in. She took note at once of the dragon in my cap and said that she must speak with me. So he dismissed his courtiers and asked if he was to retire too; but she told him to stay, that what she had to say to me concerned him, although he would not understand it. She called him 'Nonohualton,' but he her 'Civacoatzin'—one could see that he held her in high reverence. And then, if you please, she put the Master's questions to me, and I gave the answers thus—

" 'What news do you bring, young lord?' said she.

" 'News from where, your Godhead?' said I.

" 'From the Serpent's Hole.'

" 'That the fourth year will be Ce Acatl.'

"Up to that, questions and answers had been as the Master taught me them, and you may guess how thrilled I was to hear his words spoken by her. But then she put a question of her own. It was, 'What motto will you give for the fourth year that will be Ce Acatl?' She spoke in a low voice, but with a quick, decisive intentness. I said that I did not know how to answer that. 'Then this is the answer you shall report in the Serpent's Hole,' said she, and gave me that text from *The Book of Our Lord and Huanhua*: *'Thus I incarnate from age to age for the preservation of the good, the destruction of the wicked, and the establishment of righteousness.' "*

"There can be no doubt of what she meant," said Quauhtli.

"There can be no doubt. Quetzalcoatl will be born on earth next year."

"And in the north, where you were sent to prepare the way for him. Oh, the Master told me that, Nopalton. And that you would meet the princess. She too is of the Children of the Serpent."

"The Topiltzin himself told me so after she had gone. He said, 'She is of an order called the Children of the Serpent and has a wisdom I know nothing of.' But the first words she spoke told me that she was of the Master's kin. Blessed be he! I shall see him tomorrow."

Quauhtli's face was hidden in his hands. After a while he looked up and asked, "And what next?" Nopal saw a grave glory on his face, which he remembered afterward.

"Next I went to Teotihuacan, which is the chief city of their religion. The people there are called Otomis. They are quite different from the Toltecs; they have been in the Anahuacs much longer. I did not like them so well. The place is full of priests. All the priesthood of those northern nations is trained at Teotihuacan.

"I tried to get work in the guilds there, as at Culhuacan, but always I was turned away, and soon I knew that it was the Chalchiuhite Dragon that set the guild-masters against me. When all of my gold and cocoa were gone, I sang in the market to get more, for men starve to death in those parts if they have no quills of gold dust or bags of cocoa beans.

"A priest passed as I began my singing, eyed me with alarm, and went into the Market Magistracy, out of which came, a few minutes later, a party of topillies—the men who keep order in the streets—who seized me and dragged me before certain priest-judges, and I was discussed by them in Otomi, which I did not understand; no one told me why they discussed me. But there are people there who break the laws, and they are treated as I was. I was brought before the judges several times during the year, and kept meanwhile in a stone cell that—well, before they had done with me, I was too sick to know what was happening. Those priests are cruel; they do cruel things to human beings. They did to me. I could not tell you . . .

"The next thing I remember is lying in a litter under the sky, doctors tending me, and a kind and noble face in the background that smiled at me as I opened my eyes. It was that of a Culhuatec named Cohuanacotzin, a friend of the Topiltzin's. He was as good to me as you could have been. He told me afterward what had happened. Civacoatzin had bidden her brother send someone posthaste to Teotihuacan to save the life of a man on the point of being sentenced to death by the judges, and the Topiltzin had sent Cohuanacotzin. It seems that he arrived just in time; they were about to cut my head off when he arrived.

"He took me on to Tollan and nursed me back to health in the king's palace there, the time I was to spend at Teotihuacan being past. The king of Tollan, by name Huemac Tezcatlipocâ, is the Topiltzin's brother; Cohuanacotzin is a favorite with them both. Twice or thrice the king visited me, but neither he nor Cohuanacotzin knew about my having rescued the Topiltzin. Cohuanacotzin was endlessly kind. He is a great man at war, loves fighting. But you would love him, as I did.

"In four months I was well and I left him. He was loath to let me go from the palace, but Civacoatzin's orders had been definite and strict. I went out into the town and found work in the guilds. I understood that he had gone back to Culhuacan, but I found out later that he stayed in Tollan as long as I did, keeping a kind of watch over me in case of danger. For Huemac, though of noble nature, is said to be rather under the influence of the Otomi priesthood, whose power, my protector feared, might reach me in Tollan. It did not, for Tollan, in spite of its king's predilections, is by no means a priestly town. I liked its people even more than I did the Culhuatecs.

"My work there was much the same as at Culhuacan, but at Tollan no less than three-score people put the Master's questions to me, and two-score and fifteen of them pledged themselves. So I think it is to Tollan that our Lord will come. And now . . . you have something to tell me, Quauhton?"

Quauhtli sat silent for some while before answering. "We ought to sleep now," he said at last. "For both of us, there will be much to do tomorrow. If there is news, you will hear it then, Nopalton."

7

The Master

Eagle Hermitage was within a couple of score-score feet of the summit of Quauhtepetl and so girt round with precipices that there was no coming to it but by the glade, the Quinames' Altar, and the tunnel. From the cave, a long and winding canyon sloped down and southward. The cave mouth looked east, and a bow-shot or two from it, in that direction, was the place where the hermits from of old had meditated at sunrise. This was on the edge of the precipice above the Quinames' Glade. Between it and the cave were the canyon floor and a ferny hollow between two hillsides, the southern one ascending gently and of no great height, the northern one steep and lofty to the peak. On that side a rill came tinkling and pouring into a basin and flowed thence into a pool. From the basin the hermits drew their drinking water; the pool was their bath. It was rimmed round with rushes and clean sand, and was deep enough to dive into, wide enough to swim in, and of water cold and delectable with mountain vitality and sweetness.

The stream overflowing from it wandered down through the canyon, here watering orchards or flower or vegetable gardens, there filling chains of lily ponds with little waterfalls between, to be carried away at last through untraversable conduits in the mountain. The whole canyon, narrow and deep in parts and in parts wide and sunny, had been loved into garden richness by long generations of hermits. Neither crop-destroying deer and rabbits came there, nor the jungle cats that prey on them.

The hermits had always been there, and their duties had always been the same. They were to spend a certain time daily in meditation, their thought in the God-world; and they were to cultivate the garden, making themselves hands and minds for Shilonen and Centeotl in the maize rows, or for Coatlantona, who manifests through flowers—all this for the spiritual health of mankind.

The garden provided Nopal and Quauhtli with their breakfast the next morning. They ate it in the cave to the music of the stream and of a zacuan that sang in the canyon below. When these two were together, they rarely broke silence till the sun had been three hours in heaven; nor did Nopal wish to do so now, although daylight revealed to him, far more than last night's torchlight, the new grave greatness of his fellow disciple. His own mood, on the other hand, was gay; his silence covered laughter-lit anticipation. . . .

While they were at breakfast, without a word or sign, Quauhtli rose and went out.

Nopal finished his meal, put the cave in order, and expected Quauhtli's return. Then he went out himself, to wait for him beside the pool—where even waiting was joy, where existence thrilled with gladness, where purity and peace came up with the ferns and grasses and one could feel a loving mystery brooding on the heights above. The worlds visible and invisible exchanged sympathy with him; the mountain received him into its divine mood. No wonder Quauhtli had grown so great: Eagle Hermitage had become as the Serpent's Hole itself. The sun had but to be a little higher in heaven, and the hour for speech arrived, and Quauhtli would—

Ah, and here came Quauhtli—from behind him and the edge of the precipice. This was strange, as Nopal had not seen him there when he came out. He turned his head to see and then started to his feet in delight, for the One who came, and made the fern as he passed through it break into green flame for joy of his coming, and the morning to burn up suddenly deific and triumphant, made him forget even Quauhtli. . . .

* * *

It was some time before Nopal realized that he had been dreaming. Even after he awoke, it was some time. But—yes—he was alone.

It meant, of course, that the Master had sent him a thought, had turned his mind in Nopal's direction, and that had caused the dream. It had often happened before but never quite like this. In dreams, as in waking life, one could readily recognize the Master's humanity, even though it was eight thousand times more beautiful, forceful, and vivid than that of other men. But now—!

To dream of him was always to awaken with this elation and sense of momentous spiritual victory achieved, and that was what counted. The details might or might not be important; often it was one's own brain that supplied them. As now, for example, the stretch of sand by the pool. . . .

But there were no pictographs written on it, as a half-involuntary glance assured him. In the dream, he had seen Huehuetzin writing there with his finger, and he had but to shut his eyes now to see him there still, tracing on the sand the characters Nopal had understood so clearly, and remembered so . . . but did he remember them? No; they were gone.

It was not worth a moment's regret, after all, since in a few hours he would be with the Master. It was time to start now, and he would—as soon as Quauhtli had told him the news.

But . . . where was Quauhtli? He did not answer when Nopal called. He was not in the cave, nor anywhere in the canyon below. From the precipice brink, Nopal scanned the road, far away and beneath, up which he had come yesterday; bits and stretches of it emerged into view and then were hidden again behind out-juttings of the forest. His eye caught motion on one such road fragment, and he fixed his gaze on it. Yes, that was Quauhtli, making good speed northward.

Well, but one would be with the Master soon, as soon as one could get to Teotepetl and the Serpent's Hole. Quauhtli would only be carrying out the Master's orders. . . .

Nopal put fruit and a couple of tortillas in his road sack, kindled a torch to light himself through the tunnel, and started out. His way led west and down across the southern slope of

Quauhtepetl, and then northwest through lowland forests, where the wild things knew nothing of man. An hour before noon, he came out into Huitznahuatec land again and crossed the Rain-flower at the ford, and was on his own, or Shollo's, estate. A little later he passed right in front of the house, from the open-room of which anyone might have seen him come up from the road and go through the mountain gate; and more than one did see him, but he was too intent to think of it . . . because the day was more wonderful than any he remembered.

The feeling had been growing on him as he approached the Mountain that was God. The visible world hardly concealed the invisible that shone and sparkled through it. The Master must be flooding sunlight and shadow with his thought, to make the veil of sense so thin, the heart so drawn to exultant worship. As he went up by the path that had never been trodden but by feet on errands like his own, he marveled more and more. The air was soaked with holiness; he could feel the pure meditation of the trees . . . .

He came into the glade where his father had left him that morning so long ago, and there among the roots of the mahogany tree where he had waited then, a small boy was waiting now, gravely watching the head of the path for his coming.

The child rose when he appeared and with an air of portentous seriousness, said, "It *is* your Godhead, isn't it?"

Secure of his meaning, Nopal answered, "Yes, it is I."

"He said you would tell me your name."

Nopal told him.

"Yes, he said it would be that. I do reverence to you, Nopaltzin Tecuhtli." He bowed low, touching the earth at Nopal's feet, as disciple to teacher, adding then, "I am Nauhyo. Has your Godhead heard of me, please?"

Yes, in the dream by the pool at Eagle Hermitage! Of course! That was one of the things the Master had written on the sand. . . . Looking down into the grave eyes full of question that searched his own, he answered, "Yes, I have heard, Nauhyotontli!"

The child-face lighted up for a moment at hearing that affirmation coupled with the affectionate-diminutive form of his name, but then grew grave again. "He says that you are to come here again tomorrow, you and Shollotzin,"—he pronounced the name a little doubtfully—"and that you may bring me also if you wish to, but I am not to ask; and then you will do what is to be done. And He says that I am to go home with you this evening, Nopaltzin, and that I am to remember always. He said I was to go and that He blessed me, and that He would not need me anymore. So I came here to wait for your Godhead, as He told me to. Only please, Nopaltzin, I did not want to go!"

Nauhyo paused there, struggling with himself, to Nopal's amused wonderment, then added, "Please go to HIM now, Nopaltzin. I will wait here for you; only please go quickly now!"

So Nopal went. The joy and sanctity that had taken possession of the forest afternoon quieted his mind from speculation. Certainly he would take Nauhyo home to Rainflower that evening— since the Master did not want them to spend the night on the mountain. In a world so goldenly holy, there was little room for formulated thought. A secret laughter ran through the lustrous metallic greens of the foliage, the darting jewelry of the hummingbirds, the painted, lazy sails of the great butterflies, and the richness and stillness of the blooms.

It was as if some triumphant happiness were overflowing into the life of the forest, as if the Mighty Mother were laughing through all things visible her delight over the birth of a god, the emergence of some new, most sacred force from the Unknowable into the world. Never had this fold in the mountain, sacred at all times above any spot elsewhere, shone so marvelously still and intent as now.

It was a narrow ravine that began not far from the glade; the entrance to it was something that an army might camp on Teotepetl seeking, and never find. It broadened out as it wound on inward and upward into a bloom-scented solitude with green mountain shoulders high above and, now and again, blue peaks visible, or rose-dim chasms skyward; or forest slopes whitestreaked here and there with the snow-bright thread of a waterfall, or kindled by the flight of some startling-plumaged bird. Wilderness passed insensibly into garden, with fruit trees planted in no order and, on all sides, luxurious banks and tangles of blossom as the hillsides receded, winding still, and the space of flowers widened.

It was impossible for Nopal not to know that the silence was growing, that the valley was packed with a bright silence of a kind new to him. The thin, far-off drone of the waterfalls made no difference to it. He knew what it all meant. The Master would be in deep meditation, in a deeper and holier meditation than ever before in Nopal's time. Only that could account for the golden, spiritual stillness whose grip was on all things. The blossoms by the way, the green sprays of the vines, hung hushed in a motionlessness that seemed rather an assertion of eternity than an absence of sound. Great white waxlike trumpets of bloom drenched the sunlight with solemn fragrance, the aroma of their tense adoration, and one could see that they participated in the Master's lofty mood.

A turn, and the garden widened out into a large valley, lawny and well-wooded, with a lake in the midst. Shiningly blue, ripples dancing, peace and holiness brooding over it, the water lay; and yonder rose the island, green and tawny against the purple shadow beyond, with the three little two-roomed stone houses hidden by the crest of it, the midmost of which was the Master's. . . .

Nopal put off in the boat, rowing it around to the southern side of the island, where the landing place was and, above it, the houses. No one was in the open-room of the middle house, where he expected to see the familiar figure in meditation, and yet the feeling was strong on him that he had never been welcomed there so dearly and intimately as now. He went up to the house and entered the open-room, not lifting his eyes to glance into the room beyond. On the cushion seat where the disciple sat when the Master had occasion to talk to him, he took his place to wait until he should be called.

He composed his mind for meditation, or it composed itself. All the valley was meditation, and filled with the highest mood that man's consciousness can attain. The Master's thought pervaded it . . . . From blue sky and green heights, something laughter-laden was watching him, something that beckoned him into the Great Freedom, until at last he forgot conditioned existence in the splendor of a light that—

In a world of formless loveliness, the Master was speaking to him . . . of the divine fluting at Teotleco, which, said he, only the queen and Nopal had heard. He enlarged on the importance of that. Ulupi, he said, had heard it at her accession, and never a sovereign since until Chimalman. Did not that mean that Chimalman's reign would be exceptional? Her glory would exceed Ulupi's . . . .
    It was for Nopal to bring that news to her. He was to make Chimalman understand that she would be the greatest and most fortunate of Huitznahuatec rulers.
    "You are to tell her this," said the Master. "The gods promise that she shall serve them more wonderfully than any of her predecessors did. They expect more from her than they did from any of them; she is to be assured of that, and never to doubt it. She is never to forget that we are with her to guard her and lead her to her greatness. She must trust in us who trust in her; she must trust, and go on trusting, and never cease to trust, so that her trust may open a path between us and men. You are to say those words to her and make her know that they are from the gods. Say that she is to trust until her trust becomes knowledge and until all we hope of her is fulfilled. Whatever happens, she is to trust.
    "And you are to help her and be her servant and guardian. It was for this I trained you, and your father before you. It was for this I trained you, dear son!"

Nopal was waking, drifting farther and farther from his dream. The light and vision were gone, and the last words of the Master seemed to float to him from remote spaces. He was half aware of his material surroundings, though still encompassed by some laughter-laden noble consciousness that watched him from the heights. And the dream was not all gone, for again words came, far and faint. "Remember that I trust in you!"
    And again, when he thought he was quite awake—but now

whether heard by the ears or in the heart, he was uncertain—*"I give you my peace!"*

The second wonder-dream today! And surely no disciple had ever fallen asleep in the Master's house before! Strange that the divine fluting on Teotleco Eve, and the queen's and his own hearing it, should have—
A sheet of paper fluttered down from somewhere and fell at his feet; it was covered with pictographs in the Master's handwriting, and his own name was at the top of it. It was for him, and he had better read it now while he was waiting. What numbers of unexpected things were happening on this day!
No pictographs could be easier to read than the Master's, and Nopal had no difficulty in gaining the sense of these. He was to be, they indicated, in Huitznahuacan for the Feast of the Mountains next month; he was to put Nauhyo in the Calmecac on the day before; on the morning of Tepeilhuitl, he was to apply to Ameyal, the Tlaloc-priest, who would have a message for him. He was to adopt Nauhyo, whom he was to take back to Rainflower with him that evening, and tomorrow he was to bring his brother Shollo, and Nauhyo also if he wished, here to the Serpent's Hole to do what was necessary; and now he was to enter the inner room.
That last was puzzling, but he could make it mean nothing else. *Now he was to enter the inner room*—where no disciple had ever been. . . .
He rose from his cushion and on tiptoe, with heart strangely beating, went in. And knew why the valley and the mountain, earth and sky, were thrilled to such solemn elation. . . .

Nopal went out and climbed to the crest of the island, and turned toward the flushed sky above the mountain shoulders—and understood.
The sun drew to his setting in just such deep, conscious trust in the Divinity of Things as enriched himself, because Huehuetzin, the Master, going inward into the wholeness of that beautiful mystery of which they too were fragments, had held the door open, and the golden knowledge that is the air and light of that

world had shone through and flooded this world with its sublimity. Golden knowledge there; trust here. It was the same thing. All this divine glory of the sunset, this rapt aspect of the world, was but the visible manifestation of that knowledge, or trust. In the trees south of the lake, a bird gone wild with ecstasy sang out its heart in worship; Nopal could hear the very words of the song: *"Love to you, praise to you, love to you—you who are gone, you who are gone!"* Far up, the waterfalls droned their sleepy monotone as accompaniment; but louder than bird or water was the silence by virtue of which both became intelligible; and he was aware that his mood of love and faith was not his alone, but his as a part of universal nature. The bird was pouring it out into the evening, glorified by death, pouring it out on behalf of things animate and inanimate, including himself, because that force—that divinity Nopal had known embodied in the Master—now was set free into all visible beauty and the lofty places in the human soul.

Nopal was conscious of nothing in himself but the God-part, of nothing in existence but the divine. The Master was not lost, but now, for the first time, really found, since there was now no veiling personal identity between that Great Soul and the soul in himself. He was one in adoration with the universe.

"Love to you, praise to you, love to you—you who are one with us, you who are gone!" sang the bird.

8

Rainflower Reminiscences

Rainflower Manor was Nopal's by law, as well as in Shollo and Maxio's feeling. It had come to him, as the eldest son, when his father died and left him, Nopaltzin Tecuhtli, head of the family. But to own and cultivate land and leave a son to inherit it would never be for him, he thought; and despite the entail, he had resigned it wholly to Shollo, whose son, Shelwa, would one day be its lord in name as well as in fact.

But it was his home when he chose, and Shollo and Maxio wished that he would choose more often. To Shollo, as to Ketla-sho, he was of a higher order of being, at least halfway to godhood, and Shollo had infected Maxio, his wife, with much the same belief. He had acquired it as a child, thus—

Rainflower Manor was at the foot of Teotepetl. The wall, beyond which the forested mountainside began, was not more at its nearest point than seven-score strides due north of the house. It was built high against four-legged marauders from the wilds that might imperil crops or livestock, but hidden by flowers and shrubbery, so that one saw nothing of it from the garden. But at one place, a little east of the house, a flagged and winding path led in through this screening border to a gate in the wall, which was the district's heart of mystery. It was the only way onto the mountain.

Everyone knew that the gate was there; everyone knew that Teotepetl was, by the run of mankind, to be approached only spiritually. There were three sacred mountains, visible assurances of religion: this one, and Blue-wind, and Mishcoatepetl; and this one, even though King Tlaloc had his paradise on Mishcoatepetl, was the holiest, and itself one of the greatest of the gods. And yet there was a path and a gate by which men might enter and go up into it.

All Huitznahuatecs knew these things, including the children at Rainflower Manor and village. Teotepetl was forbidden ground, not only to themselves, but to the whole grown-up world, and forbidden not merely by one's parents, nor by the king, but by the Ruling of the Universe itself. By the Sun and the World-Soul; by the Blue Air, who is Quetzalcoatl, and by the Mountain, who is God; by all Benevolence Disembodied and the Invisibility we Adore. This was fundamental knowledge. One would as soon doubt the divinity of things. Ages and ages had bowed down to our Lord the Mountain and profited spiritually by doing so; and the doctrine nested naturally in every mind that put forth its first cognition buds within sight of Teotepetl. Children knew it as soon as they knew anything.

But the path and the gate asserted something they knew only less well: that there were those who had leave to go up there, invited by our Lord to visit him in his fastnesses. There were people as lofty of soul as that. "Oh, if we could but know who they are!" thought the Rainflower children, "How we would love and revere them!—we by whom our Lord is to be worshiped only from afar in the valley . . ."

And first Shollo, and then Ketlasho, very young children still, had seen their brother go all alone in through the path to the mountain gate, and had been thus made to realize that Nopal was one of those who might wander on the steep acclivities of God. . . .

When Nopal was at home in those early days, he and Shollo had had wonderful times together. They were inseparable, wandering through sun-drenched days by the river or through gardens and farmlands, the elder's arm over the younger's shoulders, counseling together—oh, so gravely and wisely—about everything but Nopal's absences from home. Or, for days together, they played games of their own devising, wherein twigs and leaves and pebbles became mysterious beings, magically gifted; or they made the tame creatures about the house and farm take part with them, consciously or perhaps not, in extemporized dramas, the characters represented being the amazing inhabitants of time-submerged worlds. Chief among these actors willynilly were Cuetpatzintli, the whimsical coati, and sleek Mizquiton, the ocelot, and the toucan, whose agility and huge bill made him a favorite in such parts as Cipactli's, where a sense of humor was required. And then there were the four or five tame monkeys of various species; and if you came to that, the turkeys and the dogs, too.

Cuetzpatzintli, the coati-mundi, with the long, inquisitive snout and feathery brush of tail, had the run of the kitchen and barns, and a marvelous appetite for crop-destroying vermin; all that was asked of him was that he would respect the big yellow mombin trees in front of the house, and here his conscience must have been effective, for the zacuans, sweetest of feathered singers, nested and sang in them season by season. In drama you had to give him rather indefinite parts and leave the interpretation of them to his own genius.

Mizquiton, the ocelot, you were to remember never to unchain while the turkeys were grazing in the fields; and religiously you were to keep her away from the sties where the hairless dogs were fattening for the Huitznahuacan market. She had learned, more or less, not to wander of her own accord into temptation; and it was not fair that you, whom she regarded as morally, though perhaps not intellectually, her superior, should lead her where her appetite could not but become unmanageable. She had gotten her name, Mizquiton—"nice little death"—not merely from the soft suddenness of her paws and her extreme lithe beauty, but from what happened once in her first days at Rainflower, when she got loose in the dog sties—a thing, mind you, that must never happen again!

But she loved the children dearly and never scratched or bit them except in affection. Generally, she must act her parts whilst rolling on her back in the dust and sunlight before her kennel, her four delightful paws sparring at the universe above; whereas Cuetzpatzintli was good, all allowances made, as a messenger; he could be sent to steal music from the Sun, or the bone from the Hell-king wherewith our Others first made men. He would nearly always come back sometime with something, though usually he ate it.

Ketlasho had less part in these memories; she was very early in taking the mistress-ship of Ashopatzin's house, and long before she took it, her dominating interest had been to learn the business of it. There was a nice gradation of character in his family, from Ketlasho to Nopal. Her being was fulfilled, and generously, in the care of her household in Huitznahuacan; the altar in her God-room was the center of her spiritual life. And in Shollo there dwelt a kindred basic home-affection, but also he must have God the Mountain above him and in daily sight, and no altar in the world would have taken its place. She must have her roof above her; he must feel the sky above his roof; while for Nopal, the sky was all-important and roofs meant nothing.

9

Nopal's Homecoming

If Maxio had gone out through the open-room, she would have seen Nopal coming up from the road on his way to the mountain gate, but because she went by the back of the house, and southward, she missed him. She always went out to meet her husband returning from his work.

On their way back, she and Shollo came on Yanesh at the end of the causeway between the fishponds, making wreaths for the evening's wear. He had finished two—no doubt for themselves—and had hung them on the tlapalizqui bush under which he sat working, and was making a third, of extreme beauty and gorgeousness.

"For whom is the royal wreath then, Yaneshton?"

The ancient chuckled slyly, his face puckered into many eight-thousands of wrinkles. For whom should the wreath of divine tlapalizquis be? Ah then, their little Godheads did not know as much as old Yanesh did! For whom should it be but the greatest of mankind—after King Ashokentzin? Not but what his Godhead Shollotzin was a very great man—

"Then it is meant for Nopaltzin Tecuhtli," Shollo laughed. "If only we knew when Nopaltzin Tecuhtli was coming—"

But on that point Yanesh had no doubt in the world. His Powerful Godhead would be here to wear the wreath, or the one that would be made for him, tomorrow or the next day . . . at any rate, while the tlapalizquis were in bloom. The shrubs, one on either side of the pathway, were covered with dark, rich blossoms, smoky maroon in color, as deep as infinity, and with a glow as of fire burning through. For the Tecuhtli had told this very Yanesh, the last time their eyes had been consoled with the sight of him, that in three years' time he would wear a tlapalizqui wreath of Yanesh's making; and that was in this same Teotleco month of Reed Ten. That their little Godheads should know less than Yanesh the Straw!

They heard him chuckling till they turned the corner by the ocelot's kennel, where a descendant of the original Mizquiton rubbed herself, rumbling, against Shollo's leg as they passed. Of course Yanesh was right, and Nopal might be here any day; and their minds would have been full of it but for—

At home, confirming news awaited them. The children had just come in after spending the morning under the mombins in front of the open-room; they were convalescent after the sickness that had kept Nopal's return from their parents' minds. Their nurse, a lean spinster by the name of Shochill, of homeliest features and rosiest imagination, had been in charge of them there; and she had seen, and had been making a great stir of it among the servants, our Lord the Mountain himself, in human or, rather, in God-guise, go in toward the mountain gate. There was this much excuse for her excitement: Perhaps only two or three living had seen that path taken. It was a startling thing to see.

"What was our Lord like, Shochill?" asked Maxio, suppressing amusement.

"Oh, like a mighty god, your Godhead Maxiotzin. Like the Beautiful Youth, or the Plumed Dragon, or any of them. As magnificent as . . . as Nopaltzin Tecuhtli himself."

Whereupon her master and mistress knew whom she had seen, Maxio having the wit to divine, though Shollo had never told her, that Nopal was one of the God-invited. If he were not, who would be? But one must not pry into the Mountain's secrets, and they were at pains to talk of other things over their dinner.

"But I shall come home early," said Shollo on leaving. "And you had better not come to meet me."

"No," she answered. "I shall be busy decorating the house. He can hardly be here till I have finished." Her conscience warned her that she had verged on the dangerous.

When Shollo had gone, she sought out Yanesh and found him dozing by the tlapalizquis. Mostly he would bask in the sun all day, without much change of place; sleeping a good deal; working at such tasks as wreath-making, that did not tax his strength; giving orders to the gardeners, his subordinates, and shrewdly watchful that they were carried out. A great man was this Yanesh, two years older than Nayna the Aged, but encouraging the notion that the two years were ten.

It was he who, ages since, had designed this great Rainflower garden. He boasted, not too hyperbolically, that he had crumbled all the soil of its flower beds between his fingers. He was a village youth when the old house, half a mile west of this one, was burned down, and the then-Tecuhtli, Nopaltzin's great-grandfather, had chosen him to lay out the garden of his new home. And with noble genius, he had carried out the work, it must be owned; and had thereby come to be a person of great authority, with many gardeners under him whom he ruled not untyrannically, and some prestige throughout the district. For years, were you the Tecuhtli himself, or his wife, if you wanted stuff from the garden, you had asked Yanesh for it.

He chuckled mightily over Maxiotzin's request for flowers. Her little Godhead might go home and judge whether or not this ancient had foresight. Copil and Coshcosh, good lads, would be at the house before her, with the wealth of Yanesh's garden for the great Tecuhtli's pleasuring. So all that afternoon, Maxio and her maids were at work upon what Copil and Coshcosh brought them: baskets upon baskets of bloom, until the whole house was fragrant. Toward the end, she grew unreasoningly fidgety, fearing that Nopal would come before she had finished, and at last she placed burnt incense in the God-room in gratitude to the Mountain, who had kept him till she was ready. He might come now when he pleased.

But the shadows went lengthening, the light turning mellow, and there was no sign of him. The turkey girls herded their flocks in the meadows with their queer, chuckling, throaty cries and, singing the "turkey song," drove them home to their pens. The dog-herds fed their fattening charges, noting with satisfaction those nearest to marketable plumpness. Turkey pens and dog sties were fortified for the night, for the one thing the wild jaguar or ocelot loved better than fattened turkey was fattened dog. Shollo came home, later than he had intended, praised the beauty of Maxio's work and retired to prepare himself for the evening. Maxio stole a quarter-hour for her own preparations, and she might have stolen an hour or two, for that matter, for the Tecuhtli did not appear.

Ishcash, the village Priest of the Mountain, came in to supper, news having reached him on his avocations that Nopal was expected. Ishcash was their cousin and very good friend. Village priest meant also village teacher, especially of music. There was no instrument he could not play and teach, nor song he could not sing. Also, all literature was stored in his memory. His presence of an evening was well-loved by the entire household.

For the evenings were the season of general culture. When supper was over in the open-room and the villagers began to come back, and the torches were lit in the sconces, and the floor was strewn with cushion seats, and the women sat at their sewing, and the talk gave place to song or the chanting of poems or the telling of stories, and the riches of the race-mind were set forth—then it was good to have Ishcatzin there. It was very good on this night, for the rumor was that he had a new story to tell, which at any time would have been a cause for high anticipation; and yet he was telling it before ever a soul had guessed it was coming.

For first he called for Catautlish and his xylophone, and for Copil with his flute, and for Tozcaykech and Toshpilli with their teponaztli and tlamalhuilili—drums of different tone and pitch. He arranged these four in place so artfully that none could see what he was leading to; and then he began talking about our Lord the Mountain, suggesting that he must have had many adventures anciently.

And all this Ishcatzin did that the evening's work might get done despite expectation of the Tecuhtli and the excitement that it would cause. And so at last he was telling them of a contest that had been of old between Teotepetl and a mighty king of the tzitzimitls who had come up out of the infinite forest to the south, intent on the destruction of mankind, and first of all, of the spiritual protector of mankind, the Mountain. Ishcash sat on the dais, the musicians below and in front of him; and soon, as the tale waxed mighty in his mouth, he was conducting them as an orchestral accompaniment. With a glance here and a motion of his hand there, he drew from them the effects he needed. The tzitzimitl made himself into a fire and came up worldwide, roaring and billowing, tossing huge branches high into the air on the crests of his flames; and the base teponaztli boomed and bellowed conflagration-like, and rose into a dreadful fury, ominous and threatening; and above all the sound that Tozcaykech could drub from it, the priest's voice rose clear. And then, at a flick of his hand, the teponaztli sank from its prominence and became distant, and phrases that seemed magical from flute and xylophone soared above its grim rebellion as Ishcatzin told of how the Mountain, beholding unmoved the fire from afar, asserted its calm divinity against the tzitzimitl and summoned the gods to do battle for the world. They gathered and arrayed themselves, and flute and xylophone and high-pitched tlamalhuilili united to describe their assembly and intent.

" 'Who will go forward and quell this uprising?' said the Beautiful Youth, said the Soul of the World.

" 'Lord Tezcatlipocâ,' said King Tlalocatecuhtli. 'Let it be for me and my princes to go; let it be for the Lords of the mountain waters!'

"Then he called up his princes, his heroes; and they rode through the heavens in their beauty. They rode on the purple clouds, the generous masters of the rain; they brought with them the waters of the heavens, the beautiful waters of the lakes and the sea."

So Ishcatzin chanted, the musicians accompanying him: flute and xylophone very sweet and lofty; tlamalhuilili throbbing out the march of the Tlalocs that turned soon into the wild, furious beating of tropical rain; the mountain gods drenching the world; trees beaten down, mighty branches snapping and crashing; the hissing and rattle and thunder of the steam-generating contest; the teponaztli growling and whining; the tlamalhuilili whipping it slowly into silence. Not for nothing had Ishcash trained those same musicians. Then he told of the gods' triumph: of how the Plumed Dragon established peace there; of how Citlalicway Teteoinan herself breathed upon the blackened world; of how the Beautiful Youth restored its beauty. And then of how they came to the Mountain to praise him, and camped in the forests about his feet.

"Even here, where Rainflower stands, the Plumed Dragon abided. And here they dwelt in the seventh silence, awaiting news from our Lord the Mountain, who then considered and pondered deeply and asserted in his heart the divinity of things. And as they waited, listening, behold, the thought in his heart became music, and they heard from the Mountain a strange, divine singing, and—"

A quiver ran through the room; voice and instruments suddenly were silent. For, marvelously, the story had come true. Breaking in on Ishcash's words, song came from the Mountain: A voice unearthly sweet and noble was singing. They rose and crowded into the spaces between the pillars and watched. From the shrubbery that hid the mountain gate, something—or someone—emerged singing, and the song ended as he came. Wonderful moment, when all those eyes might—

But Ishcash whispered to Shollo, who turned and quietly gave orders that all should leave, and that no word more be spoken by anyone, nor this that they had seen be referred to ever. When only he and Maxio and the priest were left, Nopal came in, carrying Nauhyo on his shoulder. The look of gods was on their faces, so that the three to whom they came were awed, and quickened in the heights of their being.

10

A Funeral and After

In the morning they were incommunicative, Nopal still radiantly godlike, but Nauhyo a wan, over-grave child rather than the young divinity of last night. He was much in need of her mothering, Maxio thought.

But he was to have none of it just yet. At breakfast, Nopal asked Maxio to have food packed for Shollo, Nauhyo and himself; three meals apiece, for they would be away until tomorrow at noon. If Shollo's surprise did not begin then, it was surely augmented, but neither he nor his wife thought of asking questions, or even to be inwardly curious. Shollo's astonishment was to grow before nightfall.

When they set out, it was, to his awed amazement, quite openly toward and through the mountain gate into the forbidden sanctity beyond. But as Nopal said nothing, he kept silence and forbade his mind to speculate. The path was mostly too steep for running; but even when it sagged, Nopal showed no desire to hurry. The slower the better, thought Shollo, for the place was one to be taken in with deliberate worship.

At noon they lunched beneath the great mahogany tree in the glade, not breaking the silence; and when the meal was over, they sat still speechless, Nopal and Nauhyo preparing themselves for what was to follow, Shollo content to be filled with the divine peace of the Mountain. Presently Nopal rose and led the way into the valley. Then Nauhyo, all of the God-look returned to

him, began singing. He sang as they passed through the fold in
the Mountain and crossed the garden and paddled across the
lake to the island: little songs that seemed pure conjurations of
magic—haunting, uninterpretable, triumphant. No wonder they
had thought last night that it was our Lord Himself who was
singing!

As soon as they had landed on the island, Nopal led Shollo
away to the work they were to do, and the latter saw nothing
more of Nauhyo for the time being. Their work took them to the
shore opposite, a bare bowshot from the island, by a causeway
a couple of feet below the surface, and to a cave in the cliff
nearby, where logs of ocotl wood, all cut to a length and squared
evenly, were stored. These they began carrying to the island and
building up on the highest point of it, in such a way as to leave
steps up to the top of the pile as it grew. Little had Nopal divined
in the old days for what purpose he and Quauhtli had been
bidden to cut and store those logs.

They worked hard and speedily, Shollo without speculation
but keenly aware of a sacredness in the labor. By sunset the pile
was finished, and Nopal led him into the middle house of the
three. Then Shollo understood what was toward. "The funeral of
a god," he thought. Nauhyo was there, watching beside the
frailness that now they carried out and laid on the pyre.

Night fell as the smoke, and then the flame, began to rise, and
Nauhyo to sing again, more wonderfully than ever; and all
amidst a strange silence of the forest that struck soon on Shollo's
hearing, used as he was, at Rainflower, to the concert, or pan-
demonium, for which nightfall always gave the signal. But here
jaguar nor ocelot nor puma squalled or roared; howler-monkeys
were silent; even the frogs were chorusless. Was it always like this
on the Mountain, he wondered.

The wood was very dry and burned up fiercely; the flame
leaped high, a steadfast, roaring pillar, bloom-capitaled, loosing
quivering sheets above to sail nightward and vanish, summoning
into strange, momentary visibility this point and that on the
heights—a jutting rock here, there a grand tree standing lonely.
"So may my love go up to you in song!" thought Nauhyo and

Nopal. "So has your passing illumined the lofty places of the soul!"

It grew late; the flames no longer soared skyward; Nauhyo had long ceased singing. Nopal, standing so near the fire that one would have thought his clothes would have been scorched, presently noticed his silence, looked down at him and saw that he had fallen asleep. He lit a torch at the fire and signed to Shollo to pick up the child and follow him into the southern disciple-house. It had been Nauhyo's latterly, and his bed was in the inner room. Nopal put him in it; then, while Shollo was supping, brought in Quauhtli's bed for him from the other house.

"Where will you sleep then?" asked Shollo, and was answered with a gesture that he took to mean there was another bed somewhere. But Nopal had no mind for sleeping that night. He would watch and keep company with a Sacred Memory.

So he went up to the top of the island again and sat down by the fire . . . and knew who inhabited the vast night above him, and with what keen serenity of joy. He set himself to recalling the days he had spent of old with the Holy One in this holy place; and though there had been many score-scores of them, he doubted there was one he missed, with such a light did they shine in his memory. Every day of them, with all of its incidents, came to him. He remembered Huehuetzin's laughter and playful moods; and again, the severe and lofty lessons he had learned from him: when the Master had caused him, but always wordlessly, to see, face and conquer some lurking weakness in himself that Nopal had known nothing of before. Who else could have done that? Who else could have laid such trains of happenings, seen the end, and worked for it, of such remote chains of causes and effects . . . and all of it that the disciple might learn and grow?

For your kindness manifested as kindness, Master, you were to be loved and honored; but oh, far more for your compassion manifested as severity, and for the pain you caused in your disciple! Gratitude, gratitude and utmost love to you, Great and Wonderful Being, to whom now, by death's most holy magic, your disciple is so much more closely united than ever when life stood between! Be it all that is uneternal in me, whose soul is your creation, that this fire has burnt up and destroyed!

He rose and paced up and down on the island shore, the Presence still with him, converting the night into myriad benediction. Stars rose and stars set. Above, the flames had died down, and the glowing mass, with here and there still some structure to it, was falling along its slopes in little silvery cascades of vermilion-hearted ash. Suddenly the unwonted silence struck him, and he stood still to listen.

Something fell in the fire, and a momentary flame and spark shower shot up, and as his eyes chanced to be on the shores beyond the lake, he saw why the night was silent. Or . . . had he really seen that picture of the water's rim lined with all of the forest's population: deer and jaguar side by side, gazing intent on the fire? There was just one flash, and then it was gone.

Nopal awoke in the dead time before dawn, with no memory of having lain down or invited sleep. Nor could he have been sleeping long, but the world had changed altogether. Inside and out, it had changed. The starry sky was covered away, and the air smelt of the coming of rain. His clothes were damp, and he was chilled through and through. And . . . the Master was dead.

He went down and lit a fire in the empty disciple-house which had been his own. Then, in the dying darkness, he stripped and bathed in the lake, toweled himself dry, found fresh clothes in the wardrobe, and dressed. The light grew, but it was gray and cheerless. It was months too early for rain, but rain there was going to be, he saw.

In the store cupboard he found chocolate, the only provision left up there, which he prepared and heated; it would be best for them hot. They must get back to Rainflower at once; this place was— Well, it had been the secret eye of the world, and the world's heart of holiness; and now the eye had gone blind and the heart had ceased to beat. He had better call the others now, and bring them in here to breakfast. He went across to the other disciple-house.

The rain was nothing as yet, but it would be heavy before long. Still, they must go down to Rainflower. The clouds, purple-gray and gravid, covered away the heights above and even rested over the immediate hilltops. As soon as ever they had breakfasted, and that hurriedly, they would start. He went in and called Nauhyo and Shollo, bade them hasten over to the other house, and went back to wait for them.

Soon Shollo arrived, saying that Nauhyo was not himself this morning, that he seemed depressed. They waited, and the thunder began booming and rattling overhead. The rain burst on the world like a host of drums beating, and Nauhyo did not appear. Nopal threw on a rain-cloak and went out to look for him and at last found him prostrate beside the dead fire, or where it had been until these few minutes of rain had washed away the remains of it in ashy runnels into the lake. He was soaked through, of course, and convulsed with sobbing, and Nopal, when he had carried him into the house, found little to say of consolation. Death used not to be like this; something adverse had stricken the world, to put this seeming of dire finality on things. For both of them, the high realizations of yesterday were gone; what filled the world was that the Master was dead.

There were plenty of clothes in the wardrobe, and Shollo, having children of his own, knew what to do for Nauhyo and did it. But he was sure that the child was in a fever and wished he had him at home and in Maxio's care. "But we can hardly get him down there in this rain, can we?" he observed.

Nopal, however, would hear of no delay; they must start as soon as they had drunk this chocolate. There were three rain-cloaks available: his own, that he had left hanging in the wardrobe three years since; one of Quauhtli's that would do for Shollo; and the Master's, which he made no scruple about fetching. They would wrap Nauhyo in it and then take turns in carrying him. Oh, but the rain came down!

By the time they were ready to start, the downpour had actually filled and sunk the boat at its mooring; and if they fished the craft up out of the shallow water and emptied it, it would sink again before they could get across.

"We will take the causeway," said Nopal, a proceeding that might have seemed to Shollo more impossible still but for his habit of trust.

"I know it very well," Nopal continued. "We used to cross it blindfolded when we were children, the Master looking on the while."

Who the "we" were, Shollo was not to learn, and that was the only time he heard mention of the Master.

They might as well have been blindfolded now, for there was no seeing through the rain. Nopal led the way and made straight for the causeway, Nauhyo in his arms and Shollo following with a grip on his brother's rain-cloak behind. The grim tension of Nopal's mind, allowing for no thought or consideration and so throwing the work of path-finding on his instinct, brought them over in safety. Even so, Shollo slipped and fell in the water at one point, and there was a struggle to get him on the causeway again.

Then the rain redoubled in fury, and it was hard work to come to land; and the wind rose, and they were thrice beaten to the earth before they had left the valley. And the Master was dead. What had made the valley beautiful was gone. The light of the world was put out.

It was the wildest journey ever either had made, with torrents constantly to be crossed; steep, slippery places to be descended; trees falling in front or behind; blinding rain and forest-flattening wind. They arrived soon after nightfall, the brothers quite exhausted, Nauhyo in high fever and unconscious. Maxio had him in bed at once, with Nayna the Aged—who, Maxio thanked the Mountain, happened to be in the house—in charge. Nayna, she said, was worth all the doctors in Huitznahuac, and "We simply could not have sent for her in this rain." And Nayna said that Nauhyo would be well in a month. Then Maxio gave her mind to mothering Nopal and Shollo.

Nopal remained at Rainflower for the rest of the month of Teotleco, during which time the Tlalocs, having invaded the world so unseasonably, hardly retired to their heights but deluged things incessantly, so that the Mountain was hidden always. Hidden, too, from Nopal were all the peaks and beauty of his being. It was the darkest period of his life. He knew that in the evolution of every soul—especially of one pledged, as he was, to discipleship—there is a time when the Law that teaches men must, in order that men may learn and evolve, carry them up to the lofty places of consciousness and then hurl them suddenly into the depths. It was the lesson set for Nopal now.

The god in him who had sat enthroned, as never before, during those two days of his exaltation, lord of all the provinces of his being, had withdrawn into hidden realms and left him lonely in an empty world—trying to hide his desolation from those around him.

11

The Feast of the Mountains

It was the morning of the Tlalocs' Day, the Feast of the Mountains: the first of the month of Tepeilhuitl, which took its name from this festival. But Ketlasho reproached herself with being in no mood for a time so holy.

That was not because Shollo and his family had failed to come in for the day. She loved Shollo dearly, but he was not Nopal; and Nopal *had* come, and he ought to be here. They could have Shollo any year, and mostly they did; but Nopal had not spent a Tepeilhuitl with them since they came to Huitznahuacan. And now look!

The moment he arrived yesterday, she had seen that something terrible had happened. The pain was shining through his eyes. Why couldn't he stay here sensibly and let her take care of him? Maxio was the dearest of women, but sisters-in-law weren't sisters, were they?

Didn't you see his trouble when he was telling the children about Tlaloc-cakes last night? For her part, she had never heard such wisdom, and she was sure that Ameyatzin, the Tlaloc-priest, would say so too. The children had been standing round her while she kneaded the dough, and pestering her with questions till she was sure the cake would be a failure; and then Nopal had come to her rescue and told them all that to keep them amused. Ten words were not out of his mouth before they were as quiet as lizards in the sun, and it was enough to make you weep to hear his grand and gentle language, all fired and molded with his sorrow. The Tlaloc-cake would tell you: Wasn't it the best you had ever seen? That was because she had been listening to his explanations while she made it, and lifted by them into the true Tepeilhuitl mood—

—which is like that of the thirsty earth when it receives the rain-blessing of the Tlalocs—

—and had risen this morning as happy and thankful as she could be, even at such a god-season as this. And now it was nearly time to start . . . and he had slipped out before breakfast without a word to anyone, and there was no sign of his coming back!

She had dressed herself and the children in their best; she had inspected Shaltemoc closely, patting and pulling his holiday til-matlies till they sat to her taste; she had arranged and rearranged the wreaths and garlands on herself and her daughters, and spent time on the blossoms her husband and small son were to wear over their right ears—and still no Nopal appeared. They would have to set out without him, almost the saddest thing that could happen on such a morning, because the crowd would be much too great to allow her any hope of joining him at the Top of the Town. It was very disappointing; indeed it was!

She checked herself. These were not Tlaloc-Day thoughts! One should be laying one's heart open to the spiritual influences of the Mountain-gods, ascending in thought to their lonely and lofty places, quite freed of the unrest of personality and daily business. The whole family had better wait in the God-room, bathing their minds in the religious silence there that was never broken. Even Pelashil would be quiet there, and she was sure that Shaltemoc would be no less the better for it than herself.

Besides, the Tlaloc-cake was in there on the altar; and very likely the sight of its perfections was what would best help her into silent-mindedness.

Everyone knew that the Tlaloc-cake was, domestically speak-ing, the centerpiece of the season's celebrations in every house in the land. It had to be made the evening before, baked in the night, and by dawn placed on the altar in the God-room. Its size was to be in proportion to that of the family, every member of which was, for the next ten days, to eat a sacramental piece of it lest he should lose something of the Tlaloc-benediction, which was the spiritual counterpart of the rain. One's heart, while one ate, was to be among the peaks and snows and pine forests; one's imagination with the Tlalocs in Tlalocan, that paradise of the gods that was the essence of the beauty and wildness and exaltation of all mountains everywhere.

The cake itself was designed to help one to such lofty thought. It was built up around two pottery figures—headed the one like a child and the other like a serpent—that fitted together standing back to back. The dough was made of maize flour well flavored with amaranth seeds, then modeled around these two figures to represent, as nearly as one were artist enough to do it, the mountain Mishcoatepetl, which the wise housewife had done her best to learn thoroughly in many litter-borne excursions around its base. The child-peak of Mishcoatepetl looked to the east, and the serpent-peak to the west, and thus the cake was to stand on the altar. The last perfection was certain clouds of the lightest puff-pastry set to float, as it were, about the mountain top: the supreme gift being to make it seem as if the child and the serpent were keeping them aloft with their breath.

Improbable as it may appear, there was a way to do this. But one had to be most exact, not only in the proportions and manipulations of the dough, but in having the right verse on one's lips at this crisis and that, and the right ecstasy in one's heart always. Most successes were only approximate, but hers, Ketlasho felt, was perfect this year, and that was because of what Nopal had been telling the children.

The Tlaloc-cake began to restore her peace as soon as they were settled in their seats in the God-room. Watching it, one could so easily imagine mountain things: the rocky precipices; the swish and whisper of pine boughs; the dark slither and foamy tumult of the torrent among its boulders—all those mountain sights, sounds, and scents that make gladness for the gods in men.

She began turning in her mind what Nopal had said about Tlaloc-cakes, and mountains. First, there was that we see when we look up to the slopes and peaks. We look away then, from the

common world in which we eat and sleep and do things, into a
lofty world that endures, knows itself, and is secure.

"You turn from your daily mind, where the little thoughts
drift and flutter, toward the summit of your being, where lives
the god in you who is eternal: your Lost Other, that someday you
will become."

And he had gone on to explain that the serpent meant antique
time, duration, eternity—she could not quite remember why—
and that the child meant newness and futurity and what is always
coming into being. Those two stood together he said, there in the
midst of the cake to tell us what is at the heart of men and
mountains alike: our Others—the gods, who are as ancient as the
Serpent of Eternity and as young and proper to the ever-arriving
future as childhood, and as serene and unshaken as the great
mountains we adore. And it all meant much besides, he had
assured them, saying it would be a great thing for anyone in a
whole lifetime to learn all that the child and the serpent meant.

Brooding on these things, Ketlasho succeeded in smoothing
out her mood entirely, so that when the time came to start, her
thoughts were sufficiently near the peaks, and that though Nopal
had not come.

On arriving from Rainflower at midday of the day before, Nopal
had taken Nauhyo straight to the Calmecac, intending to present
him to Amaquitzin or Acatonatzin and return at once to Ketlasho's for dinner. But Amaquitzin had persuaded him to dine and
spend much of the afternoon in his company, succeeding in this
because evidently a most unusual mood was upon the teacher,
and his face shone. It came out that he had a feeling that the gods
were nearer to mankind than ever they had been, that something
great was toward. He was agog with it and had begun to sense
it a couple of days before the extraordinary rains began.

The minds of all whom he had contacted seemed to have been
grandly ennobled in some way; had Nopal noticed anything of
the sort? "You yourself," said he, "I feel to be a far greater man
than you were when I saw you at Teotleco." Nopal was sure that
he was very wrong there, but said nothing. It was only when
Children of the Dragon died, said the priest-prince, that such

spiritual influxes came from the God-world to exalt the world of men: The great of soul could not go out without leaving their equivalent behind.

"What then," thought Nopal, "does he know what has happened?" But he did not ask, for at that point someone came into the room and the subject was changed. Later on, Amaquitzin chanced to ask if Nopal would see Ameyatzin, the Tlaloc-priest, on the next day—

At which, whether the question was asked by deep design or was haphazard, Nopal ceased to hear or heed him. That all this while he should have been forgetting! The Master had left him directions, after all: in that pictoscript he had found in the open-room on his arrival at the Serpent's Hole, telling him that he was to see Ameyatzin on the morning of the Feast of the Mountains—Ameyatzin, who therefore would, no doubt, give him directions from the Master as to his future life. Nopal rose abruptly to take leave but found that his old Quetzalcoatl-teacher was in the midst of telling him something he must in courtesy hear to the end, and he sat down again.

Amaqui was speaking of the queen, urging that Nopal should not delay in making himself known to her, just as he had done at Teotleco. Had Nopal seen the thought behind Amaqui's mind, it might have driven him out of Huitznahuac then and there by the northern road. As it was, he was merely reminded that he was to give the queen a message from the Master; he would remember presently what it was. But the priest-prince's thought was this: Chimalmatzin must marry and leave an heir to the throne; and she had met, and shown no inclination for, every young noble in Huitznahuac but this Nopaltzin Tecuhtli, whom he and his brothers thought the fittest of them all to be king.

In the morning, Nopal woke early, his mind held by something he had not thought of the night before: namely, that if he was to have word with Ameyatzin this morning, he could hardly seek him too early, for by breakfast time, the Tlaloc-priest would be much too deep in the great affair of the day to grant an interview to anyone. So he made all haste away, not troubling to leave word with the house servants, who alone were abroad at that hour. He would be back to breakfast in any case.

A walk of a few minutes brought him across the town and up through the marketplace to the courtyard behind the koo of Tlaloc: the quietest, most secluded spot in Huitznahuacan. Ameyal was sitting in his open-room when Nopal appeared. An ocelot from the forest was playing in front of him, her four white paws in the air.

It was a familiar sight. That quiet courtyard was a favored haunt of the creatures of the wild; it was said that the peccary herd came there sometimes and that the Tlaloc-priest preached to them. Whether or no, there was the ocelot pleading for attention she was not likely to get, for the old man wore on his face something more than the remote sacerdotal expression proper to official occasions. This Nopal saw at a glance. Then the ocelot saw him and vanished in a streak onto the roof; but nothing disturbed Ameyatzin.

He and Nopal had always been the best of friends. He had often been a guest at Rainflower in the old days and had made much of the lad, recognizing him for what he was. So now Nopal arrived with his old affection in his mind, and something more, for was not Ameyal now, in a sense, his link with the Master?

But Ameyal showed neither surprise nor pleasure at seeing him, apparently unknowing of who he was. What the priest said was: "I have been expecting you, King Tlaloc's Milnaoatl."

"Your Godhead, no! I am not the Milnaoatl, but Nopal of Rainflower. Your Godhead has a message for me?"

"Help me to my feet," said the Tlaloc-priest, and when Nopal had done so, he turned to the inner door. "Come! Iyaca will bring you the Milnaoatl breakfast."

"But Ameyatzin—"

"Come!" said the Tlaloc-priest and led him into the house with a manner so final and lofty that Nopal could not oppose him. But he went groaning inwardly to think that the Master's plan had broken down and that the message Ameyatzin was to have given him would not be given. When Iyaca came in, between them they would be able to break this dream of the Tlaloc-priest's and then Nopal would be free to go home and quiet

Ketlasho's perturbation, for perturbed she would be at his absence. Or at the worst, when the time came for going up, the right Milnaoatl would appear and set this wrong one free, but the Master's message would not be given. *This* Ameyatzin, his mind plunged in illusory dream, was not the one who could tell him what the Master desired his disciple to do.

Nopal had been the Milnaoatl in his time, and so he knew well that to take that part lay each year between a dozen or more of the young men at the head of the Calmecac, one of whom would have been chosen months ago and ever since would have been preparing. There were the hymns to be memorized; there was the deep searching into the springs of his life, and the severe self-discipline he would have to undergo, all the while hiding from the world the fact that he was the one chosen. The last thing possible in the world was that a Milnaoatl should be chosen on Tepeilhuitl morning.

All the same, supposing that Ameyatzin had really selected no Milnaoatl until this most preposterous moment; the old priest was bound to realize that no one would know of it but himself and Nopal.

Iyaca, in due course, did bring in the Milnaoatl breakfast; but as things went, it was impossible even to catch his eye. Ameyal was present, and it was Iyaca's business to see no one but Ameyal, whose look was that of a sage illuminated in meditation, not that of an old man lost in dreams. Nopal knew that his own mood, if he were really to be a votary, should be high and holy . . . but he could not attain to a holy mood now.

They breakfasted together in silence, and the true Milnaoatl did not appear. He should have arrived by that time, as the votaresses would soon be coming and it was his duty to be there before they came. Nopal began to think of the hymns, which he remembered in a general way, but certainly not accurately in detail. If the worst came to the worst—

But then Iyaca brought his master certain pictoscripts, and Ameyal said: "Let Tlaloc's Milnaoatl listen!" And he began reading from them the hymns that a Milnaoatl must know. Nopal listened eagerly, struggling the while with a kind of anger that arose within him. He was not fit to go.

By the time Ameyatzin had chanted all of the hymns thrice, Nopal knew them well. After all, he had been the Milnaoatl before. It was a high and solemn duty that had thus been thrust on him: one that no one before, in all history, he supposed, had taken twice, or had taken in so unhallowed a mood. The votaries were made, for the day, sacred to Tlaloc: appointed to approach on behalf of sovereign and people the Masters of the Clouds and Torrents; to set in motion that of which the reaction should be, physically, the rains of the coming year, and, spiritually, certain down-flowings of mountain grace to keep men mountain-hearted and life wholesome.

What a case was his, then, whose sole preparation for it was that hope had gone from his world! But it became clearer and clearer that he would have to take the role. The Tlaloc-priest led him into the robing room and bade him robe himself, and there was the familiar Milnaoatl costume laid ready. He could but obey, struggling with himself the while toward the mood it behooved him to inhabit, but with no commendable success. He heard the votaresses arrive, and presently the litters came, and the Tlaloc-priest and the five were borne up to the Top of the Town. And again, he was not fit to be the Milnaoatl.

In the arena, the dance ebbed and flowed about him, ebbed and flowed, and brought him no nearer to fitness. And when, in the course of it, all five votaries were led away and up into the Queen's Garden and to the gate at the southeastern corner, through which they should set out to climb the holy mountain, there was one of them, the Milnaoatl, who hated going and knew himself unworthy to go. It had never happened thus before.

12

The Votaries and Tlalocan

High up on Mishcoatepetl, and not so far from the Serpent Peak, there is a valley said to be always delicate with the blooms of fairyland, and a lake in which was the goal of the Tepeilhuitl votaries, who alone of all mankind ascended Mishcoatepetl above the town.

Before starting, they were each given by the Tlaloc-priest, a paper boat to launch on the lake, with a paper figure in it: that of a man in the Milnaoatl's; of a woman in the votaresses'. Around these figures, in some mystical way, were the aspirations of Huitznahuac centered. The boats would float out from the shore, the launchers the while intoning the prescribed hymn, until a current bore them to a kind of whirlpool under the cliff on the other side, where they sank, bearing the kindness of humanity to the kindly Princes of the Rain.

That was the purpose of the pilgrimage; and yet, a votary might, and sometimes did, serve a higher purpose and attain a nobler goal without ever coming near the lake and the valley at all. The Lords of the Mountains, on this, their sacred day, might intercept any of the five midway and take that happy one into Tlalocan—the Copal-Incense Garden of King Tlaloc—which was held to be within, or in some magical propinquity to, the mountain, and there make known to him or her the secrets of Spiritual Beauty. This was done to express the Lords' great goodwill toward mankind; for when a votary was taken, it signified the Tlalocs' promise that fortunate times were at hand. It happened once or so in a year-sheaf. A votary would return late or in unusual fashion and tell the tale—but only to the Tlaloc-priest—of his or her adventures in the Heartland, and thereafter it would be seen that his or her life had been enriched marvelously, and that for all of Huitznahuac, the noble augury of it would be fulfilled in some way. It rarely happened more often than once in a year-sheaf, and only twice or thrice in all history had more than one votary been taken in a year. But it was possible that all five might be taken. It had happened once, in Ulupi's time, and it had presaged the coming of Huanhua; and who was to know in what year so supreme a miracle might not happen again? That was the feeling in Huitznahuac in every Tepeilhuitl. Who was to know? This very Rabbit 13, for aught one could tell, might be signalized wondrously, as in their turn might be the Reed One, Flint 2, House 3 and Rabbit 4, which were coming. So it was a day very salutary to the Huitznahuatecs, one that drew them by chains of golden expectation toward the God-world.

There were paths and paths on Mishcoatepetl, made by whom, and why not long since overgrown and lost, only the Tlalocs could tell. All of them led at last to the lake and the valley, but not one of them was the path. When the votary went up into the mountain, the Tlalocs would guide him according to his own inner standing, according to the particular thing that the ages of his evolution had made him. It was said that in all time no two votaries had gone up by the same path.

The first rule was that one must go in faith; faith was to be the guide. Whether one came to the pilgrim's usual goal or to holy Tlalocan, nothing but faith could bring him to it—which is as much as to say that one must allow the Tlalocs to lead. The votary left his course to them, taking viewless divinity by the hand. He had put self away to begin with. He had been for months training himself, and being trained, to do just that. Then he followed the path at his feet, even if it appeared to lead him, at a dozen strides away, to the brink of a precipice. His thought was to be with the gods, who chose the way and led him in it.

As now they led in turn the Tepos, the Shochiteca and the Matlalqua as each passed out by the mountain gate from the Queen's Garden and walked on in sight of the rest to an open space called the Raingods' Glade and there disappeared from view. All three, after long wandering or short, came happily into Tlalocan.

After the Matlalqua came the Mayavel, who was Queen Chimalman. She went out into the forest as to a lover, her heart entirely for Mishcoatepetl. She had never had a human lover, nor looked at any man with interest of that kind; she did not know what it meant. The mountain thrilled her to a more starry elation. . . .

For the sake of impersonality, the votaries went cloaked and hooded in town and till they had passed the Raingods' Glade; it was better that none should know who they were or think of them as but the characters they represented until their return. But now, when it was lawful to do so, this Mayavel threw back her hood and went bareheaded, worshiping, singing. Until noon, she was mostly ascending. There were pleasant, lawny slopes, mysterious edges of the forest, solitary trees that beckoned, wooded heights full of whispering motion—all of them surcharged with a gay, dynamic friendliness to feed her joy. By noon, she had quite lost herself; there was no other world than this mountain world. Her path wound on mazily through silent, shallow valleys, a sunlit loneness peopled by the unseen. There was soft grass; the occasional grayness of boulder or outcropping; shrubs, scattered or in thickets, with orange-colored berries and leaves richly bronze-green or gold-green.

Someone was ahead of her; she could not tell how she knew. Someone was ahead of her at four- or five-score strides away; because of the winding of the way, she could not see that far. She sang her hymn, as was appointed, to Tlaloc Quitzetzelohua, the Down-scatterer of Jewels, and divined that the one ahead of her would be he . . . and then, at a turn and a change of the landscape, she caught sight of him for a moment: a gigantic, beautiful being, fiery-mist-bodied, who, in that same moment, became a precipice, one of seven by whose bases, she saw, she was to pass.

For now the green valley was gone, and the way wound down

in shadow between these great cliffs, which, she thought, were human-profiled at their tops, and this nearest one with the face of the Tlaloc she had seen. They were watching her with calm, eternal eyes; but when she looked up to them, the faces were gone.

But before that changing of what had been vividly living into motionless rock, the god had dropped a jewel by the wayside; she had seen it fall, and saw it now as she approached, gleaming on the ground and sparkling. Nearing, she saw what it was: a chalchiuhite dragon—*the* Chalchiuhite Dragon; and then it rose in the air on wings and circled about her head, and soared up among the peaks that she knew were watching her from above; and her song rose and soared with the dragon, which shone above there like a star, but was always visible for what it was and advanced as she advanced, lighting the crag tops that were always human- or god-visaged, except when she looked at them directly. And so it was until she had passed the seven of them; and as night fell, she came out from the defile and stood on the brink of the abyss.

A great part of her kingdom lay below, dotted here and there with the lights of farms and houses; above were the dancing myriads of the stars. Among them, brightest of all, was the Chalchiuhite Dragon; she saw it flash across the heavens and take station above the peak of Teotepetl to the west and shine there the Star of Quetzalcoatl, the Evening Star.

A whisper came down from the peaks: "Let the dragon be a sign for you!" and the question rose in her mind: "A sign of what?"

"Now, that he is coming; and then, that He is coming!" came the answer. "Look yonder!"

And there in front of her, where she had thought the abyss had been, and a great part of her kingdom beneath it, lay stretched in twilight, in daylight, in a light more brightly mysterious than day's, the lovely Garden Tlalocan, and approaching her by the path between the living waters came the Star of Quetzalcoatl, came the Chalchiuhite Dragon . . . in the hands of the Stranger of Teotleco.

* * *

When the Mayavel had passed out of sight, the Tlaloc-priest had given the signal for the Milnaoatl to start, and Nopal had gone out into the forest.

He went singing the hymn appointed: an invocation of the Tlaloc Tepahpaca Teaaltati, the Purifier. He sang it because it was the hymn appointed and had been used by the Milnaoatl at Tepeilhuitl since the beginning of the world; but his heart was elsewhere, and he was no fit votary for the pilgrimage. All the doors of the God-world were shut against him, and what he was doing was meaningless. He sang his hymn only as best he could, and it was unlikely that the Tlaloc would hear.

His way led under great trees that grew not too close together for blossomy shrubs to riot into luxuriance between. It was his business to invoke the Purifier in these and all the forest things through which Teteoinan the All-mother burns up into beauty and multiplies her occasions for joy. To invoke a god in them means to exchange consciousness with them in some sort, reminding them of their kinship with men and giving back delight for delight. What delight could he give? To the best of his belief, he quite failed in his invocation.

That, possibly, mattered little to the good Tlaloc he invoked. Teaaltati was abroad that day, intent on his grand Tepeilhuitl purposes and not to be set back by trifles. He would flood with his own divine Mountain-consciousness the mind, heart, and life of anything human he might find singing invocation to him on the mountain. By midday he had begun to have his will of the Milnaoatl, and through the afternoon he went molding him to the mountain's desire.

In the valleys, the silence became music; in the pine woods, the wind became vocal, and august voices whispered in consultation; steep rock-surfaces beckoned to be climbed. But, Nopal mused, was it not the Master who had bidden him go to Ameyatzin this morning, and therefore was he not, perhaps, Milnaoatl by the Master's own order, in obedience to him making this pilgrimage on the mountain? And the Milnaoatl he became, fulfilling the part: a disciple again, completely trusting in life and the innate divinity of things.

At the brink of darkness, he came to a torrent that must be

crossed, for in that way lay the path. There was no leaping across, but he might be able to leap to that rock in the middle. The water was deep and too swift for swimming, and the sudden darkness too near for hesitation. He leaped . . .

Nopal thought he must have been dreaming something; though now, on waking, the dream escaped him. Well, he had had many dreams as wonderful in this so-familiar room of his on the island in the Serpent's Hole. . . .

With a pang he remembered that the noble years of his life there had come to an end and that today he was to go . . . to go beyond the limits of the known world on an errand for the Master. It would not really be exile. . . .

But he must hurry; Quauhtli was calling.

When they had breakfasted, the time came to start. "We shall cross the lake with you," said the Master. Ah, yes. His dream had been that the Master was dead!

So they went down to the steps, the Master's hand on his shoulder. In the boat, Quauhtli took the paddle so that Nopal might be free to listen to what the Master was telling him. It was about the new queen. Of all the sovereigns of Huitznahuac, said the Master, only Ulupi, before her, had heard the divine fluting at Teotleco, and her glory should exceed Ulupi's, and by much.

Nopal was to tell her that. He was to say to her that none of her predecessors had been exalted as she would be. He was to tell her that the gods expected more of her than they had of any of the kings, her ancestors. She was to be assured of that, and never to doubt it. "She is never to forget that we are with her to guard her and lead her to her glory. Say that she must trust in us who trust in her. She must trust, and go on trusting, and never cease to trust, so that her trust may open a path between our world and men. You are to say those words to her, and make her know they are from us. She is to trust until her trust becomes knowledge and what we expect of her is fulfilled. Whatever happens, she is to trust. Let the Chalchiuhite Dragon be her sign."

They came to the landing place on the far shore of the lake and Quauhtli drew the boat in. "Here we shall leave you," said the

Master. "No, we will not go ashore. And now tread carefully, for the rock is moss-grown and slippery!"

The Master's hand in his, Nopal stepped out of the boat . . .

. . . onto the rock in the midst of the torrent on Mishcoatepetl. The Master's voice was still in his ears. The daylight was gone; he could not see the bank he was to cross to. The swift transition from his vision bewildered him. But he was to give a message to the queen, and at once. He looked this way and that, and—

Light broke in on the left: golden daylight, by all that was wonderful. It came through an arch in the rock and showed him that he was standing on a causeway that led in through the arch and out into open sunlight beyond. Of course . . .

He went in—into the Copal-Incense Garden. And there, coming down the path toward him, was the one he was seeking, the one to whom he was to give the Master's message.

And, meanwhile, Huitznahuacan was beginning to be agog with a rumor that none of the votaries had returned. If One were to think of what that might mean—and that unless they had been taken into Tlalocan, surely they would have come back by now. Groups went about the stepped streets exultantly telling each other so. This Rabbit 13 might be the year of years. . . .

And, mind you, next year would be a Ce Acatl. Next year would be a Ce Acatl!

13

A Huitznahuatec Market Day

A mood of high expectancy grew through the next two days, during which three of the votaries returned with tales to tell the Tlaloc-priest of the high things they had seen in Tlalocan. Then the anticipation was wonderfully enhanced on the morning following.

It was that of a market day, as every fifth day was in Huitznahuacan. All of the town, and much of the country, was in, or represented in, the marketplace, disposing of the results of its past five days of labor and acquiring what it would need during the five days to come. Your tastes would be farfetched indeed if you could not find there all that you desired.

A walk through from the Market Magistracy to the koo of Tlaloc will prove that to you; so imagine, please, that you are a farmer from Blue-wind, Rainflower or Greenjaguar and that you started out early this morning with, say, three litters—one for yourself and two for your produce—and a double relay of bearers, who made their five miles or more an hour without trouble and brought you into town in six hours. From such districts as Burntbread or Losthistory, you would have had to start out on the day before and spend the night in the guest house of some intervening village.

Arriving, you leave your litters at the posthouse in the Townmouth, where your men unload and shoulder your goods, thence carrying them to where the Street forks and up the stairs on the

right, just this side of the koo of Teteoinan, to the Market
Magistracy, a large building facing the Street. Some two-score
steps lead up to the terrace on which it stands, and it is colonaded
in front, with cornice and pillars curiously carved, and glistens
silverly in its coat of polished gypsum—as all the buildings in
Huitznahuacan do. In it, the Market Magistrate, normally the
reigning sovereign presides; but Acamapitzin for the present is
taking Chimalman's place there, as he took that of the old king,
his father, during the latter years of Ashokentzin's reign.

You could pass to the left into the Lower Market without
entering the Magistracy, but you do not. Acamapitzin is a man
you greatly respect and like; and in any case, you would go in to
greet him. Having brought those litter-loads of farm-stuff with
you, you go in as well to have them entered in the accounts of the
market by clerks whose skill and intuition in pictography fit them
for the work. When you leave, they will also note down all you
take from the market, and at the end of the day they will see to
the collecting of what suitable foodstuffs are left over, and presently to the drying, salting and storing of them. All of the buildings on the hillside to the west of the Upper Market are
storehouses and contain, as a rule, what would carry Huitznahuac through a year or more of disastrous crops.

Your business there finished, you leave the Market Magistracy
by a door in the east wall and descend by five steps into the
Lower Market. Here, to your left, is the koo of Teteoinan, with
the stalls of the flower-suppliers at its base. In front and to your
right is an irregular semicircle of pillared gallery, with houses on
houses piled up on the steep hillside above. To this gallery every
market day poets come and chant their verses for any audiences
that may gather; you will find a crowd listening to them always.
At some time in the day, everybody spends an hour here, and the
poets are kept busy. If you have luck, you may even listen to the
priest-prince Acatonatzin, greatest singer of his age. One keeps
silent here mostly; greets one's friends, but with a gesture; indi-
cates the flowers one wants without speech. All of the flower-
suppliers are women attached to the Temple of Teteoinan.

At the southwest corner of the Lower Market, a flight of some
twenty steps—with the small koo of Centeotl, the Maize-queen,

at the left on top—leads you to the next level, where the potters, cabinetmakers, stoneworkers, carpenters and goldsmiths carry on their trades and display their wares on market days. From any one of them you may have what you want for the asking. Cross this Middle Market diagonally and another stairway brings you to the foot of the koo of Shewtecuhtli, the Fire-god, at the lower end of the Upper Market, the largest of the three and the center of things socially on market days. It slopes up from there south to the koo of Tlaloc but curves to the east in the middle, so that the one koo is not to be seen from the other. Here your bearers bring the loads they brought in and then distribute themselves, unless ordered otherwise, in quest of a day's enjoyment. There is plenty to be had, here and below, to fill their time until you need them in the evening.

For instance—not to speak of the poetry in the Lower Market, and depend on it, they will all spend an hour or two down there drinking it in—the Huitznahuacan storyteller, and two or three others of that profession from the villages, will be in attendance up here during the afternoon. And the Greenjaguar jugglers, the best in the kingdom, come in, and the tumblers from Losthistory, so that all day long there will be something to see or hear, as is but fitting in this great Huitznahuacan, capital of the world. To be a litter-bearer, and run your twenty or thirty miles under a load into the city on a market day, is a privilege much sought after by the young men of the villages; it is their chance to see the wonders of the age, and it gives them matter to talk over until their turn for it comes again.

The Upper Market supplies all needs in the way of food and clothing: the latter in the long gallery under the hill on the east; the former on the other side, under awnings on the terrace of the lowest tier of storehouses. There the hunters bring carcasses of deer, peccaries, rabbits and so forth, according to the needs of town and country; and the farmers bring fatted dogs and turkeys from their herds. There come the fishermen with what the rivers afford of fish and of frog-spawn in season. And there in season you will find baskets or piles of chiles, bright green and bright scarlet; tomatoes; maize, in grain or on the cob; onions and garlic; pochotl seed; beans of many sorts; many kinds of edible roots; also of fruits—zapotes, black, yellow or green; cherimoyas and mombins; cashews and sugar-apples; soursops, texocotls, quauhtzapotls, papayas, and a score of kinds beside. Here too, to one side or the other of the Upper Market, the agave-farmers bring all the products of that master-plant: roots and sections of stem to be roasted, roasted and roasted, or stewed, stewed and stewed, into wholesome edibility; raw fiber to be dried, cured and woven into nequen cloth or pulped and made into paper; dried leaves disthorned to thatch sheds or build fences withal; pins, needles and hooks made of the thorns.

Up here, too, at the Shewtecuhtli end, are the cooks who cater for folk, like yourself, in from the country—the very best of cooks, be assured!—these mincing meat with garlic and fiery chiles, wrapping it in maize dough and with maize leaves outside all, and baking the result in their clay ovens into excellent tamales; those making a dozen different types of flat loaves or tortillas; these others preparing roasts or stews of venison, turkey or dog meat with tomatoes, mushrooms and garlic; or, farther up, pounding cocoa beans with maize flour and pochotl seed, and boiling, cooling, and frothing the mixture into chocolate, halfway between liquid and solid—food or drink as you please.

In the gallery you can get all of the nonedible products of the agave worked up into their final manufactured form, especially nequen cloth. Nequen cloth dyed or undyed, by the piece or cut into garments, wondrously little tailored, in sepias, umbers, siennas, terra-cottas, brick-reds, dark blues, leek-greens and jade-greens, rich yellows, and pale but vivid blue-greens, such as are worn now by the happy crowd that fills the place. Oh, yes—everything imaginable, you may say, is to be had in the Huitz-nahuacan market.

And the unimaginable, too, this morning, for you are delighted to see the awnings of the Saltmerchants in front of the Fire-lord's koo, and the tales you shall hear from them may well be called unimaginable. Indeed, there is a streak of the supernatural in their very existence; but for them, "human" and "Huitz-nahuatec" would be synonyms. They cannot come here without, in a sense, unsettling the bounds of the universe, and yet we are used to them, for they do come, one or another party of them, half a dozen times or more in the year. When you come to think of it, the apparition of a god would, on the whole, be less surprising. . . .

For we know the bright realms of beauty that lie inward of the man-world and of which the solid mountains are the shadowed projections, as it were; all have visited them in dreams. Between death and rebirth, we traverse and make our homes in them. But who has passed the legendary Canyon at the End of Things or walked in the unknownness of the north? Who knows what infinite mystery girdles around the eight thousand of mountains we call Huitznahuac?

None but these Saltmen. Understand or believe it who can, their very presence here proves that they do.

They are excellent, entertaining fellows: merchants and strolling players. Highly gifted men, we all think them. They call themselves Chiapanecs, whatever that may mean, as we call ourselves Huitznahuatecs, and say that they come from a land called Chiapas. They are a kind of link for us with that which, to say the truth, we never could quite find it in our hearts to believe in: a world beyond Huitznahuac. Imagine, then, what a source of wonderment they are! Our literature of humor is mainly built on the tales they tell us, and how magnificently farcical and fanciful it is!

They come with their trains out of the north, spend a day here and go back the way they came. During the morning and afternoon, they are providing us with salt—and romance—in the marketplace; toward evening we feast them in the guest house; later they perform for us in the arena. We count them very benevolent beings thus to leave their mystery-world and make the roads of space their home that our needs may be supplied, and to get nothing for it in return. Well, nothing really! Truly there are the bags of uncut chalchiuhites we press on them as tokens of our affection. Chalchiuhites aplenty are to be found at Blue-wind.

There are several parties of them, with three merchants in each, but those here today are our favorites: by title and names, the Philosophers Hax, Been, and Quicab. They have not a tale to tell, of all their countless eight thousands, but what is a keen joy to listen to: quaintly fascinating, most original, preposterously unlikely! They fill the vastness we know not with what queer figments of fancy please them—and to be sure, please us too, and marvelously! And we have much too much sense of humor ever to ask, "Is that true?"

For instance, when they tell us that their salt comes from a lake in the northern world and is, in fact, dried water, what bad manners it would be to take them seriously! And when they go on to say that in those parts—those surely nonexistent parts—there are many cities larger than this immense Huitznahuacan! And that men can speak from a mountaintop through a thing called a far-speaker and be heard fifteen-score miles away in any direction!

In brief, their imagination is infinitely fertile, and Huitznahuacan is having infinite enjoyment of it this morning. They are at their best when descanting upon a people they call the *Toltecs,* concerning whom their wildest tales are told. Not so long ago we had never heard of these Toltecs; the Saltmen were, till recently, reticent as to their native regions, and our literature of humor is not a year-sheaf old. We might well be thankful that they have changed their habit!

This morning they had needed clothes for some of their porters; the need was obvious. What they must do, then, was to accept the best mashtlies and tilmatlies in the market. The clothiers were insistent, as was all Huitznahuacan. There was no way of paying for these clothes. To offer more salt than was asked for would be to elicit the question, "What for?"—we of Huitznahuac having no conception of sale or barter. So, when they had taken what they must, Shaltemoc, Nopal's brother-in-law, sensing a trifle of embarrassment in them, switched the talk to the Toltecs with, "Let the philosophers tell us now about the clothes their Toltecs wear."

The crowd urged the suggestion. It was early, and there was plenty of time. Everyone took more or less of a holiday when Philosopher Hax and his partners were in town.

Sleek and well-fed Quicab responded; he had the glibbest tongue in the world. What that tongue could make of it here, lean Hax and large Been were interested to discover, since how could you tell Toltec tales on this matter without seeming to disparage the garments—excellent garments, mind you!—that generous Huitznahuacan had just been giving you? Philosopher Quicab felt this too; and his tongue, glib as it might be, and artful enough as it was elsewhere, in Huitznahuacan distinctly aimed at truth. "Clothes?" said he. "Oh, your Godheads must understand that the Toltecs have no such wearing apparel as you have. For your clothes, it is understood, are good clothes. They are well-made, durable, and artistically colored. Oh dear, no; the Toltecs have no such clothes as these!

"You see, they are afflicted with what is called foppishness; many of them decidedly are fops. That is, they do not dress sensibly, those people. To speak with quiet reason, they have no such sensible habits in dress as you have here."

Hax and Been applauded inwardly, imperceptibly exchanging glances. After all, Rogue Quicab was telling a kind of truth.

"They have not—" that philosopher continued, still feeling his way and with less than his usual eloquence "—they have not the art of dying nequen that you have. Indeed, they commonly use a substitute for nequen, a stuff they call cotton." He mentioned it with convincing contempt.

All very well; but we had heard of marvelous mantles of fur and feathers and felt that we were not getting all we deserved. An old man named Opochtli reminded them of these things.

"Oh, yes," said Quicab. "Those are their fopperies, you see. They trick themselves out in gauds and frippery in the vanity of their habit. A barbarous custom, you may call it."

Philosopher Been here interrupted tactfully, seeing his partner without resource. "They go into battle cotton-mailed," said he, "the cotton quilted and twisted so that no arrow could pierce it."

He had turned the matter off into humor, relieving his partner neatly. The Huitznahuatecs strove to keep face.

"Battle, Philosopher Been?" This was their most preposterous, and so our favorite, subject.

"Ah," said Hax, "That is a matter your Godheads know nothing of." Hax always vaguely disliked talking about war when visiting Huitznahuacan.

But we did know, of course. We knew well what "battle"

meant; it was what happened between the gods and the Sun of old. The absurdity was to speak of it as happening between men and men.

Philosopher Been went on to extend our ideas. "War," said he, "comes about when one king marches against another and subdues him."

"But how subdues, your Godhead?" Thus we draw our friends out, inducing them to practice their art.

"By killing his men. In this warfare, you must understand, men take bows and arrows, spears and terrible macuahuitl-swords, and ruthlessly slay those who oppose them."

For all our restrained habit, we must laugh a little at such a farfetched, quaint, fantastic imagining. Philosopher Been's expression as he spoke was quite serious—even, you might say, pained.

We drew them out on the subject of the Toltec towns, and Quicab became eloquent presently. "Are they really like that?" asked old Opochtli, wonder on his face.

"A deal better live here in quietness than amidst that pomp and bloodshed," growled Been, and the other two grunted agreement.

Just then a clerk came up from the Market Magistracy to stop the distribution of all fresh foodstuffs, because it might be needed for certain strangers who were—

"Strangers?"

Yes. It was something that had never happened before. A herald, if you please, had just come in to announce that an embassy from—the Soul of the World knew where—would be in the city before noon, so we must reserve what provisions had been brought in this morning until we knew what these guests of the queen would need. And would their Godheads, the provision-dealers, have their porters take what they had up to the guest house at once? And would their Godheads, the cooks, repair thither with all their paraphernalia and do their best with what the porters would bring? For we hear that there are score-scores coming; the guest house itself might not be big enough. And would not the rest of their Godheads present like to go out northward along the Road to meet and welcome the ambassador?

Indeed they would, and with a will! Lucky that, being a market day, all were here assembled and ready! The Chiapanecs' aspect, from serious, had turned glum indeed, but none noticed that. We had other things to think of as we poured down toward the Lower Market, the Townmouth, and the Road beyond. An ambassador was coming; but how could an ambassador come? Where was he to have come from? And after the glorious omen of Tepeilhuitl! What like of man was the herald, your Godhead Quanetzin?—this to the clerk who had brought the news. Had he human- or God-seeming? How was he clad? Had you opportunity to take note of him, for instance?

Oh, yes. Good opportunity. He had human- rather than God-seeming, Quanez thought; but how anyone, being human, could yet be so little like humanity, it was for their Godheads to ponder. "And yet, if you can understand me, noble. Noble, my conception is. And speaking so strangely that one had to guess at his meaning, though there were many words one could catch. These extra-mundane people must be sadly crippled in the matter of communication by speech.

"But the apparel! The marvelous splendor! The woven fur and feathers, such as the Salt-purveying Godheads had spoken of. The scintillant glow of harmonious colors! And this one merely a kind of servant, sent forward to announce his master's coming. . . ."

"A Toltec!" quoth Opochtli. "Depend on it, sent by that great northern monarch the philosophers have told us about." He was passing with the crowd out through the Townmouth; unlike the rest of us, he was unhumorous and had sometimes inclined to belief in the Saltmen's Toltec tales. But now his remark caused no amusement. What if it were true, after all? We had certainly heard of those cloaks of fur and feathers.

We questioned the Saltmen in passing; but those philosophers had become, contrary to nature and precedent, quite unapproachable. Tush, they had no opinion at all; they knew nothing in the world, they said. —Were their tales really true? Was there such a people as the Toltecs? —Let their Godheads who wanted salt come for it: market days were for getting in the things one needed. It might be necessary for us Chiapanecs to take the road earlier than you thought, so you will do wisely to acquire your salt now! —But would you not come down with us to see this great sight, the arrival of the first ambassador in history? —Yes, but not just yet; later perhaps. They must attend to this and that first. So the crowd passed on and left them presently alone.

And we went growing toward belief in their stories, forgetting, however, those about war. And we thought of this latest portent—the ambassador's coming and the new world it implied—in connection with the high happening of Tepeilhuitl. Oh, we were on the brink of glorious things; the Feast of the Mountains had foreshadowed them! At least men were divine, the Others of the gods themselves, for which reason we addressed each other as "your Godhead." So to come into contact with a new mankind would be to increase our wealth and knowledge of divinity, to gain untold riches of the spirit. A happy and most blessed time!

Thus Huitznahuacan, passing out through the Townmouth and trailing along the Road to the north, was uplifted, and presently meeting the so marvelous ambassador, made quite clear to him the joy it had in his coming.

14

The Toltec Ambassador

The Chiapanecs, sitting disconsolate, watched the townspeople depart. When the last had gone, Been broke a long silence with, "Our last visit here, then!"

"Half a dozen hours behind us," groaned Hax. "Had we dawdled, we should have been overtaken. A good pestilent curse on someone!"

"On the hierarch, then!" growled Been. "He will be at the bottom of it."

"I am going to see before I believe it," said Quicab, rising.

"And be recognized, and have them know we come to Huitznahuac?" said Hax.

"I won't be recognized. Wait you!"

Quicab hurried off toward the koo of Tlaloc, knowing that somewhere behind it there was a way up to the Top of the Town. He soon found it. East of the Tlaloc-priest's house, the hillside rose steeply; up the face of it, in zigzags, stairways had been cut, which Quicab took at a run. These brought him to the back of the koo of Quetzalcoatl. Ascending, he trusted that Amaquitzin would be somewhere below, busy about the ambassador. He could devise a tale, he hoped, that would satisfy anyone else.

On the top, he crawled toward the temple with a mental "Excuse-me" prayer to its deific owner; he would arrange a more formal apology presently through his own deity, the hook-nosed Yacacoliuhqui, God of Merchants. The temple was empty, as he had hoped, so now there was nothing to fear from behind. Still crawling, he made his way to the northwestern corner of the koo top and surveyed the world.

Yes, there on the Calmecac roof were the three Royal Uncles in consultation—to his surprise, without the queen. They were too deep in their counsels to be likely to look his way. Still— As he watched, they turned and went down the stairs into the Calmecac. None else was in sight, and so he might dispose himself as he would.

He stood up to get the better view. The city seemed quite emptied of its people. The whole southern half of it lay visible: there the Townmouth; there the Street; nearer, some twisted bits of the Street of the Quechol. How long was he to— Ah, there they came!

A most triumphant host, pouring in through the Townmouth: Huitznahuatecs, and islanded in the midst of them, gorgeous strangers, a litter-borne procession, at the head of which was a banner bearing the arms of . . . he peered, focusing his keen vision to make it out when the flag should front him—

Of Huetzin, King of Tollan. The coat of arms of King Huemac. Of course! Only a fool would have dreamed it could be otherwise.

He watched the crowd down there, tossing his head with impatient pity. They were treating the Toltec—who was, yes, Yacanetzin of Tollan, a great lord whom Huemac often sent on such missions—as if he were one of the greater gods come to deliver them from bondage. With flowers from the marketplace, they were piling up the Toltec litters, crowning and garlanding the ambassador and his suite, even to his bearers and escort.

These same bearers had been relieved of their loads, each one's place under a litter having been taken by a Huitznahuatec, by whose side the displaced and bloom-bedecked Toltec walked. The procession hardly moved forward at all, so great was the press of good feeling that surrounded it. "If they but knew why their guests have come!" sighed Quicab.

Well, he had seen enough. Yacacoliuhqui be thanked, the Chiapanecs had pitched their camp well to the south of the city, where these Toltecs, unless cursedly inquisitive, would not see it. Not but what Yacanetzin was a gentleman.

Soon Quicab was back with his partners in the Upper Market. They looked their question, which he answered with, "Yacanex of Tollan." They spat in silence.

Somebody appeared from below, looking for someone else, and said that the ambassador was being taken to the guest house and would not their Salt-bringing Godheads proceed thither to help entertain him? They promised to go, and so got rid of him, having however no idea of keeping their promise and thought it wise to retire behind the koo of Tlaloc, where they would be unlikely to be disturbed with more such invitations.

A score-score times in history, the *Canon of Ulupi* had been found to have foreseen things apparently unforeseeable. And so now. When the Royal Uncles went down into the Calmecac to consult it, they found everything they needed. Even on ambassadors: "Should be received in audience by the sovereign, or by four or three of his next of kin."

But the sovereign was missing; and so soon after Tepeilhuitl, it would be improper to inquire why. How long might the audience be delayed? "Must be received within four hours of his arrival." Must be received, then, by themselves and Ameyal, the Tlaloc-priest, unless the sovereign should appear meanwhile. And the Tlaloc-priest was not forthcoming; the messengers sent had failed to find him. There was nothing to be done, then, but go down with the Calmecac students to meet their guest and conduct him to the guest house with song.

They met the ambassador in the Street, where the crowd was making much of him, and they were favorably impressed. His clear-cut, scholarly face, with its air of self-possession, under that high panache of tzinitzcan feathers and above the scintillant splendor of his robes, was certainly impressive. His expression too was friendly; how could it be otherwise? To say the truth, he had been a little perturbed at the warmth of his welcome.

Cities against which they came to stir up war were not wont to treat the League's envoys like this. The ambassador wondered if these simple people could know the nature of his mission, or was it that they themselves were heartily in love with war? He had given up even trying to maintain the distant air proper to his errand, and he smiled back the affection in their eyes. His escort was overcome likewise, and fraternizing with the enemy-to-be.

These Huitznahuatecs, the ambassador thought, seemed to be the finest and kindliest people in the world, and would make splendid soldiers for the Topiltzin once they were conquered and annexed. It was even a pity that they should have to be conquered. He almost hoped for the success of his mission, which, from the first, had been intended to fail. Had they a queen, he wondered, one in a position, or who could be induced, to listen to Huemac's proposals?

The Royal Uncles found him listening with courteous sympathy to the extemporary verses of greeting that the poets had come down from the Lower Market to chant in his honor. The ambassador understood a third of them fairly well, and the spirit of all of them. He had been a student of the archaic forms of the Nahua language; this was archaic Nahua with a difference, and he was glad of this opportunity to listen to it, for presently he must make himself understood by them. When the students arrived and sang, he was still more delighted, and he came to the guest house a good friend to Huitznahuac.

15

The Audience

When the Toltecs had been nearly four hours in the city and the time for the audience drew near, Amaquitzin took upon himself a huge and, as he felt, almost sacrilegious responsibility. He left the guest house unostentatiously, taking with him—as Nopal was not there—Nopal's brother-in-law, Shaltemoc, of whom he begged a favor. Together they went to the arena, where Amaquitzin got Shaltemoc to blindfold himself with a tilmatli, after which he led him here, there and yonder, and then to the mountain gate in the Queen's Garden. He asked Shaltemoc to wait there and tell any two persons who might come by that they were needed at once in the throne room of the palace, and why they were needed.

Thus Amaquitzin made certain that if the queen was on the mountain and should return before the audience was over, she would come straight to it and not go down, as the custom was, to the Tlaloc-priest's house. As all the town was at the guest house, the blindfolding could be done unobserved and Shaltemoc's placidity could be trusted neither to be disturbed nor to be speculated upon.

At the audience, the Royal Uncles sat on the lower level of the dais, facing the Toltecs: Acatonal in the middle; Amaqui and Acamapichtli on his left and right. They were the only Huitznahuatecs present. Behind the ambassador, who was seated, stood the members of his suite: secretaries, soldiers and bearers, half a score-score perhaps, glittering richly in the shadowy light. When the ceremonial pipes had been smoked, Acatonal, in a low voice and without rising, welcomed the Toltec in the name of the queen of Huitznahuac—"There is a queen, then!" thought Yaca-netzin of Tollan—and invited him to deliver his message.

Very deliberately, and after a long pause, Yacanetzin did so. Slow speech became his office, and now he must use the archaic forms, translating his thought as he went, imitating his hosts' accent. He gave them time to get used to the result, first framing elaborate compliments on their mountains, their city and their customs, by no means without sincerity. When he felt sure that they were understanding him fairly well, he came to what he had to say. The Human Tezcatlipocâ, Huetzin, King of Tollan, Lord of the Anahuacs and Third Illuminous Potentate of the Toltec League, asked that the queen of Huitznahuac add his realm to her illustrious dominion, and Huitznahuac to the empire of the League, by becoming his wife.

An adequate silence followed, broken at last by Acatonatzin, speaking in like low, deliberate tones. He too paid lofty compli-ments with sincerity. He said that they had thought of his God-head's city as built of rainbow-stuff on some happy hillside in Tlalocan, rather than in the man-world; it was inspiring to learn that there were Toltecs, beings like themselves—human, and their brothers—to be their friends henceforth. The queen, he said, would be grateful to the lofty Huetzin for his proposals.

Then Acamapitzin spoke. But could the kingdoms be united indeed? he asked. He understood that they were far apart. Here had been kings and queens since Ulupi's days, to whom Prince Huanhua of the Mighty Bow came from beyond the western sea, forgoing his sovereignty abroad. It would be a long way for King Huetzin to travel when he desired to be with his bride.

After another silence, Amaquitzin spoke. Who could answer for a woman's heart? said he. Their sovereigns chose for them-selves, and chose from among their friends, whom they knew. Let the king of Tollan become one of these; let him come in person to ask.

While he was speaking, the queen and Nopal entered by a door on the dais, behind the Royal Uncles, and so were unnoted by them. They had come down from the mountain together; the blindfolded Shaltemoc had given them Amaqui's message at the gate. She heard only the last sentence spoken, and now her voice, with a new and sacred power in it, thrilled through the hall.

"Let the king of Tollan come," said she, "and Huitznahuac shall seem to him to be his own, and we, the king and queen of Huitznahuac, will be to him as his brother and sister. Let the lord ambassador convey this to him."

She sat down and motioned to Nopal to be seated beside her. The princes, who had risen at the sound of her voice, went up and took their places standing behind the two.

"King and queen," thought Yacanex. "The mission fails." He rose to reply and spoke very solemnly, with bent head. The news that the queen was not unmarried, said he, would cause King Huemac great grief. It might cause grief elsewhere also. Who could tell? There might be mourning among both peoples, and many cities lamenting their dead.

For now the gods were tired of their old unconcern with human things and proposed to be the masters of the world of men. They had commissioned their servants, the Toltecs, to unite mankind in one empire and one religion, and it would be impious to disobey.

The king of Tollan had hoped, as had his allies of Culhuacan and Otompan, that this far and beautiful Huitznahuac might be brought peacefully and by marriage into the God-ordained Communion of the Toltec League, so that from here to the limits of the universe southward, Toltec order, culture and religion might prevail. But now they must take new counsels and devise new means, and none knew what the end would be. But let the Huitznahuatecs be of great heart, since no disaster could overtake the brave.

"Practice yourselves in arms and discipline," said he, "lest it come to warfare between you and us!"

The Huitznahuatecs heard this phrase and, except for Nopal, were puzzled. "Lest it come to"—what?

"My sovereign," Yacanex continued, "has been mindful of your needs in this respect; understand, then, how truly he is your friend."

He turned and summoned certain of his bearers and had them unpack their bales in front. "This one first!" said he. They took from it wonders of royal raiment, woven of scintillant hummingbirds' feathers: robes for Toltec monarchs such as the kings of the south had never dreamed of; the colors of them burned in the somberness of the hall. Then came arms and armor of equal magnificence, the uses of which the queen and the princes could not guess: suits of cotton mail, terrible macuahuitls toothed with obsidian, hardwood shields, and helmets gorgeously panached. These he had the porters arrange along the sides of the hall.

When all of the bales were unpacked and the equipment of a Toltec regiment set forth, he spoke again, not to explain these strange gifts, however, but in a few words to bid his hosts farewell. His hosts had taken in the meaning of nothing before he was gone, his suite at his heels, down by the empty Street of the Quechol to the Townmouth and away, all of their spare baggage-litters laden with provisions by the Huitznahuatecs.

And meanwhile in the crowded marketplace, it was known that wonderful things were afoot, and all in connection, of course, with the so-lately mythical Toltecs, whom yesterday none had believed in at all. How propitiously they had revealed themselves! Half-gods rather than mortals, as their splendor testified. How fortunate we were that they had become our loving friends! Come, your Salt-dealing Godheads, Philosophers Hax and Been and Quicab, rejoice with us; fill our ears now with your marvelous true tales!

But their Salt-dealing Godheads, for some reason, were not to be found.

16

The Ambassador of the Gods

Ameyal, the Tlaloc-priest, should have been in consultation with the Royal Uncles that morning, but Acamapichtli's messengers failed to find him, and the princes could not afford to wait. Perhaps never before on a market morning had he been absent from his temple, where it was his duty to be. Iyaca, who watched over him lovingly, and these days with more care than ever, supposed that he was there as usual; and he would surely have been told he was not but for the excitement in the town.

Ameyal was, in fact, up on the mountainside, in meditation in the Raingods' Glade, having wandered out there early instead of ascending the koo. Since the Feast of the Mountains, he had been more than ever of the God-world, in a curious elevation of mood, with temporal things but shadowy to him, and divinities rather than men for his companions. At about midday he returned, for no reason that his mind was aware of, going down by the path through the forest and by the bridge over the ravine at the bottom of his garden. He found the Saltmen seated on the lowest step of the koo stairway, looking thoroughly disconsolate.

They had been his good friends for many years and had, as usual, begun their day in Huitznahuacan with a visit to his temple, bringing an offering. They had been as surprised not to see him then as they were to see him now—supposing him, of course, to be with the ambassador—as he came up through the garden. For all his aloofness, he noted their depression at once and would have probed for their hurt with a view to healing it, but that Hax anticipated him.

"Your Godhead need not ask," said the lean Chiapanec. "It is the ambassador who came this morning."

Ameyal's eyes, strangely lit up, questioned them. He himself had lately sent out ambassadors, the only kind he knew of, or that there were for him to know of, on behalf of Huitznahuac to the gods of the Mountain . . . .

"The ambassador of the Toltecs, your Godhead," explained Quicab. "You will have heard—"

But he had heard more than they guessed. News so holy never before had come to him. "Toltec," as it chanced, was a new word to him; he had never been in the way of hearing the Saltmen's tales. There were no human kings to send ambassadors, who could therefore but come from inner realms. So what he heard from explanatory Quicab was not "ambassador of the Toltecs," but "ambassador of the Gods"—Teteo.

They marveled at the way his face shone. He seemed to lose interest in what they had to say, to become unaware of their presence. The gods had sent their ambassador into the world, and he, as Tlaloc-priest, must go up to meet that august being. As Tlaloc-priest, as Quetzalcoatl-priest, the Plumed Dragon's emissary, the herald of the Evening Star—his thought was beyond him. He heard a music out of grander worlds, was called, and must go.

"Your Godhead—" began Been.

Ameyal turned again, blessed them with a sign, and left them amazed as he entered his house.

"Come," said Hax. "We had better go back to the market-place." He meant, "This place is too holy for the likes of us."

Ameyal dressed himself in his robes of ceremony and set out for the Raingods' Glade again. Very slowly he went. There was little strength left in his body, but he knew nothing of that; his spirit was more than in its prime. The supreme moment of his life had come. He was on his way to meet the gods' ambassador, and the flowers of Tlalocan bloomed about him as he went, and the zacuans of Tlalocan sang to him. Nearing the glade, he walked more and more in the glory of the God-world. Entering it, he beheld the Beatific Vision: King Tlaloc himself. Or, no, one greater than King Tlaloc: the Plumed Dragon, shining wonderfully, drawing to himself the worship of the worlds. . . .

He came following what Ameyal at first did not see: two shadows that were for some reason wearing Tepeilhuitl robes—Mayavel and Milnaoatl robes. Together the three passed some three-score strides in front of him and went down by the path toward the Queen's Garden—the first two in a kind of penumbral unreality; the third, shining more clearly visible than anything Ameyal had seen in his life. . . .

After some while it occurred to Ameyal to go back to the temple. That was his place, of course; and, yes, the One that had come would expect him there. He went down through woods that were flooded with divinity and vocal with melodious adoration. All things wore at last their true semblance, which is hidden usually from the eyes of the incarnate. The sky was visibly the splendor of Quetzalcoatl. At the end of every forest vista there shone the robe of celestial hummingbirds' feathers, the youth that seemed to be eternal, the beauty beyond computation by man. . . . The she-jaguar slunk at his side, purring; the mother deer with her fawn, expecting his affection. . . .

By the time he had crossed the bridge and come up into the garden, his years had dropped from him and he was a young man again—in his last year at the Calmecac, and the Milnaoatl, about to ascend the Mountain. Outwardly and visibly, it was the koo of Tlaloc he was ascending; inwardly, it was Mishcoatepetl. Every step of the way he had traveled in his youth, he traveled again now, and he came to the lake in the valley, where he launched his votive paper boat.

The craft floated out; he watched it glide across the waters, rosy with sunset, to the whirlpool under the precipice and there disappear. And still he watched—for the boat that should come for him. For he knew that he would not return to Huitznahuacan; he would not be needed there now, since the gods' ambassador had come. The boat he looked for came, rising out of the whirlpool. It seemed to be of golden and violet fire; the figure standing in it was that of a deity bodied in fire . . . was himself, but of a strength and beauty beyond human.

So that wondrous One came to land and took the frail Ameyal in his arms; and the being of Ameyal became his being, and at last the Tlaloc-priest knew himself fully for the god he was. And he went forward in the boat, the lone god in the boat, on the waters of dream-wrought Tlalocan, through gardens past imagining, by temples built among the stars. . . .

Later in the day, when the audience was over and the Toltecs were gone, Acatonatzin went up into the temple of Tlaloc and found there the body of the old Tlaloc-priest, sitting as if in meditation, and the atmosphere of the place almost a visible light with holiness.

17

Passing

At the end of that momentous market day, Huitznahuacan was
suffering from the intrusion of the external. The people had
known but of two worlds: that of men like themselves and that
of the gods. Now a disconcerting third had thrust in, to the
detriment of both of them. Or rather, of one of them, and that
the invisible and more important. The Toltecs having invaded
the people's minds, the gods were receding.

When Acatonatzin came down into the marketplace and told
of what he had found in the temple of Tlaloc, his news did
something to restore things, but not quite enough. Death was so
much less startlingly strange than were the Toltecs, even the
death of one so beloved.

From house to house that evening messengers bore the news;
and where they went, talk and speculation ceased, and the altars
in the God-rooms were draped with the Tlaloc colors. Yet there
was still that feeling that Ameyatzin was not being truly honored,
that where the death-peace should have been, and the quiet
reaching out into the light and beauty of his passing, there was,
at best, an effort to keep thought of the Toltecs out. The night
was cheapened a little, that they should have offered up clean and
holy to their friend.

The next day the tidings went out over all Huitznahuac, and
from every district those who could, set out for the capital. There
still the silence was kept all day, and on the funeral morning that

followed. But the blue serenity of that morning shone over a Huitznahuacan that shared its mood but imperfectly. The people gathered at the Top of the Town, consciously avoiding thought about the strangers. Ameyatzin had gone through the peaceful gates between this and beauty, and had held those gates open for a while to let the grace of Tlalocan shine through . . . onto a world that had been too thoroughly disturbed to feel all the benediction of it.

Nothing went quite well until Amaqui, either acting on intuition or remembering words of Nopal's, went down onto the Calmecac roof and sought out Nauhyo among the college boys, led him up onto the koo of Quetzalcoatl, and whispered to him at a break in the Ritual, "Sing, my child!"

What should have followed was silence as the flames rose from the pyre in the arena, but into that silence Nauhyo's song came stealing, and as he gained confidence, soared above the throng: songs of the Mountain Teotepetl and the holy valley there, one after another, restoring the Huitznahuatecs to their right mood, till not a soul of them but stood cleanly in the presence of sun and sky, gods and mountains, on the very verge of that beloved Tlalocan into which their friend and helper had passed. Nauhyo had come so lately to the college that few of the citizens had taken note of him, and none knew of his power of song. Not even the queen, in whose mind it sowed the seed of an intent that bore fruit presently.

Nopal, hearing the song as he came up the Street of the Tzinitzcan in search of the queen, learned from it that a funeral was taking place, and knew, of course, that it was Ameyal's funeral. That was why the Tlaloc-priest had been so much in his mind over the last two days. He stood silent and sped his farewells, with those of the crowd above, into the light into which the Shining One had passed.

This was the first that Nopal had heard of the death. After the audience, as soon as the Toltec ambassador had left the hall, he too had slipped out, but by the way he and Chimalman had come in: through a curtained doorway behind the throne. In the amazement the whole business had caused, he went unnoticed, and when he had gone, the rule applied again: One did not inquire as to Nopal's whereabouts. The people were gathered in the marketplace, and he met no one on his way. He went down to his sister's house, where he obtained food—a two-day supply—from her, and changed his Milnaoatl robes for everyday wear. Then he sought the forest on that northern side of the town and began ascending the mountain, keeping well toward the east. He had matter for long meditation and must be alone.

In an hour or so, he had reached the place he was seeking: a cabin in a little glade, with the precipitous northern side of Mishcoatepetl behind. Water came trickling down the rock wall into a basin in which, upon arrival, he bathed. Then he broke his long fast, smoked, retired into the cabin, wrapped his blanket about him, and slept. His physicality needed that much; it, at least, had had neither food nor ordinary sleep since the morning of the Feast of the Mountain.

Waking sometime after midnight, he came out, lit a fire, and sat under the stars, considering his problems.

The queen had told the Toltecs that he was her husband. And she had come with him from—somewhere. Down from Mishcoatepetl; Shaltemoc had met them at the mountain gate in the Queen's Garden and told them that an ambassador was in the House of the Kings, awaiting their arrival. *Their* arrival, not *her* arrival; so Shaltemoc had said. And she had taken him by the hand and led him across the garden and into the audience-room.

And before that . . . before Shaltemoc spoke to them, there had been something that linked him to Chimalmatzin, some bond between them. But this of husband and wife . . . had he not always known that marriage was not for him? Was he not long past the age when men married? Neither he nor Quauhtli—

But what was it that had happened on the other side of the mountain gate? He made a silence within himself, reaching out toward memory . . . as if for a dream out of which Shaltemoc's voice had awakened him.

They had come down from Mishcoatepetl, since they had entered the garden by the mountain gate; and . . . why certainly they had been wearing the robes of Tepeilhuitl votaries. Then before his mental vision there came suddenly a picture of Ameyal, the Tlaloc-priest, not looking old and worn as he had last seen him, but with a look of health and strength on him, an extraordinary light of happiness on his face. A look, too, as if he were searching in Nopal's mind for the answer to a question. Why, yes, of course; it was Ameyatzin who had given him a message from the Master on Tepeilhuitl morning, who had sent him, at the Master's bidding, as Milnaoatl onto the Mountain. And it was returning from that pilgrimage that he had come with the queen.

He lived over again his ascent of the mountain until he came to the torrent that must be crossed at nightfall; then, marvelously, his memory carried him away from Mishcoatepetl and to the Serpent's Hole; it insisted on that. The next thing that had happened was the Master's charging him with a message for Chimalmatzin; and it was clear now, word for word. In his mind, he repeated it. That picture of the Tlaloc-priest came before his inner sight again, and now the face wore an expression of eagerness, of encouragement. There was a mystery about what had followed. Had he seen Chimalman and given her the message? He could not remember that, nor anything further until Shaltemoc spoke to them at the gate. But, of course, he had come down the mountain with her.

No; there was more. Who was it that had come down with them? And where had that one left them? He was not there when Shaltemoc spoke.

The sun rose and set while Nopal turned these things in his mind. There was much he could not understand, need not trouble to understand. But this was quite clear: He must deliver the Master's message to the queen, and carry out too the commands laid upon himself in it. Then if she chose, he would—

Again Ameyatzin appeared, and now his face shone with approval. Yes, Nopal would become her husband. He could carry out the Master's orders that way. When or how he had received those orders, he could not tell, since his memory necessarily was lying when it told him that he had been with Huehuetzin in the Serpent's Hole on the evening of Tepeilhuitl Day. It did not matter. The words were in his mind, and the tones in which they had been spoken. . . .

It was midnight before he reached his decision, and having

reached it, he lay down to sleep again. The Tlaloc-priest must be
thinking strongly of him, that he kept seeing these vivid mind-
pictures of him. In the morning, but not too early, he would see
Chimalman.

In the morning, when he came up the Street of the Tzinitzcan
and heard Nauhyo singing, his decision was further confirmed.
The Master had left him word that he was to share with Chimalmatzin responsibility for Nauhyo's upbringing, which was almost as much as to say that he should marry her. He had been
accustomed to the thought that a disciple must make no such
ties, must not divide his loyalty—and yet, as he remembered
now, his own father had been in some way a disciple.

Since there would be no going up through the arena while the
funeral was in progress, he went around past the front of the
Calmecac, across the Street of the Quechol, and behind the koo
of Quetzalcoatl, and joined the crowd unnoticed on the slope of
the terrace under the House of the Kings.

As the crowd was dispersing, a messenger brought him word
that the queen wished to see him and conducted him to her in her
garden. She rose from the jaguar seat as he approached.

"Your Godhead is the Tecuhtli of Rainflower?" she asked.

"Who brings your Godhead a message," said he.

She dismissed the maid whom she had sent for him and
pointed to seat cushions by the waterside, desiring him to be
seated. "I think I knew that you had a message for me," said she.
"Will your Godhead deliver it now."

"It is this," said Nopal. "I am to tell your Godhead that the
gods promise you shall serve them more wonderfully than any of
your predecessors. They expect more from you than they did
from any of your fathers; you are to be assured of that, and never
to doubt it. They say that you are never to forget that they are
with you to guard you and lead you to your greatness, that you
must trust in them, because they trust in you. You must trust,
and go on trusting, and never cease to trust, that your trust may
open a path between the gods and men. I was to say these words
to your Godhead and to make you know that they come from the
gods. You are to trust until your trust becomes knowledge and

all that the gods hope of you is fulfilled. Whatever happens, you
are to trust."

She would have him repeat the message thrice. Then she repeated it herself with no prompting from him; and after that, she
pledged herself in silence to obey. Following a long pause, she
looked up at him.

"It was on the mountain that your Godhead was given this
message for me?"

Nopal, his mind on a mountain other than Mishcoatepetl,
answered, "It was on the mountain."

"Did you give me the message on the mountain when we were
together there?"

"I do not know. It is true that we came down from Mishcoatepetl together."

"And one other was with us."

"Your Godhead knows that too?"

"It is a mystery. When Shaltemotzin spoke to us at the gate,
that Other was there no longer. We were three days on the
mountain, Tecuhtli."

"Three days?" Nopal had not known that. The meaning of it
was obvious: They had been in Tlalocan.

"Was your Godhead given the message for me in Tlalocan?
And did you give it to me there?"

"I cannot tell, your Godhead. I remember only going up on
Tepeilhuitl Day and coming down to the mountain gate with you
and with that Other."

A long silence followed; and then, from Chimalman: "There is
another matter on which I must speak to you, Nopaltzin. You
remember what I told the ambassador?"

"I remember."

"I did not know that my words were untrue." She spoke very
slowly. "We had just come down from the mountain, and I was
not yet used to this world. I think I had memories then, long
memories, that have gone from me since. I was amazed afterward
at what I had said, but it seemed to me then that it was true, and
had always been."

Nopal bowed his head.

"You know that there must be a king here, Nopaltzin. My wish is that what I said should be true."

"It shall be true, your Godhead."

"My gratitude to you, Nopaltzin!"

There followed ten days during which much business was accomplished: preparations for the marriage, preparations for dispatching the embassy to the north. The marriage was to come first so that Amaquitzin, as ambassador, might represent the king and queen of Huitznahuac, and he was to be accredited not to Tollan and King Huemac, but to the Toltec Topiltzin at Culhuacan. Nopal's knowledge of the northern world had suggested this. And—this was the intent Nauhyo's singing at the funeral had awakened in the queen: Nauhyotontli should go with Amaquitzin. His power of song, they considered, would conquer the north; none could hear him and be unaffected.

As to the marriage, Amaqui was hugely delighted that his wish was to come true. In all Huitznahuac, he thought, and his brothers agreed with him, none was so fit as Nopal to be king. And so much the fitter, all agreed, because he was the only Huitznahuatec who knew the north; and the north would now concern them greatly. All Huitznahuac was happy over it.

The marriage took place on the tenth morning. They passed from temple to temple for the ceremony, ending at that of Quetzalcoatl with the blessing of Amaqui as Quetzalcoatl-priest, whom then, as ambassador to the Toltecs, the king and queen accompanied to the northern limits of the kingdom. Then Nopal took his bride to Rainflower and thence on foot up Teotepetl to the Serpent's Hole. Ten days they spent there, he telling her all he could of the Master and of his old life there as the Master's disciple.

They were as fellow disciples together, their whole effort to come nearer to the God-world, laving their humanity in the God-life of the mountain and of that sacred vale.

BOOK II

The Road

The Hierarch of Teotihuacan

The river filled the evening with a drone as of hoarse, worn-down voices that made a pleasing accompaniment to the tune the litter-bearers crooned as they trotted along, their faces toward the setting sun. Following them came the bodyguard, two spare companies of bearers, servants, the litters that carried the stores. It was a great company that the hierarch of Teotihuacan, ambassador of the Otomi Republic, brought with him on his mission to Huitznahuac. Beyond the river, the hills rose at once, steep and forested; but on this side, a broad stretch of travelable land lay between it and the jungle; and along this broad stretch the party journeyed. It was the Road.

The Great Road ran from the north to the south of the universe, which in north and south alike had long since been forgotten, or had become the vaguest of traditions. In the north, science might know where it began; not even superstition had imagination to guess where it ended. Neither north nor south troubled about it; although over most of its great length it was well traveled for short distances; and as little aspect of roadhood as it might now wear, those who dwelt in its vicinity never forgot that it was the Road.

No doubt the Quinames built it in the days of their power, when they were giants in stature and arrogance, and strewed the world with monuments of their glory. It still withstood the encroachment of the forest, to say how mightily they had built—

they, who so far as north or south could tell, had vanished from the world before the apotheosis of the Sun.

Many nations of old had sent their merchants and ambassadors to travel it: from the Anahuacs to Huitznahuacan, and farther. At every stage, in those days, a city, or at least an inn or rest-house, had stood, and the traveler had no need to carry food with him at all. But they had vanished time out of mind and left no material trace. Ages since, civilization had receded, the stir of it to the north, the spiritual quiet that redeems it to the south; and now these infinite leagues of hills and forests had but curious tenants humanly: wild tribes, always treacherously at war among themselves, who regarded strangers only as potential food.

But anyone was safe from them on the Road, and herein lay its last remaining dignity. To err from it by as little as ten paces was to plunge into the cooking pots of savagery; to keep to it, on the other hand, was to have the tribes in some sort one's servants and friends. Perhaps the giants who built it put magic into the building, to say, "This is the gods' property forever; let none molest who uses it as the gods intend!" Perhaps the ages that had busily used it had built into it a convention—of a beneficence more lasting than can be quarried from the hills. In any case, there remained in the air that which kept the savages from killing—on the Road. And, of course, in the worst part there was the God on Puma Rock.

So it was that man or tribe might march along it gaily, and no slinking or hiding, day after day through enemy territories, and so far from being killed and eaten, might expect to be fed, and the enemy would do it. This much did remain of the ancient rest-houses and cities: Where they had been, it was an act of piety to leave food for travelers, the one pleasant tenet in the wild men's religion. None knew why it was pious. Piety generally tended in the opposite direction; you felt better as a rule, and the gods loved you more, when you had eaten a man than when you had done him a service, but there was this supreme exception. After all, the gods were mighty and had leave to be inconsistent. Unless the traveler on their Road was fed, they hated you and prepared ugly punishments for you. This was not believed or suspected, but *known*.

Safe to say that Hierarch Yen Ranho was the first civilized
man to enter into relations with these tribal people. It is proof of
his greatness that he had not been five days in the forest before
the forest knew that he was a very powerful god. It was even
thought that the city he came from was an excellent place toward
which to face when one prayed. A few judicious miracles had
aided this belief; characteristically, the hierarch left it to his
subordinates to work them. But you cannot convert a savage
even by miracles until your native greatness has so far won him
over as to lure him forth from the dark jungle to meet you on the
Road.

Three of the wild men's great chieftains were now in Yen
Ranho's train; they might have been riding in litters could they
have brought themselves to such a peak of trust. He smiled to
think by what name they called themselves, as he had come to
learn but yesterday: *Quinames,* if you please. Though they had,
apparently, no legend of such high descent, he found it interesting to believe that they were the modern representatives of those
half-mythical giants who had ridden through the upper air and
all but dethroned the gods themselves. These squalid, murderous
forest thieves . . .

The sun rested on the hilltop in front, and his bearers, thrilled
by the sacredness of the hour, turned their hearts toward holy
Teotihuacan, because the time of prayer drew near. The hierarch
felt the hour too; but his religion, naturally, was more advanced
than theirs, and free from superstition. A stern realist was Hierarch Yen Ranho. All the facts of life proclaimed to him that the
truth he lived for and willed should be universally honored. He
looked out on the world with keen, unflinching, joyless eyes and
rejected as vicious any ideas and beliefs that did not seem to him
proven by the joyless things he saw. Sentimentalism was a lie,
and the universe abhorred a lie. The gods abhorred a lie, as he
himself did, and they would punish it. Ever eager to plague
mankind—as mankind so richly deserved plaguing—they never
forgave false opinion. It was a thing that ought not to be forgiven.

He had not invented his religion; it had grown down to him
through a long line of predecessors, most of whom had modified

it in a certain direction. Its mood had come to be greatly different from that of the antiquity in which it had, supposedly, originated. No hierarch had so rigorously disciplined it as he had—by constant observation of the facts of life. His observations, of course, were filtered through a medium, that of his character; and that they might bear a bias, due to the trend of his lives, he never suspected. Stern, clear-cut of mind, severely logical, he had hewed away error where he had found it; and he hoped that before he died, he would have led mankind willy-nilly some way toward truth. He had done so already. Let him but succeed in what he had undertaken now, and he could afford to die when he might.

Great need there was that someone should lead mankind toward truth!—as he was now reminded. Even these bearers of his, being ignorant peasants, would be feeling beauty in the coming on of evening, and reading in it the kindness of the gods. Thus too the deluded ancients had felt, not having the wit to divine, beneath the shadows and purple solemnity, death stalking through the forest. They had dreamed of beauty and tenderness, where he knew lurked only Omnipotent Bloodlust to be appeased. Our Lord Enemy Yaotzin, the Slayer who rides upon the Night Wind, they had called the Beautiful Youth, and the Soul of the World.

But he had advanced toward regarding things with eyes freed from illusion. All that vastness soon to darken above, and these wastes tree covered; earth and the waters and the caverns; day and night and the winds and stars—which of these things loved mankind, or which ceased for a moment to plot and threaten? Through which of them did not Universal Resentment glare and Detestation direct itself against man because of his sins? *Have mercy upon us! O Lord, have mercy!*

His thought traveled to the Quinames again—not to the ancient giants, but to their supposed descendants in the forest—and he reflected upon how curiously extremes might meet. Here were these savages, as deeply sunk in wilderness depravity as might be, and yet, in their outlook on the universe, very near to truth in some important respects. They knew the inner worlds to be hideous and hostile; there was no sentimental illusion-worship with them! And they carried their knowledge to its logical end in behavior, for they sought to mitigate their gods' animosity with gifts of human blood, as he had learned from the three chieftains who accompanied him. Wiser than we, wiser than we!

As usual, his camp-makers had gone on before and had made all ready for the party at the bend of the river, where, when his thoughts had run thus far and the daylight had gone, he arrived. His two-roomed tent, luxuriously severe within, befitted his dual dignity of king and priest: comfort that his arduous duties made necessary, with a cast of asceticism superimposed. There were rich, dark hangings, maroon and cinnabar and crimson; heavy carpet and low, cushioned divan throne, all in the same colors; a golden lamp hanging by a golden chain. Such was the outer room, in which they set forth his meal while he bathed and was arrayed within, arrayed in great splendor, for he kept full state of an evening on his journey. As he comes forth from his toilet, one may behold him: a tall, gaunt man, grim-faced; eyes black, fiery and impenetrable; high nose, thin lips and square jaw. It is a face full of power, alert and concentrated, but not particularly beautiful. His garb: a black, sleeveless gown, full length, sewn with jewels; tilmatlies of scarlet featherwork; peaked headdress draped to the ground behind. He comes out to a roomful of slaves and officers, the former prostrate, the latter kneeling. One of these, just entered, gestures for permission to speak.

"Yes?"

"A party just come up from the south is pitching its camp some score-score strides from us, southward."

From the south—huh! And none must come from the south but His Holiness must know their business. No, he would not dine yet. A large party? —Between a score and two-score, as the watch reports. —Humph. Let a meal be prepared for two-score men. And they were dismissed; but Secretary Mahetsi he would need, and his Godhead Tata, Commander of the Escort. From the south . . .

The two he had named remained; the rest retired. "Aye," said the hierarch, "it is an occasion. From the south, he said. Come then; we will pay them a call."

Simultaneously the two with him expressed their surprise.

"Pay them a call!" gasped thickset, methodical Priest-Secretary Mahetsi; and "By Yaotzin," exclaimed Tata, "Your Holiness would do less for the Toltec Topiltzin!"

"Yes, pay them a call, we three. Less for the Toltec Topiltzin, certainly; we must consider what is becoming. He does not come up from the south. Come! No! No torch! No torch!"

On the way, they were startled by a ripple of song from the camp they were approaching: a very marvelous child-voice; nor would the hierarch permit himself to be announced till the song was ended. Then Mahetsi was told to announce him, but in an unusual fashion; not as the hierarch of Teotihuacan, but thus: "Yen Ranho of the Anahuacs salutes you and inquires!"

The child who had been singing made answer at once: "Amaquitzin Quetzalcoatl salutes you and invites you!"

The hierarch's party was now free to come forward. Amaqui, his hand on Nauhyo's shoulder, advanced to meet them; the young men, gathering from their tent-pitching and from about the fire, followed.

At sight of them, Yen Ranho decided on his role. It was to be one of kindly and courteous geniality. The lord-priest from the south must be his guest at supper. And not only he, but all the gentlemen of his retinue. He too, the hierarch told them, was a priest: of Tezcatlipocâ. And when priest invites priest, god invites god, and it was irreligious to refuse.

Tata and Mahetsi, looking down, hid their amazement. Where was their taciturn hierarch, whose few words were wont to be commands? Who was this kindly, persuasive aristocrat who had taken his place? The end of it was that the Huitznahuatecs were led back to the Otomi camp and seated at supper in the hierarch's tent. But before that, while their feet were being washed elsewhere by slaves, Yen Ranho, without witnesses, conversed with the Quiname chiefs. In sign-language. There was nothing to overhear.

The hierarch—most cordial and engaging of hosts—hoped great results from his pulque at supper, but he was disappointed. It was perhaps the one possible product of their crops of which the Huitznahuatec agave-farmers knew nothing: a liquor that one must learn to like. The smell or first taste of it told all of Yen

Ranho's guests that it was not for them, and so their tongues and discretion were unaffected.

The hierarch wanted information. Amaqui, as genial and free of speech as himself, gave him much, but not of the kind he wanted. Nothing about his—Amaqui's—place of origin or why he was traveling north. He was an ambassador, apparently; he wore the title of Quetzalcoatl and was obviously the head of the Quetzalcoatl hierarchy of his country, but what country was that? And if an ambassador, to what king or republic was he accredited? There were no countries between here and the Anahuacs. . . .

But Amaqui, the simple and unsophisticated, yet somehow had his own way with the conversation; or at least, Yen Ranho might not have his. He talked, did Amaqui, of the Road, of the savages, of tradition, of poetry, of mythology: a charming and impersonal discourse. Nor could Yen Ranho be sure—and this distressed him—that his guest was not fencing with him.

As for the young men, they had an instinct for silence, and Nauhyo's shyness was invincible. Something within each of them was trying to make them aware that their hosts were not to be trusted, and was having huge difficulty on account of the newness of the task. In Huitznahuac, one met with nothing alien; trust was a factor basic to all human contacts, no more to be interrupted than the flow of blood in the veins. But here the unthinkable was happening; the Otomis brought disturbing concepts, impossible to be defined. So they kept silence; and Amaqui, effortlessly, enabled them to do so; and again, Yen Ranho could not tell whether he was doing that with conscious intent or not. Surely he must be; and yet—

When they left, the hierarch had learned nothing. Nothing that he wanted to know. It was perhaps unimportant.

They went escorted by his notables; he parted from them at his tent door, all cordiality and kindliest solicitude. Deep in his cogitations, he stood there for a while, watching them depart, watching the setting of the moon. Reentering the tent, he found the three Quinames squatting before his divan. Good! It was evidence of their powers. They were great men among their people, the most Quiname of the Quinames. Competition for a

living with the jaguar and the ocelot had made them miracu-
lously keen of senses and lithe of limb; they had given him many
such proofs of this since they joined him, and where they desired
to excel, he believed them unexcellable.

Their names were Ib, Guaish and Ghuggg; they were gross,
thick louts to look at, not greatly reminding one of the human;
and if one had to have them in his tent, it was extremely necessary to burn incense. A brazier with live coals stood before the
divan; he threw on a handful of copal and raised a sweet protec-
tive cloud of smoke between himself and their unwashedness as
he took his seat, then condescended to notice them. He made a
gesture translatable as an impatient, questioning "Well?"—as if
they had come not at his command and in his service, but beg-
ging inopportune favors.

Ib crawled forward and handed him, in a curious, unobtrusive
manner, a roll of pictoscript, which he received without a glance,
as if it were nothing, although he divined that it was the thing he
had sent them for. He could have spoken to them in their own
Quiname, but he preferred the sign-language, which none can
overhear. You can say in it all you can say with speech. Motions
of his hands said to them now: "I thought that you Quinames
were thieves; I thought that you had skill to search and find."

They had expected praise; having understood what he wanted,
they had brought it, but you never could satisfy the gods. A
quaint quiver went through them, expressive of deflated spirits.
After motionless minutes and covert glances of the other two at
Guaish, their best orator, that one began gesticulating elo-
quently, to the effect that the God the gods worshiped must
believe that his slaves had done their utmost. They had examined
the boxes of green pebbles, the bundles of clothing, the litters, the
tent walls. Unless they had brought what he sent for, surely there
was nothing.

And how many of the pebbles had they stolen?

There was a flurry of gesticulation, conveying denial of the
charge implied. What were small green stones to his adorers, who
could not eat them? Likewise, had he not forbidden honorable
theft? The pebbles lay unprofitably in their boxes; though to the
simplicity of his slaves, to leave them there seemed unthrifty.

Whereby he knew that they had taken toll of the chalchiuhites, as indeed was the case. But they had polluted the air long enough, and too long, with their cannibal uncleanliness; besides, the document they had stolen for him awaited his attention. So he dismissed them with the warning that their gem-stealing would not be forgiven them unless they were very faithful and obedient; and he admonished them that they must be prepared to come to him again when he should call.

Alone, he proceeded to study the stolen paper, making out its purport easily, like the scholar he was. Of course, an embassy; and here was the ambassador's name, "Amaquitzin Quetzalcoatl," written so ingeniously that he could have read it even had he not known it already. From the king and queen of—Huitznahuac. Ah! From the king and queen of Huitznahuac. And—to the Toltec Topiltzin. That could mean nothing else.

He had guessed the Huitznahuac part from the first, but this was news certainly. They were on their way to Culhuacan, not to Tollan; to Nonohualcatl, not to Huemac; though by Huemac, Yacanetzin was sent. Did they then know more of northern politics than we did of theirs? From their standpoint, Nonohualcatl was undoubtedly the better man to approach. But not from the standpoint of the gods and the hierarch of Teotihuacan.

That was why he had maneuvered with such wonderful and discreet persistence to bring about a reversal of the ordinary procedure, and the sending first of the ambassador not of Culhuacan, the leading city of the League, but of Tollan, the third and last. Huemac of Tollan was so much more religious than his brother, so much less under the most dangerous influence in the Anahuacs—that of their sister, the Princess Civacoatzin. But Amaquitzin was on his way to Culhuacan, to Nonohualcatl Topiltzin. . . .

Yen Ranho struck a gong and bade the slave who came to summon the secretary. When that one entered, he said without looking up, "The divining board, Mahetsi."

It was a low table, curiously marked on its face with squares, circles and triangles, and grooved for the movement of the pieces. These were of many shapes and kinds: pieces to represent the gods, the planets, the cities, and the divisions of time; the

kings and the agents of the gods; and the great Opposing Forces
that play for world sway and for the souls of men—Yaotzin, the
Dark, and the Bright, Tezcatlipocâ.

Mahetsi set the board before his master's divan, then seated
himself on the other side of it and watched while the hierarch set
certain pieces in their grooves. Then the two sat silent, their
fingers on the edges of the board, their eyes intent on the pieces.
Presently the board quivered, as if life had come into it; then the
pieces began to move.

"This is the past; read it and be silent," said Yen Ranho.

As he gazed at the moving pieces, Mahetsi then saw a vision.
He saw Yaotzin, the Dark Tezcatlipocâ, enthroned in the City of
the Gods, Teotihuacan. Yaotzin was enthroned through year-
sheaf after year-sheaf, raising up hierarch after hierarch, a long
succession, to represent and, to a degree, to embody him in the
world. Each hierarch handing on a secret to, and exacting a
pledge from, his successor. They point to a year-sheaf that is
coming, and to a Ce Acatl, year Reed One, in that year-sheaf,
and to the south of the world; aye, to the City of the South,
Huitznahuacan, that emerges as the year-sheaves pass.

The hierarchs fear that year Ce Acatl in conjunction with that
city; they are pledged—that is what their pledge is—to destroy
Huitznahuacan before the Teotleco month of that year Ce Acatl.
Hierarch after hierarch, year-sheaf after year-sheaf, the power of
the Dark Soul of the World has gone on increasing; but it is
threatened in this year-sheaf, they fear; it is threatened from
Huitznahuac. . . .

"Past becomes present," murmured Yen Ranho.

Yes, this present Year-sheaf of the Jaguar is the fateful year-
sheaf the dark gods fear. The years of it move across the board.
Rabbit One: Watch the cities of the Anahuacs; watch the piece
that represents the hierarch . . . recognizable now, wearing the
form and image of Yen Ranho, greatest of all the hierarchs.
What does he do in this year Rabbit One of the Year-sheaf of the
Jaguar? He has touched the foreheads of the kings and cities; he
has spoken the new word *Huitznahuac* in the north.

The north begins to be haunted by rumors of another world in
the south. *Reed Two:* Ambitious Brothers on the two thrones of

the League go conquering in the north, and their ambition is fanned by their conquests. But, O Ambitious Brothers, it is in the far south that the great conquests are to be made: in Huitznahuac. *Flint Three:* Huitznahuac, O Ambitious Brothers! They go conquering far and wide, but they have heard as in a dream of the south of the world.

House Four: Eastward they go conquering, but there is no satisfaction for them eastward. Huitznahuac, Huitznahuac, O Ambitious Brothers! *Rabbit Five, Reed Six, Flint Seven, House Eight, Rabbit Nine, Reed Ten, Flint Eleven:* And now the Anahuacs are dreaming of the City of the South; it becomes the fabulous home of men's desires. Eastward you have conquered, and westward, Ambitious Brothers enthroned! But the east and the west have grown worthless to you. *House Twelve:* Huitznahuac, Huitznahuac! Awake, kings of the north! What monarch has ever gone conquering southward, beyond the limits of the world? *Rabbit Thirteen;* and now the business is on foot; the Ambitious Brothers are bound for Huitznahuac; it is there they will go conquering.

What a flame of will in this greatest of the hierarchs that he has set the Anahuacs alight with the will to destroy what is so far from the Anahuacs, and what, but fourteen years ago, they had never heard of! Comes now this greatest of the hierarchs southward, but what meets him here in the middle of the board, which is where one reads the actual, the here and the now? A piece as powerful as he, glowing with as powerful a glow as is the hierarch-piece. It is easy to recognize: It is their guest of this evening, Amaquitzin Quetzalcoatl. . . .

"You are to read this."

Mahetsi looked up from the board, and all movement ceased there. He took the stolen document his master handed to him.

"Then he *is* from Huitznahuac. But—he goes to the Topiltzin at Culhuacan? Their ambassador. But it is to Huetzin he should have been sent."

"Read the future now," said the hierarch. "See, I take Yen Ranho from the board." He removed the piece that represented himself, that had glowed into his likeness just now. They placed their fingers as before on the board; in a few moments the thrill and the life began there again.

Amaquitzin moved swiftly into the north; the yellow light that shone from him paled the red glow of the northern kings. The red glow has faded from the king at Culhuacan at contact with him, passes from red to orange, and from orange it pales to yellow. The war glow has gone from the north. And look! Here are the kings riding south now, but not in war array; they ride south bearing gifts. *Rabbit Thirteen* still: month, Tlaxochimaco. They are riding through the forest. Month, Xocotlhuetzi—their heralds arrive at Huitznahuacan. Month, Ochpaniztli—Huitznahuac sets out to meet and welcome them. *Reed One* now, and the month of Teotleco—the month of the Arrival of the Gods. They are in Huitznahuacan now, guests of the king there . . . and who is this god that has arrived in the world? This god that arrives on the night of Teotleco, when the kings of the north are in Huitznahuacan? Not our Lord Yaotzin; not the Dark Tezcatlipocâ. For now, behold, the light from this god streams up into the north; and where are the hierarchs of Teotihuacan now? Where is our Lord Yaotzin himself, whom our hierarchs represent, if not incarnate? Gone down and vanished before this dangerous Teotleco from the south!

"No," said Yen Ranho. "That is not what shall be." He replaced on the board the piece that represented himself and set the Amaquitzin piece back where it had been. "Watch now and read."

The life came back to the board, and the thrill, and the pieces began moving again. They watched, more and more intently. Mahetsi turned cold and shuddered.

"My lord," he gasped, "he is an ambassador!"

"He is an ambassador."

"And—it is the Road!"

"It is the Road."

"My lord, my lord!"

"You are pledged to obedience."

"I am my lord's slave."

"And shall be my successor. Soon. He is an ambassador, and

it is the Road. And the gods punish crime and are relentless. But I shall have saved the gods. Bring the savages here."

In Mahetsi's absence, the hierarch busied himself. He fetched from the inner room hardwood daggers—and a little chalchiuhite statue of Camaxtli, which he breathed on, made passes over, laid his hands on, till it glowed ominously with a light of its own. This he set on the divining board, of which the pieces now were laid away. When Mahetsi ushered in the Quinames, the little figure had its due effect on them.

"He has come down from heaven to dwell in the God-house of your village," said the hierarch. "He is Camaxtli, the Invincible, the God of War, who brings his worshipers' foemen into their caldrons. Behold how great a thing I have done for you."

Their eyes glittered as they drew near, anxious to possess their god.

"When you shall have done what he demands of you."

"What shall we do?"

"Take these," said he, pointing to the daggers. "Go to the other camp. Wait till they sleep, and sacrifice them to him."

They grinned happily, took the daggers, and slipped away.

"You understood?" he asked Mahetsi.

The secretary, ghastly visaged, bowed his head. His training had gone far, but not so far that he could take this matter without shock; and he would gladly have been alone now, to accustom himself to the world he must henceforth inhabit. But he was to suffer another shock before he was dismissed.

"Listen, and write this on your memory," said the hierarch. "The Otomi ambassador must be killed by the Huitznahuatecs."

"My lord?"

"The Otomi ambassador must be killed by the Huitznahuatecs. And therefore they must have reason given for killing him. Your duty will be to provide it. You will betray me to the Huitznahuatecs. You will reveal to them that I ordered the massacre of their embassy on the Road. No word! You are pledged to obedience; see that you find a way to obey."

Again the miserable Mahetsi bowed his head.

"There must be no Huitznahuatecs left," the hierarch warned. "The League's punishment for the murder of one of its ambassadors is the extermination of the people who murdered him. The Pamxobs killed an ambassador of Tollan, and there are no Pamxobs now. What Mishcoatl Mazatzin did to the Pamxobs, his sons will do to the Huitznahuatecs. It is understood?"

"It is understood, my lord."

"Let it be remembered. You are dismissed."

For a while the hierarch sat alone, pondering over his plans. Yaotzin had been kind to throw these few Huitznahuatecs in his way. Otherwise, how could one have devised the extermination of all of the Huitznahuatecs? Well, one had built up the edifice of one's life, had brought the world nearer to truth, much nearer; and now, in one's death, one would be fulfilling the pledge, the Great Pledge that, of all mankind, had been exacted of, and taken by, only the hierarch reigning in this year Rabbit Thirteen of this Year-sheaf of the Jaguar. How fortunate, how blessed one was, to be able to pay with so small a price—

A motion disturbed his meditation; the Quinames were in the tent again. Their faces betrayed anxiety and disappointment.

"Ah? You have done your work? No. What has happened?"

"There is no camp. They have gone."

2
Ahuacatl Glade

Among the Huitznahuatecs, when their Otomi hosts had escorted them back to their camp and left them, it needed no
spoken word to make known the fact that one thought occupied
every mind: The place was not suitable for camping. They would
find a better site a league or so northward; and anyway, they
ought to be making more speed with their journeying. The young
men were by no means tired; why, no, the day had been an easy
one. What they needed was more exercise. Before moonset they
had packed and were well to the north of the Otomi camp and
could afford to light torches. When they did encamp an hour
later, they arranged watches for the night, for the first time.

In the morning, when sun and river had restored them spiritually and physically, the young men were at a loss to understand
their feelings of the night before. Once more the world was
natural, full of healing beauty and the presence of the Others;
they must have imagined that nightmarish something. The Otomis could not really have been like that; no human beings could
be evil . . . only, there was a change in Amaqui that became more
and more apparent. Pain had been stamped on his face in the
night.

They followed their college custom daily, singing their hymn
to the sunrise and then keeping silent for the first three daylight
hours. So as they swung up from the riverside into the hills, there
was no speech about last night's trouble, which trouble therefore,

by contrast, made the morning peace and beauty seem more laden with divinity than ever. It was indeed wonderful country they were passing through; full of fresh springs, the music of streams and bird-song, and rimmed around with the mauve and blue and snow of far mountains. But the inwardness of it was lovelier still. Their first contact with evil had made them more sensitive to the divine.

At mid-morning, when they were ready to halt for their meal, they came into a glade in the midst of ahuacatl trees. On the eastern side of it, about halfway to the top, a man was busy beside a fire. He rose at their approach, advanced to meet them, and invited them to breakfast. On a clean tilmatli spread on the ground, he had tortillas, newly baked, and a pile of the black-purple, egg-shaped fruit from the trees. Although they had often found food provided for them on the roadside, they had never before found the provider present to act as their host. Furthermore, to add to the strangeness of it, this gnarled and sidelong little man had nothing of the savage in him, but was well-dressed, friendly eyed, and spoke the Nahua speech, though strangely.

So soon they were seated, feasting on his fruit and bread, and chatting with him. His name, he said, was Coshcana; his birthplace far in the north, beyond the Anahuacs and the Toltec kingdoms. His master, the Hermit of Puma Rock, had sent him here this morning to prepare food for travelers, as indeed he often did. —Did he know any of the forest people? He knew their ways, which were savage and evil. They worshiped sorcerous, abominable gods, and feared them greatly. They shed blood, even human blood, in their gods' honor. There was no redeeming them, only holding them in check; and it was his master, the hermit, who did it. For, strangely enough, he was the god they feared most of all; none knew why. Because Puma Rock was over yonder—pointing to the northeast—none of the Quinames would so much as venture into the forest on this side of the Road from about three leagues south of here to as far north as the Hill of Derision, which their Godheads would come to this afternoon, beyond the loop of the Road. If when they came there, they would look out across the treetops to the southeast, they would see Puma Rock, where his master lived; and, by the by, they would have a village of the savages within a couple of miles of them on the other side. But they might meet a whole tribe of these people on the Road and there would be nothing to fear from them.

Why? —Well, none knew really. But it had always been so. Very likely because the tribes were afraid of his master, considering that he was the God of the Road, who kept it sacred and had ordained that none should be harmed on it. There had always, they must understand, been a hermit on Puma Rock whom the tribes, he thought, believed to have been the same person from the beginning; but he, Coshcana, had been the servant of three of them before his Godhead Quauhtzin came up from the south—

"Quauhtzin!" cried Nauhyo, greatly excited. "Oh, where did he come from, and when did he come?"

"He came but two months ago, little Godhead, and from a place called—"

"Eagle Hermitage?" cried Nauhyo.

"Aye, he did; and from the mountain that you will know of if your little Godhead is the Nauhyotontzin of whom he speaks. For I noted from the first, your Godheads, that you are all of the same manner of speech as my master, Quauhtzin."

"Yes, I am," said Nauhyo, and he began a flood of questions, while new thought was stirred in Amaqui's mind by Coshcana's words: "from the mountain that you will know of . . ." And then there was this wonder-child; and Quauhtli, King Nopal's friend; aye, and King Nopal himself, who had brought Nauhyo to the Calmecac. . . . "The mountain you will know of" must be Teotepetl, the Mountain that was God.

Back Amaqui's mind went to his early youth, and to a visit paid then to Rainflower Manor in the days of old Nopaltzin Tecuhtli, the king's grandfather, who had taken him up into a mountain which, since he went there from Rainflower, must have been Teotepetl. The results of that visit had shone through all of his life, but never so insistently as now. There was much that he had forgotten, but not that he had walked beside a lake with an August Being, who had given him that which had ennobled all his days. Not till now had he realized that it was on Teotepetl.

From that day till this, he had never spoken of it, and did not know why he had always thought of the One who had talked with him as the Master. The sacredness of the experience had forbidden speculation about it.

But now Coshcana's phrase brought it all back to him, and more vividly than ever. Especially he remembered something he had long since forgotten about: the Master's parting from him, and his words in answer to a question Amaqui had thought but not spoken. He could hear them now: "No, my child, you will not come here again; but I shall watch over your life, and I shall be with you on the last day of it." Whenever that last day might come, the Master seemed to be with him now. That same divine quickening that he had felt by the lakeside on Teotepetl so long ago was suddenly in the air: an overwhelming sense of a Benign Presence, infusing into forest and sky the secret Fire Divinity. Involuntarily he turned his head to see if—

But it was not the Master he saw. Instead, it was three savages who came running from the south. Coshcana with signs offered them food; they made no reply, nor slackened their speed, but grinned rather inauspiciously. Tribesmen thus traveling were no uncommon sight; there was no reason why the Huitznahuatecs should feel uneasiness.

3

The God of Puma Rock

Just beyond the Glade of the Ahuacatls, the Road makes a great loop, swerving to the west a long way, north a long way, then east and to the south, till at the Hill of Derision, due north from the glade, it takes and keeps its proper northward course again. But let none think to save time by cutting through the woods from glade to hill: a way shorter by leagues than the other, but severely to be eschewed. If there was a path, it was known only to Coshcana and his master. Very few would have considered it a path at all; certainly no litters could have traveled it.

The rock on which those two lived took its name from its appearance as seen from the top of the Hill of Derision, from whence it resembled the form of a puma, lying head to the southeast on an enormous pedestal of rock, part tree-covered and part bare, that rose some four score-score forearms above the forest tops. As Coshcana had told the Huitznahuatecs, it had been for ages the seat of a line of hermits, thought by the tribes to be an ever living god.

This was the heart of Quiname-dom, potentially the most dangerous country the Road traversed. A few weeks farther north or south, one came into milder, or lonelier, territories; but here, whatever thought stirred the inner atmosphere was bloodthirsty and treacherous. Perhaps for this very reason the hermits had been stationed on Puma Rock, with their sacred domain stretching far around them. Under the puma's chin was the cave they had lived in; thence, the tribes felt themselves watched by a power beyond their understanding, an omniscience which to disobey would be too dangerous to be thinkable. Their fathers had heard It singing since before the Apotheosis of the Sun. You peered out anxiously before you ventured from the thicket onto the Road, lest you should see its face and—

Strange acoustics in the sacrosanct region accounted in part for this terror. There were places between the loop and the rock where a word spoken on certain reaches of the Road would be heard perfectly though the speaker were miles away; from some such spots you could make the Road hear, from others you could not. On the Road, you might step out of silence into a snatch of song that seemed to come from near at hand, and at another step or two, you would pass into the forest's common daytime silence again.

In all stages of society there are things within the *knowledge*— not the belief—of everyone; and there are other things to disbe- lieve, which might prove a man eccentric, or even mad; but you might find men disbelieving in them even so. The more thought- ful of the Quinames believed that the sun would rise tomorrow morning; so far as they knew, it always did. But if a prophet had arisen to deny it, he would have obtained some hearing probably, since it was not a matter on which one could afford to be dog- matic. But if chief or prophet, fool or hero, had denied what we knew would happen to the Quiname who trespassed within the domain of Puma Rock, his career would have ended then and— insult of insults!—his corpse been regarded as too poisonous to be disposed of in the natural way.

None ever had denied it, of course; the knowledge was too certain. One step into the forest on that side and out would leap on you a demon like a jaguar, as vast as the mountains, with eyes of penetrating green fire and claws of red-hot obsidian; and thenceforth and forever, you would be diet for him—conscious, inexhaustibly tortured, as endlessly renewed as consumed. It was not clear whether this monster was the god himself or merely his servant and instrument; ordinarily, it was thought, the god wore human, though dread-inspiring, form. And if he could suffuse the forest with his voice, so of course he could with his vision, and he would leave no misdeed undiscovered or unpunished. What were misdeeds? Foremost of all, to invade his domain; after that, almost anything if you did it on the Road. Theft and murder, for example: things praiseworthy enough if done elsewhere.

Though were one of the gods to tell you to do those things on the Road, he would be speaking for all the gods, would he not? And for the God on Puma Rock as well . . . ?

Quauhtli, carrying out the Master's orders, had started for Puma Rock on the day of the Master's death. He was to leave Nopal and travel north. At such and such a point on the Road he could expect to meet such and such a man and to go where that one led him and there abide. The point of meeting was the Hill of Derision and the man Coshcana who, having made obeisance, led Quauhtli to the cave on Puma Rock. Overlooked from that height, the forest was wonderful: the treetops interflitted with winged jewelry, oversprinkled with huge blooms; and Quauhtli was happy there, waiting what should befall. There were patches of land below that he and Coshcana cultivated; while he worked on them, he sang and thus maintained the sacredness of the Road.

Although his own teacher had passed into the unseen, there were others of the same order, and he owed them the same obedience he had given Huehuetzin. In due time, the one who would be his new teacher would come to him, or send for him; the commands of that one might come from without or from within himself, and he lived to obey them when they should arrive.

Quite often he sent Coshcana to Ahuacatl Glade to prepare food for possible travelers and to watch the world for him. For aught he knew, Nopal might, under orders, be passing sometime; or some other might. Knowing the effect sight of him had on the savages, he avoided the Road. The day Coshcana entertained the Huitznahuatecs, the feeling had come on him, not to be dislodged, that some momentous thing impended, some grave danger to someone. He grew more and more anxious, waiting for his servant's return.

* * *

Seeing how eager Nauhyo was to see Quauhtli, Amaqui might
have sent him with Coshcana to Puma Rock and waited for him
in the afternoon on the Hill of Derision, except that Coshcana
had described the way as too difficult for a child. In any case, he
said, his master would meet them on the hill; Coshcana would
make haste back and tell him of Nauhyo's impending visit, and
Quauhtzin would be there before them. So with that, Nauhyo
had to be content; it did not greatly lessen his delight. The
Huitznahuatecs resumed their journey, and Coshcana slipped
into the woods.

Nauhyo could never have gone with him. It was a matter, for
almost an hour, of letting himself down cliffs, crawling by rabbit-
runs through the thicket, wading up streams, climbing granite
ridges. He started out in no mood for loitering, but his desire to
make speed increased as he went. A certain anxiety overtook
him, so that he fell to arguing with himself. "There is plenty of
time," he argued, "for me to get home and report to Quauhtzin,
and for Quauhtzin to reach the Hill of Derision." *Himself,* however, was not so to be silenced, but kept suggesting that there
might be more in it than he knew . . . more, and worse.

Perhaps he owed his mishap to this tension of the mind. It
happened while he was climbing the Ridge of Tlaloc's Well, quite
near the top. The rock there was steep and slippery, and he had
to haul himself up by a loop of outhanging pine root. As he did
so, his right foot slipped back along a sharp edge and took a cut
as deep as his thumbnail and as long as his middle finger:
a painful, laming, hindering wound. He held still for a moment
to collect himself and could hear the comfortable converse of
waters above. In Tlaloc's well, there was healing for most
things. . . .

He managed to get to it, affirmed friendly brotherhood with
the presiding Tlaloc, and bathed the wound. The water chilled
out the pain, or most of it, and stopped the blood flow. He found
the right leaves to apply and bound up the foot against bruising
contacts in his tilmatli. It was near noon already and he had lost
time; things being as they were, it would be an hour yet before
he could reach Puma Rock. Once at the foot of the ridge, the

going would be easier. He got there at last, only once hurting the foot severely . . . and did not afford himself time to consider the pain.

Then on by deer tracks and across a stream where humming-birds glittered, where he soaked his bandaged foot again, reliev-ing it, not before it was time. As he pressed on, aware of pain and blood loss as little as might be, anxiety grew on him and tinged his consciousness—driven from the normal by his wound—with nightmare colorings, till it seemed to him that his delay had been altogether culpable and was to cause enormous disaster and ruin.

So, not in possession of himself, he arrived at last at the foot of Puma Rock and took thought to give a cry that would apprise his master of his presence. He had lost much blood and was losing much now. By the time Quauhtli reached him, he had fainted.

The stairway up to the cave was long and steep, but Quauhtli was not the strongest of the Huitznahuatecs for nothing. Still, it took time to get Coshcana up there. And while he was reviving him with the right distillations, rhythms and rubbings, and dress-ing the wound—which took time again—he had to keep his mind free from the anxiety that would have made his doctoring useless. And that took strong exercise of the will.

It was mid-afternoon before he heard Coshcana's news. Huitz-nahuatecs were on the Road, under Amaquitzin; Nauhyo was of the company; Amaqui and Nauhyo would wait for him at the Hill of Derision. That was all; there was nothing to be so anxious about. He knew that even now he could reach the hill almost as soon as they would, if it was safe to leave Coshcana. He did not quite like to do that, but—

Coshcana, as anxious for Quauhtli to go as Quauhtli himself was, feigned sleep to enhance his arguments . . . and Quauhtli went.

4

Forest Voices

Quauhtli made all speed down the stairway and through the forest. A restless apprehension drove him, although heaven knew there could be nothing to fear. On the Road, everyone was safe, as safe as in Huitznahuacan. It might be that Nauhyo was bringing him some message from Nopal, perhaps some last direction of the Master's. He tried to think so and that an instinct or an intuition of its importance accounted for his mental strain . . . and failed.

He was to pass through two of those places where the weird acoustics of the forest made voices on the far-off Road audible. From the first place, he knew, one could also make oneself heard on the Road, but not from the other place. The first was a long, lanelike glade, a few strides across, that had an air, because of its windings, of being endless, or of leading into kingdoms of mystery: a place so still that one would think the work of creation was not proceeding there, or that a god was asleep nearby and infecting all nature with the deep quiescence of his being.

Often enough, Quauhtli or Coshcana, stepping out from the forest dusk into its daylight, had heard suddenly, from the distant Road but as if quite close at hand, the clucking, hawking sibilance of Quiname speech, or even, in the case of Coshcana, the mellow Chiapanec of the Saltmen. The Master had taught Quauhtli the language of the Quinames, and Quauhtli had caught, at one time and another, many fragments of speech that had never been meant for him.

As he broke into this glade now, the air that had been still and somnolent suddenly became alive with music. There was but one flautist who could draw that sweetness from his instrument: Amaquitzin; and but one singer who could so put the mellow-throated zacuan to shame. . . . So that was where they were on the Road. They would reach the hill before him, but they would not have long to wait. He would not call to them lest he break into the song.

In due course, he came to the second place where he might expect to hear them, and he did. The song burst on him suddenly, as if the singer were there under the cliff, not ten paces away. The flute was silent now, and it was another song being sung: one that startled him to hear. It was what, in the Serpent's Hole, they called *The Death-Song;* the Master had taught it to them. He could picture the scene on the Road: Amaqui and Nauhyo would be litter-borne, and Nauhyo would be making the young men forget that they were bearing burdens. He would be, as Quauhtli had so often seen him, oblivious of every created thing but the star, the god, the topmost blossom of eternal beauty toward which he was singing, drawing up every atom of his hearers' being, body and mind, toward that height. The sound followed Quauhtli down the gorge as he ran, the last line coming very clear and tender.

"The gates of deathless beauty open."

Then a moment's silence; then the young men's voices applauding; then Amaquitzin's: "Child, I know who taught you that!"

A questioning, rather awed "Yes?" came from Nauhyo.

Then Amaquitzin's voice came again: "Yes, and he is with us now. Do you not know that the Holy One is with us now? *The gates of death—*"

A scream rang out, followed by a confusion of voices, Quiname shouts and groans. In the Quiname tongue, Quauhtli shouted . . . and realized that although he could hear, he would not be heard. He dashed on, his heart straining furiously. . . .

5

The Ib Quinames

Ib, Guaish, and Ghuggg, mighty chieftains among the Ib Quinames, and sometimes that people's representatives in the train
of the hierarch of Teotihuacan, being wholly unencumbered with
baggage—but for a little green jade god, Camaxtli by name, who
was to do great things for them—were able to make much better
speed than the litter-laden Huitznahuatecs; and so they reached
the woods west of the Hill of Derision, and therein the hidden
village of their tribe, by noon. There a little gentle drumming
brought to the council house all who had right of entry and to
whom eloquent Guaish explained what great things were to be.

There were as many tribes as trees in the forest, said he, but
only to the Quinames, because of their well-known piety, had the
gods granted this great good fortune: this chalchiuhite Camaxtli,
and instructions on how to earn his protection. There were travelers on the Road: a strange people from the south, unlike other
humans, whom the gods desired destroyed. To the Ib Quinames
alone in the world, the gods had given the right, and on them
imposed the duty, of killing men on the Road. Judge, then,
whether ever again Quiname cooking pots would gape in vain for
the most delicate kind of meat! Judge!—since every traveler on
the Road must pass by the Hill of Derision, where henceforth the
Ib Quinames, lying in wait, should be blessed in replenishing
their larders.

And now these first fruits came; by mid-afternoon they would reach the hill. Moreover, they were unarmed, and were helpless and foolish. Let the warriors arm themselves and the fires be lit under the caldrons. Those whom the gods desired slain were innumerable; and yet not so innumerable as the Quinames. . . .

This was revolutionary; nor did wisdom fail to find a voice there. It was that of the mother of the three chiefs: ancient, exceptionally hideous, and by nature suspicious of gods and men. She wished to know who had told her sons that men might be killed on the Road.

"The Great Priest of the Gods' Town, who is a god and speaks for all the gods." Ghuggg took up the tale, recounting the miracles he had seen done in the hierarch's name. Guaish and Ib remembered them differently but supposed that it was other miracles they remembered; they related them in their turn as their wonder-besotted imaginations presented them to their memories. The case put forward by the three was convincing, but the hag was stubborn. The hierarch might be a god, she said, and if he had performed these wonders, he must be. But the gods were spiteful creatures, ill things to have truck with; he might have issued his orders merely to get the Ib Quinames under the claws of the Demon Jaguar. And the Road was older than the gods; and the God on Puma Rock was the Road. They had heard and seen him; they knew his power.

She might have carried the day with those savages squatting in the dark, but at that point Camaxtli silenced her with a miracle.

"Look!" cried Ib, "The god himself proclaims his power!" He pointed to the shelf where Camaxtli had been placed, surrounded with the dried heads of ancient enemies of the tribe; and all saw an aura of red light glow from the image.

"Shall we obey him, or shall we not? Shall we feast upon our enemies, or shall we be destroyed?"

"We will obey! We will feast!" cried the Ib Quinames.

Prostrating themselves, they howled a hymn to great Camaxtli thus glowing with anger, while the mother of the chiefs raged inwardly but said no more, knowing her sons in the mood for human sacrifice, and not desiring to be the victim herself. So she added her voice very audibly to the howling of the hymn to this new god, the Lord of War, who was to be their tribal patron henceforth, and who would come stalking forth from the council house into mid-village, visibly huge and grim and irresistible, to lead his people to victory whenever he desired blood to flow. In the wonder of his manifestation, they might forget other gods and attend to this one business he had in hand for them . . . and so they did.

And then, when it was all but done, and the rhythm of blood lust and the pulse of murder beat strong in the heart and brain of each of them—suddenly came catastrophe. Suddenly appeared among them, on the Hill of Derision, that Known God they had determined to forget; and he came in evident anger, and he was the most real of the gods, and the Master of the Demon Jaguar.

There might be others invisible, but he and his wroth were most visible, most potent; and the stone image they had brought with them to their triumph was nothing at all: helpless inanimation in their hands now in the moment of their disaster . . . and what was there to do but to lie down in misery and die?

6

On the Hill of Derision

An arrow a man, all of the Huitznahuatecs were fallen when Quauhtli appeared—except for Nauhyo. Him he saw stand in the midst, pale and bleeding at the shoulder, but utterly calm. Then the savages, dancing and yelling their triumph, rushed into the circle of their victims. One of them, knife uplifted, made for Nauhyo, seizing him. And Quauhtli was in time to hurl that man away, to scatter a few of the brutes on the ground, to make his presence known, and to pick up the fainting child, all before a thought could enter his mind. The Quinames lay prone among the dead Huitznahuatecs, hiding from their eyes the dreadful vision of Recognized Deity. . . .

First he must bandage Nauhyo's shoulder and stop the blood flow. Then— His silence worked upon the savages; expecting the blow to fall, their souls curdled with terror. At the right moment, he spoke: "What moved you, unhappy ones, to this damnation?"

"Mercy, O Lord God!" they moaned. "Have mercy on us!"

Yes, they thought him a god; and there was that about the Mountain-huge Demon Jaguar. It should serve him in his need.

"Mercy is for the merciful, not for ye." There was loud wailing.

Then he took a grave risk. "Am I more a god than these whose bodies ye slew?"

It was an unpolitic, thoughtless thing to say, but he could have said nothing better. Gods bodiless through their misdoing would be much more potent against them than gods or men or demons embodied could be.

He selected the savage nearest him, who happened to be Guaish, the Eloquent, and forced from him the tale. Prompting from without must have set them on, he divined, and the tale Guaish told seemed true. The Great Priest-god from the Gods' City in the north: That would bear thinking out presently. But first he must get Nauhyo safely home and tended, and leave the dead under protection. . . .

He must keep the savages where they were; willy-nilly, they must be the protectors. And he would need them here in the morning, when, somehow, he must reconsecrate the Road. Personal horror or grief had no chance to win him over; the duties imposed were too great. Guaish's tale came to an end.

"Punishment follows on crime. I cannot alter that which you have done. If ye escape from the Mountain-huge Jaguar—"

Oh, how might they escape, how might they escape? Then one of them howled, "He came not upon the Road, nor across the Road, but now he may come where he will."

"Aye," said Quauhtli, "because ye have broken the Law of the Road, the Law of the Road is broken." A plan came into his mind that he thought he might trust in. "There before ye lie the great gods whose bodies they permitted ye to slay that ye might be undone; unless ye are destroyed, they will hate me. Therefore they, and not I, shall command the Mountain-huge Jaguar tonight. Cry aloud to them for mercy. It may be that while ye cry, they shall withhold him."

They obeyed, putting passion into their wailing. "Cry aloud!" he urged them. "If one of ye stirs during the night, or forgets to cry to those gods, he shall feel the obsidian claws!"

He was lying, and he had never lied before. He left them howling for forgiveness, their faces pressed to the earth. It would still be daylight when he came to the cave. At the place from which he had heard the beginning of the massacre, he heard, as he passed, their cries for mercy, and he hoped for the best. The night must be spent in tending Nauhyo and devising a plan; if they could but be relied on to remain there, fear-enchained, till morning, something might be done. They must be driven from these parts entirely; and whither? The answer came to him: into the forest south of Huitznahuac, where no man comes. No memory of their crime must remain here, to be the seed of like crime in the future. Into the forests far to the south of Quinatepetl and Eagle Mountain they must go. . . . And he had Coshcana incapacitated, and Nauhyo maybe dying on his hands, and was quite without aid. . . .

Not quite, however, as he found when he came into that narrow glade from which he had first heard the Huitznahuatecs on the Road. Instantly he was among voices once more, and voices, surely, that he knew. Where had he heard those tones? Why, in the Huitznahuacan marketplace long since, and the language was Chiapanec, that of the Saltmen; and the ones talking were those three best fellows in the world: Philosophers Hax, Been, and Quicab, surely! He stood still to listen and soon became quite certain of it, although he had hardly seen the men since his college days. He broke in upon them.

"Ah, your Chiapanec Godheads!"

A pause, and then a startled, "Huitznahuatec!"

"Yes, I am Huitznahuatec. And you are the Philosophers Been and Quicab and Hax?"

"We are those three, O Huitznahuatec ghost in the air." There was, however concealed, a good deal of fear in the voice that answered him.

"No ghost, but an old friend who sorely needs your help. Where are your men?"

"The camp is some thirty strides behind us, southward."

"Then they will not hear me, and that is well," Quauhtli said.

And so he told them of what had happened and of how he must, at all costs, take Nauhyo home now and yet keep the savages where they were till morning; of how they considered him a god and the Master of the Demon Jaguar; and of what he had told them so as to keep them there.

"A god your Godhead must be, to have a voice and no body," said Quicab. "Where are you?"

"A goodly distance from you, in the forest. But I will come to you at dawn and explain. Meanwhile, can you help me tonight? You can do what you will with your voices, I know."

"This is our business as much as your Godhead's," said the voice of Hax. "Aye, more. You can trust us."

That night, on the Hill of Derision, the Chiapanecs divided the time into three watches, relieving each other, and played their part. The miserable Quinames heard the darkness around them full of voices: the squalling now and then of the Mountain-huge Jaguar, far more terrible than that of the natural beast; voices of angry gods wandering around them, terrible, horror-stricken, vengeful. Then the jaguar squall, eerie and jaguarish, took on human, or rather, Quiname language and implored leave to get to work on the criminals. The voices hushed and curbed it, whispering, "Not yet! Not just yet!" The wild men took no thought to escape; there was nowhere to escape to but into the jaws of the Demon Jaguar. Undoubtedly, they were being punished for their crime.

Meanwhile, in the cave, Quauhtli was tending Nauhyo, largely under Coshcana's direction, for he had much medical knowledge. He said that Nauhyo would live, he thought; but it might be a long illness. The wound was no great matter, since by the mercy of the God-world, the savages had not poisoned their arrows—not that arrow, at any rate. It was the shock, which must have been terrible, that was to be feared.

At dawn, Quauhtli was at the Chiapanec camp, where Hax and Been had risen and were awaiting him, Quicab being on duty at the hill. They breakfasted together. They agreed with him that the Quinames could never have thought of this for themselves. Such savages, said Hax, had no power to originate things but did only what their fathers had done before them. And the like of this had never been done before; for killing begot killing. Once done, it would always be done.

"Whereby the Road will no longer be safe for ourselves unless your Godhead can manage to reconsecrate it."

"Who, then, could have set them on?"

"One with a stronger malevolent will than is to be found here in the forest normally," said Philosopher Been.

"They said that it was the Great Priest of a City of the Gods in the north, who is traveling southward along the Road," said

Quauhtli. "I have heard that there is a city called Teotihuacan in the Anahuacs."

They snorted grimly. "There is, and the savages were telling you the truth, or it will surprise me." This from Hax. "He would go any length in the world, that man."

"He has gone a pretty long length this time," quoth Been. "Curse him!"

They went on to sketch the situation in the north. Much of it Quauhtli had heard from Nopal, but he was glad to have it made clear by a fresh telling, and much was new to him.

"And if it is not Yen Ranho himself who is at the bottom of this push to conquer Huitznahuac, may the savages season my carcass with my own salt, and may it poison them! A man from Tollan was at Huitznahuacan when we were there last; an embassy from Teotihuacan–Otompan would follow him in a month. As matter of fact, we slipped by that embassy's camp before dawn yesterday, and hurried, I can tell you. I say that Yen Ranho is his own ambassador and that the savages told you the truth."

They agreed that an account of it must be sent to Huitznahuacan and offered to provide a messenger. But Quauhtli explained his plan for making the Quinames themselves take the message, and for removing them from these woods entirely that none might remain who knew of the crime. After discussion, they brought him writing materials, and together they concocted a pictograph that there could be no misreading. Then Hax gave orders to his men that the camp should be struck and that the men should follow them almost to the Hill of Derision—keeping out of sight of the hill, however—and there hide in the woods east of the Road.

The morning was still gray, the trees dropping their mist-drops, when Quauhtli and the two Saltmen approached the Quinames and Quicab. Quauhtli picked his way into the midst of the savages where they lay still howling for mercy. The Chiapanecs took their places on the rim of the circle and redoubled their play of jaguar squalls and menacing voices, and the Quinames redoubled their howls.

"Silence!" roared Quauhtli, and he was obeyed on the instant.

"Now," said he, "the gods ye slew are to pronounce judgment on ye. Listen and tremble!"

The Chiapanecs began their eerie ghost-talk—gibberish, with a significant word or two of Quiname thrown in—and Quauhtli interpreted it. First, the savages were to summon to them all who might be left in the village. He did not know whether they would be able to obey, but thought it worth trying, as he was loath to trust any of them to go to the village. His command was followed by silence, whereupon he signed to the Chiapanecs, and the dreadful ghost-voices began again. Then one of the savages lashed out and caught up the signal-drum and began beating out a rhythm on it, his face all the while nuzzled down into the ground.

Who was to know what he was signaling? He might be telling the womenfolk to escape far into the forest. But no such noble thought was likely to enter an Ib Quiname's mind; being in trouble, he desired that his kin and compeers should share it. In a little while, the edge of the wood on that side was peopled with the rest of the tribe, who, when they saw the God from Puma Rock, fell prone too. Then sentence was pronounced on all of them.

The three chiefs were to take the young men of the tribe and make speed along the Road into the south of the world until they should come to the real City of the Gods, whence were the gods they had slain; and they were to take with them the litters and effects of those gods and, above all, this talisman, which alone could protect them from the Mountain-huge Jaguar, who would be in pursuit.

Here Ib was bidden to stretch forth his hand to receive the talisman, and in it was placed the pictoscript Quauhtli had written. This, and the litters, they were to give to the king of the city and then do as he would tell them to do, go where he bade them to go.

And they must pass on the way the company of that false tzitzimitl from the north who had led them into evil; they must watch and pass his camp by night and not be discovered. And the gods they had slain would be with them to protect them if they did not err or stray from their commandments. And the rest of the tribe was to follow and make what speed it could. The Mountain-huge Jaguar would not harm them as long as they were on the Road, their faces turned southward, and they tarried only by night. But the chieftains and the young men must make speed if they desired to escape him.

"And now, let your Salt-dealing Godheads hide in the woods." The Chiapanecs took cover.

"I myself will now vanish from among ye, but think not that I shall not be watching." He picked his way through them and took his stand with the Saltmen. "And now, O Ib and Guaish and Ghuggg, you and your young men and swift runners, and the litters with ye, and the talisman—to your feet, and escape if ye can from the Mountain-huge Jaguar, there is no safety for ye until ye come into the City of the Gods."

In an instant they were on foot and making as good speed south as ever humans might, and the rest were following them before long. Then the Saltmen set their porters to cutting wood for the funeral pyres.

7

The Ib Quinames' Pilgrimage

All day long, Ib and his party made speed southward. They had eaten nothing since they left the village the afternoon before; yet not one of them thought of food until, toward sundown, at one of the ancient rest-places, a man hailed them to come and feast with him.

They halted in terror at his call and, having halted, found themselves unable to keep their feet, much less go forward, so famished were they. So there they gorged their fill anxiously, then plunged on again. Sometime in the night they fell and slept where they fell, but not for long. The sun had hardly conquered the gray of dawn before they shivered and awoke, and rose, and quarreled, and went on. They heard the slain gods gibber around them and the squall of the Demon Jaguar behind, and they were least unhappy when they were traveling fastest.

After a few days, however, they were checked, and might travel fast no more. They came in sight of the Otomi party and could not pass them. Day and night, the edges of the woods were filled with cannibals armed and hungry, and the Ib Quinames were unarmed. To slip past along the open Road by daylight was impossible; even to be seen by the people of the tzitzimitl priest would be unthinkable sin. A tzitzimitl, and a particularly noxious one, they counted the hierarch now; but, if anything, a tzitzimitl was more dangerous than a god. And by night, the Otomi camp was surrounded by a blaze of watch fires, a host of sentinels. They could but loiter along, expecting the red-hot obsidian claws.

A little before noon one day, the Quinames lost sight of the Otomis, and before they saw them again, they had come to the end of the world. They reached the top of a hill, and suddenly, in front of them, there were no more trees but a great level plain, without rocks, bushes or rills, surrounded by mountains afar. If the known forest world was terrible, how much more terrible was unknowable this!

They must bide where they were till nightfall; to go out into that awfulness by daylight would be to be seen. And when night came, they must bide where they were till daylight, for where all the world was Road, who could find his way? Looking forth at sunrise, they saw that the plain was clear, that the Otomis had vanished. The Quinames had crossed it by noon and entered the Canyon at the End of Things.

There, the next day, they had soon to go warily again, not being far, by this time, behind the hierarch's party. Far beneath them, on the left, the river roared and foamed among its boulders, threatening them hideously; and the mountains on either side threatened them also, from whence the Jaguar peered down at them. In front, not more than half a mile away, their archenemy, oblivious of their presence, swung leisurely along in his litter. From this and that vantage point during the day, they watched and cursed him, their hatred of him grown to madness.

At mid-afternoon they reached the forking of the canyon, where the Road left the river and ran up through a narrow passage to the right that wound ever deeper into the mountain's heart. They had to go more warily than ever. There were no vantage points now, no watching the Otomis from afar; they must send scouts crawling forward to see that they did not blunder around some winding of the passage and into their enemies' rear. Their chance came that night.

Ghuggg, the scout, came creeping back to say that the Otomis had camped for the night, and he brought other news with him that made them, for the first time since their disaster, remember that they were the famous Ib Quinames, with great gifts of their own. Ghuggg had crawled along a ledge on the canyon wall and seen all that was toward. In the forest, the hierarch, knowing that the Law of the Road had been broken, and so might be broken again, had kept his camp well guarded by night; but here in the canyon, where there was no humanity, the need for such care had passed. There were but two watch fires, one at either end of the camp, and a single sentinel at each. They might, after midnight, pass right through. The tents were set alternately against the right wall and the left; the Devil-priest's tent was midmost; a passage wound between wide enough to get the litters through—with skill.

And they trusted that they were the famous Ib Quinames and possessed that skill, enough and to spare.

The first question was what to do about the sentinel, who stood by the fire not twenty strides away but around a bend that kept him unseen. The obvious thing would have been to creep up and kill him quietly, a matter manageable enough. But it had been burned into their consciousness that on the Road one must not kill. They must somehow lure him from his firelight and not kill him, but put him beyond the power to cry out.

They held their council in whispers, squatting in a bunch below the bend of the canyon, where they could see the red flicker of the fire on the rock in front and above. All day long the Road had been climbing; here the ascent was steep. Had the Quinames guessed how sound travels in the canyon, they would not have forgathered so near to the Otomi sentinel, and luck would not have come to them in the fashion it did.

Huhú, the Otomi sentinel, watching by the fire at the rear of the camp, could not make out what had taken the night to make it, just down below there, so full of quaint elemental noises: soft, strange sounds as if the patter of raindrops or the rustle of leaves had half-acquired articulation, or been infected with a desire to be speech—like human, and yet that could not possibly be human. Purr, hiss, ripple—a little less audible than the canyon silence itself—floated on that silence, half submerged. He must be imagining it; it was too subtle even to be some lost wind in these secret depths—some tiny wind questioning the vegetation in the darkness—or the converse of hidden waters. He would not think of it, but instead, of a cabin thatched with palm leaves far away on the road between Teotihuacan and Otompan. How many months now since he was there? Hush! there it was again— that curious elemental language! Just down there, beyond the bend. Were one to make the ten steps between this and that to lay the matter to rest, one would have peace to think about one's wife and home.

The Quinames heard his footsteps approaching and made ready. He looked down into the shadows, but with eyes his firelight had spoiled for the seeing required, whereas the ones waiting for him had little to learn in the matter of night vision in a shut-in place like this; it was only daylight on the open plain that could confuse them. Huhú took one step forward and before his foot was on the ground, found himself seized, gagged, bound, and helpless. Then he was tied facedown on a litter and all manner of things were piled on top of him—in reality, the Huitz-nahuatecs' baggage—and he was on the move toward the camp he ought to have been guarding.

While Huhú was being dealt with thus at one end of the camp, four shadows stole through and dealt with the sentinel at the other end. They served him as they had served Huhú and deposited him in the darkness beyond, then returned to report a safely sleeping camp.

Genius in action is, after its fashion, absolute. It is at one with the universe and utterly beyond the reach of human weakness; even though, in unillumined times, its possessor may be the most timorous of men. Only the day before, the Quinames, fleeing from the wrath of heaven, had been but squalid poltroons, half mad with fear. Now, when they saw work for their hands to do, and that the most congenial imaginable, giving their most prized and cultivated instincts fullest play—it was another thing alto-gether. The Mountain-huge Jaguar was forgotten, nonexistent; they trusted that they were the famous Ib Quinames again, of whose prowess so much boasting had been done. Ghuggg, one of the four who had secured the second sentinel, came back to his companions with a chain of chalchiuhites they had seen the Devil-priest wearing when they were in his train of old. Now Ghuggg wore it proudly; he had been in Yen Ranho's tent, in the inner room, and had seen him sleeping, and had come away, to begin with, with the Sacred Chain of the Hierarchate.

It fired their imagination. They moved through and left their belongings and their captive where Natzó, the second sentinel, had been deposited. Then they returned and went through the camp like ants through a carcass. It might appear so; for truly, the work they did seems more than human. They carried away the Otomi litters, with all of the Otomi stores loaded on them. They burdened themselves heavily and made their traveling difficult, but they had not the conscience to leave their labors incomplete. They left the Otomis their tents, the beds they lay on, and the clothes they were wearing, and went on their way triumphant. Soon the captive sentinels were unbound and bearing between them the heaviest of the litters.

But presently, what with their burdens and their lack of sleep, the glory of their exploit dimmed for them. Their old mood crept back, and the cold of the dawn became haunted. They dared not pause to feast on the stolen provisions; they were not making the progress they might. And who knew but that there might be something in thievery, done on the Road, that officious Omnipotence might object to? They had killed no one in the camp. At least, each hoped sincerely that no one else had, but who was to know? Man was naturally sinful; very likely some fool, for the fun of killing, had brought down on them all anew the redoubled anger of the Invisible. It was a dejected band that trailed out of the canyon at sunrise and onto the level plain, a band that wished heartily to be rid of its spoils but loath to leave them where the Otomis might find and pick them up.

Some way to their left flowed the river; as soon as they caught sight of it, they knew what to do. They would fling their burdens over the banks and go forward but lightly encumbered. But by the riverside, and high above the chasm down into which the waters roared there, they changed their minds. They needed food and a little rest; a cave they came upon would hide them from the pursuit of gods or tzitzimitls or men. So in they went. They quarreled for a while as to whether it would be safe, so near the Road, to kill and cook their captives, and decided that it would be safer to feast on what they had stolen from the camp. So they bound Huhú and Natzó again and flung them on the ground at the far end of the cave. Then they gorged without restraint and forgot about them. When their hunger was something more than satisfied, they resumed their journey. Seeing no reason to burden themselves further with their spoils of last night, they left them in the cave. Before nightfall they were brought into Huitznahuacan, and Quauhtli's pictograph had been read in the House of the Kings.

Where, however, it but confirmed the news that the Huitznahuatecs had already heard. The hierarch, on his arrival at the northern end of the canyon, had sent his secretary ahead by litter with swift runners, who left him at the edge of Huitznahuac and returned. Thence Mahetsi had made his way on foot to the city and proclaimed his master's guilt. It did not matter that he did not know whether the massacre had happened or not; all that was important was that the Huitznahuatecs should believe it had. For Mahetsi's part, he hoped it had not.

8

The Republic of New Otompan

Huhú and Natzó, with covetous eyes, watched their captors feasting. They lay bound where they had been flung down at the back of the cave, knowing nothing as to their whereabouts or of the Quinames' destination, nor that Huitznahuac was quite near, nor why they had not been killed. They had heard of the cannibalism of these forest people and had guessed that their turn would come when the stolen food was finished: a nauseating thought that quite held Huhú's mind; he could think of nothing else. But better that, Natzó consoled himself, than to fall into the hands of the hierarch again, for he supposed that he had been napping a little when captured; and although the Otomitl, or even Tata, would have given him a clean death for it, he distrusted Yen Ranho. They lay a stride or so apart, their feet toward the feasters, who were some twenty long strides from them and heeding them, apparently, not at all.

A chilled neck and right shoulder slowly made themselves felt by Natzó, the physical sensation creeping through his mental misery till at last it suggested to him an idea. He turned his head and whispered: "Huhú!"

"Eh?"

"There is a draft."

"I've been wishing there wasn't."

"There must be an opening behind us somewhere."

Huhú was much too wretched to care. If he was to go to the

Quiname cooking pots, he would prefer to go to them without a rheumatic neck.

"We might escape."

"Huh! Tied up in these vile mashtlies?"

"Wriggle this way and we'll see."

They both did some wriggling, Huhú without grasping the importance of it, bruising their naked bodies on the rough rock floor.

"Now lie back to back with me."

They contrived to get into that position. Then Natzó, over-coming huge difficulties, worked his fingers free, worked his thumbs free, groped for the knots in his companion's bindings, fumbled and worked at them until Huhú's arms were unbound. In much less time, Huhú, thus freed, untied Natzó's; then both quickly unbound their legs. The savages were no such skilled binders, after all.

Taking their bonds with them that they might dress decently in them by and by, they crept in the direction of the draft, their hearts beating wildly. But that end of the cave was fairly dark, and the Quinames, not far in from the cave mouth, were busy with their gorging. Soon they were behind a boulder and knew that they were, at least, out of sight.

Before long there was a bend in the cave, which went on diminishing into the dark: a passage that still permitted them, feeling their way, to walk more or less erect.

"There may be snakes, tarantulas and scorpions," whispered Huhú.

"Better all of them than those stinking savages," said the other. "Come on!"

On they went, groping before them with hands and feet. The ground beneath them was surprisingly smooth and level, the draft their guide. They turned another corner, and far in front of them was light.

The light was a long way off, but as they advanced, it grew more distinguishable and reassuring. They hurried on, since the walls and floor were becoming visible. They were losing their fear of the Quinames rapidly; safety seemed in sight.

"But, Natzó, what if we come out into the canyon before the Divine Hierarch has passed? What if—?"

"May jaguars eat the living body of the Divine Hierarch!"

"Oh, Natzó!"

They stopped to dress themselves, in mashtlies only, for their tilmatlies had been torn into binding strips. Then on they went, mashtli-clad, and came to the end of the passage, which they approached with caution at last, for fear of the Divine Hierarch. There was no need for fear or caution; their outlook was not into the canyon at all, nor onto any part of the Road. Beneath them lay a green valley, to all appearance quite shut in: grassland dotted with groves, a lake at the bottom. Great herds of deer grazed on the hillsides and by the water. There was an air of peace about the place found only where man is unknown. They ran down to the lake, and the birds hardly troubled to rise before them, nor the rabbits to scuttle away. The herds looked up unconcernedly and, without so much as turning aside, went on with their grazing.

They lay flat on the clean sand of the margin and drank and washed themselves free of the night's terrors.

"Natzó!"

"Yes, Huhú?"

"May vultures feed upon his entrails!"

"On whose entrails?"

"The Divine Hierarch's. May his remains be shamefully defiled!" They both roared with laughter, rolling on the sand.

They found a hiding-place above, and until nightfall watched the mouth of the passage they had come through; but no pursuing Quinames appeared. There they lay through the night, afraid to light a fire, but in that game-rich valley, not hungry. It was too cold for sleep, and they fell to devising plans.

"Huhú!"

"Yes, Natzó."

"Not a jaguar has squalled during the night, not a puma nor an ocelot."

"That is true, Natzó. It is a civilized country."

"We could live here in great peace and wealth. We could found a republic and live gloriously."

"We have no weapons, Natzó. To found a republic, one needs weapons."

"The Divine Hierarch's baggage may still be in the cave."

"In the cave, Natzó?"

"Consider! The savages stole it, but it would be of little use to them. It was the theft that pleased them, I should think, and not the spoils. What would they do with all those bales of wealth? I say they will leave them in the cave and go on wealthless about their business. We will go there in the morning and take what we need."

"What if—"

"Oh, we will sneak in quietly enough. Or, if you are afraid, I will. If they are still there, we shall see them against the light of the cave mouth and they won't see us. There'll be royal robes in the bales instead of the tilmatlis they tore up for us."

After a long silence, Huhú sighed. "I shall miss my wife and children," he said.

"Yes, that is a pity. But we may find girls somewhere to marry. We may find gentle savages—the savages here would be gentle— and teach them civilization. The Republic of New Otompan . . ."

They waited till daylight before entering the cave. Natzó was willing enough to go alone, but Huhú, though fearful, was unwilling not to accompany him. "There are other passages leading off," said he. "We may lose our way and wander forever in the desolate entrails of the mountain. I wish we had torches."

"If we had, and if the Quinames are still there, the light would be our destruction."

After groping for a while: "Pulque would be good, Natzó."

"There will be plenty in the cave."

The darkness thinned presently, but still all was silent ahead. "There would be noise enough if they were there," said Natzó. "Ah, here is that boulder we slipped behind. Now to peer out cautiously."

The Quinames were not there, but the baggage was. Of the Divine Hierarch's boxes, only three had been opened: two of food and one of garments. About half of the food in each box had been taken. The garments were strewn on the cave floor; to judge by the number left, none of them was missing. The Otomis had on new and gorgeous mashtlies in a moment, and five or six tilmatlies apiece, much above their station.

The cases were marked on the outside with pictograph descriptions of their contents, so plainly that even those illiterates had no difficulty in understanding. Here were skins of pulque; here dried yetl leaves, and pipes in which to smoke them; fire-sticks and tinder; torches. They drank, and smoked, and dreamed of the glories of New Otompan, keeping the while a sort of watch on the plain outside. But they saw no one. When the mood took them, they lit torches and carried them into the dark passage and there set them up as well as might be, thrust into crevices or a few piled up and flaring on the floor. And by their light, they began the transport of their booty into the territories of the new republic.

The passage, at the New Otompan end, opened up into a chamber, wherein they deposited what they brought. Three only of the litters were small enough to get through, but these did good service. They worked hard till nightfall, making journey after journey. Then, having supped delicately, they slept the night on the hierarch's bedding, with five or six quilts of the richest and thickest under each of them, and soft, luxurious fawn-skin blankets above.

A life began for them far more pleasant than soldiering in the Otomitl's army. The memory of their families came to trouble them little; nor did they at first push out and explore, to find those gentle savages who should be their subjects. That one valley, so far as they knew, was a world without ingress or egress but through their cave, and it sufficed them. Fruit was to be had for the picking; what game they needed waited for their shafts. They felled trees and built a cabin by the lakeside and moved their bedding there, and they used the cave, their first home, as a storehouse. There were no dangerous beasts, not even insect pests, to trouble them.

It occurred to Natzó that they must fortify their realm against possible, if improbable, invaders. So they felled more trees, trimmed the logs roughly and hauled them into the cave; there they piled them lengthwise in the opening of the passage till it was blocked. When the heavy rains began, they moved back there. They had but to put out pans then, to catch all the water they needed.

The one loving to lead, and the other to be led; the one to patronize, and the other to be patronized—they did not quarrel. Everyone that either of them knew or had known became a reality in the mind of the other. Thus, talking or silent, they spent the weeks of the rain, when the runlets on the hillsides were torrents, and often the falling waters made a curtain before the cave mouth through which some lonely buck passing, at a dozen strides or so away, could but be seen like the faintest of ghosts. They were well stored with food and firewood, and kept their fire burning always.

Huhú was standing by the cave mouth, looking out; Natzó lay on his bedding, watching the smoke from the fire travel up along the roof to its escape, and dreaming great dreams. Thus far, they had been busy with the valley of New Otompan; when the rains ceased, they would look afield. They would explore and extend their empire wonderfully. In this new, sorrowless world, there must be other territories than this. Who knew to what new realms they might come conquering? To what peaceful but gifted tribe, of which Natzó might make himself the hierarch and Huhú the Otomitl, teaching the people the arts and sciences? War, that they had never known, he could trust himself and Huhú—a good soldier, if uninspiring—to acquaint them with. They should grow great, and bless their benefactors, and set up a power to rival the Topiltzin's. And he would teach them to speak Otomi, and invent for them a pictography in which they could keep and hand down the record of his greatness.

"Of what are you thinking, Huhú?"

"Of the rain and the lake, Natzó."

"And what of them?"

"That the one is ceasing and that the other has risen."

Natzó rose and joined him, and they both stood looking out. As they watched, the white opacity of the rain vanished, and the grayness above from which it had come. Soon the sky shone darkly and intensely blue. Everywhere, sunlit jewels sparkled on the wetness of the valley.

"The lake will rise no higher," said Natzó. "Look yonder!"

The surface of the lake shone blue but troubled; beneath the blueness, tumult was to be seen, or divined. The waters had risen, certainly; it was difficult to judge how much. But—where was their cabin? They scanned the eastern shore but saw no sign of it. Of course not, for look! The water was at the base of a rock that had been a good forty strides east of it, and risen to a man-height higher than the level of its floor. Ah, and look! There the cabin went!

There it went—or the logs that had composed it—carried along toward the other end of the valley on a swift current. They watched till a fiercer force of water tossed the logs up and hurled them out of sight.

"Where we have never been," said Natzó. "A marsh was there formerly; the lake had no outflow. I was right—there are other territories in New Otompan. The Tlalocs have shown us the way; they intend the republic to grow."

They followed the waters to their outflow: a sudden fall into a gorge completely tree-hidden. When the lake had gone down and the outflow was but a trickle, they would descend and explore. They waited some weeks and finally they set off. A winding way, strangely concealed, led them out into a valley larger and more beautiful than their own. But was not this their own too? They proposed to move their stores here and annex it.

So there they built a new cabin, and lived in it till they wearied for fresh scenes. Then Natzó decided that the republic needed a navy, whereupon they cut logs and made a raft of them by the waterside, packed a tent, provisions, and cooking pots on it, and set forth on their adventures.

9
Yen Ranho Disappointed

On the morning after the Quinames passed through the Otomi
camp in the canyon, the first of the Otomis to be abroad soon
saw that much had happened while they slept, and the camp
awoke into an atmosphere of strangeness and apprehension.
This turned soon into bewilderment and then into consternation
when the store tents were visited and their foodless condition
became known. They might starve before they came to this
Huitznahuac, and anyway, what would the Divine Hierarch say?
He had no reputation for leniency. Those who served him, or the
state, were expected to be rigorously faithful and efficient; punishment was more familiar than reward. The two who might be
chiefly to blame were, it was discovered, not there to be punished,
so punishment might fall on anyone. They loitered about like
men of evil conscience; there was no stir of work in the camp, as
there would have been of a normal morning. Their stricken
thoughts made a heavy and uneasy atmosphere.

Thus Tata, their commanding officer, found them when the
unusualness of the morning brought him to the door of his tent.
He saw dejected groups discussing in low tones news that did not
seem good; none were taking down the tents, lighting fires or
cooking. What was the meaning of it?

They did not know what to say.

What! Were they rebellious? You there, Yetsú; why were no
fires lit?

Please, his Godhead, there was no firing.

No firing? Where were the cooks' firing gatherers? What did this mean?

It meant that although there had been firing enough last night, and food and everything else, this morning there was nothing at all. The case was too grave to be dealt with except by the hierarch, to whose tent Tata hastened.

He found Yen Ranho risen, and evidence on all sides to confirm his tale. Everything that could be taken had been taken. Ghuggg's prize, the chain of chalchiuhites, had been worn by score-scores of the hierarch's predecessors; and Yen Ranho was furious over the loss, although he showed no sign of it. He heard Tata's tale in silence and made sure that he had it all; then he quietly issued orders. Who the thieves were called for no speculation. It was to be given out that they were within a day of their journey's end and that the men would not go hungry for long. The tents were to be packed and all made ready to go forward, and let the commander's manner be as though nothing unusual had happened.

But, left to himself, he pondered over it. The Huitznahuatecs must have powerful magicians among them, thus to have triumphed over him. Yet the news he had sent on could not have reached them; Mahetsi must have failed, or they should have been killed last night, and not merely robbed. He was puzzled and could not read the thing to his satisfaction.

He was little used to walking, and his men were hungry and dispirited. They did not emerge from the canyon till noon, and it was evening before they had crossed the plain. Where the desert ended and the cultivated land began, some half a dozen men stood waiting for them in front of a row of litters, well loaded, that blocked the way. The leader of these came forward as the hierarch, walking with Tata at the head of the Otomis, approached.

"You are the chief priest of Teotihuacan?" His manner was reserved but touched with a grave compassion.

Tata made answer that the Divine Hierarch came as the ambassador of the Otomi Republic to—

Tzontecoma, lord of the Northern District of Huitznahuac,

cut him short. "We understand," said he. "The king and queen have sent you provisions, hearing that you are without them. Also these litters, that you may return to your homes the more easily. They request that you will turn here and not go forward into Huitznahuac." Having said that, he turned and, with his following, left them.

"We camp here," said the hierarch, completely master of himself.

He spent the evening alone. Turn it in his mind as he might, he could make nothing of it. If they had known of the massacre, they would have killed him when they raided the camp last night. So they could not know. And why stock him with provisions after robbing him? Well, they were treating him with extraordinary discourtesy; the League could not but be incensed. But he had worked for something better than this.

In the morning he set out for Huitznahuacan, with only the bearers of his litter. He met none by the way and arrived at a silent city. He knew the way to take, perhaps from Yacanetzin's description of the town. Before the shut door of the House of the Kings stood Mahetsi.

"I have failed, my lord. There will be no murder of the ambassador." The bearers waited below in the arena.

"You did your duty?"

"And was not believed. But the savages came and confirmed my news. It was they who raided the camp."

"Ah! Come then. At least they have insulted the League."

10

Acamapitzin's Plan

The Royal Council at Huitznahuacan heard Mahetsi's story with courtesy, but also with distrust. There was something about the man intrinsically that all of them distrusted, Nopal foremost. Although meanwhile the Ib Quinames arrived with Quauhtli's letter, most woefully confirming Mahetsi's tale, they scented a plot in his telling of it, and when the time came, they made it easy for him to rejoin his master.

The Ib Quinames were herded into the Upper Market. Most of the men of the town, grimly silent, were put to guarding them while the letter was being discussed in the House of the Kings. Nopal, Chimalman, Acamapichtli, and Acatonal were of one mind, claiming that "we must be cut off utterly from these peoples of the north. This Otomi priesthood is contaminated, and we can not deal with the Toltecs without suffering it."

Nopal understood that the League meant war; he alone of the Huitznahuatecs had some slight idea as to what war was and of the nature of armies. And he alone knew the Canyon at the End of Things. Tradition had always been strong that the canyon was the only door to Huitznahuac from the north. He placed his knowledge before the council, and Acamapitzin seized upon it and conceived the beginnings of a plan.

"We must explore the mountainside," he said. "It is there that we shall find what we need."

So Nopal and he and the queen would go with them. They

would set out at once for the north, taking with them the litters and stores that Yen Ranho later had from Tzontecoma. Having given the latter the news and his instructions, they went on, skirting the plain to the west and so avoiding the Otomis, and up onto the mountain. At nightfall they camped high up; and in the morning they found what they wanted: boulder-strewn declivities sloping on either side down toward the cliff tops of the canyon—eight thousands upon eight thousands of boulders, an inexhaustible supply. The biggest of them stood right on the brink. Elsewhere placed, no human power could shift it, but being where it was, it might serve.

"Give me the Ib Quinames," said Acamapitzin, "and we will get to work here."

It would be convenient, anyway, to have the Quinames segregated and busy, well away from the city. When the rest of the tribe arrived, they could be hauled up over the barrier and, all together, packed off into the forests of the far south. Meanwhile, things could be set in order throughout Huitznahuac and the country reorganized to meet critical times, the women to raise the crops, the men to be drafted here, more each week, to work upon this civilization-saving barrier of which, said the king and queen, Acamapitzin should be in charge.

The first big boulder fell soon after the Otomis passed northward. From either side, the dozen bearers who were left with Acamapitzin poked the cliff's edge from beneath it with poles and shoved it from behind. It blocked the passage from side to side when it fell, scarring the cliffs, and stood two good man-heights high.

Soon the Quinames arrived with an escort of twice their number. They were in a kind of daze, their whole reliance placed upon these magnificent visible gods, the Huitznahuatecs, who could and did protect them from the gods unseen. They set to work feverishly, obeying the orders given them in the sign-language; they adored God Acamapitzin, and were but half aware of their surroundings.

And all the time, more and more Huitznahuatecs arrived. They made timber runways down the slopes and slid the boulders to the edge and over. Behind the first great rock, others and others had fallen, graded according to size, with the largest in front, so that the barrier should slope down toward Huitznahuac. Tons of earth were loosened and pushed over. Then men working below raked the soil into a level earth-bed to cover the last rock layer. Discovery was made of what depth of earth, and how loosely settled, would make a bed for what size of boulder dropped, so as to keep it from jumping, and in time, the need for the raking ceased. The gods who loved Huitznahuac had provided for her needs, and the barrier rose and rose.

When the Culhuatec ambassador arrived, a twenty-day month after the Otomis' departure, he found the rise several man-heights high and the work going on lustily. He was Cohuanacotzin, who had rescued Nopal from the priests of Teotihuacan; he was the Topiltzin's closest friend, a great general, and a master of military engineering.

This barrier was something to admire, thought he. If there were no way around, they should be put to it. But Yacanetzin of Tollan, whom he had met on the Road, had been wrong about these peoples' ignorance of war. This work of theirs would puzzle, and might confound, the Topiltzin himself.

All of his trumpets could attract no attention from above; thud, thud, crash, the great rocks kept falling. It was no courteous way to receive an ambassador; Yacanetzin had been wrong there, and the hierarch right. For the latter, whom he had also met, had been bitter about the way the Huitznahuatecs had insulted him. It was a pity. . . .

Cohuanacotzin unloaded the gifts he had brought and left them not too near the foot of the barrier. Then he departed, wondering how the problem would be solved. Not even the Topiltzin's armies could pass while those rocks were falling.

BOOK III

War

1

The Little Gods of Forgotten Plain

Forgotten Plain lay north of the Canyon at the End of Things. It was the Saltmen who had given it its name. To the tribes of the forest, it was unknown—forgotten possibly; but that was not why the Saltmen called it Forgotten Plain. Their idea was that the gods themselves had forgotten it.

Which may have been largely true, at least of the greater gods. Tlaloc could have known nothing of it; rain never fell there. Would Citlalicway Teteoinan be aware of a land where no green thing grew? As for the Beautiful Youth and the Plumed Dragon, was not their compassion chiefly concerned with the regions where most are men? So the Saltmen argued, and they concluded that the gods would have forgotten a place like that.

Still, it had godlets of its own.

It was rimmed around, except on the forest side, with barren mountains, blue-purple and rose-purple, with a dim glint of silver where the polished rock reflected the sky; and these mountains were the strongholds of the godlets. They knew themselves—in the third person—as Pweeg and Pfapffo and Ttang, and not one of them had ever heard of either of the others. Not one of them but believed that he was the sole deity in existence. Of course there were the coyotes and vultures, but they did not think of *them* as gods.

Each regarded a third part of the plain as his playground and workshop, school and house of dreams. Their duty—but none ever knew who appointed it to be their duty, or when—and their pleasure were to flow out over the plain, occupy it, and be absorbed in its vast, clear sunlight, and in its dust and stillness, and, as it were, to pattern the silence of it with the clicking, stridulous, chirring rhythm of their song. They were creatures of routine, loving to do what they had always done.

Needless to say, they occupied no lofty position in the grand deific hierarchies; incense burned to them in never a temple in the world. But they had gifts of their own and served their purpose, doing the best a godlet could do. They had genius for the inhibition of mental activity and inquietude. They absorbed thought and turned it into sun-soaked loneliness and silence. And they did it without the slightest idea that they were doing anything at all.

Not that much thought came their way, or had come for sheaves and sheaves of years. But it was the same to them whether it came or not, or from whence it came. No rumor could pass them, northward or southward; and so, to Huitznahuatecs and people of the forest alike, the plain was something outside cognition, beyond the End of Things.

As one to these godlets were the speech of men and the *ki-yi* yeowing of coyotes on the horizons of the night; whatever of desire, thought, or feeling lay behind either, the godlets absorbed them and remained untroubled. They could make their consciousness like a clear pool that reflects only the cloudless sky; it was the easy and natural thing for them to do. Whatever emanations of the human mind were blown to them from the south or north fell into them without a ripple.

So it happened that in the northern world, although there had been a rumor through the ages of a road that ran south into the forest as far as to the Brink of Things, there had been no rumor of a kingdom Huitznahuac lying beyond it, not until the priesthood of Teotihuacan, omniscient for its own ends, spread it about. And so it happened that in Huitznahuacan, although the Saltmen told their tales well and wondrously, none believed them till the Toltec ambassador arrived.

The place of Ttang was in the south of the plain, nearest the canyon; Pweeg took the northeast, toward the river; Pfapffo the northwest; and there daily they worshiped the sun. When anything human approached, they shrank back into their mountains like a snail's horns withdrawn at an unrecognized contact, or as if on a light breeze blown outward from the center of the plain. Only, for ages and ages, nothing human had approached, not ever, except the Saltmen.

And they, really, were very wonderful people when you came to think of it. They did not destroy the potency and value of Forgotten Plain, because they knew better than to affront or inconvenience the Little Gods. They made always the proper apologies for their intrusion, which the Little Gods in due course absorbed and enjoyed. They had the right poems to chant: those the vibrations of which were peculiarly pleasing to that class of deity. And furthermore, the poems they chanted toward the south were of the kind most delectable to Ttang; nothing could have pleasured Pfapffo like those they chanted to the northwest; those they chanted toward the northeast were calculated to produce a noteworthy complacency in Pweeg.

Again, their predecessors had, in their great wisdom, set up three altars on the plain, and it had been the custom of the Saltmen from time immemorial to burn a pictoscript on each whenever they passed. It was essential that each pictoscript should have a meaning. Gibberish would not do. Something in the nature of human thought must be liberated when the paper was burned. It must be the soul—as what the flame consumed was the body—of the sacrifice. It might be "For every man there is a god," or "The universe is indestructible, without beginning or end," or it might be "People eat food." Nothing could be too abstruse and lofty, nothing too jejune.

The Little Gods would scent the thought, and it would be to them a call to what was both duty and pleasure, and they would say, each to himself, "Ah, this is something I must absorb; this is food delicately cooked for me. Were I to neglect this, I should sin!"

So out they would flow from their mountains as soon as the Saltmen had passed and establish themselves on the plain again, lolling luxuriously, and gather up, each of them, every mental trace of human passage, which they would then digest in the sun-soaked vacuity of their consciousness, and make all vacant and nonentitous again, and the plain as lonely as ever. The coyote, as gaunt and fleet as a shadow, would pass over the very footsteps of the Saltmen and scent nothing, and never dream that anything alien had passed.

That way things had been for ages. Each of them believed that he had been there always, and always would be; or certainly it had never occurred to them to think otherwise. But change is the one thing certain in this universe of ours. Change came at last, and their world became different.

It was when Nopal passed that way, sent by the Master into the north. He came out of the canyon and onto the plain. He had nothing about him, mentally, of the kind that the Little Gods were on the watch for or delighted to absorb. He came out in the early morning, and all he was doing was worshiping the sun. There was not a thought about him more personal than that. To worship the sun was so much the Little Gods' natural mode of existence that they did it unconsciously; it was the disturbance of sun-worship that they heeded. So no thought-scent, as it were, was blown ahead of Nopal to apprise Godlet Ttang of his coming, whereby Nopal almost ran into that deity. He passed within a span of the center of Ttang's consciousness and saw nothing but a little whirl of dust rise from the ground a stride to the right of him, and he paid no heed to it.

But to Ttang, this was the most momentous event in history. His attitude to humanity had been one of mixed fear and attraction, as heaven, no doubt for its own purposes, had arranged it should be. But now the fear could not come into play, because what had happened had come too suddenly for anticipation. He had contacted the human thing without injury and had received huge exhilaration from the contact. It had dilated his being into a vast, magnificent surprise; he was no longer receptive and quiescent, but active, volatile and whirling.

He rolled himself out over the plain, self expanded to extreme tenuity, and encountered simultaneously Pfapffo northwestward under the mountains, and Pweeg northeastward toward the river.

"Ay-yah! ay-yah! ay-yoh!" Nopal heard it whispered over the plain . . . by the wind, he supposed.

"Ay-yah! ay-yoh!" sighed Godlet Ttang. "Behold what cometh!"

At contact with him, Pfapffo here and Pweeg there were kindled from their quiescence into tumultuous bliss such as his own. They reared themselves up like waves and expanded outward like ripples on water. They took cognizance of Nopal as he passed, and the three of them, like flames over dry grass, ran and whirled out, their forces no longer in equipoise. Nopal felt the place somehow in commotion. Sometimes he heard on all sides a faint sound of crackling, snapping, and roaring, as if some far inner world were on fire. Sometimes it was as if the ghost of a great wind were howling, or as if the hissing and drumming of rain pursued him and passed and died afar—although no wind blew, and no rain was falling.

Had he but consulted the Saltmen before starting out, no doubt they would have taught him their own procedure, and he would have gone through without upsetting the balance of things. Then perchance the Little Gods would have remained in ignorance of each other's existence. But now no longer did they dwell solitary, each in his station performing his duty; but they converged, and met in the south or the northeast or the northwest to brood on their ancient sorrow and present bliss, for they were convinced that before they knew each other, their lives had been wretchedly lonely. Or they would riot and dance together from forest to canyon and from mountains to river. But brooding or dancing, they paid attention to nothing but themselves. Thought might come and go, and they remained oblivious of it; it was no diet for them now. They worshiped each other and forgot how to worship the sun.

In the forest, quite near the plain of the Little Gods, lived the Viridian Pygmies; their village was within two-score strides of the plain's edge. But the plain's edge was a thing not for them to know about. They looked and went the other way; not one of them had ever seen or heard of it. They knew that it was impossible to go south of the huts, that the world ended there, and one might come upon something frightful. The lucky thing was not to think about it at all—and these people were good at not thinking about things. So it had always been.

And then, the day after Nopal passed to the north, Quahh, a youth among them of whom great things had been prophesied, was seized by a tremendous inspiration, which was that if one walked that way, by taking only two-score strides, one would live forever! Either the scheme of things had been changed or the ancestral spirit—a howler-monkey—had lied lest his descendants, attaining immortality, should become his equals.

Quahh resolutely turned his face southward and pressed on, daring ineffable terrors . . . until he looked out through the leaves and thicket onto a world most unimaginable, most sublime. Pressing forward, he stood on the plain's edge, unabashed now and unterrified, because thrilled through with the immortality the wondrous spectacle had created in him. From height to height of dizzy speculation, it sent his mind soaring. Here, then, was no snapping of the Universal Jaws, no End of Things. There was a beyond, and beyond. Howler-monkey, howler-monkey, look to your throne!

He turned back and was seen coming into the village *from the south;* and thenceforth he was worshiped, for on his forehead was the light that marked him as one who had conversed with heaven.

He said nothing of his discovery, knowing that the language had no words to describe it and that the brains of his people lacked the expansion that would enable them to understand. But on that very night, three men of the tribe dreamed that they journeyed southward and were none the worse, but rather the better, for it; the End of Things was not just beyond the huts.

And then someone in the tribe north of them got the same inspiration, and it was bruited abroad in the villages. These people had no means of communicating with the Viridian Pygmies, whom they regarded only as potential food; they did not, therefore, get the news from them. They had indeed known that the plain was there, as the pygmies had not; but they had known of it as the limits of the universe. Now they were telling each other that beyond it there were other forests, other tribes.

People by people, all at war with each other, became obsessed with this wonderful knowledge, till it reached the Quiname tribes—from the Gholb Quinames in the south to the Appa, from the Appa to the Hlun, and from the Hlun to the Ib Quinames to the north. From them the news spread on; it was as though a wave of thought had gone rolling by, stirring utterly new concepts and interests among peoples whose languages lacked words, mostly, for things beyond the range of present vision. It followed Nopal northward and reached, in due course, Quiche and Maya, Chiapanec, Zapotec and Tarasco, and, finally, the Toltec and Otomi lands.

There Yen Ranho's propaganda was marvelously aided by it. Since there was a south beyond the jungle, men said, of course it must be conquered by the League. *Since there was a south*—for now men began to "know" that there was. By the time that Nopal went to Tollan, it was a matter of common belief, or knowledge. The wonder is that he was never suspected of being Huitznahuatec himself.

But as for the Little Gods, their dominions came to be disturbed more and more by human passaging, and less and less did it trouble them. They knew nothing of it when Nopal returned south, or when Quauhtli passed to the north a few days later. Yacanetzin of Tollan came, but the Little Gods were busy under Pfapffo's mountains, and it was to them as if Yacanetzin had never been born. They were trying to remember the ancient times and the age when they had known each other as brothers; for they had concluded that such an age had been.

And then came the Otomi embassy, and then the Ib Quinames, intent on expiation. Then the Topiltzin's own ambassador, Cohuanacotzin, the Culhuatec, his the greatest train that had passed there yet. But the Little Gods knew nothing of their comings or their goings.

Then the plain became no more alien to humanity than another place; its old aloofness and desolation vanished. Pweeg now played host to his companions; they related to each other histories antique and endless. It seemed to them that they remembered what had been before they were commissioned to the plain. They had forgotten, however, how to absorb thought and turn it into sunlit silence. Their minds had lost the art of reflecting, like calm waters, only the sky; they could no longer make themselves vacant but for the slow traveling of the sunlight. One or another of them was always talking; all three of them were busy with what they listened to or told.

And so presently they knew nothing of it when the plain was covered with a great host. They sat beyond the river, where no one came, whilst the solitude they had loved became filled with the business and disciplines of men.

2
The Toltec Topiltzin Arrives

The shadow of the Topiltzin had fallen on the Road, from Culhuacan to Forgotten Plain. His agents were everywhere enlisting the tribes and paying them munificently for their service. Their task was not difficult, since the savages knew that the gods were in this affair. It had to do with the revelation, lately vouchsafed to them, that there were men, kingdoms and mysteries beyond the forest and the End of the World. These, of course, the gods would wish to conquer. What had not been known to the tribes would not have been known to the gods; the newly discovered was as much as to say the newly existent. Above all, that Master wonder-worker, the Great Priest of the Gods' City, had let them know that the Topiltzin's agents were not different from agents of his own. It was by his will that they were at work, and so the tribesmen must help them.

However, the forest peoples were not enlisted to fight; the League had its well-trained army, which no savage on earth might hope for the honor of joining. What was wanted of the tribesmen was their power to carry burdens and provide food for the hosts of the north. The Topiltzin had the world mobilized for this unique campaign, and there never had been a time when the Road was more crowded. At every stage—each half a day's journey from the last—a camp had arisen, at which masses of food were stored. Hosts of porters ran back and forth, day after day, from capital to first stage, from first stage to second, and so on.

In the forest, hunting was done systematically. Herds of deer were driven daily by wary savages to this stage or that and slaughtered by the regiments as they arrived; what was not eaten was dried or salted and sent on. Word had gone out that there was to be peace and cooperation among the tribes, and men who had been for ages stalking each other through the thickets with murderous and dietetic intent now beat the woods in company, Toltec officers superintending them.

Forgotten Plain came to be the apex of all this vast activity, the reservoir into which it flowed. A Culhuatec noble named Cocotzin was the first of the Topiltzin's generals to arrive there. He came with a huge army of porters and a force sufficient to protect them. With these he transformed the plain. He dammed the river not far from its emergence from the canyon and led it by a score-score of ditches over the land that had been dry and sterile. He set up rows of tents and interspersed them with kitchen gardens. He found building clay and built storehouses. He burned back the forest a mile or two all along, and under the ashes he planted fields on fields of maize and beans and squash.

One might complain that this burning back would dislodge the Viridian Pygmies; in fact, it did leave them and other tribes homeless. Nonetheless, having no gift for foresight and faring for the present excellently under the change, they rejoiced and re-garded Cocotzin as a very great god. They had no foes to fear now, and the Toltecs, being of a strange, superior order, were kind to them and enjoyed their sense of fun.

Of all the forest people, the pygmies were perhaps the most adept in forest craft. They had need to be, having no warriorlike qualities wherewith to meet their better-statured neighbors, who would have eaten them all long since but for their quicker wits. The beast that could outwit the pygmies was hardly to be found, a result of their long training in the fear of men.

As was proved, for instance, by the fact that no less than thrice they drove great herds of peccaries out onto the plain, inducing the doomed creatures, as though by magic, to go out by the Road, keeping clear of the newly planted fields on either side. If peccaries know that they are being driven, it is a poor thing for the would-be drivers; so one must influence them, as it were, psychically, throwing vague notions of distress or desire into their very warlike consciousness, whilst keeping one's own presence unsuspected. Once out in the open, these herds thought nothing of meeting the Topiltzin's armies in battle—every man of them, if need be. They perished, poor beasts, under arrow fire, with no chance of striking back and no shadow of fear in their breasts.

Whoever knows enough to cheat a herd of peccaries need fear nothing in the forest; the she-jaguar with her kittens is child's play to him. The pygmies drove out onto the plain, eventually, every jaguar, puma, ocelot and other wildcat in those parts, and the soldiers finished the work of exterminating them. No food pleased the pygmies so well as the flesh of these creatures, which they understood nourished lithe, sly, fierce and catlike qualities in the eaters. They relished this flesh far above meats edible by civilized men.

Well, the fewer the beasts of prey, the more numerous the beasts they preyed on; and jaguar and ocelot skins made noble cloaks for officers. So Cocotzin kept bowmen and spearmen always at the beck and call of the pygmies to kill their quarry for them, and to be, to the best of their ability, kind and fatherly to the little knaves. What more pleasant meat was driven in was dried in the keen sunlight and stored, or eaten, or smoked over brush bonfires and stored; and every day there came armies of porters with stores; and every day the arrivals of the day before set out northward again, burdenless and at good speed, for the appointed station on the Road, there to rest, reload their litters, and thence to return.

On the plain too, and in the kitchen gardens, and on the burnt forest lands, the first crops were ripening. Soldiers hoed and irrigated and weeded; and presently they harvested their labors' results. The Topiltzin had given this work to a man with high genius for it; Cocotzin deserved praise.

He went far beyond what he imagined was necessary. The Topiltzin made his conquests without difficulty or great delay, and no doubt he would do so now. But one could not predict

with certainty, for this was a new kind of war. Cocotzin was there
to see that nothing devised by gods or men could happen to make
the army hunger or go unfed.

So the camp grew—the vastest that history had ever seen. In
due course, the fighting regiments began arriving and kept on
coming in day after day, eight thousands upon eight thousands,
in ranks a score abreast, with their litter-borne officers. They
came swinging up out of the forest at a wolf-lope, until the
innumerable tents that had been erected were filled with their
complement of men. Thereafter it was the pomp of war that
flaunted itself over Forgotten Plain. Daily, from dawn to dusk,
some or another of those eight thousands, to drummed commands—wolf-lope, dog-trot, quick march, slow march—went
through the mazy evolutions of their war drills.

And then at last, when all was ready to receive him, came
Nonohualcatl Totepeuh Camaxtli, the Toltec Topiltzin himself.
And the other chiefs of the League were with him: Huemac,
king of Tollan, and the two heads of the Otomi Republic. They
came escorted by their bodyguards: three wonderful regiments,
the flower of the north; giants, with their gianthood enhanced by
yard-high panaches on their helmets. It was a fine emblazoned
thread that had been drawn through the green of the forest.
Ahead were the Culhuatec guards, flashing in gold and ocelot-
skins and scarlet; then the kings and their allies; the Otomis in
black and gold and crimson; King Huetzin's guard from Tollan
in their jaguar skins and purple and silver.

From north to south, the Road had been lined to watch such
splendor go by; it seemed to the savage watchers that the panthe-
ons verily were on the march. Even the litter-bearers appeared to
be more than human; and as for those wondrous figures they
carried—what forest speech of theirs, they wondered, could be
framed into the telling of their glory?

That Golden Being (the Topiltzin) in the gem-encrusted litter,
the second from the left there in the midst, where most of the
banners flashed and glinted—no sane tribesman could mistake
him for less than the high-commander of the God-world, the
strongest strength in universal nature. And the one on the left
(Huetzin), borne in a litter only less splendid than the other,

although not quite so mighty a deity, would be darker and subtler. Possibly he had keener insight into the wicked contents of men's hearts than even that third one, the hierarch, undoubtedly had. The latter's atmosphere of lofty benevolence, coupled with what was already known of his power, was impressive. On his right rode one of whom little could be ascertained; he was possibly the more dangerous for that. This was the Otomitl, military head of Otompan: a spare, tough little man without sympathy for ostentation, who rode where he did only because the Topiltzin, knowing his worth, insisted upon honoring him.

In due course, they reached the camp on Forgotten Plain and were received by Cocotzin and the army. And now the world undoubtedly was about to be shaken. Tremendous events portended. But the Little Gods knew nothing of these things.

3

Exploration

The morning after his arrival, it was the Topiltzin's whim to go exploring the canyon; he wished to see for himself the barrier the Huitznahuatecs had raised. He took with him the Otomitl for his sagacity; Cohuanacotzin because he was his closest personal friend and always his companion on adventures; and Yacanetzin of Tollan because, as Huemac's ambassador, he had been in Huitznahuac.

They assembled while the sky was graying with dawn and made their way quietly through the camp southward. They took no weapons; their wear was the patternless nequen of peasants and of a dusty, indeterminate color that would blend well with the landscape. Only King Huemac and Cocotzin were to know that they had gone.

The sun was well in heaven before they had left the plain and come to where the Road, bearing eastward, entered the mountains. Side by side with the river, it ran through a valley that ever grew narrower and deeper. There was no occasion for great vigilance as yet, and they came upon no branching of the way a man, much less an army, might take. The gorge was not yet so narrow but that now and again great sweeps of mountainside, slope, and cliff were visible above. At one point they sighted mountain sheep, minute specks skyward, cascading down what seemed sheer precipice; and again, a little later, a flock grazing on an emerald slope between the forests. Those heights, at least, were untroubled by men; no Huitznahuatec outposts were on the watch.

But Yacanetzin, enlarging on the unmilitary nature of the Huitznahuatecs, scouted the idea that they would know what outposts were.

"But that can hardly be," said the Topiltzin. "Where there are men, there will be war. It is the natural way of things."

"Your Godhead will find these Huitznahuatecs thoroughly unnatural," chuckled Yacanex.

They wasted no time; hosts of way-finders would be crawling over every inch of this territory presently. The object now was to see the barrier before nightfall and form conclusions. Cohuana-cotzin, who had seen the beginnings of it, held that it implied the presence of skilled military engineers in Huitznahuac and a knowledge of war unreconcilable with Yacanetzin's views of Huitznahuatec civilization. The Topiltzin, and by his desire, the Otomitl, would see and judge for themselves.

They were at the fork of the canyon by noon, and there they rested and lunched. After refilling their water-skins by a climb down to the river, which now they were leaving, they turned to the right and struck up into the canyon proper. The enormous height of the cliffs on either side increased always; they seemed to jut inward above and to almost meet overhead; but along the Road, fifteen to twenty men might travel abreast anywhere.

When they reached the barrier, little daylight was left; although above, the sun might still be some way from his setting. The Huitznahuatecs had raised their obstruction at the point where the hierarch had camped on the night the Quinames had despoiled him. The venturers turned the corner where the savages had captured the sentinel Huhú and saw it at the end of some four-score strides, perhaps, of straight road. No work was being done on it; no rocks were falling. They judged it to be about a dozen man-heights high—not beyond a man's climbing, but if defended reasonably from above, utterly beyond an army's. Its foundation was a thing to admire: an enormous rock that must have been dropped from the cliff tops; but dropped, apparently, neatly into the place intended for it, so that it filled the whole width of the canyon. It was a nice piece of work, one that certainly suggested military engineering.

It was impossible to leave the destruction thus imperfectly examined, and they had two days' supplies with them. Near the spot where the Quinames had ambushed the exploring Huhú, there was a cave in the western wall of the canyon; it suited the Topiltzin's mood that they should not only spend the night in it, but they should have a fire in its mouth for their comfort. —A fire, and reveal themselves to possible watchers? —Why, certainly. The glow would flicker on this opposite cliff, which had its back to the barrier, on which, anyway, no work was being done tonight. All was silent there, as they knew. And it had never been intended, that barrier, to be climbed down and up by casual explorers of the canyon. The Huitznahuatecs had probably raised it and left it, trusting in it and the gods. Start that fire, and dismiss them from your minds.

A fire needs fuel, however, and where was that to be found? —Look at all this kex on the ledges—the lifeless, one-time tenements of the green growth that last season had gained what foothold it could find on the canyon walls. Would that not serve for a beginning? And then, had they not seen excellent fuel some two-score strides or so back? Ah, his Godhead, the Otomitl, had noticed it!

Two-score strides or so back the Topiltzin led them and pointed it out. On that western wall of the canyon, four or five man-heights up or more, was what appeared to be a wide ledge. Up there the light was a little better, and one could make out that pioneers from the pine forest above had found lodgment there, and had captured a dozen such small citadels on the cliff's face. Not much more was visible than the dark treetops; the way up to them seemed none too difficult.

"This is work for us, not for the head of the Otomi Republic," said the Topiltzin. "Come, you two!"

Up then the three went. But the Otomitl, amused inwardly at the implication that his greater age was at a disadvantage—thus he interpreted it—had a mind to follow them, and he did so, as agilely as any, he considered, as soon as Yacanex had disappeared over the edge above. Yes, there was a little wood. None of the trees were much over a man-height high, and several of them dead. The ledge might be twenty strides deep at its widest. The Toltecs busied themselves breaking off dead trunks and branches and throwing them down. It occurred to the Otomitl, whose coming they had not seen, to explore a little.

He found a narrow passage, or gully, behind the wood, leading upward and toward the barrier. He scrambled past obstructions and came out onto a small platform well in view of the barrier's top, an easy bowshot away. Although by this light he could see little of what might be doing there, by daylight the place might be useful: for spies, and perhaps for sharpshooters. Returning, he was down in the canyon before the others. Having discovered really nothing, there would be no need to speak of it now.

In the cave, when they had made their fire and supped, the Topiltzin developed a vein of geniality. He dropped his military wisdom and became the holiday schoolboy out for fun. None but mountain sheep had seen them all day long, said he. No one was coming down over that barrier to molest nequen-clad nonentities like themselves. Why, then, was it needed to keep watch? Yacanex, suiting his mood to his leader's, opined that the enemy certainly did not know what watch-keeping or spying meant. The enemy would, he said, spend their nights abed, to the last man of them, wishing us well as they went to sleep, if they thought of us at all. Cohuanacotzin demurred and thus roused the Topiltzin to overruling him.

"Think of a man," said Nonohualcatl, "and your thoughts will go buzzing in his ears like mosquitoes, drawing him to remembrance of you. We will forget the Huitznahuatecs for tonight, and that is all the protection we shall need."

"Is none to keep watch, then?"

"No, none. We are all to have a good night's rest."

"But it is true that to think of a man is to set him thinking of you," said Yacanex, and he related a story in point.

To that the Otomitl added another tale, a memory from his boyhood. "Aye," said Cohuanacotzin, "and I will go further and say that to think of a man means often that you will come upon him, though you supposed him at the other end of the world."

"Were that true," said Nonohualcatl, "I should have come on that Quanetzin of Quauhnahuac before now."

"Your Godhead certainly thinks of him often," said Cohuanacotzin.

"Aye, I do. I dearly wish that I could find him."

"May we know who that Quanetzin was?" asked the Otomitl. Then Nonohualcatl told the story of the attack on him in the Culhuacan marketplace and of how Quanez had saved his life. "Nequen-clad he was, but never born to wear nequen, by Cipactli!"

"Your Godhead is right there," said Cohuanacotzin. "He was a very great gentleman."

"You knew him then, Cohuanacotli?" the Topiltzin asked.

"Does your Godhead remember sending me to Teotihuacan, at the instance of the Divine Princess, to rescue a man from the priesthood there?"

"Yes, I remember that."

"It was Quanetzin I rescued."

"What became of him? Where is he now? Why did you not tell me it was he?"

"Your Godhead must ask the Divine Princess that last question," said Cohuanacotzin. "By her request, I took him to Tollan and nursed him back to health in Huetzin's palace."

"To health?" asked the Otomitl.

"Aye, to health, your Godhead. Your colleagues at Teotihuacan have a way of treating their prisoners . . . as you know."

"It must be owned that they are an unsoldierlike lot," said the Otomitl.

"You must judge the republic by Otompan, not by Teotihuacan."

"But what became of Quanetzin, Cohuanacotli? Where is he now?"

"Why, I was a year at Tollan watching over him, by the Divine Princess's orders. Then he disappeared."

"She has her reasons for what she does," said Nonohualcatl. "She must have wished me not to know. But I wish I had known. The business of this war has kept many things from my memory, but I shall have a search made for him one of these days. Was he

really a Quauhnahuatec, Cohuanacotli? It did not seem to me
that he spoke with a Quauhnahuatec accent."

"He had a very marked accent, but it was nothing like the
Quauhnahuatec," said Cohuanacotzin. "I was puzzled a good
deal over that. I am quite sure that he was not a man of the
Anahuacs at all, but he said nothing as to his place of origin and
I could not ask him. I am sure too that our civilization was new
to him, and yet that some form of the Nahua was his native
tongue."

"He must have been a Huitznahuatec," volunteered Yacanex,
not seriously, "for they speak a dialect of Nahua that was never
heard in the Anahuacs."

But Nonohualcatl failed to smile at that. . . .

When the time came for sleep, the Otomitl chose his place with
care; he, at least, had no intention that no watch should be kept.
He waited till the others seemed to be sleeping, then vanished
into the darkness without; two who were on the alert in the cave
saw nothing of his going. He went around the bend and toward
the barrier, feeling his way, and satisfied himself that none was
breathing in the gloom there. The moon crept over the cliff's edge
above, and soon her blue-gray witchcraft brought the barrier
into visibility. Nothing stirred up there.

A footfall from below sent the Otomitl deeper into the shadow
and close against the wall before the Topiltzin came into view.
There was no real reason why the Otomitl should be undiscovered; he was an ally, not a subject. The Culhuatec king's decision
against watch-keeping was, with respect to him, but as much as
to say, "We Toltecs will sleep; let your Godhead also spare
himself." But the Otomitl ever loved his own counsels too well to
part with them till he must. Nonohualcatl passed him and made
no sign, and he proceeded to watch for what might happen.

The Topiltzin advanced to within a few strides of the barrier
and stood still. The Otomitl could make out that his head was
thrown back as he scanned the Huitznahuatecs' work. Was he
going to attempt to climb it? For a moment his ally thought so
and prepared to come forth and stop the venture at any cost. A
great soldier—and one could not but love the man—but the dark
gods take this unmilitary spirit of risk-taking! However, after a

while, Nonohualcatl turned and came slowly down the canyon, relieving the Otomitl of his apprehensions. The latter followed him when he passed, as far as to the cave, and there ambushed himself to await the Topiltzin's return. Thus these two spent the night that was to be watchless: Nonohualcatl from time to time on guard against possible Huitznahuatec reconnoitering parties; the Otomitl on guard against rash doings by the Topiltzin. At dawn they were both in their places in the cave. And with daylight, they were astir: all three of them. Three, for Cohuanacotzin was missing. They were out in the canyon in search of him in a moment, the Topiltzin disturbed and alarmed, the Otomitl mainly ashamed that Cohuanacotzin could have cheated his vigilance. But he showed them the Culhuatec's tracks from cave mouth to barrier foot and made it evident that Cohuanacotzin had climbed the barrier and that he had not been captured down here. Huitznahuatecs had not been in the canyon during the night. What was to be done?

A sudden event provided the answer: nothing! For a great boulder fell from above onto the barrier, followed by another, and another. The enemy was at work on the cliff tops; there could be no passing the barrier or exploring it now. There must be a truce presently. They must parley, bargain for the return of the prisoner—"If they have not killed him," said the Topiltzin.

The Otomitl suggested that His Godhead consider that if they had killed him, they would probably have thrown down the body to tell us so. But Yacanetzin would have none of it. They were far more likely to spend the day feasting him and reciting poems in his honor. And very fine poems too—once you caught the trick of understanding them.

4

Cohuanacotzin's Adventure

Ever wary against his daredevil moods, the Culhuatec lords were
wont to watch over their Topiltzin, and none so carefully as his
closest friend, Cohuanacotzin. So when that one, chancing to
wake, missed Nonohualcatl from the cave, he came at once to
alertness and anxiety. The Human Camaxtli had, in truth, been
tempted to climb the barrier; it was just the sort of thing he
would do. Cohuanacotzin caught the thought and did not stay to
question it, but made straight for the barrier. Coming in sight of
it, he thought he saw something nequen-clad disappear over the
top. Moonlight cheats the senses; perhaps it was the shadow of
a wind-swayed tree he saw. He did not doubt where his duty lay.

The ascent was not too difficult. The moon served him till near
the top. Then came a tense darkness that made the last man-
height the worst; but he achieved it. And all the while, Nonohualcatl and the Otomitl were prowling in the canyon beyond the
cave. And now, where was the Topiltzin?

Cohuanacotzin gave an owl-cry that Nonohualcatl would understand, and as chance would have it, he was answered from in
front, perhaps by a real owl. His lord was ahead then, and
summoning him to follow. He dropped to hands and knees, the
only way to move in this thick darkness.

The ground seemed to be fairly even; the boulders dropped
had been well covered with earth. If the Huitznahuatecs had
abandoned their work at this stage, it would take no time to

surmount the barrier—even if they attempted defense, using the weapons the Toltecs had provided. He himself had left the war furnishings of half an eight thousand at the barrier's foot when he came as Culhuatec ambassador. (It was the League's custom thus to arm its enemies.) But arms would not serve here. Their true defense would be to go on dropping down— What was that? He crouched motionless. Could it have been breathing he had heard? No, the black night was soundless, tenantless. He felt his way forward again and crept on, and could not free himself from the feeling that he was not alone. He whispered once, twice, "My Topiltzin?" and, naturally, was not answered. But the darkness, he came to be certain, was full of silent motion that surrounded and went on with him. It could not be the Human Camaxtli or he would have answered; it could not be wild beasts, or he would smell them. Then it must be Huitznahuatecs. It was so dark that, passing his hand before his eyes, he could not see the movement of it. And then, as he felt forward cautiously, he touched— human flesh.

A foot. He was certain of that, although it had been withdrawn at once. He waited, breathless. Then, with infinite caution, he rose to his feet and felt out on this side and that, before and behind. On all sides there were nequen garments, covering human bodies; and he might call himself a prisoner. It was just as well, since presumably the Topiltzin was a prisoner too, and would need him.

With a laugh in his voice, he said, speaking slowly and clearly in view of Yacanetzin's report of their speech: "If your God-heads could produce a light—"

Several surprised voices answered. He could not make out what they said, but the tones were reassuring—as courteous and friendly as his own. And, by the Sun and Cipactli! for all their unfamiliarity, somehow familiar, waking an echo in his memory. Fire-sticks whirred; a little flame was born; soon torches were alight. He was in the midst of some twenty young men, unarmed and magnificent of physique; more than his equals in that way. His equals, too, he was quick to see, in other ways: They were nobles. Their faces were lit with interest and appeared quite friendly. They were his captors, of course, and he their prisoner;

but not until the next day did he realize that he had been the only
one there conscious of that.

"Your Godhead is a stranger here, a Toltec perhaps?"

So he made out their question and answered that he was; and
then it broke on him why their tones seemed familiar. Quanez of
Quauhnahuac used to speak with that accent. Surely! Quanez of
Quauhnahuac, of whom they had just now been talking in the
cave! Think of a man and— But it was miraculous if Yacanetzin's jest should prove to be truth and that Quanez was really a
Huitznahuatec!

They invited him to accompany them and showed solicitude in
lighting the way for him. They said—he was beginning to understand them now—that he was most fortunate to have come on
that night and at no other time, but surely Acamapitzin must
have known he was coming? Seeing that he was puzzled, they
went on to explain: The rocks usually were dropping night and
day, but Acamapitzin had ordered that on that night the work
was to stop and they were to remain on the barrier top. But he
had not told them why. His Godhead would see Acamapitzin in
the morning. That, they supposed, was what he would wish?

Cohuanacotzin postponed forming conclusions, but he took it
that the Topiltzin had not been captured; probably he had not
climbed the barrier at all. But . . . had this Huitznahuatec really
been Quanetzin's method of speech, or had the earlier talk in the
cave misled him into imagining it?

He slept out the night in a tent farther up the canyon, careless
as to whether he was guarded or not. In the early morning they
woke him; a litter and bearers were in waiting, and he was invited
to mount. It certainly was Yacanex, not the hierarch, who was
right about these people who thus made an honored guest of
their prisoner. He had not to persuade himself, but knew that he
was as safe with them, although caught spying, as an ambassador
would be in Culhuacan.

By daylight they were out on the plain, where now Huitznahuac had come northward; it was not the empty place it had
been. A small town stood by the riverside, and houses were
scattered elsewhere. To the little town they brought him. In the
open-room of its chief house, an old, most princely man rose to

greet him. He guessed rightly that this was the Acamapitzin his captors had spoken of, and he gave his own name in reply to the announcement of his host's name. Cohuanacotzin of Culhuacan. Acamapitzin's manner, which had been gravely courteous, took on some color of interest and cordiality, as if the name meant something pleasant to him.

When they had all breakfasted together, the young men went out, and with a certain reserve, Acamapitzin began to question his guest. "Your Godhead," said he, "is from the far north of the world, I think?"

"Your Godhead is not in error."

"I am glad it is you who has come." A long pause ensued. Then, "Of late, an ambassador came to us from those regions, from Huetzin, king of Tollan." He pronounced the names with some caution.

"Your Godhead has the names accurately. Yacanetzin of Tollan would have been with you in the month of Tepeilhuitl."

"And then came another."

"Another ambassador, in the month of Quecholli."

Acamapitzin was slow to go on, as if doubtful of how the next point should be presented. "Priests, perhaps, are but little honored in the Anahuacs?" he brought out at last.

"There your Godhead is mistaken. Priests are highly honored in all civilized lands." There was something of conventionality in his tones, though.

"In the Anahuacs there is a practice called 'war'?"

That startled Cohuanacotzin, who, in spite of Yacanex's report, had settled it in his mind that the great gentleman he was talking with, who certainly would imply no falsehood, was also a great soldier. Acamapitzin's mien and bearing evidenced it, and there was that grand piece of engineering in the canyon to confirm the impression.

"War?" said he. "Yes. It is the Toltec League's custom to punish by war peoples who oppose or disobey the wisdom of our kings."

"And your Godhead has come with the kings of the Toltec League to punish us of Huitznahuac?"

"It is true that my sovereign has come to include your God-head's country in the domains of the League."

"Your Godhead's word was 'punish.' We are wondering for what crimes the Huitznahuatecs are to be punished."

"Your Godhead drives me to embarrassment. But did not the king and queen of Huitznahuac insult the ambassador of the Otomi Republic?"

"Your Godhead then thinks that it would be possible to insult . . . that person?"

It was a hit, expressing an opinion not uncommon in Culhua-can itself. Cohuanacotzin recovered with, "I also came here as an ambassador, your Godhead, but you refused to receive me."

Acamapitzin was startled in his turn. "It was your Godhead who left the gifts in the canyon? Then we did unwisely; we did ill." He drew in and blew out a cloud of yetl smoke, and another. "And your Godhead is Cohuanacotzin of Culhuacan, and you are a friend of the king of that city. But not, I think, of the Priest of Teotihuacan?"

"Your Godhead asks—"

"There was a Lord Quanetzin, said to be of Quauhnahuac—"

"Your Godhead knows Quanetzin?"

Acamapichtli rose, Cohuanacotzin thought, with the shadow of a smile in his eyes. Said he: "An affront was given, and now amends must be made. Your Godhead will deign to ride into the city, where the king will make amends for the affront."

His manner said so clearly that the conversation was closed that the Culhuatec, bewildered a little, found nothing to say. The litter outside, to which Acamapitzin led him, was a closed one, for the morning was gray and sweet-aired with the expectation of rain. The bearers had prepared for it by discarding hats and tilmatlies; they would run in mashtlies and sandals alone.

While the litter was crossing the plain, the air darkened and filled with moisture, and a cool wind rose. The Huitznahuatec hills, when they reached them, glowed heavily green under the wild slate-purple of heaven. To Cohuanacotzin, there seemed nothing unfriendly in these aspects; it was as if the Tlalocs of this far southland had been gods of his own; they were as companion-able as their human Others, the Huitznahuatecs, the friendliest of mankind. He had settled it in his mind by this time that Quanez, called of Quauhnahuac, must have been Huitznahuatec. How else should Acamapitzin know about him?

Then the Tlalocs spoke. Rain leaped out of the air; its silver spears aimed themselves at the greenness, hid away hills and trees with its glinting opacity, rioted and rejoiced over the world. Were the young men not to consider themselves and take shelter? —Not unless his Godhead insisted. For their part, they were on splendid terms with the mountain Tlalocs, who loved mankind. They spoke with sincerity, and the Culhuatec, thinking of floods in the north, which often slew men and beasts, wondered. He thanked them and begged them to follow their inclinations, using the terms of courtesy: the "your Godhead" that at home one used only to equals or superiors, but that here seemed appropriate for all. There could be no danger, he thought, if they felt there was none.

He wondered whether they knew that he belonged to the host that had come to conquer their country and that he was a prisoner of war. Clearly, they had little understanding of what was taking place. They themselves, he supposed, would be killed, or enslaved, presently. There were unattractive aspects even to war, he was surprised to find himself thinking. But great human ends often worked themselves out through the sufferings of individuals. Nothing could count against the supreme advantage of being brought under the just and civilized Toltec rule.

So they brought him into Huitznahuacan, and up to the House of the Kings.

"Cohuanacotzin, my friend!"

"Quanetzin of Quauhnahuac!"

Nopal laughed. "Yes, in the Anahuacs. But here, Nopal, the queen's husband." He turned to Chimalman. "Cohuanacotzin rescued me from the priests."

Her welcome to him had in it a womanly cordiality and affection, but with some leaven of queenly reserve. "Your Godhead comes here as an ambassador?" she asked.

But no, he did not. He was, in fact, a prisoner of war. Or worse still: To be exact, he was an enemy caught spying. "In the Anahuacs, I should be put to death. Only, now that I find there is no

war between us and that my Topiltzin is your Godheads' devoted
friend—"

"Your Godhead is our friend, Cohuanacotzin. But the Topiltzin . . . has he come with his armies?" This from Nopal.

"He has come, but by the Sun and Cipactli, he has not come against Nopaltzin-Quanetzin of Huitznahuac-Quauhnahuac!"

"Would it make a difference? Would he not attack any land that remained unconquered?"

"Never think it! When he finds that your Godhead is king here, he will propose paying Huitznahuac a yearly tribute. Only last night he was talking of you, of his longing to find you."

"Your Godhead will take him the news?" asked Chimalman.

"It is the first thing that must be done. You will come with me tomorrow, Nopaltzin? The Human Camaxtli must see his deliverer with his own eyes."

But then the hierarch's bitterness came to his mind, and his report of the insult he had received in Huitznahuac: a complication that might make the happy issue less easy to come at, if only slightly. And there was Acamapitzin's cryptic question about the possibility of insulting such a man. Cohuanacotzin determined to come to the heart of things at once, to break through the reserve he felt in their cordiality.

"Would it displease your Godheads to tell me what happened when the Otomi ambassador came?"

They told him. Of the massacre of their embassy on the Road, and of Yen Ranho's guilt in the matter. "And we decided that none should come into Huitznahuac from the north."

His face paled at the story, then darkened with anger. He was aghast and furious by turns; not even of Yen Ranho could he have believed this. And yet he did believe; he had no option. The one feature of the League that no Toltec gentleman, except for religious King Huemac, loved too well was the alliance with the Otomi priesthood; with the military side of the Republic, they were friendly enough—the military had their code and their religion of war, their point of honor and their punctilious observances. But every fine traditional instinct in this Culhuatec gentleman was outraged, and violently, by the priest's crime.

"It must be atoned for," he said when all was told. "My

Topiltzin will know what to do; the Otomitl will be the first to demand the criminal's life. Yes, there will be full atonement." His mind kept harping on that, and the thought framed itself, "Unless Yen Ranho is executed, I will pay for it with my own life." But no, they said; Huitznahuac would have none slain. To kill the priest would not right the wrong, but make it wronger: a point of view that Cohuanacotzin did not understand. So they dismissed the matter; Nopal would go with him to the Topiltzin in the morning. In the meanwhile, they made much of him.

5
The Hierarch Acquires Information

The Otomitl might be judged to have been secretive; he was, perhaps, not more so than a great soldier ought to be. If he was judged also an honest fellow, it is well. Many had had good from him; none, but in the way of his business, harm.

Being an honest fellow, without personal ambitions and incapable—except in the science of tactics—of plotting, some part of his mind had been vaguely troubled by the hierarch's presence with the army. War was a soldier's job, not a priest's. It was the greatest of sciences; more, it was an art capable of evoking the best of which one's wits and will were capable. Killing was no essential part of it. You did kill people, but you must not blame war for that.

Someday, when the whole world had grown civilized, common sense would prevail, and undesirable features would disappear. Then, when the war season came, the League would march out under a great strategist, its Topiltzin, and a great tactician, its Otomitl, and seize fine positions in the territories of enemies who, realizing their military and cultural inferiority, would do the sensible thing and thereafter enjoy the blessings of Toltec-Otomi rule. Thus the whole world would be at last united: an end surely to be desired.

Meanwhile, what one had to do was to make the best use of one's faculties and to give the weight of one's opinion toward achieving magnanimous terms for a conquered nation. An

enemy, in any case, was a man to whom you had much to be
thankful for; there was no sense at all in hating him. When hatred
came into it, the pleasure had gone from war. Without an enemy,
how could one exercise one's art? Rather should the enemy be
loved than hated; respected; held to be noble; so, surely, should
the greater glory accrue to his conqueror.

But hatred had been brought in here, and by His Godhead,
Yen Ranho, and by religion—a matter that ought to be kept
clear of war. Or rather—how shall one put it?—every true war
had, of course, its plain and honest religious motive: desire to
extend the power, glory, and dominion of the Toltec-Otomi
gods. The hierarch had, no doubt, his own ideas as to the nature
of these gods; but to a soldier's way of thinking, they must be
held to be magnanimous. Why, then, should Yen Ranho be
injecting what would blur the cleanness of our warfare, foment-
ing hatred against the Huitznahuatecs? Why could not the hierarch have stayed at home?

The Otomitl would have been still more disquieted had he
known what went forward in the hierarch's tent on the day he
spent with the Topiltzin in the canyon. Yen Ranho needed information that day, and he had his own means for acquiring it.

The Blue-Hummingbird Pygmies dwelt northeast of Forgotten Plain, a league or so into the forest. They were a wonderful
people in their way. Yen Ranho feasted the tribe on the river-
bank near his tent and selected one of them as being likely to
serve his purpose. He gave them potations so marvelous that it
was a wonder so much of blissful heaven could slide down the
gullet of man. They were a great-eyed people, with a look of
seeing into the secrecies of night in the forest; and this Ikak,
whom the hierarch chose, had more of the look than any. His
imbibings were different from the others', and more blissful.
Where they were sodden in common drunkenness, he was let
loose into space, a bodiless delight floating and soaring. *He,* or
his body, was carried into the hierarch's tent; *they* were kicked
and rolled down to the water's edge by humorous Otomi soldiers, put on boats, rowed down and dumped unceremoniously
in their own part of the forest, or somewhere near it.

In the tent, the hierarch remained with the entranced body of the pygmy during the rest of that day and the night that followed. Those on guard about the tent knew that Yen Ranho was not to be disturbed.

No one ever knew what sorceries went forward there to bring about what happened. What Ikak remembered was that he flew through the air along the canyon, watching four men, noting every action, aye, and every thought of them, seeing all they saw and understanding all they said. Then, as he remembered, he followed one of them over the barrier, to Acamapitzin's house by the river, to Huitznahuacan and into the palace, hearing, seeing and understanding all. What Yen Ranho got from it was the knowledge he wanted.

There was some talk that the voices of those whom the pygmy watched spoke audibly through the pygmy's entranced lips; some talk of all he saw being reflected—in the air, in a mirror, in a pool of blood—for the hierarch personally to see. This, history does not know; there were mysteries, and unclean ones, not wholesome to be recorded.

Blue-Hummingbird Ikak never saw his forest home again. When he—that is, his body, with himself in it by that time—left the hierarch's tent, it was to take the way his soul had taken in the trance, or in part of it. He went as far as to that platform on the cliff's face, over against the barrier that the Otomitl had found, and noted that an arrow might be shot from it to kill a man on the barrier's top.

Blue-Hummingbird Ikak went by night, armed with a bow and a sufficiency of poisoned shafts.

6

Cohuanacotzin's Return

Early in the morning after his arrival in Huitznahuacan, Cohuanacotzin set out on his return to the Toltec camp; Nopal, of course, was accompanying him.

The Culhuatec had his reasons for hurrying. Today the army would begin to move, and it would be as well to get their business done with the Human Camaxtli before any major steps had been taken. Not that it would make much difference to Nonohualcatl, who might be relied upon to turn his war plans into an immediate ovation for Quanez of Quauhnahuac. But Cohuanacotzin himself was a general, and hated irregular ways.

The sun came up over Mishcoatepetl as they left the House of the Kings, which was still in shadow, although the Calmecac roof across the arena shone gilt with morning. Chimalman was for showing her guest the city. She would walk down with them to the Townmouth; they should take litters there. Nopal, who knew what the Culhuatec was used to in the way of urban grandeur, was amusedly pleased to help acquaint him with another kind of city; he felt that he knew Cohuanacotzin well enough to believe that he would appreciate its quality.

So down they went by the Street of the Quechol: Chimalman, gay and unreservedly friendly now, explaining; Nopal smilingly watching; Cohuanacotzin touched strangely by the dear little place he saw, with its wonderful atmosphere of quietness and clarity. The Street of the Quechol was rain-washed like the air, and here and there sunlit. Its twists and windings, landings and stairways, were engaging, as were the gardens on either side, accessible up steps or down steps, and the houses scattered throughout. All was clean, well-kept and prosperous-looking; here and there an early riser was at work among the plants and shrubs, and every face was aglow with that strange Huitznahuatec friendliness. It all confirmed in him the idea that he had come among a people simpler, nobler, and sweeter than one could find in the north, and he was happy to believe it. What joy the Human Camaxtli would have in these newly discovered royalties of the far south: the king, his savior of old; the queen, so amazingly sovereign and girlish! How, above all, the Divine Princess would delight in her, should they come to meet, as, heaven knew, now that things had taken this turn, they well might. . . .

For Nonohualcatl would be little content not to come down this way, long as the journey might be, as often as affairs allowed; and this royal pair, no doubt, would be seen at times in the Anahuacs. There was a vitality in this Huitznahuacan that made one walk like a boy again. It might be, after all, that its innocence of war had kept the country holy. A month in the south, one suspects, would have quite converted Cohuanacotzin from his belief in war.

At the posthouse in the Townmouth, litters and bearers were awaiting them; also deer and jaguar skins to wrap about themselves against the chill of the early morning. So there Cohuanacotzin took leave of the queen of Huitznahuac—for the day, perhaps, or for two days. Tomorrow, or the next day, he would surely return, most likely with his sovereign, or else their Godheads would be his sovereign's guests at the camp. Until then, then!

Taking leave of her husband, the radiant queen whispered to him, "The Divine Companion go with you!"

They started out at a good pace; some of the best runners in Huitznahuac were carrying them. It was a morning of mornings for seeing that country, with the most gracious of suns lighting diamonds everywhere. The Culhuatec found himself in love with the scenes he passed through, half wishing that this mountain land were his own. So he told Nopal; by no means speaking insincerely. There was something piquantly magical about it, an antiquity, a romance, a gentleness; it seemed to share in its people's fineness and kindness, to bear some kind of spiritual affinity with their character.

Cohuanacotzin had met many Huitznahuatecs in the House of the Kings the night before, and he had been quite alive to their quality. It was the same quality that had made him love Quanetzin at Tollan and on the way thither, a couple of years and more ago. He was convinced that that quality would be universal here; that go where he might among these mountains, he would meet Nopals and Chimalmans, Acamapitzins and Acatonatzins—women and men to respect, wonder at, and love.

Well, from this time out, the Topiltzin would, of course, keep an ambassador at Huitznahuacan; might he be the man! He told Nopal of this hope of his as they rode side by side between the hills and the river. Nopal reciprocated the wish earnestly and spoke of it to the litter-bearers, and they too joined in it; they were well within the circle of their king's and his guest's friendship. So they passed on through the Northern District and across the plain.

At his house by the river, they gave their news to Acamapitzin, who then signaled word up into the mountains that work on the barrier was to stop. He had his means of thus giving orders: men stationed within sight and hearing of each other from there to the mountainside and to Huitznahuacan, who by daylight backed their shouts with the sign-language and by night with torch signals. The old prince's relief startled Cohuanacotzin, who still could not quench the feeling that this was a man born for war preeminently, by nature a very great soldier. It made him eager to introduce Acamapitzin to the Human Camaxtli; he was not sure but that those two were the most warriorlike men living. He urged therefore that the prince should accompany them to the Human Camaxtli's camp, which Acamapitzin was very ready to do.

Cohuanacotzin had great delight in Acamapitzin now. What reserve there had been yesterday, on both sides, was gone, and he saw that the prince's great strength was founded on gentleness and benevolence. He might be akin, indeed, to Nonohualcatl;

nature might have designed him to be a conqueror, but— Warfare as an ideal went receding in the consciousness of Cohuanacotzin; his conversion was proceeding apace. They must both, he said, take advantage of the Topiltzin's return northward to visit the Anahuacs. They must be his guests, supposing the Human Camaxtli would allow anyone less than himself to play host to them. They should see the world in a manner that Nopaltzin had had no opportunity to see it when there, for they would move courted among the great, and not in disguise among the trades. He made no mention of Yen Ranho, and kept himself from thinking of religious Huemac's friendship with that priest. But he spoke of Yacanetzin of Tollan and his admiration for what he had seen in Huitznahuac, and of the Otomitl, who would convince them that his race produced fine gentlemen, worthy of their friendship. And he spoke of the Divine Princess and of his desire that she should come to know the queen of Huitznahuac.

Thus cheerfully conversing, they rode through the canyon as far as to the tent where the Culhuatec had slept out on the night of his capture. There the youths who had captured him had prepared lunch for them. They met as old friends. In a happy mood, he gave them the news that their king was counted a great hero in the Anahuacs and that there would be no attack on their country. They replied that they had known it was for some happy purpose that he had come to Huitznahuac, and they could not make enough of him.

"Is the rope ladder ready?" asked Acamapitzin. It was; nothing remained but to lower it. "Let your Godhead see to that," he ordered one of the young men, who then went out barrierward. "And when we are down, let the bearers follow, and then lower the litters to us."

That would not be difficult to do, they said; they had the ropes and tackle in place. So then all climbed the slope to the top of the barrier. —And now, has any man been seen down there this morning? —None, nor yet yesterday. —All well then; it is but to make the descent.

"Your Godheads must allow me to precede you," said the Culhuatec. "Should any of our people appear there before we are all down, it would be as well for them to find me, and not either of you, there."

They saw the force of his argument and begged him to proceed. But they did not see Blue-Hummingbird Ikak on the platform over against them, nor the bowstring drawn back to his shoulder.

Cohuanacotzin stepped forward to the top of the ladder.

Pat, pat, pat, came the arrows. A cry of horror issued from the Huitznahuatecs. But between the second pat and the third, old Acamapitzin, lightning-swift, while the arrow that killed him was flying, shot the shaft that killed the pygmy, and fell.

7
Nopal Returns

Nopal, since his marriage that had made him king, had been
filling the royal office of Market Magistrate, leaving Acamapitzin
free to direct the work on his barrier. The morning he rode out
with the Culhuatec to visit the Topiltzin being that of a market
day, Chimalman determined to take his place. There was a certain grave brilliance about the queen that morning: a new aspect
with her, to be accounted for perhaps by the ending of this
trouble with the Toltecs.

She found no difficulty in her duties in the marketplace; with
the help of the clerks of the market, she mastered the whole
business of it before she had been there half an hour. It was a
very different affair now from what it had been; even the clerks
were women. One never saw a man under fourscore in the marketplace; it was women who brought in the foodstuffs from the
farms, and women who, after what was needed in the town had
been taken from it, bore the rest out in litters to the mountainside, where all Huitznahuac was at work. From the districts
north of the town, the farm produce was taken there direct, and
not brought to Huitznahuacan at all.

At noon, because of these abnormal conditions, the work was
finished and the market closed; and Chimalman went home,
crossing, however, to the north side on the way and seeking there
Shaltemoc's house. That was because she wanted Pelashil, the
need being on her, for some reason, for the company of a small
child.

"May I have her until the evening, Ketlashotzin?"

"But she will be a trouble to your Royal Godhead," the mother expostulated.

Expectable protestations on both sides followed, which ended with the queen's capturing Pelashil and marching off with the mite in her arms. When she had gone, Ketlasho made note of the cause of her changed appearance. Chimalman's hair was done up in a pile on the top of her head, in wife-fashion; but yesterday she had been still wearing it, although married these many months, hanging loose on her shoulders, maidenwise. Well, queens determined their fashions for themselves!

Through the afternoon Chimalman devoted herself whole-heartedly to entertaining her small guest with songs and stories and picture-books. The theme of all of them was the life—and lives—of Quetzalcoatl: his victory over the Sun and the doom it imposed on him, that he should incarnate among men from age to age; his rejection, life after life, by the people he would save; his unending purpose that would triumph at last.

They dwelt in that high story, Chimalman inspired with the reality of it, Pelashil listening, eyes wide with wonder. It mingled with a kind of love new to the heart of the queen: mother love. She had had joy in Pelashil before, but now it was different. . . . And she was to trust, and go on trusting, in the gods who trusted in her. How near the gods were to her today!

In the evening, she took the child home to Ketlasho; then she had the whim to go down to the Townmouth, to meet possible news from the canyon and the Topiltzin's camp. She did not expect that Nopal would return today. No, the Topiltzin would keep him for a while; Cohuanacotzin had said so. But something, through her high mood and faith, she expected.

At the Townmouth, the posthouse master's wife, now in charge there, showed a desire to keep her chatting for a while; and she, expecting news now in some keen way, was compliant.

"Your Royal Godhead brings such serenity," the woman said. "It is as if our Lord himself were here."

But she had no more than seated the queen before sounds of a party coming townward from the north called her away, and as she left Chimalman, she mused, "As if our Lord himself were here . . . our Lord Quetzalcoatl, the Divine Companion . . . Take refuge there now, Queen of Huitznahuac! Fortify yourself in the knowledge of that Wonder-Presence!"

Chimalman became aware of lowered voices, with something ominous in their tones. But the woman had been right; it *was* as if our Lord himself were here—the Divine Companion, who had come down with her and Nopal from Tlalocan. So real, so actual now, that should she turn her head, she might see him; should she reach out her hand, it might be clasped. . . .

"Your Royal Godhead!"

At her side stood the posthouse mistress, such a look of grief on her face as Chimalman had never before seen on human countenance. Chimalman rose and took her in her arms, eager to provide comfort, her lofty mood turned now into instant compassion. But the woman's tears, it seemed, were mainly for Chimalman.

"Your Royal Godhead must be prepared, my darling—"

"Come, dear soul," said the queen. "I will go; I will see to it."

She went out with the weeping woman, accompanied by . . . Overshadowing Divinity? She had no tears to shed—not even when she saw the burden the litter-bearers bore.

She issued orders quietly and incisively. To one, "Take a message to Ishmishutzin Teteoinan that the king is sick and needs her instantly at the House of the Kings".

Others had come beside the litter-bearers, to meet such a need as this. One of them she sent up in haste to Eeweesho and Ocotosh, to bid them prepare. Then, "Come," she said. "We dare not delay; you shall tell me later."

What she was told later was, of course, of the arrows shot by the tzitzimitl: the first, that had killed Cohuanacotzin; the second, that had grazed Nopal's shoulder; the third, that had slain Acamapitzin.

8

Nonohualcatl's Anger

Cohuanacotzin had risen early to go to his Topiltzin; his Topiltzin had risen even earlier to send in search of him. The sun rose
over the camp on Forgotten Plain to find it the scene of great
activity: the army, to the last man, on parade in full splendor of
accoutrement; the Human Camaxtli, a figure of glinting glory,
enthroned to review it.

They had built a triple throne facing north over the wide space
that Cocotzin had left open for drill field and parade ground: a
raised dais ascendable on either side by flights of steps; highest
in the middle, where the Topiltzin's seat cushions were set; with
lower levels to right and left, where were the seat cushions of his
allies of Tollan and Otompan.

Here these three sat now, with the Culhuatec guard below
surrounding them, to watch regiment after regiment thunder
past at their quickest pace, the wolf-run; all of them encased in
their cotton mail and tossing up in salute hands that held their
regiment's favorite weapon—bows or spears or javelins or hardwood swords—and shouting, an endless musical shout taken up
by rank after rank as they came by; now swelling into bass
thunder according to the privilege of this regiment, now sinking
into sweetness according to the duty of that—the Toltec Zacuans, for example, whose business was rather to sing their com-
rades into battle than to take any foremost part in it themselves.

And then the sound would change from song to squall as the

Otomi Jaguars followed in their cloaks of jaguar skin, their hardwood helmets carved to a likeness of the head of that jungle topiltzin and terror of the woods; and from that to an eagle's bark with the coming of Huemac's Quauhtlis and Cozcaquauhtlis, eagles and vultures, the first eagle wing helmeted, the second helmeted hideously like their namesakes of the air. They came late onto a battlefield and cleaned things up as cozcaquauhtli cleans up a skeleton.

Then came Otomi Tlilcuetzpalins, with their curious, swaying, lizardlike rush and the scalelike green lizard-glitter that art had imparted to their cotton mail; and the Culhuatec Thunderbolts, and Ometochtlis—strict and sober men, these last, for all that they were named after Two-Rabbits, God of Drunkards and Drunkenness. For it was said that to express the stupidity of the drunkard, you had to double that of the stupidest creature living, the rabbit; but Ometochtli acquired a certain fell dignity when considered as a peril to mankind, and the name of the regiment signified that it was as dangerous as pulque to the Human Camaxtli's enemies.

Regiment after regiment, they came past and took up their stations in order: the armies of Culhuacan, Otompan and Tollan. Before mid-morning, a great part of them was on the march. A regiment was to go west with Huetzin into those barren mountains from which the Little Gods originally came, to seek in that direction a feasible way into Huitznahuac. A regiment was to cross the river and go east, under the Otomitl, with the same end in view. Three regiments of sappers and miners under Yacanetzin were to advance at once into the canyon. Arrived at the barrier's foot, Yacanetzin would signal to the Huitznahuatecs, learn the fate of Cohuanacotzin and negotiate for his return. Yacanetzin was the man to do it, being famed in the Topiltzin's circle as the Huitznahuatecs' friend. . . . Nonohualcatl himself had much to do in the camp.

Late that night a runner bearing a pictoscript letter from Yacanetzin in the canyon arrived before Nonohualcatl's pavilion and demanded access to him. A secretary came out from the inner recesses and brought the man before Nonohualcatl, who was seated smoking among the cushions of a low divan, dictating orders to seven scribes, expert pictographers. Each of these wrote according to his individual genius; thus, with seven versions for the receivers to compare, there could be no doubt as to the imperial meaning.

Nonohualcatl took the letter, glanced at it, scrutinized it with face grown rigid. Then he called to the first of the scribes and gave it to him, bidding him read it and pass it on to each of the others in turn. Each groaned as he read it.

"Now," said the Topiltzin, "what is it that Yacanetzin reports? What is this that has happened?"

"May the glory radiate!" said the first scribe. "It is news too foul for divine ears."

"Yet must your ears hear it. Speak!"

"The Huitznahuatecs have murdered Cohuanacotzin, and thrown his body from the barrier-top."

"Go!" said the Topiltzin. "Wait in the pavilion; I shall need you presently."

His face was drawn and taut; it was not the insult to his dignity that he was feeling then, but the loss of his friend. Of all his subjects, Cohuanacotzin was the one he loved and trusted most, the one who was nearer to him, and more like-minded, than even Huemac, his brother. That had been so ever since their school days. His grief was not long in changing to anger, however.

The drums were beating soon; at once the plain was covered with lights and with the grumbling of drums. The Topiltzin would do honor to his friend before he avenged his death. So all night the army was at work: cutting trees in the far-off forest and building a pyre on the plain. He would have everyone at work, for the pyre should be gigantic. He himself felled trees, striking grimly and savagely. None slept or breakfasted till all was over. He set the torch to the pyre at sunrise and dedicated himself, as he did so, to his new and bitter purpose. It was a grim and sullen Topiltzin, whom none had seen before.

Afterward, when the camp was resting, orders were sent abroad and up the canyon. No communication was to be held with the Huitznahuatecs; no faith was to be kept with them. They were to be killed without quarter or question. Written messages from them, should they attempt to send any, were to be burned unread by the finders; nothing from them was to come to the Topiltzin, or to any of his generals or officers. And when the time came, all Huitznahuatecs were to be exterminated. Meanwhile, where was the man who could take Cohuanacotzin's place? The *only* man in all the Anahuacs who could take his place? He had worn nequen in the Culhuacan marketplace; he might be wearing a private soldier's uniform in the army now. Search was made, but Quanez of Quauhnahuac was not in the army. Swift runners started north; search was to be made throughout the Anahuacs. Quanez was to be sent to the Topiltzin. The desire to have him there grew in Nonohualcatl's mind as the days passed. Superstition entered into it; he could not succeed without Quanez. It became a passion with him, as strong as his passion for revenge.

The camp was a sad and silent place. The son of Mishcoatl Mazatzin, whom none could help loving, had gone; in his place was a Human Camaxtli none too human. . . .

9

Road and Barrier

Cocotzin was again in command on Forgotten Plain; headquarters had been removed into the canyon. At a wide lateral break in it, whence vistas of peak and precipice were to be seen, among the fruit trees by a stream Nonohualcatl had pitched his tent. Daily he sent out scouts into the heights and kept them searching, searching and searching; and based on their reports, he issued new commands and plans. He pressed the work against the barrier; thought out, contrived and fashioned new means of hurling energies against the barrier; nursed his will for revenge; hated the Huitznahuatecs; and waited anxiously for Quanez, or news of Quanez, to arrive from the Anahuacs.

The scouts sought among the high precipices for a way through, and sought in vain. The gods who loved Huitznahuac had made it inaccessible except through the canyon. Runners, too, came in from Huemac and from the Otomitl, who had gone groping west and east seeking a passage; they brought the same message always. West and east, the mountains had pushed those generals back northward, and no passage was to be found.

From the Topiltzin's pavilion to Forgotten Plain, the canyon was one long camp, filled with regiments, whose quarters always left room for a continuous stream of food-litters to pass. Their route lay between headquarters and the barrier. Relays worked there day and night digging out sections in the canyon walls; a man to every stride and a half. With the earth dug out, they filled baskets, each of a size to contain a man's load; then came other regiments in files, two endless processions. They shouldered the baskets and bore them south as far as to the bend in the canyon where one came in sight of the barrier, there and on the way emptying them, till the road had a new level and sloped upward to that point. And still and always came the two processions, and the tons and tons of earth; and still and always the level of the road went rising. From the road-head thus raised, new tons were emptied down into the canyon, and the road-head drew nearer to the barrier.

And day by day, the barrier-top was raised also. The Toltec officers in charge at the road-head rarely saw men at work up there; but always the great rocks came down, then the cataracts of earth that filled in the spaces and made a bed for the next boulders. As far as they could see, the falling rocks never rolled or jumped, but sat at once where they were meant to be: in front, where one could see them; or behind, where one could but hear their thuds. "With the start they have," thought the officers, "it will take us an age to catch up with them."

And whilst they thus looked up and thought, the endless files of men came on with their basketloads, dropped by the way or dropped from the road-head, trodden down hard by other endless files of men; and the road-head advanced and mounted. How was it that the officers could stand there superintending, and the endless files come up with their loads, and never a shaft or a boulder was directed at them by the enemy? They might make what havoc they would here, thought the Toltec officers, if they dropped their rocks from farther up the mountainside. Let the gods see that they will not think of it!

A great shield of basketwork and quilted cotton had been prepared to shelter the men at the road-head from arrows, but it was discarded after a while as a hindrance: No arrows came. The Topiltzin himself was often at the road-head, in all the blaze of his imperial accoutrements; but though the enemy might have stationed sharpshooters at a score of safe points, never a shaft was aimed at him. He was hate-blinded against understanding, or he might have guessed that they had no desire to harm him or his people, that they could never be made to think the killing of men justifiable. In truth, it was a tzitzimitl, and not a human being, that Acamapitzin had shot at and killed.

The Huitznahuatecs had nothing in their own nature by which to interpret their enemies' mood. They divined, indeed, some appalling, incomprehensible inhumanity in the northern peoples that made it necessary to keep them out, and for that reason, they raised their barrier. But they made excuses for the Toltecs; their feeling for them was pity, not hatred. Perhaps it was only here, and in relation to Huitznahuac, that by some unlucky star influence, they became evil. In their own land, and under proper conditions, perhaps these killings would not be committed. And perhaps they would tire of their will to enter Huitznahuac long before the rocks on the mountainside gave out.

The Toltecs practiced war, they had heard; and war meant killing. But that could be only a legend. They had had Cohuana-cotzin's word for it that the Toltec king would condemn and abhor the murders in the forest; and it was a tzitzimitl who had done the murders they had seen; and it could not have been the Toltecs who had set the tzitzimitl on, because the first it had killed had been the Toltec Cohuanacotzin. . . .

On with the work then. Drop the rocks and raise the barrier; it was for the Toltecs' own good, since here they worked only evil! The princes murdered; King Nopaltzin lying between death and life with his wound. It would take generations to get the poison of these times out of their memories; generations of the old, clean, quiet peace—and hard work every waking moment now.

Why the poisoned arrow that grazed Nopal's shoulder had not been quite effective, none knew. Those arrows were designed to kill if they but scratched the skin. Perhaps a god, for his own purposes, interfered to delay things. Cohuanacotzin fell down into the canyon, Acamapitzin on the barrier-top.

"I am not hurt," Nopal had said. "A scratch—nothing!" But before they had laid him on a litter, he was vomiting and staggering; and then he fell.

Not a Huitznahuatec in all time had heard of, or conceived of, the possibility of poisoned arrows; but a youth came forward who behaved as if he had. He threw back his prostrate king's tilmatli then and there, saw the wound, and sucked it for his life. No one knew what his action may have served; all were inclined to fall back on divine intervention. Nopal was still alive when they brought him into the House of the Kings, but the youth who had sucked his wound was dead.

And since then the king had lain wasting in a kind of trance, and the queen had reigned from his bedside, fighting for his life, with Ishmishutzin, the Teteoinan-priestess and chief repository of Huitznahuatec medical science, for her aide. Acatonatzin, priest of Tezcatlipocâ, took command on the mountainside, with Shollo and Shaltemoc, Nopal's brother and brother-in-law, for his chief lieutenants.

The work was not allowed to suffer by the loss of Acamapitzin. The barrier-top went on rising; all Huitznahuac was intent to hasten its rise. There was but one will in the country: The north should be kept out. But the road-head went on rising too, as the files of men came up and and dropped their basketloads of earth. Acatonatzin, watching, saw that sooner or later, if they kept on, road-head and barrier-top must reach the mountainside above. Or perhaps—for sometimes the road-head gained on him, so furiously did Nonohualcatl impel his Toltecs to their work—they would come to where they could climb onto the barrier-top. If so, work here must be stopped and no more boulders thrown down: He could not risk killing them. Oh, that he could afford to draft men from here into the south; into the far, unknown south beyond Quinatepetl and Eagle Mountain, there to build a new Huitznahuacan where the Toltecs could never come!

The road-head had risen to a certain height and turned the bend, so that now it faced the barrier. Nonohualcatl came up on his morning visit. "Phew!" said he. "What a vile stench is here!" Up came the files and poured down their earth in front. Up came the files and emptied their earth at his feet. He stepped up onto the earth thus last emptied out and saw what lay on a shelf in the cliff face now level with his head. "Empty your baskets there and cover it," he said.

Although he thought no more of it then, the significance of the remains of Blue-Hummingbird Ikak was perhaps lodged in his mind. A dead forest pygmy, the arrow in his breast of a different type from the arrows on the shelf beside him: a picture perhaps later to be remembered . . . and understood.

10

Civacoatzin's Message

When the first of the Topiltzin's hosts passed southward, Nauh-yo, watching from the Puma's Head, saw them as they came down the Hill of Derision, and called Quauhtli to come see. Quauhtli could make nothing of the procession beyond that it was a new thing. But when the Road had quite lost its loneliness, and go where you would along its length, troops of bearers passed you, their litters piled high with heaven knew what, Quauhtli thought of his last night at Eagle Hermitage, and of what Nopal had told him then about the warring kings of the north. Before long, he had guessed what was going forward.

One day he all but came out upon a camp that was being built in Ahuacatl Glade, which soon became the site of huge activities. The strangers felled trees and built storehouses there; also a rest-house of some pretensions, and lodgment for many men. About half of the bearers who came there, he judged, left their loads and returned northward; the rest went on. He spent much time watching them from secure places along the forest edge and soon found that there were others beside bearers on the Road. They came in from the north, rested the night and went on south, and more came to fill their places in the barracks. They traveled in regular formation and moved to drummed or shouted commands; they carried dangerous-looking things that were . . . weapons of war, he divined.

From the moment he first heard these people speak, a curiosity as to their language awoke in him. Soon there were words he understood. Presently he was catching sentences, and realizing that it was intelligible Nahua, he set himself to mastering the trick of it. He had no doubt but that it was the Nahua of the Toltecs; had not Nopal told him that they spoke the Nahua language? Only, they spoke it slurred and softly, Nopal had said, and not with the grand and crashing mountain tones of the Huitznahuatecs.

One day Quauhtli took Coshcana with him to listen to it and found that he had surmised correctly. Coshcana had lived among the Toltecs years ago and had known their language thoroughly, and the knowledge came back to him when he listened to the soldiers for a while. After that, Quauhtli took lessons from him, foreseeing that he would have need to speak as the Toltecs did.

Ever since the day of the massacre, he had been thinking that as soon as Nauhyo was well enough, it would be his duty to take him back to Huitznahuacan, seeing that it was in Nopal's charge the Master had left him. But then this change in the Road's habit intervened, and farther southward there might be war—heaven knew what. Under the circumstances, he would not risk traveling with Nauhyo.

And where could they be taking this war business but to Huitznahuac? he reasoned—since there was nothing but forest between this and that. War, in Huitznahuac: an easy thing to say; but Quauhtli's imagination, confronted with the seemingly unbelievable was a slow traveler. War meant man-killing on a great scale, Nopal had told him. But how could that be done in Huitznahuac? Those you intended to kill must surely have the same intention toward you. Still, there was much room for anxiety.

And then, Coshcana was wise and true, and Nauhyo loved him, and he Nauhyo. Coshcana could take care of Nauhyo. . . .

Thus gradually Quauhtli was coming to the view that he must go south himself, but alone. He knew that it had been Nopal's destiny to marry Queen Chimalman. He knew also that the Master had had some special feeling about her, or plan for her, divining indeed that hers might be the most precious of human lives. Was there no call for him, then, to be in Huitznahuacan at his fellow disciple's side? Coshcana all his life had been a servant of disciples, was pledged to that service, Quauhtli thought; he could be trusted to guard Nauhyo. . . . So he turned it in his mind, and then awoke one morning with the certain knowledge that he was to go. To set out at once; that was imperative. He awoke Coshcana and told him, laid a hand on the sleeping Nauhyo's head, and went.

It was long after the Topiltzin's passing, and the traffic on the Road was not what it had been. There were troops of porters daily, indeed; officials with their retinues sometimes; messengers in plenty: but there was no unbroken stream of men as before. Beyond Ahuacatl Glade, he kept to the forest as long as it was safe to do so, not wishing that his first encounter with Toltecs should be too near home. Then he came out boldly onto the Road and began systematically putting the leagues of it behind him. That morning's stage was empty of northern humanity; he neither passed nor met anyone.

At midday he came to another Toltec station much like that at Ahuacatl Glade, except that it was without stir or voices. It was empty of humanity, apparently. He had tortillas with him, and with the knowledge that one did not starve on the Road, he had given scant thought to the food question.

But he was hailed from the rest-house when he had passed it. "Don't go past your dinner, Toltec! No wise man will do that, when the caldron that Papantli of Quauchinanco put on the fire is within ten breaths of its taking off." A merry, plump little man stood in the rest-house open-room, beaming at him in most friendly fashion.

"Aye," said Quauhtli, turning, "your Godhead is right; it is later than I thought. My thanks to you."

"Eh? *My* Godhead?" quoth Papantli, shaking with laughter. "*My* Godhead, say you? And never a tone in your voice to tell that you are laughing! From what part of the League's dominions do you hail, O strange-spoken brother? Such terms are not bandied between folk who cook meat by the roadside or travel on foot through the forest."

So he chattered, shepherding Quauhtli to a seat in the open-room; but his curiosity stopped pleasantly short of being embarrassing. All he wanted was company, and company that would praise his cooking. *"Your* Godhead shall dine today as if the title belonged to you; aye, you shall!" he ran on. "Ten breaths and you shall judge; you shall know. It would not become me to speak. But if Papantli of Quauchinanco does not deserve to be the Human Camaxtli's cook—but you shall judge! You shall judge!"

He was hospitable though, this little man. While he talked, he was setting a basin of water before Quauhtli, with soap-root and a towel; busying himself in the kitchen; issuing thence with bowls, knives, spoons, and thick paper napkins; then dishes of fruit and sheets of bread; lastly a notable tureen steaming savorily. It was but to taste of what came from this to know that his self-praise was modesty, as he himself remarked; and Quauhtli, who had the Toltec tongue of Nahua well enough by this time, had no difficulty in keeping him incurious with praise.

Thus a Huitznahuatec turn of speech flicking the little man's inquisitiveness into action evoked, "From what part of the League's dominions—" but there wise Quauhtli had but to come in with, "In all parts, such cooking should be known. The League's subjects should be blessed with such knowledge."

"It is a joy to serve you," cried Papantli, "even above the run of our great Human Camaxtli's messengers"—something of that kind, then, he took Quauhtli to be—"all of whom I enjoy serving, for they are men who can appreciate a Great Cook."

"Great you may say, and not merely good," said Quauhtli.

"Wise you are, and subtle your distinctions! Good cooks there are in the world; perhaps not many, but some. I am told that in Tollan there are two or three, and in the kitchens of more than one Culhuatec noble. The Hierarch of Teotihuacan has a cook whom even I do not despise. But a Great Cook comes not into the world more than once in a year-sheaf of year-sheaves. Aye, we are not more common than the Incarnations of our Lord."

"And when they do come," said Quauhtli, "would one not rather expect to find them in the palace of the Topiltzin of their time than by the roadside in the wild forest?"

Papantli held forth beamingly in reply; perhaps a little blasphemously too. "It is a point for theologians to argue," said he, "whether our Lord, incarnating, would really be born to a throne, as we are taught. For a Topiltzin is Lord of War, and what would He make of war, who is the King of Peace? I have thought it might well be that He would be born among the virtuous downtrodden, sweetening their lot. And how could He sweeten it better than by feeding them divinely? Yet blaspheme not, O Quauhtli of the Forest! Genius is genius; but whatever people think, I am not Quetzalcoatl! Nay, think not that!"

Quauhtli promised that he would not. Then, by degrees he drew the man from theology to passing on what news had come up from the south. Papantli spoke of the great barrier the barbarians had built against the Toltecs passing into their land, and of the road being raised in the canyon to surmount it. When the road had caught up with the barrier—that was when they should see things happen, and Quauhtli was helped to a realization of what the "things" would be. Papantli told it all very happily, much as a joke that he did not doubt his companion would enjoy. News of the murder of Cohuanacotzin had traveled thus far, and perhaps farther, and of the Human Camaxtli's will and oath to avenge him.

"None of the barbarians will be left, not one!" Papantli chuckled. "The Human Camaxtli always does much more than he promises to do, and his anger over this is terrible, they say."

Quauhtli was depressed by the hearing, but still more puzzled. How could they pretend that the Huitznahuatecs had killed the man? It was obviously impossible. The whole tale must be ill-founded. But no; the Quauchinantec had heard a dozen official bulletins read. They were terrible people, these Huitznahuatecs: murderous, irreligious, unspeakable. It was hard to imagine how men could be so base; the gods willed their—

His chatter was disturbed by a shouting from the road northward, which resolved itself into, "The Divine Princess arrives!" A couple of men, stately of attire, came into view, shouting as they trotted, "The Divine Lady Civacoatzin arrives! Prepare!"

"So *that,* maybe, is why I am here," thought Quauhtli.

Before the men had halted, Papantli was out in the middle of the Road, bowing. "Your Godheads will stop here to dine and rest," he besought them. "Ten breaths, and the pots will be taken from the fire, and your Godheads shall judge if one is not here who should rather be lording it in the Topiltzin's kitchen.''

The heralds followed him into the open-room, where they seated themselves, talking together, wasting hardly a glance on Quauhtli, whose nequen clothes, had he known it, betokened him a peasant, and no company for them. Papantli, having bowed them to their seat-cushions, beckoned him into the kitchen. "It is no place for us in there," said he, "with those great dignitaries.''

They were not the kind of Toltecs whom Quauhtli was eager to meet thus early in his dealings with the race, and he was pleased enough, little as he understood Papantli's feeling. The one thing he wanted was an excuse for not leaving at once, and that the Great Cook was prompt to supply.

"Quauhtli of the Forest, Quauhtli of the Forest," said he, "need you of a truth hurry to go? I am alone here and shall need help, and truly we have been more than brothers. Need you hurry to go?''

"No," said Quauhtli." "I will stay and aid you till the Divine Princess is gone.''

So then Papantli set him to washing and cutting up vegetables whilst himself, taking a pot from the fire, waited on the heralds and, in and out of the kitchen, favored him with scraps of information. "The gods be thanked, it is ever the Divine Lady's way to travel retinue-less," said he. "There will be but herself and a waiting-lady and the bearers to provide for." And again: "And but shortly announced, as now. Were she not the most merciful of the merciful, there would be grave trouble for the unprepared.''

In due course, the heralds went on, and in due course, the princess arrived, in a great room of a litter, built of some very light, strong wood and borne by a score and a half of young nobles of great strength and stature. Retinue or bodyguard else, there was none, as Papantli had said. They set the litter down at the southern end of the clearing and then came very quietly to the open-room and seated themselves. One, their leader, brought a message from the princess that they were to be served first and that no food was to be brought to the royal litter till they were dining.

"For her Godhead considers us more than we consider ourselves," the young man volunteered, "and thinks we need rest after eating."

So now Quauhtli was kept busy carrying their meal to them from the kitchen. They spoke little and in low tones as they ate, and were markedly courteous in their manner toward him. When about half of them had been served, he heard a gong struck in the litter and saw the leader of the bearers rise and hurry thither. It chanced that he was kept in the kitchen for a while then, attending to something for Papantli, who returned in a few minutes with an altogether new manner on him.

"Quauhtzin," said he, "the Divine Princess would speak with your Godhead." The honorific came now with awe and unction. "She orders that you are to be dressed in noble costume and sent to her. I go to make ready the garments, the best we have here." He bowed low and retired, leaving Quauhtli by no means as surprised as he might have been.

Thus soon after, dressed in the cotton and feathers of a Toltec noble, and looking the part well, Quauhtli announced himself at the door of the royal litter: "Quauhtli of Huitznahuac waits." Bidden to enter, he mounted the steps, drew aside the curtain, and stood in the doorway, bowing in the Huitznahuatec fashion—by no means as one should bow on coming into the presence of Toltec royalty; this he surmised by the look it evoked from the princess's attendant, which disapproval and Civacoatzin's gesture of reproof thereof, and the rich furnishings of the litter, he noted but half consciously. What held his attention, and, in a sense, illuminated the whole place, was the princess's eyes.

There was no feminine allurement in them. Hers was a broad and rather rugged face, much seamed; her age would not have been much less than three score. But there power shone, and life, and energy, and above all, boundless compassion; pain, solemnity, laughter, indomitable will, and again and again, above all, compassion. She sat on a divan facing him, garbed in a headdress sown with jewels, and clothes of a glow and richness that no

Huitznahuatec could have imagined; but all was a mere setting for the great, deep glory of her eyes.

She made a sign to which he responded, then dismissed her attendant and bade him enter and be seated. She kept silence for a few minutes, perhaps to give the lady she had just dismissed time to get out of hearing. Then, in a low voice, she said, "Quauhtzin of Huitznahuac—of the Serpent's Hole?"

"Of Puma Rock in the forest, and of Eagle Hermitage, and of the Serpent's Hole."

"The One that was there has taken dragon-wings."

"He has taken dragon-wings," acknowledged Quauhtli, knowing that she alluded to the death of Huehuetzin. "It is your Godhead who is now my Lord and Teacher, and I your disciple and servant."

"For a while," said she. "And now I need your service. Your Godhead is bound for Huitznahuac?"

"I am on my way."

"And I also am on my way there. It is our Master's will; we both have work to do there. My brother has gone south with his armies to conquer Huitznahuac. That was to be. Nations live through their life cycles and die; and death is at hand for Huitznahuac. But Huitznahuac has not sinned or fallen as other nations have, and her death will illumine the world. I know that great good for the whole world will come of it, but it is for us to ensure its coming. For the men of the Dark Tezcatlipocâ are at work to prevent it. One of them, the worst and greatest, is with my brother's army. Where is the disciple who saved Nonohualcatl's life in the marketplace at Culhuacan?"

"Your Godhead knows that he is Huitznahuatec? That he is Nopaltzin Tecuhtli, my fellow disciple?"

"I did not know his name, although I guessed his nation. What you tell me makes clear much that I did know. He is in Huitznahuac?"

"Either he is king there, or is to be king."

Her eyes lighted. "King there? That should make our task easy. But the conquest was to be; no, there is no preventing that. What can have kept him from making himself known to my brother, if he is king of Huitznahuac? He must make himself known. But there are things you can explain to me perhaps. Your countrymen have built a great barrier in the canyon between Nonohualcatl's armies and Huitznahuac, to keep our Toltecs out. But nothing can keep my brother out; he will go through or over the barrier, for all the bravery of your warriors."

"We have no warriors in Huitznahuac, your Godhead."

"True; I had forgotten. It is the land where war is unknown. But that will not save the Huitznahuatecs. Oh, why did they not welcome Nonohualcatl? Now he is angry with them, and nothing can save them from utter destruction unless I can get word to him before the barrier is passed. How came it that his friend, Cohuanacotzin, was murdered? It was he whom I sent to rescue Nopaltzin from the Teotihuatecs. Your Godhead knows about that?"

"I know."

"And I know that he and Nopaltzin became close friends. How came it that he was murdered?"

"No man was ever murdered in Huitznahuac, your Godhead. If they accuse the Huitznahuatecs—"

"But they do. Cohuanacotzin's body, shot through with an arrow, was found at the foot of the barrier, which, it seems, he had climbed a night or two before."

"Yet it is impossible that Huitznahuatecs should have killed him. We know nothing in Huitznahuac of the killing of men."

"*You* know nothing of it—have never seen or heard of it?"

"I have heard of it from Nopal as a thing that is done among the Toltecs. He said that the armies you have there are trained for the killing of men."

"But here in the forest? I have heard that—"

Quauhtli, shuddering, stayed her with a gesture. "Yes," said he, "I have come on it here in the forest, and on this Road."

Then he told her of the massacre on the Hill of Derision, by whom it was done, and at whose command. She had no difficulty in recognizing Yen Ranho as the man whom the Ib Quinames had described to Quauhtli. And Yen Ranho would have been on the Road at the time. She wept over the tale, not for a moment doubting its truth. The hierarch was the priest and agent of the Dark Tezcatlipocâ.

"He who compassed the murder of Amaquitzin Quetzalcoatl may have compassed the murder of the Culhuatec lord as well," said Quauhtli. "Your Godhead says that Cohuanacotzin had climbed the barrier; if so, he would have met Nopaltzin in Huitznahuacan. The Huitznahuatecs could not have failed to come on him, and they would have conducted him there in all honor. Then he and Nopaltzin would have set out for the Topiltzin's camp. And fearing Nopal's meeting with the Topiltzin, might not the priest have set men in the canyon to murder Cohuanacotzin?"

"But then Nopaltzin too would have been murdered, as I pray the gods he has not. His body was not found with Cohuanacotzin's. No; he is alive. And Cohuanacotzin's body was thrown from the top of the barrier, and the barrier is high; no arrow could have reached a man at the top of it from below. . . . Well, I must do what I can; I must use power. Your presence here makes that possible."

She sat silent for a while, in deep concentration. Quauhtli, having the understanding of silence, did not speak or stir. Then her face lit up again. "Yes," said she. "And now I must write to my brother."

From a cabinet at her side she took writing materials and was busy for some time. Then, "Is your Godhead trained in pictography?"

Quauhtli answered that he was.

"Is the meaning of this apparent to you?"

He took the paper and examined the script. It was like the pictography he knew, but with a difference that puzzled him at first. Then, almost suddenly, he saw the trick of it and read on. "The meaning is very clear," said he.

"Will your Godhead let me hear your interpretation?"

"Your Godhead has written—

" 'My Divine Brother,

" 'I implore you not to offend the Bright Gods by heeding the counsels of the Dark Tezcatlipocâ, who presides over anger and revenge. Not the Huitznahuatecs killed Cohuanacotzin, whose death hurts me. This I know; and you know that sometimes I have means of knowing. From the face of the cliff over against the barrier, the arrow was shot that killed him. The one who shot it lies buried there.

" 'Heed this, I implore you: Until you have come face-to-face with their king, slay none of the Huitznahuatecs, or your life will be made mournful till you die. I, your sister, could tell you who their king is, but you are to discover that for yourself.

" 'You know that I never advised you but according to the will of the Bright Gods, that you might prosper and be happy. I have never advised you so urgently as now.

" 'From your sister, Civacoatli,

" 'By the hand of Quauhtzin, her friend' "

"In all things, your Godhead reads as I thought and wrote," said the princess. "And now I pray you take this letter to my brother—in his camp, in the canyon, in Huitznahuacan, wherever he may be. You are a swift runner; the world and the gods need your swiftness now. You will get there many days before I can, and you will carry with you much that your Toltec runners cannot. Carry the letter in this wand," she continued, taking a rod about an arm's length long, opening it with a twist and pressure in the middle, and putting the rolled-up letter in the hollow discovered within.

"Let this be the most visible part of your equipment," said she, handing the reclosed rod to him, "and you will be obeyed and aided by all. Should you tire, it will secure you the best litter and runners on the Road. Take night-litters by night and learn to sleep in them; be traveling always, night and day. And now go. May Zacatzontli and Tlacotzontli tear away the distance from beneath your feet, and the Bright Tezcatlipocâ be your companion!"

"My service is your Godhead's," said Quauhtli, and he set forth. Zacatzontli and Tlacotzontli, the gods whose business it is to do so, tore away the distance from beneath his feet. . . .

11

The Rocks Fall

Nonohualcatl watched the rain of great boulders and brooded gloomily. If the Huitznahuatecs could keep it up, it would strain his genius to pass their barrier; indeed, his genius was strained already. He hurried the raising of his road and drove his galleries forward and up, realizing that it was all a makeshift course, to fill the time till he could find a better.

The barrier now was mountain-high, halfway to the cliff top; how long would it take him to pile his road equally high? As high as to the mountainside above, for example; for, if their rock supply held out, the Huitznahuatecs would reach that with their barrier-top in time. A stupendous work, but he would do it— unless a way through were found—if it took him a year-sheaf of year-sheaves. He would never go northward unvictorious.

There came a day when no rocks fell, and he was filled with hope. His raised road now ran steeply up to the barrier's face; and the incline, from the bend in the canyon, was notably increased by nightfall. He turned in his mind the possibility of sending an army up that precipice, and had an idea that he would do it somehow. All day long his army worked like ants. But in the evening, news was brought to him that the rocks were falling again.

That night the unprecedented happened. The officer in charge at the road-head had sent his report to the Topiltzin when the first rock fell: at the far end of the barrier, where its fall was to be heard but not seen by him. As he directed the work he went on more or less subconsciously counting the thuds of the falling rocks. His place was at the bend in the canyon; some man-heights beneath his feet lay the remains of a noted archer of the Blue-Hummingbird Pygmies.

This officer was familiar with the Huitznahuatec technique. First would come a rock from his right as he faced the barrier, to be followed immediately by one from the other side, the two cliff tops thus alternately dropping their boulders, beginning at the far end and advancing toward the near end and the top. Three-score thuds, he reckoned, would bring the falling stones into view. No; three score and three; there it came on the right. And now three more to fill the last spaces. It was a thing to marvel at, the precision these barbarians used, dropping the great masses as if by magic into place. Four on three-score. The two last ones now, which would put a new head and front on the barrier. At one time one had felt uneasy as one saw those last stones fall into their place.

Down came five on three-score, a monstrous boulder; you could feel the ground tremble at its thud. What? Has it jumped a span toward the middle of the canyon? That is unusual. By rights, one should clear this stretch of road while— Here comes number six on three-score, and . . . no dull thud now, but *crash!* Its edge strikes against the edge of the jumped other and— *Tezcatlipocâ!*

A runner carried the news to the Topiltzin. There would have been five-score men on the incline, and most of them were killed. Smashed by the great rock, the very first thrown down that had not lodged in its place. It jumped where it struck against the other, so that the weight of it leaned outward and carried it over, to roll and leap down the raised road and lodge at last against the cliff at the bend in the canyon, where it killed its last victim: the officer who had been counting the thuds.

The news brought Nonohualcatl hurrying to the spot, where help was already arriving. The rock half blocked the opening. There was no getting litter through onto the slope above; the living must be carried out on tilmatlies. The Human Camaxtli pushed his way through, and those whose business it was followed him. There was really no danger; a new rock had fallen in the place of the murderer rock and lodged safely, and the thuds from the far end of the barrier were audible; it would be many minutes, anyway, before boulders would be falling in front and at the top. Besides, a whole layer had fallen since the disaster; there was no more danger now than there had been at any time. The thuds and tremors drew nearer; but Nonohualcatl was not to be disturbed by them.

Upward of three score had been killed outright; of the rest, some ten, the doctors found, might survive. These were attended to first. While their broken limbs were being set, the Topiltzin spoke kindly to each of them, stroking their heads or the like. Then he turned to the fatally injured; not one of them but he knelt beside him and gave him consolation; and it was worth having, since was he not the Holy Topiltzin, humanity's chief link with the God-world? Four died smiling as he spoke to them, knowing that he would care for their widows and children. When he had comforted them spiritually, the surgeons came, and with a drug gave those still living the physical comfort of death.

Thud, thud, thud, the fall of the rocks came nearer, first on this side, then on that. Those who might live had been removed and carried to the hospital; the fatally injured had been given their peace. Remaining now were only a few more corpses to carry away. The Human Camaxtli—strangely turned human again now that his war had chosen to behave like war—was moving down toward the bend in the canyon and the gap that the fallen rock had left. Above, the final rocks in the course were falling. The last rock but one fell—in place, no doubt; he was not attending to it. And the last—in place? No, by heaven! Thud, crash, crash, thud, and here it comes bounding down the incline and—

He was very near the gap by that time. He turned to look at what they were yelling at, and a giant of a common soldier leaped through the gap, caught him, and hurled him through, just in time. The priest-doctor he had been talking with was killed when the monster boulder, as if malignantly conscious, made for the place where the two had been standing, pounced at it, and then smashed at last, striking out fire and earthquake, against its murderous predecessor.

The impact brought a dozen men to the ground on top of the Human Camaxtli where he had been thrown, his rescuer among them. By the mercy of the Plumed Dragon, the first rock held; for a minute, heaven only knew whether or not it would go rolling down the canyon, mangling its score-scores. But it held; and presently Nonohualcatl, grim-featured, was on his feet, and those whom the shock had brought down on top of him were trying to look unself-conscious. —Earth here! Pile up your basketloads, you coming up, at the base of this rock! So! And now, who was the man who had thrown down his Topiltzin?

A gigantic Otomi prostrated himself in a quivering silence. "My life is forfeit, Lord Human Camaxtli," he got out.

"It is," thundered the Topiltzin, checking his laughter. "Take him away; let him be given five-score—"

"Lashes," thought the Otomi.

"Quills of gold dust," thundered the Human Camaxtli, "and the uniform of a sergeant in my bodyguard. Stop! Who are you? Of what regiment?" Being employed on the earth-carrying, the man wore but a nondescript mashtli.

He was an Otomi of the Tlilcuetzpalins, it seemed; his name—

"Your name is Cuetzpalin, and you are a Culhuatec of the Guard, my personal servant." His Majesty was to be troubled with no unpronounceable Otomi names. "Station him, when properly dressed, at my door. He shall fight beside my litter in battle and stand at my back in peace. Go, Cuetzpaltzin!"

The fellow was ennobled, no less: to be styled *Cuetzpaltzin,* and *your Godhead!* He went off with his escort as if in a dream.

12

The Tzo Family Reunited

In the Republic of New Otompan, all the days were golden. No day passed but was golden. They wandered free in their paradise, did Huhú and Natzó; they traversed the lakes of a Tlalocan of which they themselves were the Tlalocs undisturbed. Daily they made for themselves duties, at which they worked strenuously, responsible to none but themselves; and when the mood to lounge overtook them, they lounged. Did they desire change, there were always new scenes and valleys in which to wander.

They explored at leisure their carefree, pestless world, so wonderful in its inaccessible isolation. Unless they had not escaped into it, they thought, men would never have known of it.

In a great belt of land north of Huitznahuac, leagues and leagues deep, hidden away marvelously, lay the pleasant valleys of their New Otompan. The river made a magnificent loop and nearly encircled it; the mountains had cunningly arranged their precipices to keep it from the knowledge of prying men. Nonohualcatl would have given ten cities to get news of it, ten cities and their provinces. Perhaps even the mountain sheep that bred in it knew of no way out, but had bred and remained there for ages.

Valley opened into lake-floored valley, and by these waterways the two Otomies went cruising, fishing as they went, paddling anon in the deeps, or in the shallows punting their raft with a pole, but mainly carried by a gentle current. Rarely did raft and stores need portage over land, but it had happened once or twice. The valleys were a maze, their waterways continually winding. They came on herds everywhere that knew no fear of man; and now and again they came on groves of fruit-bearing trees, or fruit trees that stood alone on hillside or meadow. The fruit was as good, they told themselves, as if men had cultivated it; but there was no sign that it had ever been cultivated. At first they would land and load their raft with it after eating their fill; later, they would land only to feast on it when the desire took them, and then go on, confident of finding more. In the evenings they would moor their raft when and where the fancy took them, and pitch their tent for the night. Or not pitch it, but sleep under the stars, with or without a fire. When the fancy took them, they would remain in one place for days and, as they said, found a city there. It would be a hut or a shelter of some kind. To all of their halting places they gave the names of cities in the north.

One evening they discovered squash, a whole wilderness of it, ripe for the cooking. They spent a five-day week beside it, till their taste for squash was sated; then they moved on. One noon Huhú espied, five-score strides or so up the hillside on their left, what surely was maize, almost hidden by a ridge of rocks between, and they left their raft to explore. Maize it was, and ripening. They fetched their tent and possessions and camped beside the maize-patch waiting for the cobs to ripen, planning the bread they would make. In the end, they made nothing but common tortillas and atolli; and of the latter, a porridge against hunger and a pleasant drink against thirst. The maize, they held, was but little poorer than the best you could buy in the Otompan market. As they harvested it, they sang the proper hymns in praise of Lady Centeotl, the Maize-queen. Not that they called her by that name, which was of the Nahua tongue; but their Otomi allowed for a proper substitute.

They built an altar on the hillside above the maize patch and sacrificed an armadillo that providentially appeared; it knew no better than to render itself up peaceably to these beings whose like neither it nor its forebears had seen. Its spirit went up, they supposed, as a fitting gift to Centeotl; its corporeal part, picked out of the shell after the roasting, went well with their first maize feast.

There they remained for many days, hunting or fishing or idling . . . and praying, for the finding of the divine food awoke a religious instinct in them. When they embarked and went on their way, it was with sacks, once priestly robes, of ground maize—they had devised a mill with stones—cobs, and grain for planting.

"We will burn down a copse somewhere and plant them beneath the ashes in the way our Lady ordained," said Natzó.

They embarked in the morning; they had worked hard the day before, and feasted until late. It was a hot and golden day; the waters were unrippled, apparently utterly still. But they would not trouble to paddle. They did not care whether they made progress or not; who were the lords of New Otompan? They lay on the raft and grew drowsy basking in the sun. And in New Otompan there could be no possible danger, they had long since given over keeping watch at any time. Blue here; yonder the reflections of the trees . . . no possible danger. . . . But a current was carrying them while they slept.

When Huhú awoke, black night covered him, and he was shivering. The strangeness of these facts crept slowly into his mind; then suddenly came fear. He sat up and felt for Natzó. "Natzó," he cried, "awake!" and shook him by the arm. "Awake! Death has overtaken us!"

"Fire-sticks!" cried Natzó, himself at once. He felt for and found what he wanted and twirled them till he had a torch alight. He contrived in the process that a spark should fall on the trembling Huhú's leg.

"Ha, you felt that?" said he. "Your body is on you, friend; you have not passed from life."

He stood, holding up the torch. A cavern roof was above them, not far away; cavern walls were a few arm's lengths off on either side; the dark water flowed placidly beneath, a gentle current.

"Let us paddle back to the world of men," urged Huhú; and Natzó was willing; though as they went, he talked incessantly of this great and secret empire they had won for themselves; their palace should be a mountain.

They passed through great halls, sometimes water-floored, sometimes with but a narrow waterway through; and by mid-afternoon, they came out into a spacious cave mouth and daylight. Mountain-high precipices reared here, making an angle in the valley at its forest-clad extreme. This was the limit of New Otompan, or of that part of it which lay open to the sky.

"For all that is in the mountain is ours," Natzó brooded, his imagination on fire.

By the cave mouth they built their city: their capital, they decided it was to be. New Teotihuacan this should be, appropriately named The City of the Gods—"For who knows what deities inhabit our mountain?" They might voyage on those dark waters and come out into Tlalocan itself; yes, the city should be New Teotihuacan, situated at the northern limit of the republic, as New Otompan was at the southern.

They built their city and made their plans. There was to be a great naval exploration of the dark subterranean sea. They would load their raft with food and firing, and discover the inmost of things.

Now that war was behaving like war and he had suffered losses, Nonohualcatl Totepeuh Camaxtli was freed for the time from the gnawing of his gloom. The rocks had fallen and slaughtered his men; his whole scheme was obviously at the mercy of the Huitznahuatecs. It appeared that the end of things had come as far as his expedition was concerned, which might have depressed a lesser man. But not Nonohualcatl Topiltzin. Having dismissed his Otomi rescuer, he remained an hour or so at the road-head infusing the highest of high spirits into his officers and men, who were made to feel, before he left them, as if a great victory had been won.

It may be that a lurking superstition in him whispered that without losses, there could be no gains. At any rate, the gloom was gone; tomorrow a new plan would present itself. In his mind he had already abandoned the raising of the road. He was Nonohualcatl Totepeuh Camaxtli, and he could not but be victorious.

He found his new Otomi bodyguard on duty at the pavilion door: a promptness that pleased him. "Here already, little rogue?" he condescended.

"To do you service, Omnipotent Camaxtli!" said the Otomi, hesitantly bringing out the foreign tongue he had had to learn in the military school.

"Service perish!" quoth Omnipotent Camaxtli. "Find me a way through the mountains and I will call that service."

"The Omnipotent Camaxtli behaves sensibly. Let him not be troubled further about this, since at last he has given the work to a man."

"Eh? Learn the Nahua, knave! Learn the Nahua! Who is to understand your jargon?"

The man was not afraid to explain himself laboriously, without regard to the conventions. "Your slave said that Camaxtli had at last bidden a man find the way who would certainly find it, and not fail as others have done."

Well, well, well! the Camaxtli thought. It seemed that he had found something of value tonight, something novel and amusing. He arrayed his brows in kingly thunder to hide the chuckle in his throat.

"Find it, rogue! Find it! And before tomorrow dawns or the whipmen shall deal with you!"

Cuetzpaltzin, who had been flogged before and could endure it as well as another, gave himself to no unpleasant anticipations. He had done his Topilzin a kindness and intended him another; and his Topiltzin was as decent a man as himself, or almost. Besides, he knew that he would find a way through the mountain before morning; he had not the slightest doubt of that. Otomis were mountaineers, and had brains; Toltecs were but crude plainsmen.

When, shortly afterward, he was relieved of duty, instead of seeking his quarters and sleep, he slunk off into the cross canyon behind the royal pavilion. At that point it was quite a bowshot wide, but it narrowed rapidly eastward as he advanced, till he must push a sidelong way through narrow intricacies and windings beyond the place where the runlet had sunk into the ground. This was the way to take, he considered; there were no busybodies here. He would be uninterrupted and unnoticed; this was a time when greatness of soul demanded solitude for its work: a grand project that must not be disturbed by encroachments of the envious imitative. Certainly the Human Camaxtli had been wise at last. . . . To an Otomi mountaineer . . . and of Otomis, to a man of the Tzo family. . . .

He was deep now in the intricacies, where a hue and cry might not have found him. He had climbed the southern canyon wall to other intricacies and windings. Despite his lofty musings and the treacherous moonlight and shadows, he went competently to his work; he was not the man to forget an inch of the way he had traveled: not an inch of the way, nor a bush nor crevice, nor rain-worn wrinkle in the canyon wall. He was a man of the Tzo family—the one man, alas, now available, of that so-gifted line. For where now was he of whom their sacred father, Yetzó, had prophesied that he would found a new republic if there should be room in the world to hold it? Room enough in these southern wilds, had the sainted Yetzó but known of them! Room enough for many new republics here! Ah, where was—

Eh—what was that?

Some kind of movement on the moonlit cliff face above, nothing so definite as a shadow . . . but something! A ghost, or—smoke it was. It was to be investigated, certainly, by one commissioned to find a way through for the Omnipotent Camaxtli. Some stiff climbing brought him out onto a moonlit ledge that widened out on his right toward the place from which he judged the smoke, or ghost, had emerged.

He sidled along the ledge till it was wide enough for decent walking; it was quite impossible that he could be seen. Yes, there it was again. Smoke certainly, and rising from behind that clump of bushes below. And—what was that? There were sounds . . . like far-off voices in conversation, like mountain goblins talking together. Well, they might know something, could one but overhear them. He lay flat along the ledge, craning out his head to catch something, curiosity precluding the possibility of fear.

What? The mountain goblins of these parts spoke Otomi?—as, naturally, all things would that had not perversely been taught to do otherwise. Craning out his head here and yonder, he brought an ear to the right place again, and once more he heard the tones, the rhythm. Yes, of Otomi. All the better; for mountain goblins might be bribable; one need not hesitate to offer from the Topiltzin's wealth. . . . He turned his head, brought it lower, and lost the sound; moved it again and regained the hearing of tones and rhythm, but he could make out no words. Could one lower oneself into that clump of bushes? One could, and did, although for most it would have been a risky business. Now he needed something to stand on, and room at least to move his head and neck a little so as to catch those tones and accents again. He swayed to the right and the left, his head close to the cliff, eager to pick them up.

Then suddenly, in the midst of a motion, he heard quite plainly, ". . . thinking, Huhú?"

"Of my wife and children, Natzó."

"*Natzó!*" gasped Nratzó-Cuetzpalin from above.

"Since I have none, I can but think of my brother, my only relation in the world we have left."

"Divorced your wife, Natzó?"

"Aye, I decided that at the maize patch. We will not speak of her, but of my brother Nratzó. He was said to be the most talented member, but one, of the talented Tzo family. To me he seemed dull at times, but a good fellow. My good Nratzó. I wonder where he is now."

Nratzô put his mouth to the crevice and shouted into the mountain, "Here in the world, you fool!"

"Ha—what was that? Natzó, I thought I heard someone whispering."

"You did, Huhú. We are here on the brink of Tlalocan; you heard the voice of the dead. O Soul of my brother in Tlalocan, speak to me, I conjure thee! How camest thou to die and be taken into the company of the Blessed?"

"Die, brother? It is you who are dead! I am here in the world of men, on the canyon wall, seeking a way through into Huitznahuac for the Human Camaxtli, my patron!"

"It was the soul of my brother speaking, Huhú. I caught but faint sounds, a word here and a word there."

"I caught this, Natzó: that he is seeking a way through into

Huitznahuac. What should the soul of a dead man desire in Huitznahuac? Maybe it is where the wicked are punished; maybe Mictlantecuhtli is the king there."

"No, Huhú; he was my brother; he was not of the wicked. I am puzzled indeed. O, that thou couldst come to me, my brother! For Huhú and I, alone of mortals, know the way that thou seekest."

"You do?" Nratzó soliloquized. "Then if you do, I do."

Soon he was below in the cross canyon, shouting at the top of his voice, "O Human Camaxtli, the way is found!"

Of the brothers' meeting, some day or two later, nothing need be said here.

13

A Place of Refuge

During all these months, Chimalman, watching at her husband's bedside, was, in a sense, keeping guard over her thoughts. Only in a sense, because her thoughts naturally and without constraint were with the gods. Many times a day she repeated to herself the Master's message, and she found it not difficult to obey his command. The shocks that time had brought her—the murders of Amaqui and his suite, of Acamapichtli and Cohuanacotzin, and of Nopal himself, for he was dying—had but served to drive her inward to a lofty mood of trust. The Master would not have asked for her trust had he not known that her path would be arduous and trouble-strewn. So she trusted in the gods, knowing they needed her trust, and lived in a world she made for herself.

Her feeling for Nopal may be called love; it was deep enough not to be dismayed by his approaching death. What was hers, was hers forever; and he was hers in a way. Together they had been in Tlalocan, and together commissioned to a work; his death, or hers, would be no break in that. She felt that although he lay unconscious, he was carrying it on still; quite unreasonably, she never doubted that wherever he was, he shared her mood to the fullest. He was not thinking of her, she felt, nor she of him; but their thoughts were together on the Master's work, on the Divine Companion, on that which was to come.

There were times when she felt that he was with the Master, times when she believed that the Master and he were there with her in the room and that a light and beauty on the wasted face on the pillow confirmed her belief. Ishmishutzin, living now for her patient's sake in the House of the Kings, marveled at two things: that her science, or something beyond its scope, had kept the king alive for so long, and the serene untroubledness of the queen.

The state rested on the shoulders of Acatonatzin—the wise and indefatigable. Poet and philosopher he had been; now he found within himself and put to use energies and executive power not less great than his brother Acamapichtli's. He was in the palace, in the marketplace, on the mountainside. Chiefly on the mountainside, where Huitznahuac was at work. There he kept alight Huitznahuac's courage, watched to alleviate its weariness, and kept its hope singing. Chimalman left all decisions to him and followed all of his suggestions; and he, seeing what was to happen, was eager to give her peace.

What was to happen was the birth of her son.

Son, and not daughter, she was convinced it was to be. She would hallow for him his way into the world. The Divine Companion and the Master's message, the glory that was to be more than Ulupi's, all had to do with this. And the Chalchiuhite Dragon had to do with it. The dream she had dreamed about it returned to her. Once more in her sleep she was watching the Evening Star, and Quetzalcoatl enthroned in it. And a star fell from the star. Our Lord, stooping, tossed it down, and she saw the shining thing before it fell into her heart; it was the Chalchiuhite Dragon. Waking, she found the little image on the bed beside her; there was something altogether strange about the way that little image would appear and disappear, be found and lost.

She went in radiant gravity through the day, and through the days that followed. So as not to lose the Chalchiuhite Dragon again, she placed it where it might be seen: on a shelf in the alcove by Nopal's bedside. Ishmishutzin Teteoinan, coming in, regarded it curiously, with something like awe.

"Does your Godhead know anything of that strange jewel?" asked the queen, and the old priestess by way of answer repeated the passage from *The Book of Our Lord and Huanhua:* "Thus I incarnate from age to age for the preservation of the good, the

destruction of the wicked, and the establishment of righteousness," and then changed the subject determinedly, busying herself with attention to Nopal. But the Inner Sun shone bright in
the mind of Chimalman.

The Huitznahuatecs had thrown a bridge across the canyon
something to the north of the barrier; and it was on this bridge
that Acatonatzin was generally stationed, accessible from either
side and in a position to observe what went on below. There he
was on the night when the two boulders fell onto the road and
killed the Toltecs. He heard the shrieks of the victims of the first,
and by the Toltec torchlight saw enough to guess more.

His face turned ashen; the sweat dripped cold from his forehead. His mind cried out in the silence, "On me only be the
guilt!" Fortunately, he was alone on the bridge. "They must not
know of this!" was his second thought; no Huitznahuatec must
know.

Except from the bridge, there was neither seeing nor hearing
what went on below; the cliffs cut off the sound and threw it
skyward. He went out among the men on the western cliff and
spoke with Shollo, who was directing things there; it was the
earth-course that was falling then.

"There must be greater care," he said. "The front rock on this
side has fallen."

Alarm shone on Shollo's face: "Did it—?"

"No", Acatonatzin said. "But there must be much greater
care. Let the barrier-front be put back ten paces, with very deep
earth-beds at the top."

So Shollo gave that order and was for sending a messenger
with it to the other side, but Acatonatzin stayed him; he would
go himself.

But before he could start to go, men came and represented to
them that the wooden runway was prepared for the front stones
of the next three courses and that men were actually holding
back the boulders with ropes; not to loose and drop them now
would involve great expense of labor, and might even be impossible. —Well, those three courses might go, but double the earth-
beds at the top. And then alter the grades of the runways and set

them back; let the new face of the barrier be ten good strides back, and not so steep. Push the runways back a stride at each course.

He left Shollo then, and crossed over and gave like orders to Shaltemoc, to whom it seemed that he had aged suddenly. The second boulder to reach the raised road fell while they were talking.

In the morning Acatonatzin was on the bridge again and soon began to note that the Toltec work below was lagging. As the day went on, he grew more certain of this. When night fell, no torches burned there; no work was being done. He called Shollo to him on the bridge and pointed into the unlighted depths beneath.

"They have given it up," said Shollo.

Then Shaltemoc was summoned; he would have it that the boulder-dropping should not be halted, and Acatonatzin agreed with him. But that dark silence could only mean that the work had ceased down there; activity that had never flagged before now was quite at an end. "And it has been decreasing all day," said the priest-prince.

Shollo supposed that the Toltec was tired of his folly and had returned to his kingdom, or was preparing to return. Shaltemoc was less hopeful: They might be planning to climb the barrier tonight, relying on having thus put us off our guard. Acatonal sensed inwardly that the Topiltzin had not departed, and would not; and he was vaguely troubled. The boulder-dropping must go on through the night, but without strain or hurry.

The next morning he sent out scouts: a thing, strangely enough, that had never been done before. Except for the place where they were working and the road they had made to it, this was unknown country to the Huitznahuatecs. But there was no possibility of these scouts coming where they could see the cross canyon behind the Topiltzin's pavilion, or the territories of the Republic of New Otompan.

One of the scouts who went out westward had news to tell in the evening. Some score of miles away he had seen, far beneath him, a great company of Toltecs who seemed to be lost in a maze of chasms; they appeared to be hungry and in desperate plight. So Acatonal had food-litters dispatched and their contents let down by ropes to Huemac's contingent thus entangled in the mountain; it was what saved many of their lives.

The priest-prince kept them raising the barrier all that day, but halfheartedly, for most of the men were resting. In the night he had bonfires lit on the barrier's top and watch kept, but no work was done. Nothing was going on in the canyon below now; that fact was certain. The Huitznahuatecs, learning of it, were in a gay mood. They had known that the invaders would tire and go; and now they were gone. They waited for a word from Acatonatzin to turn their backs on their work and on the mountain; but the word was slow to come. The Toltecs might still be waiting for them to stop work and go. . . .

It was by no means clear in the priest-prince's mind what a Toltec invasion would mean. He had heard that they killed people, but he could not realize the possibility of slaughter here. It did not occur to him; his anxieties and forebodings were formless. It would be an evil thing, a very evil thing, if these northern people got through; that was as much as his thoughts formulated. The wish was still with him that he had been able to draft the menfolk off to build a new Huitznahuacan in the unknown south. But he did not know that they would get through; he did not know that they had found a way. It appeared that all but he were certain that they had not.

It began to rise on his perceptions that it would be well to hide the queen. And the king too, perhaps, if he were still alive. The Toltecs might get through; they might have found a way, and they might still be harboring the scheme their first ambassador had broached, that of marrying the queen to one of their kings. Yes, we must hide Chimalmatzin; if they get through, they must not find her. Ulupi's line must not be broken.

Long ago, as a boy, he had been taken to a hidden valley on Teotepetl; a God-man had sent for and talked with him, perhaps with this very eventuality in mind. For it grew on him now that that God-man's will would be that he should send or take the queen there and place her under his high protection. If only he could find the way, but he knew that he could not. Who could? To that question, put to the Unknown, the answer drifted into his mind: Shollotzin Tecuhtli, now Lord of Rainflower since

Nopal had become king. Rumor, hardly even whispered but widely believed nonetheless, was that the lords of Rainflower had a mysterious relationship with the Mountain that was God, a kind of lay-discipleship as it were, or perhaps hereditary guardianship as against the world. He would take Shollotzin Tecuhtli with him to Huitznahuacan.

They arrived there at noon of a gloomy day, the third after the fall of the boulders, and found Chimalman at Nopal's bedside, with Nayna the Aged from Rainflower, whom Acatonal did not know, and Ishmishutzin Teteoinan. To them, in a low voice, he told his news. It might be, he said, that the Toltecs had given up their attempt—

"They have not given it up," said Nayna the Aged. "Even now they are on the march through hidden valleys, and there can be no stopping them."

"Your Godhead knows this?" asked Acatonal.

"Alas, I know, although I cannot tell how. And therefore I must hide Chimalmatzin; she must not be here when they come. I must hide her in a secret place on the Mountain that is God."

"Your Godhead suggests that? You know of . . . a certain valley? It is what I came here to propose. There is a valley there wherein she would be safe?"

The old woman drew him down and whispered in his ear: "Hast thou heard of the Serpent's Hole, Acatonatzin Tezcatlipocâ?" Their eyes met then; his, lit with awe. He turned to Chimalman.

"My child, you must go," said he. "They would not find you where her Godhead has leave to place you, though all their armies were on the mountain searching."

"I have been there," said Chimalman. "I know the way, and I will go. But Nopaltzin—?"

"The Light awaits him here," said Ishmishutzin. "To take him would be to disturb his passing."

"He shall live to confront the Toltec king," said Nayna. "Aye, and he shall confront him. I will bide here and see to it; it is a promise. A place is prepared for you, little Godhead. Shollotzin Tecuhtli shall take you. He too knows the way. You and Ketlashotzin and her children shall go."

Shollo, although he had known Nayna all his life, and knew that but little was hidden from her, was startled to hear her announce that he knew the way. "Yes," said he, "I will take your Godhead; I know the way."

"Leave me with my husband till the litters are ready," said Chimalman. So they left her.

When, a little later, she parted from Acatonatzin at the Town-mouth, he saw no sign of grief or fear with her at all. Under dark skies, indigo and purple with their storm clouds, she rode away.

14

Quauhtli's Journey

The princess's despatch-rod stood Quauhtli in good stead. At posthouses where there was but one night-litter, it was he who got it, though messengers from the Regency at Culhuacan might be thereby delayed. They never questioned his precedence. On foot during the day and but for one meal at a rest-house, eating the little he needed as he ran, and sleeping by night in the night-litters, he made as much speed as a human being could. Day after day his pace was the wolf-run, where normally all that was asked of a messenger on a long journey such as that was the dog-trot. He found the sway of the night-litters excellently conducive to sleep.

One morning he awoke aware of a change in his surroundings. The forest solitude had gone, and he was in the midst of human life and works. The litter had been set down in the southernmost rest-house of the camp on Forgotten Plain.

In no long time he was on his way again. The Road, which had been quite unmarked here, now ran between rows of tents and was everywhere well crowded with soldiers and porters, the latter bearing loads southward, or returning with empty litters from the south. In spite of the crowds, an excellent order was kept; at sight of the despatch-rod, all made way for him.

At every seven-score strides or so there stood an official who cried as he came up, "Straight on!" or "This way!" or presently, "On through the canyon!"—and he understood well enough that they were directing him to the Topiltzin. He was making better speed than any litter could; or these same *topillies,* or whichever of them first saw signs of flagging in him, would have drummed up a litter and bearers then and there and seen that he mounted it.

When he came into the canyon, he found it, in comparison, empty. The camp that had been there had been struck and the tents repitched elsewhere. Porters going and coming; a regiment on the march that he passed; a stretch of solitude; more porters; another regiment—thus the need for speed was borne in on him.

In mid-afternoon he passed the cross canyon where the royal headquarters had been. The topilli stationed there gave him a direction, to which Quauhtli, in his intentness, and knowing the way very well, paid no heed. Then the man's attention was diverted, so that he took no immediate note of the fact that the Divine Princess's messenger had gone on by the raised road. Quauhtli after a while took thought to wonder why this new work, this rising incline, that had cost such tremendous labor, had been deserted, for his way led through solitude now. It was ominous, and urged him to new speed, whereby the runner the topilli sent after him failed to catch up with him.

Past these two great boulders; and, ah, there was the Huitznahuatecs' barrier: high, but it must be climbed. They were not at work on it now; in any case, he must take the risk. The Toltecs were beyond, of course; they had gotten through. Or had they? He went up to the top without too great difficulty. A buzzing of flies that rose, blackening the air at his appearance, sickened him. *Soul of the World!*

He was left in no doubt now. The Toltecs were in Huitznahuac. These smashed bodies were those of the Huitznahuatecs, and they had been thrown down from the cliff tops. The place was piled thick with them; it was difficult to pick a way. And there . . . one face not damaged at all: Shaltemoc's, Nopal's brother-in-law, whom he had known since they were together at the Calmecac. The face was almost lifelike, the body shapeless . . . *Soul of the World!*

He staggered down the slope, his muscles gone loose and flaccid, and vomited by the roadside at the bottom. Speed, speed,

Quauhtli! A great wrench of the will and he mastered his physical misery and ran on. Ah, here a tent, and a jar of water in it, not too stale. They were here not long since, then. He drank, and poured what remained over his head and body and ran on. It was a mystery: The Toltecs had not come this way, but they were in Huitznahuac. There was no time to give way or thought to one's sick physicality now. . . .

Night had fallen when he came out onto the plain and found it a camp crowded with warlike northern humanity. He held high his despatch-rod as he came into the torchlit ways, and it brought him the same deference as in the morning. Ahead! The Human Camaxtli is ahead! Make way for the Divine Princess's courier! The first topilli he passed drummed up a litter and courteously ordered him to enter it. He did so, for the sake of better speed, so insistent was one's physicality in its reaction to its first glimpse of war. . . .

His bearers were of the best and went along splendidly. Though inwardly he fretted at their slowness, he knew that their speed was better than his own could be just now. But, resting, he was also recovering himself. He contrived to ask them where was the Topiltzin and understood their answer to be that he was at the end of this torch-starred plain—on the verge of Tzontecoma's district, in fact, where populated Huitznahuac began.

And there, indeed, they halted before a pavilion which, had he had attention to pay it, would have astonished him; but his mind was on the talk exchanged between the leader of his bearers and a group of officials at the door. One of the latter pointed along the road to Huitznahuacan, whereupon Quauhtli made his decision. His body was his own now; the rest had restored him. He leaped down from the litter, overthrowing—quite unintentionally—a couple of the bearers, and sped on his way south.

Despite all that he had done that day, he knew well that he had never run as he was running now. The way was well lit for him by the full moon above the hills, and by the glare of burning farmsteads, whence came the shouting of havoc-working Toltecs and the screams of their victims, which set him shuddering though he was scarcely conscious of hearing them, or aware of anything but that he must reach the Topiltzin before the Topiltzin reached Huitznahuacan.

At a bend in the road, a shrieking girl and the soldier in pursuit of her ran out in front of him; the man was about to seize her when Quauhtli felled him and passed on, hardly knowing what he had done, or that the girl escaped into the woods on the other side, or that the man lay still where he had been thrown. A mile or so from the city, the Road rose, then swerved to the left and downward. At the top of the rise, he saw lights at the Townmouth and that the Toltecs were there. Still, he might reach the Topiltzin before that one and his tzitzimitl host came to the Top of the Town; thus he might save the queen. Speed, Quauhtli! Speed!

With Civacoatzin's staff held high, he tore down that last, long incline, the sweat in his eyes half blinding him. And then, opposite the Townmouth, he came upon the man he was seeking, and was left in no doubt of that fact. He was enthroned there, enjoying his revenge.

"Stop!" yelled Quauhtli, and hurled his messenger's staff at the executioner, felling him. It was Acatonatzin's life he saved thereby, at least for the moment. And then, loud above the outraged commotion while they seized him: "Here is a letter from the Princess Civacoatzin to the Toltec Topiltzin, and this vile killing must cease till the Toltec Topiltzin has read it!"

Someone handed up the despatch-rod to the Topiltzin, whose fury had been quelled by the news that Quauhtli had shouted. A gesture from him put a stop to all further activities while he read. Executioners and their victims—the old men, the women and children of the town—awaited his word for the massacre to begin again. Two burly Toltecs held Quauhtli but did not molest him otherwise.

By the light of the torch held up to him, the Topiltzin first glanced down the letter, then became intent on it, his face losing its brooding savagery as he read. That was because the letter enforced conviction, on one point at least: The dead pygmy he had seen on the ledge opposite the barrier came to his memory at once. Yes, it was with an arrow such as the pygmies used that Cohuanacotzin had been killed.

Civacoatl knew; he did not know how, but he knew that she had means of knowing what she wished to know. So his fury against the Huitznahuatecs was foundationless; he, whose pride and whose instinct it was to be magnanimous, had been led into this. . . .

"Repeat the order. Let there be no more Huitznahuatecs killed or molested in any way!" he commanded, and immediately the drummers began drumming out the order. Drums farther off took it up, and drums would repeat it till every Toltec in Huitznahuac had heard.

"Does the courier know the contents of this letter?" he brought out at last.

"I do," said Quauhtli. "The lady who wrote it discussed it with me."

"You are that Quauhtzin who is mentioned?"

"I am."

"Of what city, O strangely mannered Quauhtzin?"

"Of Huitznahuacan."

"Of Huitznahuacan! And yet you bring me a letter from the Divine Princess. There never was a Huitznahuatec in the Anahuacs."

"There was, and he was known to the Topiltzin. And the princess is on the Road and will be here before long. What she says is true, king of the Toltecs."

"That it was the forest pygmy who killed my friend? Yes, I see that that is true."

"And that the Topiltzin's life will be made mournful till he dies because of the Huitznahuatecs he has murdered."

The onlookers gasped. Here was one speaking to their sovereign with tones of pity, as from a superior to an inferior; they had not heard the like before. They waited for the sign that would be Quauhtli's death warrant, but no sign came. Nonohualcatl sat there embarrassed and uncertain, quite unlike himself.

"Who was the Huitznahuatec that was known to the Topiltzin?" he asked at last.

"He was called Quanetzin of Quauhnahuac, O king of the Toltecs."

"*What?*" cried Nonohualcatl, down from his throne in a moment. "Quanetzin a Huitznahuatec? Where is he? Your life is forfeit if you lie to me, Quauhtzin!"

"No Huitznahuatec is to die, Toltec, till you have met the king of Huitznahuac."

"No. No Huitznahuatec is to die. But—where is Quanetzin?"

"You shall know, if the king of Huitznahuac permits."

"Yes, I was to see the king of Huitznahuac. Can you bring him to me?"

Quauhtli addressed Acatonatzin. "Can your Godhead bring the king here?"

"No," said the priest-prince. "Nopaltzin lies dying in the House of the Kings."

Dying? It was news for Quauhtli to digest. Only not now. There was this business of the Topiltzin to attend to first.

"The Topiltzin is answered," said he. "But if the prince whom you would have murdered permits, I will bring you to the king of Huitznahuac." The Topiltzin's eyes sought Acatonatzin, who inclined his head in assent.

"Come then; I follow your Godhead, Quauhtzin," said Nono-hualcatl. "Drummers, summon all the army to this place. Until I return, all shall be under command of this lord"—and he indicated Acatonatzin, adding, "If your Godhead permits." Then he admonished his men: "See that no Huitznahuatec is harmed."

He followed Quauhtli through the Townmouth. The Huitz-nahuatecs had not killed Cohuanacotzin; his anger had been baseless. And Quanez of Quauhnahuac was a Huitznahuatec. Perhaps one of those thrown from the cliff tops . . .

15

The Kings Meet

Quauhtli hurried on, the Topiltzin following him: past the koo of Teteoinan, up the Street of the Quechol, across the arena, and up the steps to the House of the Kings. They did not speak on the way. Quauhtli's mind was filled with a stern pity for this man who had worked such mischief in his blindness and who must now, in mercy, be made to see and realize the harm he had done. He kept silent lest, speaking, he might interfere with the workings of the Law.

The Topiltzin could not feel himself Topiltzin in Quauhtli's presence. He could assert no superiority; shame and remorse were working in him; above all, uneasy apprehension. His anger had been reasonless; and he wished to be thought magnanimous, and indeed, was magnanimous in his better moods. Civacoatzin had said that if he killed Huitznahuatecs before meeting the king of Huitznahuac, his life would be made mournful till he died; and he had killed perhaps the whole manhood of Huitznahuac.

Who was the king of Huitznahuac? And why was he to see him? Where was Quanetzin, the so-called Quauhnahuatec—the one man, as he had superstitiously come to feel, who could solve all of his problems and make the world again sane for him? These questions were on his lips to ask, but Quauhtli's demeanor kept them from being spoken.

Thrice Quauhtli knocked at the palace door, not loudly. Then a shuffling footstep was heard from within, and old Eeweesho opened to them. "Quauhtzin!" said she. "Ah, Quauhtzin!"

"Eeweeshotzin, where are the king and queen?"

"The queen is—hush!" said she, noting the presence of a stranger. "And the king—ah, Quauhtzin, your heart will be wrung! Your soul will be wrung to see him!"

"What has happened, Eeweesho?" Then he remembered. "Acatonatzin said that he was dying. Yet we must see him, Eeweeshton!"

"Ocotosh, Ocotosh!" she called softly. "Bring a light!"

The old servant, her husband, came with a lighted torch, and the two went in, following the servants. "Ah, Quauhtzin, Quauhtzin, you will mourn!" murmured Eeweesho. The aged creature was weeping. "He is in the sunroom," said she, "if he is in the man-world at all."

"How comes it that he is sick and dying, Eeweeshton?"

"The tzitzimitl shot him in the canyon; the same who killed Acamapichtli and that foreign lord, Cohuanacotzin."

Nonohualcatl caught his friend's name, and as much of the rest to know that reference had been made to his murder. "What is this, Quauhtzin?" he whispered.

"The demon that shot and killed your ambassador shot also the king of Huitznahuac, and he is dying of the wound," said Quauhtli. "Cohuanacotzin was your ambassador, was he not?"

A door was opened, and Eeweesho ushered them into the dimly lamp-lit sunroom, then retired with her husband. Heavy curtains hung in the arches, shutting out the moonlight and muffling the night noises of the forest. On a low bed of quilts lay a motionless figure, deathlike. Beside it, on a stool cushion, sat an aged woman who lifted a hand to hush them as they entered; also to beckon Quauhtli over to the bedside. And there, she holding the light, he saw his fellow disciple wasted to utter death semblance, to all appearances, dead. He felt a new wave of stern pity for the warmaker who had brought all this to pass. . . .

Nonohualcatl must see this fruit of his ambition, however; if it—that is, if the dying, or dead, Nopalton should be recognizable by him—as the God-world grant he might be! That thought in his mind, Quauhtli caught Nayna's eye, and she turned and beckoned to the Topiltzin, who came on tiptoe across the room, curious and apprehensive, and looked intently at the dying man.

He could not tell who it was, nor yet escape the impression that he should know. Quauhtli himself might hardly have recognized Nopal, had he not known who lay there.

"It is the king of Huitznahuac?" whispered Nonohualcatl.

"Yes. Do you not know him?"

"No . . . no."

There flashed through Quauhtli's mind then a herb that grew nowhere but at the Serpent's Hole, which, rightly used, would bring the dying, or the dead, back from this side of the Clashing Mountains and give them semblance of life and health, and all of their mentality, for a few minutes at least. To have that herb here might be the saving of the rest of the Huitznahuatecs from slaughter, and this Toltec's soul from the hideous damnation of the crime he had contemplated. But—

Nayna the Aged touched his arm. "I have it here," she said. "I brought it against this need."

"You have what?" asked Quauhtli.

"The Serpent-herb from the Serpent's Hole."

Neither paid the least attention to Nonohualcatl, but spoke in low whispers so that he might not hear. Indeed, he realized that he counted for but little here. But something in Quauhtli's tones had reminded him of someone, and the dying man in the bed reminded him of someone; and he thought that he was within a little of guessing who. And till this interview was over, he would hear no news of the man who had saved his life once and would save—perhaps it was his honor he would save now.

"Wait," whispered Nayna. She took a packet from the breast of her gown and produced from it two or three sprigs of an herb, well dried. Breaking off a leaf, she put it between Nopal's lips, then touched a sprig to the lamp flame till, slowly, a spark glowed at the end of it, from which rose at once a surprising volume of silvery-yellow smoke. This sprig-censer she waved slowly before Nopal's nostrils and across his face. They watched her do this for a few moments till the smoke cloud had grown to envelop her.

"Out, both of you!" she whispered, troubledly, as Quauhtli thought, and with a curious emphasis, pointing to the curtain in the nearest arch. Quauhtli held it back, motioned to Nonohualcatl to pass, and followed him into the moonlit garden. As he

went, he saw that the room was quickly filling with the pearly
lamp-lit opacity.

They were both glad to be out of it, for the fumes, pungent and
acrid, had begun to hurt their eyes and nostrils, and even their
skin. From a few paces away in the garden, they heard Nayna the
Aged chanting in a strange rhythm that rose and quickened, then
sank and grew slow, and at last ceased in a kind of gasp or sob.

Then Nopal's voice, as strong as ever in his life, called,
"Quauhtli, are you there?"

"I am here, Nopalton!" Followed by the Topiltzin, he reen-
tered the room.

Nayna was not in sight, but there was Nopal, sitting up in the
bed, with no death-seeming on him at all, but as Quauhtli had
last seen him at Eagle Hermitage; as Nonohualcatl had seen him
in the palace at Culhuacan.

"Quanetzin!" cried the Topiltzin.

"Yes," said Quauhtli, "your deliverer from the assassins in the
Culhuacan marketplace: Nopaltzin, king of Huitznahuac,
against whom you are at war."

"Quauhtli, Quauhtli, what does it mean?" began Nopal.

"Nopalton, Nopaltontli, listen! Dear heart, it is death the
bright that has come to you."

"Death?" exclaimed Nopal, his face lighting up to serenity.

"Yes. We have called you back from the edge of the Clashing
Mountains that this man may recognize you and know who you
are."

"This man?" Nopal peered closely at Nonohualcatl. "Why, he
is the man I told you about: the Toltec Topiltzin, my good friend.
It is a happy thing to me to see your Godhead."

But the Topiltzin, standing with bowed head, had no answer
to make.

"But . . . but . . . where am I, Quauhtli? How does the Toltec
Topiltzin come to be here? I thought I was in the House of the
Kings at Huitznahuacan."

"Yes, you are in the House of the Kings; you are in your own
house, Nopaltontli."

"Yes, but . . . I was dreaming before you woke me, and I am
to tell you my dream. I was going with Cohuanacotzin, the

Culhuatec—did you know Cohuanacotzin, Quauhtli? It was he who rescued me from the hierarch at Teotihuacan; I told you about that. The Topiltzin sent him to rescue me; your Godhead sent him, you know." This last was spoken to Nonohualcatl. "We were going to visit you; you had come to conquer Huitznahuac. When was it? This morning, I think. Or yesterday, for I must have been sleeping a long while. Yes. We were going over the barrier and down through the canyon to the Topiltzin's camp, for it seems that he had brought an army here to make war on us. Don't laugh, Quauhtli! If I had not been in the Anahuacs and come to his rescue when those men attacked him, fearful things might have happened here; for you know—I told you—they do practice that ghastly business of war, although they are not tzitzimitls, but men; and good men, many of them. Their Topiltzin is of a noble and magnanimous nature. I thought I saw him here just now, but that must have been a bit of my dream. Yes, fearful things might have happened if Cohuanacotzin had not come to us and if he and I had not gone to the Topiltzin's camp on Forgotten Plain.

"But did we go to the camp? Did we, Quauhtli? Because . . . hush! There was something . . . there on the barrier." A look of horror came over his face. "There was a demon . . . on the face of the cliff opposite. I can see it now: a demon with a bow and a quiver. Look! He changes. No, there is someone standing over him; can't you see? Look! Can't you see, Quauhtli? Nonohualcatl Topiltzin, your Godhead, can see him there—standing over the tzitzimitl, there on the cliff face: the priest who was my judge when you rescued me at Teotihuacan, Quauhtli: the hierarch of Teotihuacan. And he, or the tzitzimitl, shot three shafts; and the first killed Cohuanacotzin, my friend; he fell down into the canyon. And the third killed Acamapitzin, there on the barrier he had devised and built; and the second . . . did something; it grazed someone's shoulder, and he said, 'It is a scratch, nothing!' but he fell; it killed him. Who was that third man who fell? The dream became indistinct at that point."

Nopal sat forward, leaning on his elbows, gazing intently into the invisible. "Yes, it was the king of Huitznahuac, a fellow disciple of yours, Quauhtli. It was Nopal of Rainflower. . . .

Curious! By the Soul of the World, Quauhtli, that is who *I* was! I was Nopal of Rainflower—in my last life!''

He spoke with growing excitement and intensity, the power of the herb burning up in him, reaching at this point its brightest; then, suddenly, dying away. Quauhtli's arms were about him as he died . . . to lay back his body in the bed.

16
Nonohualcatl's Debt

No armed men, though many Toltecs, were left in Huitznahuac. On all of the farms in the country, soldiers worked for the Huitz- nahuatec women, and woe betide the man who was lazy or disobedient. The officers in charge of them—Culhuatecs all— never knew when to expect the visits of their Human Camaxtli, who permitted himself no rest in the labor he had undertaken. One day at Losthistory, inspecting the work of his men there, the next at distant Burntbread or Rainflower, he saw to it that the women were reverenced and obeyed. He was driven by remorse, possessed by desire to pay the debt he felt he owed to the gods and to Huitznahuac, depressed by a sense of the inadequacy of his efforts to pay it.

It preyed on him that his warmaking had brought about the death of Nopal. Setting a superstitious value on his own life and greatness, he set a superstitious value on the saving of his life back then in the marketplace, and felt himself accursed because he had been the cause, however indirectly, of the death of the man who had saved it. Yet there was a manly element in him too; his remorse expressed itself not in brooding apart and inactivity, but in this active will to repay. Quauhtli accompanied him on his tours and mediated between him and the widows left owners of the land.

He had wished to give Nopal a funeral more magnificent even than Cohuanacotzin's; but that, Quauhtli forbade. There should

be no meretricious and spectacular atonements. Life should
teach unhappy Nonohualcatl its great lessons; he should take no
refuge in unrealities. Uncondemning, sternly compassionate,
Quauhtli played, one might say, a fellow disciple's part to him,
watching for what signs of spiritual reality might appear in the
man thus chosen by the Law to meet the full blast of experience—the effects of his own actions, his own thought, his own
soul and being.

There were times when Quauhtli believed that the result of it
all would be the awakening in Nonohualcatl of that will, that
fire, that soul-dedication leading to discipleship. Nonohualcatl
made no attempt to play the king in Huitznahuac, but deferred
always to Acatonatzin, who reigned in the House of the Kings:
a frail and silvery old man now, utterly impersonal, waiting on
the gods.

Huemac, with the remains of his army, had been rescued; the
Otomitl had been found and brought back; both of them were in
the camp on Forgotten Plain. Nonohualcatl had not seen Huemac, but he had sent for the Otomitl to come to Huitznahuacan,
where Acatonatzin had given him the Calmecac to be his headquarters. There those two, the Topiltzin and the Otomitl, had
talked over the hierarch's exploits.

"He never should have left Teotihuacan," said the Otomitl. "It
was unwise; war is not a priest's business at all."

"Is massacre a priest's business then?"

"It is not, and for that reason he shall cease to be a priest."

"Your Godhead will—"

"Conduct a revolution, an easier thing to do here than it
would be in the Anahuacs. Otompan shall depose Teotihuacan
and assume full headship of the republic. He is here with a few
score priests, and I am here with the Otomi army."

"But there is my brother, Huemac. He loves the hierarch."

"The thing shall be done with some privacy, your Godhead. It
might be well if an invitation were sent to Huetzin to attend you
here in Huitznahuacan."

And it was done with very great privacy. The Otomitl, returning to the camp, brought an urgent message to Huemac, which
caused him to set out immediately for Huitznahuacan, where

Nonohualcatl told him of the crimes that had been done but not, at first, of the name or identity of their perpetrator. Huemac's religious susceptibilities were tremendously wrenched by the news that the Road had been violated.

"But the savages do not do such things, Nonohualcatl." He paced up and down the room. "They would never have thought of it. Someone must have set them on to it."

"We know who set them on, Huemac."

"Then he has been punished? He is dead?"

"You give your word and your judgment that he shall die?"

"I? Of course I do, Nonohualcatl. It was their ambassador who was killed, you say, and on the Road. Divine *and* human law broken; the gods would forsake us unless we executed the criminal."

"Good. And now we will talk of other things."

That night the Otomitl called on the hierarch in his tent. "What brings your Godhead here so late?"

"A matter of instant business. There was a massacre sometime since on the Road; an ambassador and his suite were slain."

"Well?"

"Your Godhead is no longer hierarch of Teotihuacan."

"That is a matter, sir, that concerns only the priesthood at Teotihuacan."

"Truly your Godhead is right," said the Otomitl, "and therefore you will start tonight for Teotihuacan. As I shall be here for some little time with the army, it should be easy for your Godhead to arrange things at home to your satisfaction."

"Think of another course, Otomitl. King Huetzin—"

"Is visiting his brother at Huitznahuacan, your Godhead."

He clapped his hands, and a guard of ten men entered. "Take his Godhead, the ex-hierarch, to his closed litter," said he. "Then you know your orders. Yes, a gag, and bound hands and feet; it will be wiser. You will loose him and leave him a day's march into the forest; his priests will be his bearers from that time on. No, you will have no other escort, Yen Ranho. It was you who desecrated the Road."

So that night the priestly contingent disappeared from Forgotten Plain. It never reached the Anahuacs. The Road had been desecrated; the spell that kept it free from murder had been broken. The Ib Quinames were no longer at their village by the Hill of Derision; another tribe, which came from deep in the forest, had taken possession of their territories and knew nothing of the tradition of the Road. And there was no god now on Puma Rock. . . . When the army passed that way, going north, it was found necessary to burn leagues of forest on that side of the Road, in the neighborhood of the Hill of Derision, and to exterminate the folk that lived in them. But Huemac, first of the allies to return, was careful; if a savage got onto the Road, he was safe; he was merely enslaved and taken to the Anahuacs.

Ochpaniztli, the last month of the year, was drawing to a close when Civacoatzin arrived at Huitznahuacan. Nonohualcatl was not there when she came, and she did not go to the Calmecac: Acatonatzin, having heard that she was coming, met her at the Townmouth and brought her to the House of the Kings. Those two understood each other well from the first. It seemed to him that although a Toltec, she was utterly Huitznahuatec in outlook. While talking with her, he remembered his vision on the koo of his god at Teotleco and understood that what had happened was what had to happen, and even knew that some great good was to come of it. The untimely deaths of his two brothers, of the king, of all of the manhood of Huitznahuac—each one of them now in antiquity and along the path of his evolution—had sown the seed whose dark fruit was this. But must they be considered unfortunate? Must it be thought that what they had suffered was other than the experience they needed in order to advance? Not death nor suffering, but ignobility, was to be mourned, and not one of these who had died had been less than noble. He remembered the light that had shone from dying Huitznahuac, in his vision, over a vaster world than Huitznahuac had dreamed existed, and he was able to take thought for the future.

It was the princess who suggested to him what that future should be, but his own mind had almost formulated it before she spoke. War had made its way into Huitznahuac; and where it had come once, it might come again. Wild tribes, with their dangerous weapons, might wander south, and for many years there would be none but women to oppose them. It would be wiser to abandon Huitznahuac and take what remained of the population into the north. That northern world, so vast and powerful, was weak in all of those gentle greatnesses in which the Huitznahuatecs had been so strong; and they would be held in high honor there, Civacoatzin assured him. Nonohualcatl would see to that. And they would be, he was to consider, wick and tallow for the Flame that was to be kindled there. . . . So it was decided between them; together, later, they would convince and comfort the people. Acatonatzin, meanwhile, would take litter for the districts and prepare the people.

An hour or two after he left, Nonohualcatl arrived in Huitz-nahuacan; messengers had gone seeking him on the day Civa-coatzin had come. Eeweesho brought him to her in the sunroom; he would have taken Quauhtli in with him, but Quauhtli preferred to wait in the garden. Nonohualcatl had aged much since she saw him last; he might now well be between his two and three score, although his years were but a score and twelve. All that belongs to youth had gone from him.

"Civacoatzin!" His tone showed that what hope he had was centered in her.

"My poor Nonohualton"

"Your letter was true. It was in this room that I saw the king of Huitznahuac die. He was the man who saved me from the assassins; we called him Quanetzin of Quauhnahuac."

"And Huitznahuatecs had been killed before you saw him—before you knew!"

"All of the men had been killed."

"My poor Nonohualton!"

"I owed him my life. You know how I sought for him in the Anahuacs. The desire was on me then to make him chief among my nobles."

"He had other work to do, Nonohualton. It was I who prevented your finding him."

"Your Godhead is wiser than I. But if I had known that he was Huitznahuatec—that he was king of Huitznahuac! I owe a debt, Civacoatzin, a heavy debt! And Cohuanacotli is dead too. You know the truth about that. It was a pygmy of the forest killed him, and I know who set the pygmy on to it."

"It was the Dark Tezcatlipocâ, Nonohualton. Through his servant, Yen the Hierarch. I passed that one in the forest, but he was disinclined to communicate with me. You should have sent a strong escort with him; the Road had become dangerous for him because of his crime. He had the Huitznahuatecs massacred on the Road and sent information of it to Huitznahuacan, hoping they would kill him for it when he came here and that the League would then exterminate the Huitznahuatecs. And he had Cohuanacotli murdered with the same end in view: that you might go mad with anger against them. Ah, Nonohualton, Nonohualton! Men who cherish anger in their hearts are under the power of the Dark Tezcatlipocâ, and he betrays his servants to suffering. It is a heavy debt you owe—to the king who died here, and to the Huitznahuatecs, who gave you no offence, and to the Bright Gods, whom you have sinned against."

"I would make expiation, Civacoatzin."

"There may be a way; even now there may be a way. Listen, Nonohualton. The gods had preserved Huitznahuac until now for their grand purposes. It was very old, but it was sinless, and therefore they were able to preserve it. Nations, like men, have their hour to die; they cannot live forever. Do you think that Culhuacan will endure forever, or Tollan, or the League? They will die when their time comes. They will be conquered and absorbed by their conquerors, and their conquerors will be conquered in their turn. But none of them will live through long ages as Huitznahuac has lived, and none of them, dying, will leave the world a benediction as Huitznahuac will.

"For, because of the sweetness of the life that has been lived here, and because the Dark Gods have never here been worshiped, from the death of this nation a great light shall shine. A star will rise from this sunset and it will beautifully illumine the darkness to be. That is true, Nonohualton.

"I knew—the Children of the Serpent knew—that this should be. The Dark Tezcatlipocâ knew, and plotted against the star's rising. His hierarch, Yen Ranho, plotted, as we knew. Their will was that Huitznahuac should be utterly destroyed, and not a soul

left living. To that end, the hierarch hoped to be killed in Huitznahuacan. But the Huitznahuatecs lived very close to the God-
world; it was a beautiful people your destiny ordained that you
should destroy, a destiny you made for yourself. The Huitznahuatecs would kill no man. That hope failing Yen Ranho, he
plotted further, as you know, and brought you under the power
of his god. It is a power that destroys the soul, and revenge and
hatred lay the soul open to it.

"When will you understand this, my poor Nonohualton? But
perhaps you understand it now. The Law leads us on from our
thoughts to our actions, and from these to their consequences,
which teach us, in the end, to be wise. You assuredly have done
great evil and earned heavy suffering for yourself. Grow wise
thereby! It is what the Law intends. Not by conquering Huitznahuac, for that was to be. You might have conquered Huitznahuac and shed no blood, and taken the people to the Anahuacs
to make the life of the Anahuacs sweet. It was your anger that
was the evil, your anger that caused so many to be murdered.
You do not guess what the gods may have lost through that.
Their will was that the Huitznahuatecs should dwell in the cities
of the north. Child, I would weep for you did I not know that
through this crime and its punishment, you may learn to be a
man!"

"To be a man, Civacoatzin?"

"Aye, poor heart, to be a man! Do you admire your warmaking now? Does conquest seem desirable now?"

For answer, he but hung his head, and she went on.

"The Huitznahuatecs who are left—the women and the aged
and the children—you must take to Culhuacan and see that they
are held in highest honor, because this great light, this great help,
is to come from the Huitznahuatecs. I have spoken with King
Acatonatzin, and he understands. It must be the business of
every Culhuatec to guard them against what might cause them
sorrow."

"All this shall be done, Civacoatzin. They shall be the highest
in Culhuacan. But it will leave my debt to the man who saved me
unpaid."

"You grow, my Nonohualton! Take courage; you are learning! Your debt to the man who saved you, Nopaltzin, king of Huitznahuac—yes, that must be paid, to the last quill and bean, or you are dishonored. Now listen and understand.

"War—that is your trade, as it was our father's. Well, it is the business of time and the universe. Forever and forever the gods make war on hell, and hell is the shadow of the gods. Where there is light, there also is darkness. The gods are our Lost Others. For every man there is a god, the Star within and above him, out of which his being proceeds; and for every god, and for every man therefore, there is a tzitzimitl, the dark shadow of the god. The war that endures forever is the war between our Bright Others and their Dark Others; and the souls of men that stand between are the spoils they fight for.

"Who is Camaxtli, the god you worship, Nonohualton? He is the will of all the God-world to oppose and hold back evil and to liberate mankind. He is the war of the gods against the tzitzimitls. And the Dark Camaxtli, his shadow, is the one who moved you to hurl the Huitznahuatecs from the cliffs. So with all the gods. The Bright Tezcatlipocâ is the delicate wisdom that keeps the brightness in the stars and unfolds the fern frond's tracery. The Dark Tezcatlipocâ is the fountain of all sorceries, of evil you could not endure the knowledge of.

"If you must have war, Nonohualton, there is but one way you shall escape the Dark Camaxtli. Follow this rule: Love your enemies! For hatred is the widest gate of hell.

"They are plotting all the time, the dark gods are, to bring the world to sorrow, violence, ignorance, and destruction. They are marvelous plotters, secret and sinister, infinitely cunning. But the Bright Ones watch their plottings unperturbed, because they know the cycles of time and that what has been sown must be reaped, and that men's thoughts are the seeds whose fruit is destiny. Huitznahuac was holy, and is dead. When that which is holy dies, the world is lighted. Passing into the Light of Light, holiness holds open the gates, and the glory streams through into our darkness to purify us."

For a while she sat silent, gazing out and up toward Mishcoatepetl; then, slowly, as if reading words written in a difficult script in the air, she said, "Nopaltzin saved your life; you caused his death. What do you owe him?"

"Two lives of mine, each to be his slave while they last, I think."

"You look too far, Nonohualton. But there are two lives to consider: that of the queen, his widow, and that of their son." He caught the thought and answered eagerly: "May it be thus, Civacoatzin? She shall be queen of Culhuacan, yet I will never touch her. I will be her servant; she shall rule and I will obey. I will know no woman till I die. Her son shall be my son, my only son, and my heir."

Her face lit with a grave happiness. "Yes," said she. "In this way, you shall make expiation. Poor little heart, you must suffer, but in your suffering, you shall do what the gods desire of you, and that is the path that leads to the end of suffering. It is a pledge, Nonohualton!"

"It is a pledge," said he, the beginning of hope in his voice.

17

Teotleco—The Arrival of the God

Yanesh the Straw sat drowsing in his flower garden at Rain-flower Manor. It had gone wild a little in these last months, but he might still take pride in its profuse beauty. Bushes, billowing over with bloom, had thrown out long, irregular trailers and grown to what shapes they would; seedlings had sprung up and blossomed in the paths. It was a long time since he had had men under him to order about. No matter! It was but a new kind of loveliness that overtook the garden. Copil and Coshcosh were good boys, though one had not to let them know one thought so. What had become of Copil and Coshcosh? He had not seen them for months, nor any of the menfolk. And one never saw the Tecuhtli now, nor even Shollotzin.

Who was it, desiring to be facetious with ancient Yanesh, had told him that the Tecuhtli was king? Ha, ha! you could not take in Yanesh the Straw with a tale like that! Ashokentzin was king, of course, and was so when this Yanesh was a boy, and it was not likely things would have changed.

But now there was none to carry Yanesh's blossoms into the house, none to come asking him for flowers—none, since Little Godhead Maxiotzin went, to wear of an evening the wreaths he made. No Tecuhtli; no Shollotzin; no Maxiotzin. Still, one never knew. They would come back sometime. It was wisest to go on making wreaths for them; they might be here this evening. Well now, and of course they would! Wasn't this the last of the No-month Days—the Eve of Teotleco—the last day of the year? Of course they would be here for Teotleco.

And the tlapalizquis were in bloom by the causeway between the ponds; and had not the Tecuhtli said that he would be here to wear a wreath of tlapalizquis? Up, Yanesh the Straw! You must be busy! Wreaths for their three Godheads—tlapalizqui wreaths for Teotleco!

So, with that rare thing, a purpose, born in his dream-bewildered soul, he rose slowly and came to the causeway and the place where the wonder-bushes bloomed. There he cut blossoms and sat down to make wreaths of them, and to dream. Mostly to dream, whereby it happened that the sun was within an hour of setting when he hobbled up to the house with his three wreaths. The world might call Shollo what it pleased: Nopaltzin was the Tecuhtli for Yanesh.

And he was not disappointed. There they came in their litters, up from the road, and dismounted under the mombin trees. He met them in front of the open-room.

"Ah, Yaneshton!" said Quauhtli.

"Ah, Shollotzin!" replied he. "Yanesh has not forgotten your Godhead's Teotleco wreath." And to the princess, "Ah, Maxiotzin! Sacred blooms for your little Godhead tonight."

Her voice was all tenderness as she answered him: "Ah, Yanetzin, you do not forget!" And she bent that he might hang the wreath about her neck.

He advanced then toward the Topiltzin. "Ah, Tecuhtli!" said he. "I knew that you would come when the tlapalizquis were in bloom. Deign to receive a wreath from Yanesh Ancient; never has he made it better." Nonohualcatl inclined his head in thanks and took the wreath, but said nothing.

"It is a good omen, Yanetzintli!" said the princess. "It is a good omen, Nonohualton!"

"Is there no one here, Yaneshton?" asked Quauhtli, but the old man had grown vague in his thoughts and was wandering off.

They left the bearers under the mombins and followed Quauhtli into the open-room; he then went on into the house and called, but no one answered. Everywhere there were signs that the place was quite deserted. It did not matter, since they had brought food with them, and one of the men, shown where to go by Quauhtli, brought water from the well. They supped in silence in the open-room; the bearers, five-score strides or so away, rested under the trees. Civacoatzin bore an air of suppressing information. Nonohualcatl, as dependent wholly upon her, was listless still, but with a gleam of hope in him. Quauhtli, awaiting events, was reverent in manner toward the princess. As for the Topiltzin, he was noncommittal and unpartisan.

When the meal was finished, Nonohualcatl broke the silence, almost nervously, with, "Do we go farther? Is it time for the bearers to make ready?"

"There will be no bearers, Nonohualton; we shall walk."

"But you, Civacoatzin?"

"I also shall walk. No bearers could come where we are going."

"Nor must they see us go," Quauhtli said.

"Where can we put them?" asked Civacoatzin.

"There are lakes and orchards yonder," said he; "The house would hide us from them."

She rose at that and went out to the bearers. "Children," she said, "you have had a long journey. Beyond the house, over yonder, there is a lake, and there are pleasant orchards in that neighborhood. You are to go and refresh yourselves now. After that, come back to the house for your sleep. I can trust Culhuatecs to harm nothing. We shall need you in the morning or sooner. Go now!" It was her way, they knew, to think of the comfort of those who served her, and bowing and murmuring their thanks, they went.

"I will show you the way," said Quauhtli, accompanying them. Returning after a while, he fetched torches from the storeroom: "We shall need these," said he. "And now will your Godheads come?"

He led them across the lawn and by the path through the flower bed and shrubbery to the door in the wall, and out into the forest beyond.

"Through the forest—by night!" exclaimed Nonohualcatl.

"Yes, through the forest, Nonohualton, and by night. Quauhtzin Tecuhtli knows."

"But it will be dangerous—for you, Civacoatzin!"

Quauhtli asked, "Why should it be dangerous, your God-head?"

"Are there no wild beasts—no jaguars, no peccaries, to stumble on?"

"Yes, there are jaguars, and peccaries; but why should they be dangerous?"

"You don't understand, Nonohualton," said Civacoatzin. "We are in Huitznahuac now, where men have never killed each other. The wild beasts would not be dangerous if men were not."

No moon was in the sky, so Quauhtli twirled fire-sticks at once and soon had the torches alight. The sunset finished as he did so, and with the sudden fall of darkness, the forest awoke, with all of its noises. Close by, a jaguar squalled its hunting cry.

"We should have brought arms," said Nonohualcatl.

"We shall not harm the creatures," said Quauhtli. "Arms are not brought onto the mountain. See here, your Godhead!" He gave a long, purring call and then repeated it lower. In an instant two green stars shone out of the darkness that rimmed the circle of their torchlight, and into that light, unafraid and unangry, stalked the king and terror of the forest, tail swinging. It sniffed at one after another of them, then elected to walk by the princess, purring, pleased that her hand should stroke its head.

"It is the Land of the Gods," said Nonohualcatl.

They went on, the path proving not too rough or difficult, though there were fallen trees to clamber over at times. "Where do we go?" asked the Topiltzin.

"To the Serpent's Hole, little brother."

"It is a holy place, Civacoatzin?"

"Aye, it is a holy place. It is where you shall pay your debt, Nonohualton . . . or begin to pay it." Nonohualton answered with only a sigh.

The path ascended and crossed hilltops and ridges under the stars, where the gloom of the forest tops made black abysses beneath. "The night grows quiet," said Civacoatzin. When they spoke now, it was in whispers.

A howler-monkey that had been ululating in the distance had gone silent; the squalling of the great cats had grown infrequent and ceased; the rhythm of the frogs was dying out; a pulsing soundlessness had fallen on the forest. As they went on, they became aware that this unnatural quietude was rife with rustlings and hushed patterings. A macaw in startling plumage flashed across the sphere of torchlight against the lighted tracery of branches above, from the darkness behind them to the darkness in front.

"The forest makes pilgrimage," whispered Quauhtli. "Look!" He turned, holding up his torch of ocotl wood, and pointed to a herd of peccaries coming on; deer amongst them; a tapir; three tapirs; jaguars, ocelots, pumas. And the trees were alive with monkeys, but there was no noise or chatter from them. Like all the creatures, they came on in silence, a curious intentness on them, something resembling awe.

"Aye, the forest makes pilgrimage!" said Civacoatzin. "And well it may!"

"It is Ce Acatl," whispered Quauhtli, a catch in his breath. "It is the Teotleco night of Ce Acatl!"

"Ah, Quauhtzin Tecuhtli! It is written in the *Book of Our Lord and Huanhua.*"

"It is written," said he, and he quoth: " 'I produce myself among creatures whenever there is an insurrection of vice and injustice in the world.' "

And Civacoatzin took it up: " 'Even though myself unborn, of changeless essence, and the Lord of all existence.' "

"Then it will be tonight?"

"Yes," she whispered. "I think it will be tonight. Look!"

They had come out onto an open ridge under the stars and could see the cone of the mountain in front, and all the forest: opalescent, mystical, every tree outline illumined by the glory that shone above the cone. Light, or fire, played up from it into the dark infinities. It was a fountain magical, displaying blooms snow-white, cream-white, rose-rimmed, yellow, momentarily changing. And then song broke from the songbirds in the forest; it seemed that every winged musician in Huitznahuac had flown hither, making pilgrimage, to add its power to the hymn of adoration.

Ah, but more than the birds were singing! "Hark!" whispered

Civacoatzin and laid a hand on an arm of each of her companions; and they heard the stars singing, the anthem of the Hierarchies of Light. "Come!" said she, tears of joy streaming from her eyes. "Our Lord is born among men!"

In the inner room of what had been the Master's house on the lake island in the hidden valley on Teotepetl—the Serpent's Hole—a white form reclined on the bed, the face white, wasted, joy-lit, serene. Ketlasho, standing by, was certain that a heavenly radiance, actual light, shone from the mother and the newborn child. The child with the wonderful eyes, the child who has not fretted at all . . .

"What is it you say, my darling?" she asked Chimalman.

"That I am wonderfully happy, that the gods have been dearly good to me, who has trusted utterly in them. Read to me the message, dear."

Ketlasho read: " 'The gods promise that you shall serve them more wonderfully than any of your predecessors did. They expect more from you than they did from any of them. You are to be assured of that, and never to doubt it. You are never to forget that we are with you to guard you and lead you to your greatness. You must trust in us who trust in you; you must trust, and go on trusting, and never cease to trust; that your trust may open a path between us and men. You are to trust until your trust becomes knowledge, and all we hope of you is fulfilled. Whatever happens, you are to trust."

"Thank you, dear." Very faint and far away was the dying queen's voice. A long silence followed; then: "My trust *has* become knowledge. What the gods hoped of me is fulfilled. Oh, if I could tell you! Let my eyes rest upon my Lord!"

Ketlasho took the child from the cradle and held it before her. Slowly she opened her eyes, and her face lighted with adoration. Then, closing them in weariness: "Our Lord's father will come. Listen, Ketlashton! Do you hear them coming?"

Ketlasho smothered a sob and went out into the open-room to listen, seeing that it was what the queen wished her to do. The child's father was dead; everyone was dead, or dying. But the dying goddess had sent her out twice to listen and to see if he were coming; this was the third time. She did not understand, but she obeyed.

And now she saw three coming up from the landing place, and waited for them. "It is I, Ketlashotzin," Quauhtli said. "I bring the Toltec Princess Civacoatzin, of whom the queen has heard, and the king of the Toltecs."

"She is expecting you," said Ketlasho. "Come!"

They went into the room. Civacoatzin knelt beside the bed and whispered to the one who lay there.

"Lift my hand," said Chimalman, and when it was done, she contrived to caress the princess's face with it. "You have brought me the one who is to be our Lord's father?"

"Here, Nonohualton! Kneel here, and pay your debt."

The Toltec Topiltzin, weeping now, knelt and took the queen's hand. "He shall be my only son," he vowed. "He shall reign over my empire."

"Peace, poor heart! It is you who were to be his father." Very, very faintly the words came. "Go now!"

The Topiltzin rose and went out, a hand over his eyes. Civacoatzin leaned over the queen and put an arm under her head. "His name shall be?" she asked, whispering.

"Ce Acatl; and the name he bears in the God-world. His name shall be—"and then, out loud "—Quetzalcoatl, Prince of Peace." And, whispering again, "Oh, I am happy!" she passed on.

But Quauhtli's eyes and adoration were for the Lord thus born again among men; born to inherit not little, lone Huitznahuac, but the mighty empires of the north. With bowed heads, they stood while Quauhtli repeated the scripture—

" 'Even though thyself unborn, of changeless essence, and the Lord of all existence, yet in presiding over Nature, which is thine, thou art born thus through thy mystic power of self-ideation, the eternal thought in the eternal mind. Thou producest thyself among creatures, O Lord of the Universe, whenever there is a decline of virtue and an insurrection of vice and injustice in the world; and thus thou dost incarnate from age to age, for the preservation of the good, the destruction of the wicked, and the establishment of righteousness.' "

* * *

All night long in the holy valley, the songbirds of Huitznahuac sang, hymning the Teotleco of the ages, the Arrival of the God. All night long the bloom-fires of beauty played over the peak of Teotepetl, signaling the event for whose sake Huanhua of old had crossed the western sea to Ulupi.

Afterword

It is rather unusual that a novel, completed and ready for publication a few years before its author's death, should make its debut some fifty-odd years later. Such an event demands at least some brief explanation; in this instance, it necessitates a biographical exploration of the author, Kenneth Morris. However, as space here is limited, I must refer the interested reader to my introduction to the forthcoming volume of the collected short stories of Kenneth Morris, where a more extended study will be found. Here, I am restricted to a brief sketch.

Kenneth Vennor Morris was born at his grandfather's manor house in South Wales in 1879. There he lived until after the deaths of his father, in 1884, and grandfather, in 1885, and the failure of the family business. Rosa Morris, with her two young sons, Ronald and Kenneth, moved to London, where, in 1887, Kenneth was enrolled in the school at Christ's Hospital. He graduated in 1895 with a thoroughly classical English education, yet he retained a strong loyalty to his own Welsh background.

In 1896, Morris visited Dublin, where he encountered a group of writers and mystics associated with the Dublin Lodge of the Theosophical Society, including George Russell (Æ), Violet North, William Butler Yeats, and Ella Young. This encounter shaped the rest of Morris's life. He enthusiastically joined the Theosophical Society and began contributing to the Society's publications—poetry, essays, dramas, and short stories. Over the next forty years, nearly all of Morris's writings would be found in theosophical publications. Morris stayed in Dublin for only a few months, after which he returned to Wales, where he became active in the Cardiff Lodge of the Theosophical Society. He continued writing, and attracted the notice of Katherine Tingley, leader of the Universal Brotherhood and Theosophical Society. Tingley's great vision of an ideal community and international headquarters, where the theosophical life could be realized, was already being fulfilled in Point Loma, California, a picturesque and peninsular headland between San Diego and the mountains to the east, and the Pacific Ocean to the west. Tingley invited Morris to join the staff of the headquarters, and in January, 1908, Kenneth Morris arrived at Point Loma. He would spend the next twenty-two years of his life there, and it was at Point Loma that Morris would write and publish the majority of his output.

In addition to his duties as Professor of History and Literature at Point Loma's Raja Yoga College, Morris managed to contribute numerous essays, poems, and short stories to the theosophical publications. His first novel, *The Fates of the Princes of Dyfed,* a retelling of parts of the Welsh *Mabinogion,* was published in a handsome edition by the theosophical press at Point Loma in September, 1914. The Welsh form of his name, Cenydd Morus, appeared on the title page, and the volume was illustrated by Reginald Machell, another distinguished Point Loma resident, who also illustrated many of Morris's short stories as they appeared in the Point Loma periodicals.

Other book-length lecture series by Morris appeared in the Point Loma magazines, including "Golden Threads in the Tapestry of History" (1915–16; collected in book form in 1975), "The Three Bases of Poetry—A Study of English Verse" (1917), and "The Crest-Wave of Evolution" (1919–21). Ten of Morris's short stories were collected in England in November 1926, in a gorgeously produced volume published by Faber & Gwyer entitled *The Secret Mountain and Other Tales.*

Sometime in the late 1920s, Morris became reacquainted with Ella Young, whom he had known in Dublin. She, too, had come to California, where she lived and lectured and wrote. Her children's books were published in America by Longmans, Green and Company. She convinced her editor, Bertha L. Gunterman, to consider for publication Kenneth Morris's second recension of Welsh legends, *Book of the Three Dragons.* It was accepted, and when it was selected by the editors of the Junior Literary Guild as the selection for "Boys and Girls between the ages of 8–12 years," upon publication in September 1930, it reached a larger audience than had any previous book by Kenneth Morris.

But by this time Morris was back in Wales. After Katherine Tingley's death in July 1929, followed shortly thereafter by the stock market crash, the Point Loma headquarters found itself in a desperate financial situation. The new leader encouraged members who could do so to leave Point Loma, to "earn their living in the outside world, and if possible to contribute part of their earnings to Point Loma."

Kenneth Morris returned to his beloved Wales. There in the next seven years before his death in 1937, he would found seven Welsh theosophical lodges. His output dwindled, but he began in January 1933 a publication of his own, *Y Fforwm Theosoffaid* (the Welsh "Theosophical Forum"), a four-page, stenciled, monthly publication (in English) of theosophical instruction and philosophy.

Morris's health, never good, worsened under a heavy lecture schedule. Part of this was due to a malfunctioning thyroid gland, and in April 1937 Morris entered a Cardiff hospital. To friends he confided that without an operation, he stood to live only a year at best, but if he could stand the operation itself, he would have a new lease on life. It was performed on 20 April 1937; Morris regained consciousness for only a few minutes afterward and gradually slipped into a deeper coma. He died at 4:00 A.M. on 21 April 1937.

His passing was mourned mainly in theosophical periodicals, but notices appeared in the general papers in Wales and in San Diego. Over the years, his memory has been venerated principally in the theosophical communities, where his writings have continued to be published and republished. Morris's lecture series, "Golden Threads in the Tapestry of History," achieved book form from Point Loma Publications in 1975, and three of his Chinese stories, together with a long Taoist poem, were collected by the Ben-Sen Press under the title *Through Dragon Eyes,* in 1980.

Morris's name among the general readership has long been forgotten, although his name is not unknown among those of the most assiduous and persistent readers of fantasy literature. Lin Carter included a small section from *Book of the Three Dragons* in his anthology *Dragons, Elves, and Heroes* (1969), in the acclaimed Ballantine Adult Fantasy Series. But it is to Ursula K. Le Guin that we owe the most credit for calling Morris to our attention, for it is in her landmark 1973 essay on style in fantasy literature, "From Elfland to Poughkeepsie," that she has singled out Morris along with J. R. R. Tolkien and E. R. Eddison as the three master stylists of fantasy in the twentieth century. Perhaps as a result of this, *Fates of the Princes of Dyfed* was reprinted by Newcastle in 1978, and *Book of the Three Dragons* was reprinted in a library edition by Arno Press in the same year.

Several short stories by Morris were soon thereafter reprinted in various anthologies, most notably in the excellent series of fantasy anthologies edited by Robert H. Boyer and Kenneth J. Zahorski (1977–81). Zahorski and Boyer also pioneered the study of Morris's bibliography in their collective study, *Lloyd Alexander, Evangeline Walton Ensley, Kenneth Morris: A Primary and Secondary Bibliography* (1981), which also includes the only published information to date about Morris's life. More recently, David G. Hartwell included three previously uncollected Morris stories in his superlative anthology, *Masterpieces of Fantasy and Enchantment* (1988). Still, however, only about half of Morris's excellent short stories have been reprinted since their original appearance. This imbalance will be rectified with this novel's forthcoming companion volume, which will contain the collected tales of Kenneth Morris, including thirty-three of his mature tales and five of his previously unrecorded early stories.

Kenneth Morris during his life never sought any acclaim or reknown, and little found him save for that within his theosophical circle. His indifference, I think, accounts for some of this neglect. To a number of people, including Ella Young and Morris's young friend and Point Loma student, W. Emmett Small, with him at Point Loma in the mid 1920s, Morris expressed the desire that he be discovered, if at all, some hundred or so years after his death. We needn't wait so long, especially with a major work, newly published, and a long-needed omnibus of his best work, his short stories, coming soon.

Kenneth Morris's last major work, *The Chalchiuhite Dragon,* was written for Katherine Tingley, after her request on Christmas Day of 1925 that Morris write something on a pre-Columbian subject. Evidence suggests that Morris had finished the book before he left Point Loma in January 1930, for on 27 November 1930, he wrote to W. Emmett Small's mother at Point Loma that he was "busy with *The Chalchiuhite Dragon* again, and am able to shorten and concentrate it with very good results." However, it wasn't until 1935 that he sent back to Point Loma the final version. Typescripts of the novel have been carefully preserved by the Society librarians, and by W. Emmett Small, foreseeing eventual publication.

For assisting in the preparation for this publication, it gives me great pleasure to acknowledge the help and friendship of John P. Van Mater, Head Librarian of the Theosophical University Library (Pasadena); R. Kirby Van Mater, Archivist of the Theosophical Society (Pasadena); William T. S. Thackara, Manager of the Theosophical University Press (Pasadena); W. Emmett Small, of Point Loma Publications (San Diego); and Alex E. Urquhart, friend and literary executor of Kenneth Morris (Cardiff, Wales).

—Douglas A. Anderson
Ithaca, New York
July 1991

Glossary

In compiling this glossary, I have found it expedient to follow Kenneth Morris's own example in his two novels *The Fates of the Princes of Dyfed* (1914) and *Book of the Three Dragons* (1930). In these imaginative expansions of Welsh mythology, Morris provided succinct glossaries of the major characters and place names, with enough information to remind the reader of the referent without giving away any of the story. I believe this an admirable principle, and I have tried to follow it.

The glossaries were necessary in Morris's two earlier novels owing to the confusing and eye-splitting Welsh names. A glossary is necessary with this novel because of the bewildering complexity of the Nahua names. Nahua (or Nahuatl) represents a group of languages of the Uto-Aztecan family, spoken by various native peoples of North and Central America.

Morris used as his primary source for this novel, in all matters of myth, history, language and culture, the works of Hubert Howe Bancroft (1832–1918). Bancroft, whose voluminous "works" bore his name alone even though he depended heavily on the research and writing of numerous assistants, became known as the first great historian of the West Coast with his *Native Races of the Pacific States* (5 vols., 1874–5), *History of the Pacific States* (28 vols., 1882–90), and other works. Today his work has been superseded and is largely confined to the shelves of university libraries.

In the five volumes of *Native Races of the Pacific States,* Morris found all of the basics for his story. And I have found it a useful resource in providing collateral information about the entries in this glossary. However, this glossary remains primarily based on the material as used by Morris, and I have not felt it necessary to elaborate on just how Morris used (or did not use) Bancroft, or on how Morris used the Nahua language as presented in Bancroft.

I have also resisted the temptation to provide the story with a map. To pick precisely where Morris might have situated his mythical Huitznahuac seems to me wrong-headed. Huitznahuac should remain just off the map. Suffice it, simply, to describe the general area.

The Toltec League was centered in and around the Anahuacs, in the valley of central Mexico, where were located the cities of Tollan (Tula), Culhuacan, and Teotihuacan. The Otomi lands were to the east and southeast. Goazacoalco, near which could be found the Serpent's Hole, centered around the modern Coatzacoalcos, at the lower tip of the Bay of Campeche. The Zapotecs lived to the north of the Gulf of Tehuantepec; the Chiapanecs, to the east of it; the Quiches and Maya farther to the east (and northeast). Huitznahuac, therefore, would be somewhere in or around the southernmost part of Mexico.

A few general comments should be made concerning the pronunciation of the names of places and persons, which as given here can only approximate the complex Nahua sounds.

c   *(in* ca, co, cu*) is pronounced* k.
     (in ce, ci*) is pronounced as in 'city.'*
hu   *(or* uh*) is pronounced as* w *or* hw.
qu   *(in* qua*) is pronounced* kw.
     (in que, qui*) is pronounced* k.
tl   *is pronounced as in 'atlas.'*
x   *is pronounced* sh.
z   *is pronounced* s *as in 'song.'*

The accent nearly always falls on the penultimate syllable.

Last, I should mention that I have listed personal names under the most commonly used form, and included variations of the names in parentheses immediately afterward. Thus under "Nopal" will be found his full name, Nopaltzin, and the affectionate and familiar derivatives, Nopalton and Nopaltontli.

—D.A.A.

Acamapichtli (Acamapitzin), son of King Ashokentzin, and great-uncle to Chimalman.

Acatonal (Acatonatzin), the Tezcatlipocâ-teacher, eldest son of King Ashokentzin and great-uncle to Chimalman, joint head of the Calmecac with his brother, Amaqui.

Amaqui (Amaquitzin), the Quetzalcoatl-priest, second surviving son of King Ashokentzin and great-uncle to Chimalman, joint head of the Calmecac with his elder brother, Acatonal.

Ameyal (Ameyatzin), the Tlaloc-priest, the oldest man in all Huitznahuac, cousin to King Ashokentzin.

Anahuacs, the area around the valley of Mexico in the northern world, with its three most important cities, Culhuacan, Teotihuacan and Tollan.

Ashokentzin, previous king of Huitznahuac, great-grandfather to Chimalman and father of Acamapichtli, Acatonal, and Amaqui.

Ashopatzin, father of Nopal.

Been, one of the Saltmen, a trader from Chiapas who visits Huitznahuac.

Calmecac, the college where the Huitznahuac boys were educated (the girls went to the Girls' College).

Camaxtli, the Toltec God of War.

Catautlish, a young lad at Rainflower, a xylophone player.

Ce Acatl, a year (Reed One), the fourteenth in any year-bundle of 52 years. Quetzalcoatl is always born in a year Ce Acatl.

Centeotl, the Maize-queen, a goddess of Huitznahuac.

chalchiuhite, a precious green stone, variously identified with green quartz, jade or turquoise.

Chiapas, land to the north of Huitznahuac.

Chiapanec, a person from Chiapas.

Chimalman (Chimalmatzin), queen of Huitznahuac, great-granddaughter of Ashokentzin.

Cipactli, the great Sea-creature of the Wave beneath the Sun.

Citlalicway Teteoinan, the Mighty Mother, a goddess of Huitznahuac.

Civacoatli (Civacoatzin, Civacoatl), elder sister of Nonohualcatl, the Toltec Topiltzin.

Coatlantona, a flower goddess of Huitznahuac.

Cocotzin, a Culhuatec noble and general.

Cohuanacotli (Cohuanacotzin), a Culhuatec and favorite of Nonohualcatl and Huemac.

Copil, a young lad at Rainflower, a flute player.

Coshcana, servant of the Hermit of Puma Rock.

Coshcosh, a young lad at Rainflower, a gardener.

cozcaquahtli, a vulture; also the name of a regiment in Huemac's army.

Cuetzpalin (Cuetzpaltzin), name given by Nonohualcatl to the Otomi Nratzó, who saved his life.

Culhuacan, city in the Anahuacs, capital of the power of the Toltec League, whose king was Nonohualcatl, the Toltec Topiltzin.

Culhuatec, a person from Culhuacan.

Eeweesho (Eeweeshotzin), servant to Queen Chimalman, wife of Ocotosh.

Ghuggg, one of the chieftains of the Ib Quinames, used by Yen Ranho.

Guaish, one of the chieftains of the Ib Quinames, used by Yen Ranho.

Hax, one of the Saltmen, a trader from Chiapas who visits Huitznahuac.

Huanhua, ancestor of Chimalman; he who came to Queen Ulupi of Huitznahuac from beyond the western sea.

Huehuetzin, the Master at the Serpent's Hole.

Huemac (Huetzin) Tezcatlipocâ, king of Tollan and brother of Nonohualcatl.

Huhú, Otomi sentinel, founder of the Republic of New Otompan, and member of the Tzo family.

Huitznahuac, kingdom of Queen Chimalman.

Huitznahuacan, capital city of the kingdom of Huitznahuac, on the lower western slopes of the mountain Mishcoatepetl.

Huitznahuatec, a person from Huitznahuac.

Ib, one of the chieftains of the Ib Quinames, used by Yen Ranho.

Ikak, one of the Blue-Hummingbird Pygmies.

Ilanquey, daughter of Ketlasho and Shaltemoc.

Ishcash (Ishcatzin), the village priest of the Mountain (Teotepetl) at Rainflower. He was also a cousin and good friend to Nopal and his family.

Ishmishutzin Teteoinan, healing woman of Huitznahuac.

Iyaca, disciple and servant to Ameyal, the Tlaloc-priest.

Iztaman, son of Ketlasho and Shaltemoc.

Ketlasho (Ketlashotzin, Ketlashton), sister of Nopal and wife of Shaltemoc.

koo, a truncated pyramid with a temple at the top.

macuahuitl swords, heavy wooden swords with a line of sharp stones firmly set along the two edges.

Mahetsi, secretary to Yen Ranho.

mashtli (or maxtli), a loin cloth eight yards long and nine inches wide, worn in and about the middle, with fringed and painted ends hanging down before and behind.

Matlalqua, *see under Mayavel.*

Maxio (Maxiotzin), wife of Shollo.

Mayavel, one of the Four Votaresses of Tlaloc, who, with a fifth youth, would climb Mishcoatepetl at Tepeilhuitl, the Feast of the Mountains. The other three votaresses are the Tepos, the Shochiteca, and the Matlalqua. The fifth, a young man chosen from the Calmecac, is the Milnaoatl.

Mictlantecuhtli, king of Hell (Mictlan).

Milnaoatl, see under Mayavel.

Mishcoatepetl, the Cloud-Serpent Mountain, on whose western slopes was the city of Huitznahuacan.

Nahua (or Nahautl), a group of languages of the Uto-Aztecan family, spoken by various native peoples of North and Central American.

Nayna the Aged, healing woman.

Natzó, an Otomi sentinel, founder of the Republic of New Otompan, and member of the Tzo family (brother of Nratzó).

Nauhyo (Nauhyotontzin, Nauhyotontli), young boy sent to Nopal by the Master at Eagle Hermitage.

nequen, a coarse fabric woven of the agave, or century, plant.

Nonohualcatl (Nonohualton) Totepeuh Camaxtli, king of Culhuacan and head of all the Toltec race, with the title Toltec Topiltzin, whose god-name is Camaxtli, the Toltec God of War. All other kings are his subordinates.

Nopal (Nopaltzin, Nopalton, Nopaltontli), son of Ashopatzin, brother of Shollo and Ketlasho, and husband of Chimalman. During his travels in the north, he used the name Quanez.

Nratzó, Otomi name of Cuetzpalin, brother of Natzó and member of the Tzo family.

Ochpaniztli, month-name of the last month of the year.

ocotl, a type of pine.

Ocotosh, servant to Queen Chimalman, with his wife, Eeweesho.

Ometochtli, God of Drunkards and Drunkenness, whose names means "two-rabbits"; also the name of a Culhuatec regiment.

Opochtli, an old man at the Huitznahuacan market.

Otompan, city of the Otomis, near Teotihuacan.

Otomis, the race of people dwelling in the Otomi Republic, around Teotihuacan.

Otomitl, military head of Otompan.

Panquetzaliztli, a month-name.

Papantli of Quauchinanco, cook who befriends Quahtli on the Road.

Pelashil, daughter of Ketlasho and Shaltemoc.

Pfapffo, one of the three Little Gods of Forgotten Plain.

pulque, a fermented drink made from the juice of an agave.

Pweeg, one of the three Little Gods of Forgotten Plain.

Pygmies, a forest race, including the tribes of Blue-Hummingbird Pygmies and Viridian Pygmies.

Quahh, a youth among the Viridian Pygmies.

Quauhtepetl, Eagle Mountain, on which could be found Eagle Hermitage.

quauhtli, an eagle; also the name of a regiment in Huemac's army.

Quauhtli (Quauhtzin, Quauhton), fellow disciple with Nopal at Eagle Hermitage, the tallest and strongest of the Huitznahuatecs.

Quanez (Quanetzin) of Quahnahuac, disguised name of Nopal in the north.

quechol, a large aquatic bird with plumage of a scarlet color and a black neck.

Quecholli, a month-name.

Quetzalcoatl, the Plumed Dragon, God of Huitznahuac, periodically reborn among men (always in a year Ce Acatl) to teach peace.

Quicab, one of the Saltmen, a trader from Chiapas who visits Huitznahuac.

Quinames, a giant race of a previous age; the surviving tribes of the Quinames may possibly be descendants of this ancient race; these tribes include Gholb, Appa, Hlun and Ib Quinames.

Quinatepetl, a mountain in Huitznahuac.

Rainflower Manor, home of Nopal and his family, at the foot of Teotepetl.

Saltmen, the name given to Chiapanec traders by the Huitznahuatecs.

Shaltemoc (Shaltemotzin), husband of Ketlasho.

Shelwa, son of Shollo and Maxio.

Shewtecuhtli, the Fire-god of Huitznahuac.

Shilonen, a goddess of Huitznahuac, probably another name for Centeotl.

Shochill, spinster nurse to the children of Shollo at Rainflower Manor.

Shochiteca, *see under Mayavel.*

Shollo (Shollotzin), brother of Nopal and husband of Maxio.

Shuquentzin, queen of Huitznahuac previous to Chimalman.

Tata, Commander of the Escort of Yen Ranho.

Tatzin ("Lord Father"), honorific used by Nopal to his father, Ashopatzin.

Tecpatl, the Flint-stone hurled at the earth by Citlalicway Teteoinan, the Mighty Mother, whose sparks kindled the gods.

tecuhtli, a title meaning lord.

Teotepetl, "the Mountain that was God," near Rainflower Manor; on it could be found the Serpent's Hole.

Teotihuacan, city in the Anahuacs, the capital of religion in the Toltec League. The people there are called Otomis, and they have been in the Anahuacs much longer than the Toltecs.

Teotleco, "the holiest of festivals," in the month of the same name.

Tepeilhuitl, "the Feast of the Mountains," in the month of the same name, which follows the month of Teotleco. It is the festival and holy season of the Tlalocs.

Tepos, *see under Mayavel.*

Teteo, the gods.

Teteoinan, *see under Citlalicway Teteoinan.*

Tezcatlipocâ, the Soul of the World, a god of Huitznahuac.

tilmatli, a piece of cloth about four feet square, worn tied over one shoulder and covering the other, or tied over the breast and covering the shoulders. Women wore tilmatlies over long, sleeveless gowns.

Tlacotzontli, one of the Huitznahuac gods of the roads.

Tlalocan, the paradise of the Tlalocs, which was the essence of the beauty and wildness and exaltation of all mountains everywhere.

Tlalocs, the gods of water and rain in Huitznahuac, a few of which are named: Tlaloc Quitzetzelohua, the Down-scatterer of Jewels, and Tlaloc Tepahpaca Teaaltati, the Purifier.

tlapalizqui bush, a red-flowered plant.

Tlaxochimaco, a month-name.

Tlilcuetzpalins, a regiment of the Otomis.

Tollan, city in the Anahuacs, capital of culture of the Toltec League. Its king was Huemac.

Toltec League, dominion of the Toltec Topiltzin.

Toltec Topiltzin, title of the head of the Toltec race; *see Nonohualcatl.*

topillies, the men who keep order in the streets of Teotihuacan.

Topiltzin, title of the Toltec king.

Toshpilli, drummer at Rainflower.

Tozcaykech, drummer at Rainflower.

Ttang, one of the three Little Gods of Forgotten Plain.

tzinitzcan, a bird with splendid plumage.

tzitzimitl, an evil spirit, or demon.

Tzontecoma, lord of the Northern District of Huitznahuac.

Ulupi, ancestral queen of Huitznahuac, to whom Huanhua came from beyond the western sea.

Xocotlhuetzi, a month-name.

Yacacoliuhqui, the god of merchants in Huitznahuac.

Yacanex (Yacanetzin) of Tollan, ambassador from Huemac.

Yanesh (Yaneshton, Yanetzintli) the Straw, the very old gardener at Rainflower Manor, who had designed the great Rainflower garden.

Yaotzin, the Dark Tezcatlipocâ, the dark shadow of the god Tezcatlipocâ.

Yen Ranho, the Hierarch of Teotihuacan, sent to Huitznahuac by Huemac of Tollan.

yetl, a pipeweed.

Yetsú, an Otomi cook.

Zacatzontli, one of the Huitznahuac gods of the roads.